'Tom Haddock, the story's main character, is the hilarious English equivalent of Agatha Christie's Poirot, as he stumbles through each twist and turn of the murder investigation. Witty, intriguing, with a tongue-in-cheek caricature of life in 1980s Singapore, *Waiting for Venus* is a page-turner. Beneath it runs a parallel story of the country's history and its people.'

— CHAN LING YAP, author of *Where the Sunrise is Red*
and the *Sweet Offerings* quadrilogy

'Vengeance and Love are merely items on Tom's anthropology curriculum until the deceptively cosy covers of campus life are drawn back to reveal dormant hostilities fermenting since WWII and ripe for resolution ... and love must wait. Great interplay between realistic characters, episodes of laugh-out-loud humour, well paced and so well written the pages seem to turn themselves.'

— COLIN COTTERILL, author of the Dr Siri
series of murder mysteries

'It's David Lodge meets J.G. Farrell: a dead professor, a guileless narrator, and a compelling window into wartime and postcolonial Singapore. University politics were rarely more entertaining – or deadly. Robert Cooper's book will keep you guessing (and reading) to the very end.'

— SIMON CHESTERMAN, author of *I, Huckleberry*
and the *Raising Arcadia* trilogy

WAITING FOR VENUS

WAITING FOR
VENUS

ROBERT COOPER

Marshall Cavendish
Editions

Published in 2021 by Marshall Cavendish Editions
An imprint of Marshall Cavendish International

A member of the
Times Publishing Group

Other Marshall Cavendish Offices:
Marshall Cavendish Corporation, 800 Westchester Ave, Suite N-641, Rye Brook, NY 10573, USA • Marshall Cavendish International (Thailand) Co Ltd, 253 Asoke, 16th Floor, Sukhumvit 21 Road, Klongtoey Nua, Wattana, Bangkok 10110, Thailand • Marshall Cavendish (Malaysia) Sdn Bhd, Times Subang, Lot 46, Subang Hi-Tech Industrial Park, Batu Tiga, 40000 Shah Alam, Selangor Darul Ehsan, Malaysia

Marshall Cavendish is a registered trademark of Times Publishing Limited

National Library Board, Singapore Cataloguing in Publication Data

Name(s): Cooper, Robert George.
Title: Waiting for Venus / Robert Cooper.
Description: Singapore: Marshall Cavendish Editions, 2021.
Identifier(s): OCN 1236386447 | ISBN 978-981-4928-51-9 (paperback)
Subject(s): LCSH: Murder–Investigation–Fiction. | Revenge–Fiction. | Singapore–History–20th century–Fiction.
Classification: DDC 823.92–dc23

Printed in Singapore

To my 5 Ts

Tess, Tintin, Tip, Toby & Top

1

Waiting…

I LIVE IN A cosy little vein between two arteries; my evenings are quiet as the grave, or they were until the night Uncle Bernard got hanged. Truth be told, the vein, Evans Road, is more a capillary than a vein, more a lane than a road, but don't tell Evans, whoever Evans is or was. In 1980, it sneaks across the university from Tanglin-side to Bukit Timah Road. Anybody crossing the campus at night, unless they skulk through the grass and bushes, uses Evans Road and I see them – if I'm looking. Not that many make the crossing, so the normal pulse of my Evans Road evenings, once the girls in the dormitory opposite switch off their lights at ten, is almost imperceptible – a deathlike silence. Well, silence broken by the episodic shrill of male cicadas trying to attract a mate. When on, they fill my mind; when they snap off, my mind floats, free, empty, waiting … for Venus.

As I hang on in hope, waiting for Venus to show up, Professor Bernard Fox, my best friend in the world or by this time out of it, is just up the road hanging by his neck from a rope. I do nothing to save him. Uncle Bernard is dying and I'm doing nothing. I'm not heartless; I'm really quite sensitive. And it's not quite true I'm doing nothing; I'm waiting for Venus to call by. Well, to call by *maybe*. Venus only half-promised. 'I'll try to call by, Tom, after work.' She's done that before. Lucky I'm good at waiting.

Tonight, it's pretty much waiting as usual: still life with whisky. Nothing suggests the world is turning turtle on me; I'm the same tiny speck I always was – in the same enormous place it always has been since the Empire built it in 1924 and since I moved in a couple of years back – in 1980 a young man full of dreams and nothing in the bank. A place defined by its 'nos': no aircon, no TV, no telephone, no hot water, no glass in the windows. Just 'Hard Furnishings': chairs with no cushion, beds with no mattress, cold water, and overhead fans that wobble on long stems from a high ceiling. My flat's a bit of a desert island. I love it.

Outside my space, suicidal flying insects explode soundlessly on dimly-lit old-fashioned street lamps. Same most nights; why do they do that?

I go into the kitchen to get a tub of ice cubes from the second-hand fridge I bought for a song because its door won't close right and the seller delivered and installed it, saving me the bother. I don't think this simple journey from window to fridge has significance but it does, although at the time it doesn't. I notice the dirty shirt I tossed in the basket last night is still there and still dirty; Norsiah has not been in to clean today, hope she's not sick or something.

I return to sit by my glassless window, looking through open shutters to the deep outside. I semi-focus on the old wind-up clock with luminous hands beside me as my eyelids close … 9 o'clock and already the whisky's taking over. I'm not thinking, just being. I don't think, therefore I am not; no, that's not right, but never mind. My mind is somewhere, I don't know where. Is that important? I suppose it is. Everything on that night is important.

★   ★   ★

'Professor ...?' A whisper from outside. My eyes open. Inches away, a silhouette. It doesn't startle me. I am beyond startling.

'I wish.' I sigh.

'*Bitte?*'

'Bitter?' The whisky talking, trying to be funny. 'Not much. This is my first teaching job. Can't become professor overnight. There's still time.'

'It is five minutes past the 10 o'clock.'

I look at the clock; he's right. An hour has gone by and I didn't notice it go; lost time, not waiting, not wasted, not killed, just lost. 'Yes, I know. Most of the lights have gone out in the girls' dorm.'

'*Bitte?*'

This brief encounter with a Germanic shadow I recall because I remember everything that happened that night – well not quite everything, there's the lost hour. Then the cicada starts again and the black shape at my window shouts to be heard above the insect's scream. I don't answer; I've just noticed what's behind him.

'Professor Haddock?' The voice is accented. Must be German.

Behind him waits a black Citroën of the large-bonneted World War II type with double chevrons on its grill and its engine ticking over, ready for a quick getaway. It must have come onto campus from the Bukit Timah side; I'd have noticed had it turned the corner from Dalvey – but maybe not if I'd been transported back forty years during the lost hour; doubtful I suppose, time transmogrification, but after half a bottle of whisky, and with a German at the window saying *bitte* and a WWII Citroën in the driveway, I can't be completely sure. The silhouette glances back at the car. The owl-eye headlamps light up its face. Blond, bronzed, square-jawed and built to last a thousand years; can't get more stereotype than that – although I suppose you can if you pop in a WWII backdrop. Now I know what it feels like to be invaded by Olympian sculptures from old war movies.

'Haddock, yes, professor, no,' I say. 'I am Doctor Tom Haddock. What do you want?'

'I vant to see Professor Fox, but he does not answer his door. I knock very hard. May I call him from your telephone?' VW-problem. Definitely German. Definitely stereotype; although I tend to stereotype too readily. I'll never be a novelist.

'No. Don't have telephone.'

I must sound brusque; he leaves without a thank you. I could call out and tell him there's a public phone at Guild House a hundred metres down the road just opposite Bernard's front door but I don't – *he didn't say thank you.* Doesn't he know there's a courtesy campaign on? An unseen hand inside the Citroën opens the passenger door for him and off he goes Tanglin way. I wonder why on earth a German in a WWII Citroën would visit Bernard after lights-out in the girls' dorm, but I don't wonder hard enough to go and check on him; I could, I have the key, but I don't.

I sit on in the room we call the living room, as if all the other rooms are dead. Funny language, English. Still, it is my language; my mother tongue as they say. Well, I suppose it is, my mother spoke English, though when I started to talk, I probably spoke more Malay; the *amah* was Malay and I loved her as only a very young boy can love the woman who washes behind his ears and foreskin. Most of the other kids in the *kampong* were Malay, except for some Chinese in the market and a few Tamils from the rubber plantation and I would speak Malay with them all; it was the language of fun and games and *sandwic ais krim dan kek*. I didn't distinguish the two languages much back then; Mum and Dad spoke English but everybody else in my world spoke Malay – so Mum and Dad were the odd ones out. I grew into English and Malay grew into the national language of Singapore, one of three official languages, no, four, I tend to forget Tamil, a minority language, but aren't they all? Then again, Malay is the language of the national anthem so it can't be all that minor, can it? I slouch in my armchair, ask myself senseless questions and tenderly sing Majullah Singapura.

I'm not in the habit of sitting alone singing the national anthem, so maybe the whisky's really taking over. I love the tune though and I know all the words; more than I can say for God Save the Queen. In Singapore, we sing the national anthem in the home language of the nation next door. Nobody questions that. As an academic, it's nice to have something I don't need to question, form into a hypothesis, test and prove. And I suppose it keeps the neighbours happy.

Why do I remember singing the national anthem? No reason really; perhaps I imagined it. I am young then: gathering memories without reason. Imaginative. I'll live forever. Life has yet to gift me its fear of death. Although death must be in the air. I should smell it, sense it; I should do something about it. But I don't. Instead, as Uncle Bernard dies, I make Venus a present of the most valuable thing in the world I will ever have: my time. And Venus, bless her, doesn't even know I'm giving it to her.

Shall I wait for Venus or pop her into my pending box and

nip down the road for a few beers with Madhu to celebrate the coincidental start of both our birthdays at midnight? I didn't tell Venus it's my birthday – well, it will be in an hour – I didn't want her to feel obliged to come or do something silly like buy a present.

I'll wait. Hang on. Hoping Richard will let her come.

★   ★   ★

A few minutes to midnight, another face comes to my window and it's far from my image of Venus. It's a collection of bones held together by the kind of brown-spotted yellow skin you peel back from bananas past their prime: it's Li Fang. Unassuming, a bit distant, Li Fang takes his time to grow on anybody. But he's a hero dressed as anti-hero; and he's likeable – if you like bananas and stick-insects, and I do and he's grown on me. He's cook-manager of Guild House, the restaurant-bar for lecturers and graduates just two minutes down the road and right opposite the front door of Professor Bernard Fox, my uncle and only known living relative, although I never mention the family connection – he insists I do not.

'Doc-tor-Tom-come-quick-lah.'

Chop-chop-chop. Doc-tor-Tom-come-quick-lah. Chickens, crabs and the English language, Li Fang attacks them all with two rhythmic cleavers on a chopping block. After the stereotypical German, another cliché, although this time a deliberate one: the colonial native servant. But this cliché is only a game Li Fang plays; if he wants to, Li Fang can speak English to put Dr Harry Chin, my head of department, to shame; but he doesn't want to – he wants to keep his job. Li Fang's pigtail, if he ever had one, which, knowing him, I very much doubt, is long gone.

Any hint of *kao-tao* is trimmed to a wise tortoise-bobbing of a crusty head and his frugality of language is trimmed to the needs of a public world – and charades at my window. Bernard told me never to underestimate him. And Bernard knew Li Fang better than anybody.

In public, Li Fang the linguistic museum piece is as representative of the Empire-gone-by every bit as much as his curiously intimate comrade-in-arms, the Oxford-vowelled Professor Bernard Fox. Publicly, both men are the Empire's children, its heirs and its victims. I am one too: one of the Empire's last sons. After the Japanese surrender and the British return, I was born into what we then called British Malaya, a country fresh out of war and rushing into what Dad, an Empire's policeman, called the *Emergency*. But one thing I'm not, is *colonial* and neither is Uncle Bernard or Li Fang; if the three of us fit into colonial typology at all, it must be within the subset of wild colonial boy.

'Come-quick-lah.'

I know it's Madhu's birthday as much as mine and I know we sort of agreed we'd see our birthdays in together at the Guild House at midnight. I'd half-promised to be there when Madhu suggested it – half a promise. Not that I mind sharing a birthday with Madhu, I just have a better offer, or maybe I have, although it too is a half-promise; when Venus gets off work, she will try to come. Maybe she will. Maybe she won't. Half a promise, I suppose, is better than none, but it's still no promise at all.

I can hear, coming from Guild House, a lot more noise than the coincidence of two birthdays should merit – that obscure clamour a lot of people make when talking above each other like a flock of crows coming in to roost. I look at my wind-up clock. The big hand clicks to midnight. I don't turn into a pumpkin but

I do realise the chance of Venus coming is now sinking below any reasonable stretch of likelihood. And it is my birthday. I decide a quick drink with Madhu won't hurt, not if he wants me there so much he sends Li Fang to drag me out. I slip out of my Malay sarong and climb into blue-jeans ethnicity.

⋆   ⋆   ⋆

Madhu stands in the middle of the road looking like the frizzy-headed golliwog who used to advertise the best-selling English marmalade before golliwogs stopped being cute and became racist. Around Madhu a small clutch of lawyers clatters alcoholically. They can all speak Tamil but use English as their language, setting themselves apart from the thinner and darker monolingual Tamil labourers who stand in silence in the shadows, roused from their sleep by something more interesting than sleep. Cars and motorbikes fill the street – must have all come in from the Bukit Timah side. Quite a birthday turnout; I never realised I am so popular.

Madhu's car stretches across the tarmac like a road block. Its headlights shine into Bernard's open front doors. Detective Madhu, off-duty at midnight on the birth of his birthday, is in plain clothes. For Madhu, plain means a flower-power shirt three buttons open on a bushy chest. The whites of his eyes and the glint of ivory teeth on a moonless night conjure up conflicting pictures of an avuncular black-and-white minstrel and a half-crazed cannibal. My pal's a nice guy but he's not the spitting-image of the bobby on the beat. If this guy turns up at your door to babysit, your liberal conscience might be tested.

'Happy birthday, Madhu,' I say and reach for my birthday-twin's hand. My fingers close on a snub-nose revolver in a tension-gripped fist. Madhu just made it up to the lowest of several junior ranks of inspector, something that carries a gun and a license to kill within regulations. He always has a nice smile on his face. But no smile now.

Madhu raises his lethal-weapon hand and places it on my shoulder. I feel the weight of hard metal and hope the barrel is pointing at something other than my head. He looks confused. Later, I understood why: this is the first time Madhu finds himself, as they say, the first person at the scene of a crime, the guy marked out as the prime suspect, although he is never the one who did it. I'm not sure if his hand on my shoulder is to steady him or me.

'I'm s-s-sorry, T-Tom.' Madhu's dormant stutter wakes up. I wait as he tries to swallow it away before learning what he is sorry about. 'Your f-f-r-iend ...'

*   *   *

Madhu waves the gun barrel along the shafts of his car's headlights that pierce Bernard's living room. I don't want to look. I try not to look. But curiosity, as Bernard used to say, is always stronger than fear; that's why Man is in such a mess. I look.

At light-beam's end, I make out what seems to be an old, discarded puppet that nobody wants to play with anymore. It turns alone on a cranky roundabout, dipping into light, ducking back into shadow, round and round. As my eyes focus, the marionette becomes a person; a person swinging by the neck on a rope arcing out from a central capstan, rotating to the lazy revolution of a grouchy ceiling fan.

The body circles face up towards the ceiling; the knot pushing the chin jauntily to one side. The neck that in life had almost disappeared in the academic's hunch is in death stretched out so long that, at first, I think it's not Bernard's at all. But it is. It's Uncle Bernard – turning at the fan's slowest speed, the speed he likes best, enough to circle the air around him yet leave papers undisturbed on his desk. Under his orbiting feet, a brown mongrel dog snaps at the intruding light.

⋆   ⋆   ⋆

I'm one of those who respond slowly to surprise. I don't think myself amazingly cool-headed, dim-witted or hard-hearted. It just takes a few minutes, hours or days before I burst into tears or yell yippee. I'm not expecting to find Uncle Bernard dead; I know we talked about suicide last night but had I supposed Bernard to be in any danger, I'd have done something about it, at least I hope I would, although I did nothing, so maybe I wouldn't. Truth is, I'm more wait-and-see than do-or-die. Even this afternoon, when witnessing Bernard and Li Fang divide up the diamonds, I didn't ask what they were doing; I just witnessed what they wanted me to witness: the two tiny pyramids looked equal. It might have been two small boys cutting a chocolate bar in half; I was just there to witness fair play, not to ask questions. Anyway, had I asked a question, neither would have answered me. I'm an academic; I ask questions; it's my job. But I'm a Singaporean academic, I know when to ask questions and what to ask; I ask one now: 'Have you called the police?' All pragmatic Singaporean.

'I am the f-f-fucking police.'

'Yes, of course you are, Madhu. I mean the murder squad and ambulance and so on.'

'Li Fang te-li-pon,' says Li Fang beside me. He seems

unfazed; still playing pidgin. Maybe after what he lived through under the Japanese, when hangings, he says, were daily events, and after surviving the Emergency, when whole villages were razed and commies like him buried themselves so deep in society they couldn't climb out, he takes the death of just one *ang mo* in his stride. But it's not that; I know how close Li Fang was to Bernard. Maybe, like mine, his emotions take a bit of time to kick in. Or maybe it's the diamonds.

I dont' want to look, now I can't tear my eyes away from Bernard's slow-motion revolution. Mesmerising. Like a cobra's dance. I am only vaguely conscious of a large shape untying itself from the dark knot of birthday guests and entering my space. 'This must be a terrible shock to you. I know you were the very best of friends. Like father and son. You must be devastated. Such a terrible thing...' It's Tambiah, the solicitor and Madhu's closest friend and drinking partner. I cut him short. The reality before me is coming through in bits and bursts. I hit Tambiah with a burst. 'Too much to hope you and Madhu found the killer as well as the body?'

'Steady on old man,' says the solicitor. 'Nobody can establish the cause of death at this point.'

'Well, it doesn't look like an accident.'

Tambiah lets the sarcasm pass. 'I can see you're upset,' he says. 'But suicide seems the likeliest explanation ... empirically speaking. Murder by hanging's just not practical. Thing is, until Madhu can get to the body, nobody can even establish that Bernard is legally dead – although it is obvious, I'm afraid.'

Legally dead? Can anyone be *illegally* dead? Are the *illegally dead* arrested and charged? And if Bernard hanged himself, how did he manage to turn on the fan?

2

Meanwhile in Limbo

IT'S A GAME I play alone when feeling myself in limbo between the known and the unknown; solitaire playing people not cards. I imagine where other people fit in at any critical point in my personal history. It's a coping mechanism, a way of getting out of myself and into them without surgery, putting myself in their shoes, so to speak, walking their walk. It helps me fill in the blanks between known pieces, fits the bits together to form a bigger picture and put myself in that picture. I'd rather be part of a big picture than have the big picture gobble me up. I know I'm trying to escape the inescapable and I know the picture is fuzzy-logic. It might be precise or it might be completely wrong, or it might be a bit right and a bit wrong, but it always makes sense at the time. It's subjective, of course, and all a bit academic. But on a university campus, there's nothing wrong with being academic. And there's nothing wrong with avoiding the unavoidable, if that's possible, which it's not, at least not for long. And so, as I watch Bernard turning circles, as my world rotates in limbo and as the roulette wheel of my life slows to click-click a new direction, I imagine...

★   ★   ★

K drops his evening's transvestite, his anonymous accomplice, on Tanglin Road to get a taxi into her alternative night and drives home fast, all windows open, glad to be rid of her. The smell of her irritates his nostrils; a souvenir of his own making but one he'd happily do without, a reminder of how much he hates what he can't resist, indeed goes in search of.

As he drives, he takes an air freshener from the glove compartment, sprays all around him and soaks his crotch. He hates the smell of canned fresh air – nothing fresh about it, almost as bad as the tranny. But his wife put the can in the car – so he sprays, he tells himself, to protect her from the ugly truth; to spray away what never happened. Not that Dija would ever sniff too hard for signs of her husband's duplicity; she's not like that. She'll be fast asleep by now.

He pulls quietly into his driveway. The light's on. She's waited up. She won't make a fuss. She knows making a fuss would be bad for the baby, although she'd never make a fuss anyway. After all, it's only 11 o'clock, 17 minutes and 10 seconds – Dija checks the clock as K comes in the front door, pecks her on the cheek and strokes her stretched tummy.

'Still awake? You should get your sleep. Soon be time for the little chap to keep you awake at night.' No need to worry, she can't smell the tranny, nor the air freshener, not over the pong of stale beer.

'Long rehearsal at the thespians?' she asks, as if concerned the star of amateur-dramatics might be tired.

'Yes, you know how it is. Time flies by.'

'Doesn't it. By the way, you left your play-script thing behind at the club. David phoned to say he's taken it with him and will give it to you tomorrow.'

'Good old David. I'd forget my head if it wasn't nailed on. Must be tired. These rehearsals do drag on.'

'Don't they. David said he was on his way home for an early night as the rehearsal had finished at 8.00 – *8.30 he called.*'

* * *

Ra'mad is feeding his rats. He feeds them at night. That way, they get a good sleep for whatever trials they face the next day. 'Now you all get a good night's sleep,' he says in English, as if tucking in the children he never had. 'And never mind that noise. That damn dog again and those noisy Tamils. Don't worry, you're quite safe with your Uncle Ra'mad.'

His rats look through the bars at him with the fear of God in their eyes as they gnaw their pellets. Only Snow, the one Ra'mad trusts enough to let out for some exercise within the flat, who always comes when called, the one with him for two years now, only Snow comes close to the door of his cage and smiles. Ra'mad opens the door and takes him out for a bedtime stroke. 'There, Snow. The world's now a better place.' Stroking completed, Ra'mad places Snow back inside with a square inch of cheddar cheese to sweeten his night. Snow is Ra'mad's favourite.

'That noise is too much,' he says to Snow. 'All those drunken Tamils. And that dog yapping. That's no way to behave on a university campus. I suppose I'll have to go along and see to it.' Snow chews his cheese.

* * *

Harry Chin lies awake. He wakes his wife and complains that with all this noise, he can't get to sleep. 'Take a Valium,' says

Agnes in Mandarin. They always speak Mandarin together. Agnes, Malaysian from Ipoh, is from an English-speaking Chinese family. Harry's weighty legacy from his China-nationalist father required he be raised and educated only in Mandarin. Harry's father thought the world should speak Mandarin. Harry wishes it did, life would be a lot simpler.

Harry is pleased with the new *Speak Mandarin* campaign, although it took a long time coming and only comes now because China is an enemy no more; father would approve of the campaign but would not be happy about snuggling up to Communist China. Not that chatting to China bothers Harry, as long as the chat's in Mandarin. Language apart, he neither shares his father's political views nor opposes them. Harry has no political views. He's Singaporean.

'I've already taken two,' says Harry.

'That's twenty mgs you've taken already,' says Agnes.

'Yes, I know, but it doesn't matter. Give me another.'

Agnes pushes another pill from its pod and gives it to Harry with a glass of water, thinking in English, *Yes, Harry, please take them all.*

★   ★   ★

Norsiah, too, can't sleep. She's wondering why she is where she is.

★   ★   ★

David's resolve to get an early night hasn't worked; after half an hour trying to sleep, he's tried so hard he's wide awake. So out comes the weed and up comes David to sit on the top-floor veranda of Wolverton Mess in his pyjamas, puffing what he shouldn't. He looks out over the top of the girls' dorm, across the trees and cricket pitch to Tom's place and a bit further on to Guild House, where earlier he'd phoned K and K's wife had answered, as always. He hears a growing racket coming from Guild House. 'Oh Christ,' he tells himself. 'It's the birthdays of Tom and Madhu, and I clean forgot.'

David never misses free beer and knows that by now everybody will be so drunk it doesn't matter how he's dressed. He puts his magic dragon back in its matchbox and, pyjama-clad, skips down the stairs and across the grass to the Guild.

*   *   *

Venus is thinking thoughts befitting the most beautiful woman in the world.

I bet he's waiting for me right now. He always does. I wonder if he'd wait forever. That time we went to an afternoon movie, he waited outside the cinema for half an hour. I thought we'd arranged to meet there to go somewhere else, so for me it was an accidental movie. I don't like cinemas in the afternoon; sad to lock myself away from the daylight like a vampire, and I don't normally sit in the dark with a man: Richard definitely wouldn't like that. But when I got there, Tom had two tickets in his hand already so I wimpishly followed him inside, not holding hands or anything ridiculous. We missed the beginning and I never knew what I was watching until we came out and I saw the title was *Lord Jim* with Peter O'Toole. First time I'd seen him – Peter that is, not Tom. I could see why Tom loves the story: young white man in Malaya goes native to save the natives, becomes a sort of hero, gets the beautiful girl who calls him *Tuan* and all that. Pity he has to die in the end, paying with his life for the sins of others – same old story. The movie was an old one – the kind they show in the afternoon.

We sat there, side by side in an empty theatre, me on an aisle seat in case I needed to escape the dark. Tom never tried to touch me or anything. I wondered if I was too rigid for him – I can't relax in a cold, dark place – but maybe he was just mesmerised by Lord Jim's story which even I could see was about some sort of moral dilemma, although I was a bit too occupied inside my own dilemma to pay much attention to the message. I don't know what I'd have done had Tom stroked my thigh, but he didn't; it wasn't a thigh-stroking film. I was glad when it was over and the lights came on. We sat in the foyer and had ice cream and talked about the film – I enjoyed talking about it more than watching it.

He's quite a romantic, Tom, just like Tuan Jim in the film, and I like talking to him, and I suppose there's nothing wrong with that. Then I had to get off to work; I'd only just wheedled myself into the evening slot – us newsreaders love it, it's about the only time anybody under sixty watches TV. I dropped him at the university entrance then; I didn't want to drive in past all the students.

'Siggy. I told Tom I'd try to drop by his place after the 10 o'clock news. Should I go?'

'Tom Haddock? The sort-of Englishman born in Malacca? The one I met when you interviewed the orang utan at the zoo?'

'Yes, that's him. The man Professor Fox introduced me to at the amateur dramatics play. Nice person and never tries anything on. Well, he did once hand me a fruit juice and our fingers touched and he kept his there – but I flexed my ring finger and told him about Richard and he took his hand away and sat on it as if punishing it; that made me laugh. He keeps asking me out, which is nice in a way, but having landed the evening news, I don't have time except in the mornings and late at night. Do you think I should go now? It's well after 11.00.'

'If you fancy him, Vee, why not? You won't find many men who sit on their hands to keep them under control. And you can't use the Richard excuse forever. You've done the 10 o'clock and nobody's watching now, so why not? Where's the harm?'

'Because, you know, going to his flat at this time, you know.'

'Not really. Don't see how I could know; I've never been to his place at any time – will though if he invites me; nice looker. You think going to his flat is going too far?'

'Yes. It's a bit creepy at night. It's nice in the daytime. But last time it was late and the campus was deserted; I just picked him up and we went for supper at Newton Circus.'

'No harm in that, whatever the time. If his place feels a bit spooky that's one thing, it's one of those old buildings and now staff's moving out to be near the new campus I hear it's empty apart from him and the mad chemist upstairs. But does Tom also make you feel creepy?'

'Oh no, he's nice; quite the gentleman. Always behaves. But the way he looks at me, I know what he's thinking.'

'Probably thinking what most men in Singapore think when they look at you, Vee. Let's face it, you're a sexy girl. I'd be over the moon if boys looked at me the way they look at you.'

'I bet you would, Siggy! But you're a man, sort of. Perhaps I should take *you* to Newton Circus for supper.'

'Well, you'll be safe enough! I do fancy some porridge. Let me wrap up here and then we can go. But won't Doc Tom be disappointed if you said you're going to see him?'

'I didn't promise or anything. Just said I'd try to drop by.'

'It doesn't look, Vee, as if you're trying all that hard.'

'You know me, Sig. Maybe It's not fair on Tom. Not fair on me either. You know, not fair…'

'On Richard?'

'Sorry, Sig. You know me *too* well. Okay, I'll do my face then let's go for supper. Nobody's going to think anything's up if they see me with you in the middle of the night.'

'Well! Thanks very much! Compliment accepted. But hadn't you better call Tom, lah. He might be waiting for you.'

'He's got no phone. I could call Li Fang – you know, that nice old bag of bones who runs the Guild – and ask him to take a message. You're right, I should let Tom know I'm not coming. It's actually easier to send a message through Li Fang, no need to make excuses. I'll call him.'

And she does. But when she asks if he'd mind taking a message to Doctor Tom, Li Fang cuts her short and says something's just happened and he's about to call the police. Then he tells her what it is and she promises – a real promise – to be there in 10 minutes and then tells Siggy to get his stuff super quick.

3

Death in the Living Room

'G-G-GET THAT d-dog out of there or I s-s-shoot it.' Madhu is nervous. He wasn't expecting to find a body, not in Singapore, not on Bukit Timah Campus and certainly not on his birthday. His threat brings me back to face my world as it is now.

'You don't have any tranquilliser darts, I suppose?' I'd heard Singapore's police are prepared for just about everything.

'F-f-fuck that.' Madhu only says *fuck that* when he sees the bar bill. I forgive the language but can't let him compound the death of the master by killing the master's dog. I like that dog. 'The super will be here any m-m-minute and we can't g-g-get into the h-h-house b-b-b-because of that d-dog.'

Madhu doesn't care much for dogs – a flaw in an otherwise decent bloke. Since there's little chance of Bernard's dog coming out with its paws up, something has to be done and it seems I'm the one expected to do it.

I look around for help or inspiration. I see the crowd of onlookers includes my neighbour from the flat above, Ra'mad bin Ra'mad bin Ra'mad. What's he doing here? I didn't invite him to my birthday party. He's grinning. Probably waiting for the gun blast to silence the dog. David's here, too. David in his horizontal broad-stripe pyjamas; he looks like an escapee from a Vietnamese prison. David, the night rover from the Wolverton

Mess. He never misses a show. He, too, is grinning. But David loves dogs, particularly Bernard's dog, so his grin must be from substance abuse. There will be no help for Bernard's dog coming from the onlookers; it's a dog's life and it's in my hands.

'Okay, Madhu, I'll do what I can. But don't shoot the dog. It might be your only witness and one that can't be a suspect.' My inner mind flashes my outer mind an image of the defendant-suspect: an overweight brown mongrel bitch called Barnaby, forepaws over the edge of the witness box, trying desperately to sway the judge with a whimpering defence. I didn't save Bernard, but I have to save his dog.

'Madhu, can you turn the headlights off? Any dog will protect its home if it's under attack.' Madhu nods and Bernard disappears at the flick of a switch. I move into the darkness, trying to look Joe Cool-Calm-and-Collected and ignore the sweat trickling down my spine. The crowd hushes, the cicadas take a rest, I approach the snapping jaws of a tormented bitch.

'Come on, Barns. Good girl. You don't want to bite me, lah.'

Barns lunges at me, teeth bared. The audience *oohs* like *aficionados* at a bull fight and a high-pitched scream escapes David's pursed lips.

I wait at the door until Barnaby puts her fangs away. I ease myself across the threshold of her tolerance. I keep talking, using that silly little voice we hold in reserve for dogs, babies, the terminally ill and dangerous drunks. 'There, there, Barns, everything's all right. Good doggie. There's a good girl.' I inch across the floor and Barnaby's growls turn to whines. As I reach out to her, she throws herself at me and I catch her. A very nervous dog, desperate for a friend in a hostile world. I hold her tight. Her struggles nudge me off-balance in the dark. An arm brushes

29

against me as it passes in orbit and I sit down hard on Bernard's favourite armchair, Barns in my arms and nervously licking my face. It's not at all the love scene I'd been waiting for.

I keep my eyes on the open doorway, away from the figure stirring the air around us. I hear the sound of the fan; it's the normal creak plus some. The *some* must be the weight of Uncle's body; weight transformed to sound. It's a surreal conjunction of images: the laboured circling of fan and Uncle, me sitting in the armchair Uncle sits in when I visit, the big brown bitch on my lap. Unreal. I'm not really here; Uncle isn't really dead. The word *denial* comes to me. Am I in denial? I do know Uncle's dead; I don't deny it. But I don't *feel* he's dead. Not yet. I don't feel much, to be honest, other than the weight of Barnaby and a wish to be somewhere else; but I can't move, I'm stuck in Bernard's armchair.

★ ★ ★

Sirens sound. Red lights flash blue. A car draws up. Uniformed police get out. From Guild House TV news, I recognise Superintendent Wong, top cop; he does up the buttons of his police shirt and pulls on his hat. Behind the police car, an ambulance. And behind the ambulance a little red Toyota Starlet. And spinning out from the back door of the little red Starlet, Siggy the faithful cameraman, crouching and weaving to avoid unfriendly fire, battery lights blazing from a shoulder saddle, camera capturing the spot-lit descent of Venus into the theatre of crime. Divine intervention is here.

★ ★ ★

Bernard's lonely circling is upstaged by Venus snuggling up to the superintendent of police for the sake of those few Singaporeans – if the Corporation has not already closed down for the night – watching Breaking News as it breaks while spooning down their midnight rice porridge and the many more who will be watching the already broken Breaking News while they chopstick-up their morning noodles.

Camera lights arc towards me. Bernard's shadow flickers around the walls. Barnaby reverts to body-shaking growls. All good television, I'm sure. Madhu is still gun in hand but now he's a TV cop I doubt he'll use it: the decision is now in more senior hands.

I think I see Superintendent Wong wince. The last thing he must want is an interview on TV before he's even glimpsed the hanging man. But there is no way to brush aside this particular newsperson's microphone without insulting half of Singapore. Certainly not today. The banners and posters went up just this morning proclaiming the Island Republic's latest Huxleyan campaign slogan: *Courtesy is Our Way of Life.*

Within the uneasy juxtaposition of courtesy as a way of life and hanging as a way of death, Superintendent Wong pulls Madhu firmly – but politely – into the camera. 'This officer was the first to arrive after the death was discovered; he will brief you on the situation.'

Venus swings the mic to the quivering lips of Madhu and purrs. 'Who discovered the body?'

'I d-d-d-did.'

'That's a bit unusual, isn't it? A policeman actually *finding* a body. I mean, were you *expecting* to find a body? *Suspecting* perhaps the professor was *dead*?'

'N-no. Er. Yes.'

'You were expecting to find the professor dead?'

'It w-was m-m-m-y b-b-irth d-d-day...'

The superintendent stabs a look of horror at Madhu and interrupts. 'Please try to understand, Miss Goh...'

'*Mrs* Goh,' Venus corrects, somewhat sharply.

'Yes, well, Mrs Goh...'

'Was the professor celebrating your birthday with you?' Venus turns the mic back to Madhu. Madhu rolls his eyes and opens his mouth. Before he can form an answer, his articulate superior jumps in.

'Mrs Goh. It is a shock to anyone to find a person hanged by the neck until dead.'

'That sounds like a judge ordering an execution.'

'Does it?' Superintendent Wong seems to be wondering if he should apologise for something. The official memo he'd received that morning said *all* authorities and role models are to *lead* the courtesy campaign by *example*; being another 'role model', I'd got the same memo. Wong looks like he's considering asking Madhu if he would mind awfully putting that wavering gun away, but a commanding, 'Gun away, man!' jumps out.

'Well, the fact is, Mrs Goh, the body has only just been discovered and discovery was made by a policeman – coincidentally. The policeman was off duty and in the Guild House when the manager of the Guild informed him things didn't look right at the house of Professor Fox – the front door was open in the middle of the night. The case is so fresh I'm rather surprised to see the national TV network arriving at the scene within seconds of the police.' The tone sounds slightly critical; Wong immediately softens it. 'I mean, I really must congratulate you on your up-to-the-minute news coverage. Your source of information seems almost as good as our own.'

'Exactly as good.' I notice Venus flash thankful eyes discreetly towards Li Fang. 'And I do believe *we* might have got here first if *I* had a siren and didn't have to keep to the speed limit and stop for red lights.'

The superintendent laughs just a little. Not too much. It must be no easy matter striking a balance between sympathetic appreciation for the charm, wit and beauty of Venus Goh – by far the most popular newsreader of the Singapore Broadcasting Corporation – and the serious face appropriate to an investigation of a hanging body. The superintendent's compromise between charm offensive and crime offensive achieves the look of a clown smiling with his painted mouth turned down.

'What seems to be holding up the investigation, Inspector?' I hear Venus ask. Siggy mouths 'Superintendent' at her. The superintendent looks very much as if he wants to shout '*You are!*' Instead, he waves an ambulance man and Madhu towards Barnaby and begins explaining to the TV camera.

'It's poor Professor Fox's dog...' The super stops as Barnaby interrupts, leaving ambiguity over the object of pity. Barnaby gives out her loudest growls as the body snatchers approach. She's a good Singaporean and knows her values: honour will not allow her to give up her master without a fight to the death. Madhu and the paramedic sensibly stop at the open door.

I speak quietly to the ambulance man. 'Have a tranquilliser handy?'

'For you or the dog?' the ambulance man jokes. He works very fast, as if he does this kind of thing every day, maybe he does. A full syringe is placed in a pouch and skimmed across the floor to my feet. Barns shrinks into my lap.

'Just stick the needle in her bum and push down quick on the plunger. It won't hurt her. Just knock her out for a couple of hours and give her sweet dreams.'

I've never stuck a needle in a bum before. Not even in the Red Cross first aid course, not even a polystyrene mannequin's bum. But there's a first time for everything. Barns yelps and snaps at the syringe as the drug races towards her brain. I hold her on my lap as she gets ever heavier. She looks up trustingly into my eyes and slips into the type of whimpering dream that only dogs have.

As I walk out carrying Uncle's dog, the house lights go on and the fan stops turning. The front doors are closed behind me and a uniformed man sets his feet firmly at ease on the step outside. Bernard's home is now a crime scene waiting to be processed.

My exit with the dog into the glare of Siggy's floodlights prompts a splattering of applause. Given the circumstances, a bow might be in bad taste. I acknowledge my fifteen seconds of fame with a modest smile in the direction of my lady Venus and the camera of the Singapore Broadcasting Corporation, both covering their first-ever hanging.

*   *   *

David flounces up in his prison-stripes and asks are you all right dear, a silly question, of course I'm not, but what do I expect from David? He means well, most of the time. Venus says to put the dog on the seat, lah, and holds open the back door of the Starlet for me to tuck deadweight Barnaby nicely into her Thai silk cushions. 'You were fantastic,' she says – three little words that mean so much more to any man than 'I love you'. I can taste the honey in her tone. 'A real hero,' she continues – another blessed trilogy; I've always wanted to be a hero. Through the dark cloud of Bernard's death, a silver lining struggles to glimmer.

'Lucky you came after all,' I say, opening her passenger door. 'I'd given up hope. Well, almost. Then here you are. Beautiful as ever. Bit of a coincidence you turning up practically as the news happens. But you came. That's what matters.'

'I'm sorry, Tom,' she says, patting the seat next to her for me to get in.

'That's okay,' I say, misunderstanding. 'I'm just glad you're here now.'

Venus looks at me. 'Tom, that's not quite what I meant. Of course, I'm sorry if you were waiting for me and I didn't show. But when I said I'm sorry, I meant, well … you know.' She's heading into a commiseration over the death of Bernard, I think. But wrong the second time. 'It's the same old thing. You know I wanted to come, don't you, but the voice inside held me back. I'm still not ready … you know.' Sure, she's sorry about Bernard, perhaps she's sorry for my hanging around waiting, but essentially Venus is sorry for … Richard.

'But you're here? Or am I dreaming?'

'I worked late at the studio. Can't you get a phone, Tom? How does any girl break a date with you if she can only get to you through Li Fang? Actually, the Li Fang link was lucky this time, I was calling him to send you a message that I couldn't come when he gave me the tip about the professor's death and a ten-minute start before he called the police.'

'Good for Li Fang.'

'Yes, he'll get a nice present.'

Venus has managed a tricky reverse and is pulling away through the Tamil lawyers. Tambiah is looking down over his tummy and through the car's open windows to Venus's long and lovely legs. 'Lucky, lucky bastard,' I hear him murmur; maybe so.

I know Venus has only just passed her test and now she has to cope with changing gears, looking in mirrors, dodging portly Tamils and talking to me. Venus, normally so fully in control, sounds a bit nervy as her words staccato out in a breathless ramble. 'It's a good story, Tom. You'll have to help me flesh it out. You knew the professor better than anyone. You saw him every day. Professor Fox's special friend. Everybody needs a special friend. So, I want you – for the news. Background interview outside the Prof's house. We can do that in daylight, when the coast is clear; no hurry. I can't remember there ever being a hanging on campus. There should be mileage in this one. Unless there's anything political about it, of course. If it turns out to be murder, this could be big. Feel like a fruit juice at Newton Circus?'

Venus pauses her wordy cascade just long enough for me to ask, 'What about Barnaby?'

'Is that his name? The faithful dog defending his master even after the master's death. He looks like he'll sleep for a week.'

'*She*. Barnaby is a bitch.'

'Funny name for a girl.'

'I'll tell you how she got it one day. What about your cameraman?'

'Siggy? He'll hang around here getting what gossip he can and shots of the body going to the morgue and then jump into a taxi back to the studio. No midnight supper for him. Big news at dawn. Another scoop over the printed word. Fortunately, my bit's in the can, so I don't have to be there at daybreak.'

'Does this mean ... ?'

'What it means is I can take my time with you at Newton Circus and come back and help you tuck in Barnaby. I presume she'll be staying at your place?'

'Yes. *If* she'll stay.' As I speak, I suddenly find myself choking back tears and turn my head away. Bernard died and all I did was wait for Venus, who wasn't coming anyway, not until Bernard died.

'Tom, what's the matter?'

'Grief, Venus. Good, honest grief. I loved that guy hanging from the fan.'

'Well, that's certainly a feeling I sympathise with. You know that, Tom Haddock, don't you?'

I certainly do. Venus cannot be faulted on her sympathies.

'Like some chewing gum, Tom?'

'What flavour?'

'Mango and lime.'

Chewing gum in Singapore: embryonic social deviance. I pop it in and chew it over. Barns is jerking away in her doggy dreams on the silk cushions; her pungency rising from the back seat to merge with the sweet smell of Venus. Sweet and sour. I quiver on a sneeze and again choke back the tears; I never did like mango and lime flavour.

I'm feeling unreal again. It's all like watching a film and being in it. Come on you bastard, I tell myself, it's not a movie, there's more to losing your best friend and only known living relative than choking back a few tears and chewing gum. Surely the black hole of Bernard's death can't so easily be filled by the glow of Venus ... can it?

Well, yes, maybe it can, for now. No sackcloth and ashes just yet. I'm too busy tingling at each light touch of Venus's bare arm with every change of gear. Our eyes meet for a split second and my thoughts space-warp a million light years from Professor Bernard Fox. Bernard's mind expanded my universe, the eyes of Venus capture it – perfect magnets pulling me irresistibly towards those full red lips.

I don't normally think in clichés, really, I don't, but I am now. Must be the effect of Venus so close and so utterly head to toe flawless. Long hair, a Malay wave or two in a silky black Chinese sea, flowing softly over amber skin. She's so insanely impeccable, a fusion of sanity and inanity, beauty and banality. She could win Miss Singapore on the curves of her nostrils alone. Can't get more cliché than that. The perfect blend, that's Venus: Chinese delicacy and Malay magic. Venus – the Strait's own breed, *Peranakan*, perfect Singaporean – and it's at *my* elbow she sits on the way to Newton Circus, chewing gum.

★   ★   ★

'Come on,' a familiar voice chides deep inside my head, a voice that struggles to rise from the director's chair and call *cut*. 'I don't want to spoil your fun, if that's what it is, but I'm dead. Your Uncle Bernard's dead. Venus is only here by accident. You are touching her arm early in the morning only because I'm dead. If I were alive, Li Fang would have brought a different message, a she's-not-coming message. How am I supposed to know I'm dead if I don't hear wailing and crying?'

Sorry, Bernard, you haven't picked the best of times to solicit the tearing of hair and rending of garments. The dead may always be with us but they are always dead, while not every day does the most beautiful girl in the world call me a hero, pat the seat beside her and drive me away. There's a time to grieve and a time to lust; perhaps, with practice, the two might go together, but I don't feel like practising right now.

★ ★ ★

I spit the gum out the window into the lawless black night. That's the kind of role model I am. And I kiss Venus gently on a perfect cheek, letting my nose loiter in that perfect hair. The cheek comes lightly salted. As I draw my lips away, a passing headlamp lights up a parade of teardrops rolling slowly over the perfect skin of the perfect cheek of perfect Venus. Perfectly contoured teardrops, of course. Now what, I think, does *she* have to cry about?

4

Woolf at the Door

MY DOORBELL RINGS only once in a blue moon and there hasn't been a blue moon for ages. When I'm in, my door is open, no need to ring; when I'm out, I can't hear it, and if I don't hear it, it doesn't ring, does it? I wouldn't say it's ringing now – it sounds more like an angry AK-47 attacking my door. A rude awakening. Oh Buddha, for whom does the bell clang?

'It tolled for me last night; it must be your clang now, sleeping beauty. Answer the door!' A cultured voice that sounds like Bernard orders me awake. It's all in my head: Bernard's voice, not the rasping doorbell. My clang now? Oh yes, consciousness clangs, this is the morning after Bernard was hanged by the neck and I enjoyed supper with Venus and now there's somebody at the door – better get sorted.

I open onto the familiar, spotty face of David. He no longer wears the broad stripes of the convicted; he now looks almost like a teacher of English at Singapore University should look. He keeps a finger on the button as the angry bell's snarl bounces around the empty circular stairwell; he's making a statement, I suppose. I karate chop it off.

'David, why you attack my rusty ding-dong?' The rougher the treatment, the more David loves it. Usually. Usually, he of all people can be relied on for a parry-riposte to opportunity-lines.

Usually, but not this time. David seems to have lost his parry-riposte. He stands at my door looking at me as if *I'm* the one a bit cuckoo.

'Are friends now supposed to have *reasons* to call by?' he whines, playing little boy offended. David is twenty-nine but looks like a teenager and behaves more like a student at an English red-brick university than a teacher at Singapore's second most prestigious establishment. I do too, I suppose, but not as much as David.

I look at David's Mickey Mouse watch; it's the ungodly hour of 7.30. Ra'mad comes skipping down the stairs. He's sixty-three years old, a year older than Bernard and the senior member of faculty. Sixty-three-year-old department heads don't normally skip down stairs, not in public, but there's not much of the normal about Ra'mad. Swinging on the Art Nouveau metal flame set at the end of the curly banister, Singapore University's own Doctor Frankenstein smiles as if he has just received the Nobel Prize for the perfect poisoning. 'Good morning, David. Good morning, Dr Haddock.' First name for the juvenile delinquent and formal address for me, his only neighbour in an otherwise empty block of resonantly hollow flats that has seen better days and will never see them again.

David, who boasts he can get his tongue around anything, machine-guns back: 'Morning, Doctor Ra'mad bin Ra'mad bin Ra'mad.' Ra'mad son of Ra'mad son of Ra'mad breaks into a chocolate-box smile, his pomaded moustache crackling with static. Now what, I think, brought Ra'mad skipping down from seclusion to smile on the likes of David? He isn't exactly exuding grief, so it can't be the death of Bernard, can it?

'Don't forget, 8.30. And better get that bell fixed; it could wake the dead.' Ra'mad throws the words joyfully over a shoulder as he bounces out the lobby with a spring in his gait that looks like it will take him across the cricket field in a single bound.

'Isn't she the happy one,' David pronounces in his saucy-tart personality. 'Wonder what miracle drug the old goblin's on today. Maybe she's born again. There's a lot of that going around.'

'He's Muslim, David. Muslims can't be born again. That's reserved for Buddhists, Hindus and Singaporean Christians.'

'Must be sniffing formaldehyde, then. Anyway, can I come in, darling, or is the magnificent Venus reason to lock all the bleeding doors and shutters? Trying to keep her in, are you?'

'Want to know why the door's locked, do you? Into the bedroom, David!'

'Oo I say, lovely.' David scampers to the bedroom and opens the door on Barnaby struggling to lift her head from the pillow. 'Don't get up, Barns old chapess.' David sits on my bed and cradles Barns' head in his hands. Barnaby sighs from the stomach up and closes her eyes. 'I say, Doctor Hard-Cock, what have you been up to with this canine beauty? Collar undone. Hairs all over your sheets. Saliva on the pillows. Even the *Straight & Narrow Times* couldn't resist a front-pager on this one: "Drugged bitch found sighing in lecturer's bed".'

'The tranquilliser wore off at four this morning,' I say as I fasten back onto Barnaby the dog collar Venus found on the kitchen counter top the night before. It has a robust lock that's a bit over the top on a dog collar but Venus insisted Barnaby wear it – especially now the place will be crawling with police – to avoid her being rounded up as a stray. Clearly last night I had not been up to fastening a collar on a sedated dog; the distraction of having Venus on my bed – only to tuck in Barnaby.

'Apart from undressing her, squire, what have you been doing with this lady dog?'

'Bitch,' I correct.

'Wish you wouldn't use that word. Makes me go all goosy. Anyway, you going to tell me why Professor Barnaby is asleep in your knocking shop?'

'Yes, David, I am.' I pause for effect. And pause again for added effect.

'Shall I make an appointment or are you going to send me a letter?'

I laugh. 'No, David. If you're good, I'll tell you *now*. After supper at Newton Circus, we came back here and put her into my bed; I think Venus saw her as a surrogate. When the sedative wore off, Barns almost clawed her way through the bedroom door. Well, I couldn't have her zooming back home, not with trigger-happy Madhu around, so I crushed a few Valiums and sprinkled the dust on her tongue.'

'A few Valiums! Christ, Haddock old fruit, this is our Barnaby you're messing with, not one of your little undergrad sweeties. You can't keep stuffing Valium into her to keep her quiet. Where'd you get the stuff anyway?'

'Venus left them with me last night. Thought they would help me sleep. A dozen or so.'

'A dozen or so? My God, Haddock, you'll kill her. She's a dog, not an elephant.'

'I was trying to keep her calm.'

David sighs in reproach. 'You know, there are other ways to calm the excited.'

'Such as?'

'Well, normally darling, I'd say sex. But since you're not into bestiality we must try the next-best non-narcotic thing, mustn't we? Which sounds like it's time for Tosh. I've been trying to find a use for him for a week now. Never had a house guest quite like Toshi. Only opened my heart to him because Bernard asked me to give him a home. Imagine, staying a whole week with *me* and Toshi still can't bring himself out of the closet and admit he's bent as a coat hanger. Every time I lie down, he starts massaging me. Spends hours at it, toe to head but never the middle thing. If I get any more relaxed, I'll melt. A Toshi-san massage for Barnaby might keep both of them cool. Who knows? They might fall in love and get married. I'll prance off and get him.'

David's Toshi is a guest in David's place at the request of Bernard? News to me. I wonder vaguely how Bernard came to know a Japanese masseur. After all, on the whole, Bernard's not over keen on the Japanese – a war thing.

'What the hell do you mean, a *war thing*? I take a perfectly balanced view of the Japanese. I approve heartily of the way they kill themselves; I disapprove of them killing others.' I don't answer; I know it's my imagination playing Bernard in my head. I don't believe in dead relatives contacting the living. I'm an anthropologist; there's always a rational explanation. Bernard was the biggest influence on my life. He was a Fox not a Haddock, the younger brother of my mother. He came over from Malaysia to England just for Mum's funeral. As Mum went up in flames, Uncle Bernard and I picked up a relationship interrupted when I had left to be educated 'back home'. Following the funeral, Bernard had extended his stay to see me into university and had received me in his home in Singapore every summer after that. He looked after me like a father and in many ways was closer to me than my real Dad; he was my friend, I could and did tell him everything. And after helping me through my doctorate, Bernard supported my application to lecture in Singapore – on strict condition I tell nobody he's my uncle. And when I got here, I found he'd arranged for me to have a flat on campus just up the road from him; maybe he too needed a relative, albeit a secret one. Still, I can't tell anybody he's my uncle, or *was* my uncle, and I can't tell because he made me promise not to tell. Ours was a secret relationship; nobody else allowed in. Perhaps that's why he's in my head now; he's too secret to let out. But much as I loved him, I'm not talking to him now.

Given our special relationship, I thought there's not much I didn't know about Bernard. But there's a whole Japanese masseur called Tosh who entered Bernard's life and has been passed to David without my having any idea he exists. Of course, my mind has been so nicely tangled up lately with images of Venus that I might have missed the odd roaming samurai. Anyway, a voice in a sleepy mind doesn't mean it's time for the straight-jacket, does it?

⋆   ⋆   ⋆

Tosh, when he appears, is not the Samurai Superman I expected. He's more a Japanese version of David, painfully thin, transparently effeminate and well-mannered. Not David's type at all. 'Good morning, Doctor Hard Rock. I am derightful to meety. My name it is Toshi and I am massage.'

'Good morning, Toshi. You speak excellent English. Where did you learn?'

'David teach me good. She teach me Engrish rike in Engrand. No Engrish rike in fucking book.'

'Yes, David very good teacher,' I agree.

'She is good man. Invite Toshi in her house. Better than Hirton.'

'Hirton?'

David intervenes. 'Tosh got thrown out of his job as masseur at the *Hilton*. Some bastard tried to get him to do dirty things. When Toshi refused, the rat complained that Tosh had made the advances.'

'Toshi no do dirty things,' Tosh confirms.

'Glad to hear it,' I say seriously.

The canine patient is lifted gently from the bed and carried limp and forlorn into the living room. Toshi directs precisely how Barns is to be positioned. I open all the shutters and doors. Barns turns her eyes towards the light but makes no effort to leave her inert state. She looks nicely stoned.

Tosh kneels and croons to Barnaby. 'Okay, baby-dog?'

Barnaby grunts that baby-dog is very okay, rolls over on her back and places a rear paw into Toshi's lap to be thumbed. She looks as if she regularly pulls into the Hirton to massage away the stresses of life in Singapore's dog-eat-dog fast lane. Sighs of contentment come from both Barns and Tosh. At this point, Venus breezes through the open door bearing huge paper bags. 'Coffee,' she says, 'two gallons of it, croissants and Danish pastries. Plenty here.'

Venus always takes my breath away. She left me at two in the morning and is back looking as fresh and stunning as when Uncle Bernard introduced her to me. Bernard had insisted I go with him to the opening night of a Singapore Thespians play

– 'I've ordered a taxi and two are the same price as one'. He rarely went out in the evening and we could have sat comfortably in Guild House and watched it on TV, but he insisted we go. He also insisted we go backstage when it was over. Venus was interviewing the players. Bernard made a point of introducing me as his very close friend who lives next door. Then, having brought us together, Bernard said he had a taxi waiting outside and that I should stay and introduce Venus and her cameraman to the lead actor, Kingsley Woolf, my colleague in the Anthropology Department and self-proclaimed star of the Singapore stage, 'He'll give you a lift home'. I stayed. Venus camera-interviewed the cast, we all had a drink or two and I ended up being driven home by Venus, who knew my place because it was next to Professor Fox's house, which I'd never thought of as a national landmark. She dropped me at the door and gave me her official-looking Singapore Broadcasting Corporation name card, writing her home phone number on the back. I called her from Li Fang's phone the next day.

I never did get around to asking Bernard how he got on such friendly terms with the most beautiful girl in the world and now I never will. That was a couple of months back. Since then, Venus and I have shared two late suppers, three early lunches, an afternoon viewing of the incredibly old and boring *Lord Jim* – that would have sent me to sleep had the scent of Venus not been stirring my nostrils – and one trip to the zoo, where Venus interviewed Singapore's new poster girl, Ah Meng the orang utan. I'm not sure that constitutes courtship. But I haven't touched her; Richard won't let me.

Venus sets out a picnic breakfast on the coffee table. We seem to have progressed overnight from sharing supper to sharing breakfast, missing out the rather important bit in between.

'Venus Goh,' Venus holds out her hand to David.

'I know,' says David. 'I've seen you on the news. I'm David.'

'And what do you do, David?' Venus asks.

I stiffen. Last time somebody asked David that, he'd replied, 'I suck cocks.' But David clearly likes Venus, who has no cock to suck but bears proxy Danish pastries. 'I try,' he says with feigned resignation, 'to get Singaporeans to speak a whole sentence in one language, preferably English, leaving out the *lahs* and the *is-its*.'

'Ai yah, 怎能, mana boleh? Very difficult job, susah lah, isn't it?' Venus, in three of Singapore's four official languages, makes David grin and turns her charms to Toshi.

'I am Toshi,' says Toshi. 'I am massage.' Toshi bows his head towards Venus without taking his fingers from Barnaby.

Ra'mad pokes his head – just his head – around the front door frame and says in a colloquial Welsh accent, 'You do know about the meeting at 8.30, don't you, like?' Then, seeing Venus, he smiles. Definitely a smiling day for Ra'mad. He makes no move to advance the rest of his body into our line of vision. 'Venus Goh! Quite a surprise to see you here. I suppose you're following up on the story, like?'

Venus smiles back. I frown. 'In a manner of speaking, yes,' she says. 'Have you had breakfast, Doctor Ra'mad?'

'Yes, yes, thank you. I'll be popping along. See you as usual on Sunday, like?'

See you as usual on Sunday, like? Little hairs rise on my neck. What on earth can the lovely Venus have in common with the Rat Man that would bring them together on the Sabbath? Not church, that's for sure.

While I wonder *what* meeting at 8.30, a very bleary-eyed guardian of the law places himself in the open doorway. Seems like this is open day at Haddock's.

'Superintendent Charles Wong. May I come in for a moment, Doctor Haddock?' The super stands, a courteous if somewhat awkward stranger at the gate.

Venus tries to put him at ease by patting a chair and saying, 'Come here, Inspector, and have some coffee. Did you see yourself on the early show today?'

The superintendent takes the coffee gratefully and ignores the demotion in rank. Yes, he saw the early show. His crumpled police shirt suggests that what the super has not seen is his bed. He wastes no time in getting to the immortal words that open Chapter One of the TV detective's handbook: 'I was wondering, Doctor Haddock, if I might have a quiet word with you?'

I suppose nobody ever says no to such a wondering. Superintendent Wong clearly is going to have a word with me, quiet or not. The 'wondering' is not intoned as a question and there is no pause for an answer before the super continues with what seems a total non-sequitur. 'Somebody will be coming to take a blood sample of the dog shortly. It should be done as soon as possible.'

'What do you want to talk about, Superintendent? Can we talk over coffee?'

'I'd like to see you in private, Doctor Haddock. After the meeting, of course. If you could just make yourself available. It is about the ... er ... death of Professor Fox.'

It's the first mention in the early morning-after of the death of Bernard. Until this moment, my flat has been a hub of denial. With the superintendent's words blackness enters, as can only happen in Singapore. Everybody looks at the super as if he has angered the heavens. The poor man falls into a pit of silence and nobody helps him out.

Within consecutive seconds: darkness envelopes us, blue lightning sends veined fingers searching through the heavens, a slap-clap of thunder shakes the plastic coffee cups and rain hammers down. Humbled by the elements we sit in silence; but not for long. The Ride of the Valkyries surges over us in full quadraphonic. Battling its way through the downpour, a powerful engine announces the arrival of the man in a Mustang.

Kingsley Woolf – K – *the* leading light of the Singapore Thespians – is here. K the actor. K the gift of the gods to women. K the world's best driver. K the academic authority on female genital mutilation. K the only proper lecturer in Singapore University, having come down from Oxford rather than up from Hull. K, the only other full-blown anthropologist in town. Together and separately, K and I teach about Man, under which K very much subsumes Woman. Slipping into a guise of mortal man, K hitches his Mustang outside and walks in through the doorway.

Wow, look at me, K screams without words. *Aren't I something!* He certainly is. Tight-fitting trousers carry to the left the groin bulge that always rivets David's attention and makes the undergrad girlies giggle. Pink linen shirt with two buttons open, sleeves turned-up one-fold below the elbow, pince-nez dangling on a silken neck-cord, a silvering mop of hair at the head and polished black shoes at the foot. And the signature K-kerchief knotted cowboy-like on the right side of the neck. Above it, a cheeky half-smile dances perpetually between a sneer of contempt and a beam of irresistible charm. Even his enemies have to admit that K, at forty something-something, looks after himself.

K hates neutrality. He has what those who love him call charisma and those who hate him label affectation. He holds to the Oscar Wilde principle: the only thing worse than being talked about is not being talked about. Kerchiefed K carries his love for amateur theatrics fully into real life – presuming a university campus is real life – and counts on exaggeration to confuse the sarcastic pith of his humour. His word games don't always work, particularly with Chin, the Department's Chinese-educated leader, whose English is, as K would have it, as nominal as the tits on an apprentice ladyboy.

''Ello, 'ello, 'ello. Now what?' K throws out as his entrance line. 'Morning party broken up by the police? Ha, ha, ha.'

The super remains in his pit of silence and his face registers nothing. K's punctuational laugh persistently annoys his enemies more than anything else about him. I have got used to it – just – and in a funny sort of way K is a very good friend. Now Bernard's gone, he might move up a notch and become my best friend. There's really only K and David in line for the position. Of course, there's Barnaby, who might be far less demanding. If you want a friend, get a dog.

K doesn't introduce himself to the super but addresses him directly, recognising his rank from his uniform insignia – more than Venus can do. 'Hope you'll excuse us, Superintendent. I'm under orders of the Vice-Chancellor to get Haddock to the meeting at 8.30 and there's only five minutes to go.'

'Could I ask you for a lift?' The superintendent asks politely, almost humbly, and I feel K warm to him. 'I'm to attend the meeting and my car is on the other side of campus. In this rain, I'd get drenched getting to Staff House.' The super's unassuming manner, I am to realise later, is no indication of his investigative capacities.

'Of course, my pleasure. David, you come too. Even those too poor and wretched to have telephones – like Haddock – are to come to the all-staff meeting. Didn't Ra'mad mention it? Just like the bounder. Never mind, jump in the car.'

'What about Toshi?' asks David.

'What *are* you talking about?' K replies, his half smile dancing towards a sneer.

'The nipple massager,' David explains, nodding his head at Toshi.

'I am Japanese,' says Toshi, smiling up towards K.

'Sorry about that,' K answers in a that's-not-my-problem tone. 'This isn't a party. *No* Japanese nipple-raisers. Definitely *no* Barnaby. *No* Darling of Singapore. Invite only. The noble few … and David.'

The noble few are folded into the back-seat of K's beloved Mustang, leaving behind a neutered bitch, her masseur who has yet to come out of the closet, and the Darling of Singapore who, I think, has yet to work out how her affections, once given unreservedly and forever to Richard, can be transferred to me without destroying a few millennia of Asian values *en passant*.

5

A Regrettable Inconvenience

STAFF HOUSE IS a canteen, not a meeting room. It dates
from the last fling of the Raj. The cavernous roof sheltered colonial formal dinners before it capitulated in February 1942, to
offer a collaborative welcome to Japanese officers of the Co-pros-
perity Sphere. It hosted a mix of old and new masters during the
post-war decades in which Singapore and its university popped
in and out of Malaya in its various forms and moved on with no
substantive identity crisis to serve the pragmatic needs of the
open-necked lecturers of Singapore Inc. Bernard, in the manuscript of *The Social History of Singapore University*, refers to the
colonial building as a symbol of all who survived the uneasy
birth of his beloved Singapore.

In my mind, I congratulate the Vice-Chancellor for holding this congregation within the spectre of ghosts and history
instead of inside one of the more impermeable and spirit-less
air-conditioned lecture halls. Staff House is a modest archi-
tectural hybrid of Imperial Empire, the Costa del Sol and a
kampong *kedai makan*; something for everyone. Curved white-
washed arches open the house to the elements on three of its
sides; on the fourth side, out of sight under a corrugated iron
roof on which the rain machine-guns, is an afterthought kitchen.
Long eaves provide some protection from the more aggressive

of nature's moods while ensuring a continuous circulation of mosquitoes inside and reducing the light on a cloudy or rainy day – most days in Singapore – to something like the inside of a smoky London club. It still amazes me how dark and broody the equator can be once the sun goes out. The mood, I feel, is appropriate for the occasion.

A ceiling-less high roof extends up into invisible heavens. Li Fang swears the murky cavernous overhead harbours the ghosts of Japanese officers who committed suicide on hearing on the radio their Emperor's surrender. Li Fang himself is already here, with a little group of non-academic staff; Bernard's death belongs to all. The restive mutter of the gathered is stilled to silence as the amplified VC comes through loud and clear above the drumming rain.

'The reason we are here is a sad one. Professor Bernard Fox died last night. His death is under inquiry by the police and I am pleased to say Superintendent Wong is taking personal charge of investigations.' The VC looks appreciatively towards Wong. Siggy zooms in. 'All of us must help the police by cooperating with them. Superintendent Wong's team will be interviewing all of us over the coming days and fingerprints will be taken as a matter of course. The police investigation will tell us all we can know about this tragic death. There is no room for rumour.'

The congregation murmurs agreement as Siggy pans across the serious face of academe. The VC is a practised if unexciting speaker. He allows a pause to mark the end of point one before point two.

'The death of a dean ... well ... *the* Dean of the Faculty of Arts and Social Sciences, is a regrettable inconvenience.' So, Bernard's demise is a *regrettable inconvenience*. I suppose it is,

Bernard was always something of a regrettable inconvenience when alive and I think he'll be happy to retain that distinction. 'Classes and all university activities will be suspended for three days effective immediately with a possible extension. This is for two reasons: firstly, as a mark of respect and mourning for Professor Fox and, secondly, to allow the police to conduct their enquiries without having to work around teaching schedules or undergraduates coming and going. All students are being informed of the suspension and sent home today. You are, at the request of the police, required to remain accessible for interview, either in your offices or in Guild House, which will be the temporary police field-quarters as it is conveniently close to the scene of the ... er ... event.'

The VC plays things as straight as the causeway. There is absolutely no hint that the murderer, if murderer there be, might be among us. My mind stands at ease and begins to wander to thoughts of Venus and Danish pastries, only to be drawn sharply back to attention by the VC's third point.

'We will all mourn our departed colleague and friend but university life must go on. That is, I'm sure, what Professor Fox would have wanted. Thus, the position of dean will be filled *ad interim.*' Murmurs of supportive agreement ripple obediently through the House, although nobody could possibly think of any need to rush to fill the post even *ad interim*; Bernard had been almost banished from the policy body of the university for months before his death and everybody knows it. I wonder benignly if the VC wants to do Bernard the posthumous honour of suggesting he played some kind of important role that must be maintained. Wrong. The VC's next sentence drops like a guillotine blade. 'Doctor Harry Chin will be Acting Dean of

Humanities pending a permanent appointment. I know you will all support Dr Chin.'

Ra'mad gives an audible gasp; eyes turn to him. A very wet man standing on the edge of shelter in a world full of electricity searching for an earth, Ra'mad looks as if he has been struck by lightning. His intake of breath is epidemic and for seconds the building itself seems to draw in its sides. Chin of all people! Support Chin as a replacement for Bernard? Impossible! Harry Chin, my Head of Department, characterised by his principle antagonist, Kingsley Woolf, as *the one man on faculty staff who could be replaced by a cardboard cut-out without any of his students and certainly not his wife noticing other than a change for the better.*

One year only as Social Studies Head, Chin has nothing to show for an academic career except an eight-hundred-page *Demography of Singapore*. This singular work was attacked by a *nom de plume* review – of suspected Woolfish origins – and dismissed as: 'A thoroughly original work – eight hundred pages of tables and charts pulled from all over the place and stuck together with no discernible thread of meaning and serving no function other than the ambition of an unknown academic to get to somewhere he should not be.'

K's attempts to discredit Chin before he took over the Social Studies Department achieved only the eternal animosity of Harold Chin. Few members of faculty read reviews of anything other than their own publications. Even fewer are ever likely to open an eight-hundred-page book unless they have their names on it or at least in it. Chin's eight hundred large pages of heavy paper, solidly hardbound, weighs in at over a kilo. The book and his attractive wife Agnes, especially Agnes, had been enough to land Chin the department leadership. But Acting

Dean? How on earth did Chin wheedle his way overnight into Bernard's yet warm chair? Bernard had led opposition to Chin getting the Head of Department position; what would he be thinking now?

I search for Chin's face in the crowd. Nothing registers there, no surprise, no exhilaration, nothing. He remains wrapped in his impenetrable cocoon. Inscrutable. As the VC calls for a minute of silence to remember the dead and end the meeting, questions buzz around my suspicious mind. Where was Chin last night? At home I suppose, I saw his BMW outside his house. The nearest neighbour to Bernard's place, on the other side of it to my flat, Chin's house had remained dark throughout all the activity surrounding the discovery of Bernard's body. Who could have slept through Barnaby and the sirens?

I doubt any one of those present thinks of the dear-departed but the silent minute does work some kind of miracle. As the VC finishes mouthing his count of sixty and raises his head, the clouds roll away as rapidly as they came and the rain fades to a steamy mist. The sun sends a rainbow over the university and Siggy films it. The end lands smack in the middle of Acting Dean Harold Chin's house.

A few of the more ambitious members of staff hang back to congratulate Chin. David, K and I meet at the car. 'What bloody humbug,' K spits out, winding down a window. (We are in 1980: cars are an extravagance, air-conditioned cars a luxury and electric windows a novelty.)

Ra'mad walks past us, face set like brown granite, and agrees very loudly, 'Really. Bloody humbug!'

'Christ,' says David. 'Things must be really bad if K and Rat Man are in the same bed. Can you believe it, Chin as Dean?

Truly, we are all in the gutter but some of our noses are in the shit while others are looking at the fucking stars.'

The super holds up a hand for a lift. K waves for him to jump in and guns the Mustang into reverse. We see Chin walk out from Staff House into a halo of sunshine, his star rising faster than the Singapore dollar.

'Well, Davey-boy, that twisting, crawling turd you see in front of you,' K stabs a finger towards Chin to make it quite clear to which particular turd he refers, 'will very soon be a falling star face down in the gutter.' The super looks genuinely puzzled at K's words. I suppose he holds the naïvely popular view of academic life as something removed from the rat race of perpetual in-fighting. By the end of the investigations, he will be more tuned in to the reality of life in Ivory Towers.

On the narrow road back to the flat, the Mustang's tires shed screaming rubber on every turn. It seems K is taking Chin's good fortune worse than the news of Bernard's death. The super braces himself against the dashboard and his tired face looks as if he regrets asking for a lift.

'You know what I reckon, K?' K tosses his locks to indicate that he cares not what I reckon, so I continue. 'I reckon the VC just placed a non-entity in the job to keep it open. Chin can't remain as dean. He's not a senior faculty member.'

'Fat chance. Chin's a limpet.' K cuts a corner so violently two wheels briefly leave the road. The Citroën of the night before pulls off onto the grass for safety ahead of us. K toots and waves cheerily at the scowling blond as he brushes past Black Beauty with barely a paint job to spare. Had K's reactions been a smidgen less than perfect, that magnificent French car, one of those that fearless blond officers chose over their own Volkswagen to ride into their thousand-year Reich, would have been forced down the steepest slope on campus – hopefully to combust in a rage of flames on the cricket field and save me lots of grief later.

'No way Chin will let someone take his place now he's in it. If you think that, Haddock-me-lad, you ain't learnt much about the chinks during your time in Singapore.' K glances sideways at the super, who is too busy trying to stay upright to take offence at a racial diminutive. David's eyes fix on K's flowing silver mane; hero worship in his eyes. Where, I think, is all the sadness that should be spilling from each of us? 'Mark my words, Haddock,' K continues. 'Chin will want a clean sweep of Bernard's men – beginning with us, no doubt.'

★   ★   ★

'Good news for you,' Chin says, in Mandarin, of course. And in my imagination, of course.

'You don't gamble so we haven't won the lottery,' Agnes replies, happy to put a damper on anything her husband considers good news. The events of the night before have drained her vivacity, not that she wasted much of it on Chin.

'Much better than that,' says Chin, who thinks the national lottery should be banned along with chewing gum. 'I'm the new dean.'

'Darling!' Agnes can't remember when she last used the word – probably, she thinks, when Harry bought the BMW. Her mood doesn't swing, it positively leaps from depression to elation. 'So fast! The position's only been vacant twelve hours. How did it go through Faculty so quickly?'

'It didn't yet. The VC just announced it. That's why he called me in at 8.00 before the meeting. Wanted to know: if he offered it, would I accept? Of course, I said yes and he's just announced it. It will have to be confirmed by Faculty but that's a formality. Until it is, I'm *ad interim*. That's good in a way as it gives me a few weeks to clear away the opposition and the status to do just that.'

'Well, Darling, I don't know what you mean by opposition. I suppose you mean Ra'mad, he must be the longest-serving member of faculty. Not much opposition there. He doesn't even have a wife.'

'Yes, he does. But she's well out of things in a nursing home. I'm not thinking of him – he may be senior but he's in place as Head of Malay Studies only because they couldn't find anybody qualified – I'm thinking more of those foreigners. Not all of them, but those who have voting rights.'

'Internal politics. Don't expect a simple girl like me to understand. I'm sure you'll manage whatever's necessary. Now, this is cause for celebration.' Agnes takes the hand of her husband and leads him through to the bedroom to give him his reward.

6

Quiet Words with Wong

AT SUPERINTENDENT Wong's request, K drops both of us outside Bernard's front door. 'We can have that talk now, just the two of us, inside the professor's house.' The super tells the policeman outside to open up then go get himself a cold drink in Guild House opposite. We enter the house quietly and respect-fully, like going into an empty church. Barnaby, having finished her massage or maybe just coming home, or just being Barnaby, who goes wheresoever she likes, when she likes, on *her* campus, pants in after us.

'You were pretty good friends with the professor, Doctor Haddock?'

'Yes. Very good friends. I knew him well enough to know if he had any enemies. That is one of the first things you'll want to know, isn't it? The police always ask that question in the movies.' Super Wong gives the smallest nod of affirmation. 'On campus, there were two. Ra'mad, the longest-serving head of depart-ment after Bernard, who no doubt expected to be the new dean. Maybe enemy is too strong a word for Ra'mad – the two just weren't friends. And Chin, who lives next door. Their enmity goes way back. Chin is the new dean *ad interim*.'

'To judge from Ra'mad's remarks outside Staff House just now, it seems Ra'mad and Chin don't exactly get on, either.

What do you think is the reason for their particular antagonism? Or does everyone hate everyone around here?'

'Perceptive of you, Superintendent. Ra'mad and Chin have a lot in common but are worlds apart. Bernard told me Ra'mad was hand in glove with the Japanese-led anti-colonial movement in World War II. Chin's too young to have been involved in the darker history of Singapore, but Bernard said Chin's father was nationalist-Chinese and that he too cooperated with the Japanese. Chin's Chinese-educated all the way. That's why his English is so flaky. His father, Chin Jin-Hui, was convinced Mandarin would become the primary language of Singapore and the whole of Southeast Asia. Harry Chin is said, at least by Bernard, to share his father's dreams regarding language.

'It's the language question that sets Ra'mad and Chin apart. Chin has no place for the Malay language, while Ra'mad not only *is* Malay, he is Head of Malay Studies, although his PhD is in Chemistry and his thesis is entitled "The Use of Poison in Malay Communities" and his interests lie less in analysis of the Malay Annals than in the analysis of poisons. He got to be Head of Malay Studies because nobody else with a doctorate wanted the job. Rumour has it he would still like to see a pan-Malay union embracing the peninsula, Singapore, Borneo and Indonesia. But rumour is rumour and Bernard thought him harmless. So, while Chin and Ra'mad share origins that had no love for the British or for Bernard, they have no love for each other.'

Wong surprises me with his next remark. 'If the truth were known, we might say the same for many members of Singapore's multi-ethnic society; I can remember the bloody riots of 1964 between Malays and Chinese, but violence was even worse between Teochew and Hokkien speakers. That sort of thing is gone but not forgotten. Fortunately, although you might not share my opinion, today we do not discuss issues of race and language in the public forum.'

Super Wong is a pretty good psychologist under his crumpled uniform. He manages to draw me out from the academic's usual hedge of qualification and on-the-other-hand-ness, although I can't give up my double negatives. 'I'm not sure I do not share your opinion, Superintendent. Even if Singapore's ethnic harmony is only skin deep, race relations are much better here than in just about any country in the region, perhaps in the world. I only hope that racial distrust is disappearing and not just brooding beneath the surface waiting to explode.'

'You're the anthropologist, Doctor Haddock, what's your long-term prognosis for Singapore?'

'I share the opinion of Bernard there. He was optimistic short term and pessimistic long term. He thought there would be few problems as long as things were getting better all the time for everybody but that people might close ranks within language and skin colour when the pickings are less abundant. He would have loved things to be otherwise but he thought the history of Man to be one of different peoples living happily side by side for decades or generations and then suddenly hacking each other to death for no particular reason.'

'Or hanging each other from fans?'

'Then you don't think Bernard's death suicide, Superintendent?'

'Let's leave that one for the moment. Let me first ask you another of those questions you will be expecting: when and where did you last see Professor Fox alive?'

'Soon after lunch yesterday, about three in the afternoon. Right here.'

'Did you use the front or the back door?'

'Both. Had lunch at the Guild, crossed the road, spent half an hour or so with Bernard, then left by the back door.'

'How did he seem?'

'You mean were there any signs of depression? No. Bernard had taken his nap and was back into his work at his desk.'

'Anybody see you leave?'

'Li Fang was already here; he saw me. There's a little path between Bernard's back door and mine. I always leave my back door open – so did Bernard; he started locking it just last week, don't know why. Bernard's housekeeper is away and I just dropped in to see if he needed anything.' I'm aware this is a revision of our last meeting but there is nothing to be gained by making known what Uncle made me swear to keep secret.

'And you say, Doctor Haddock, that you sat alone all evening, until Li Fang came for you near midnight. Can anybody confirm your presence at home?'

'The blond man in that vintage Citroën we passed just now came to my window soon after 10 o'clock at night. I'd never seen him before and don't know his name – he had a German accent. He wanted to use my phone to call Bernard. Bit late for a social call on Bernard.' I try to sound helpful. 'He said Bernard didn't open his door to him.'

'Not surprising if he were dead,' says Wong. 'I'll be interviewing everybody, but thanks for that. It's always good to confirm who was where, when and why, and fit it in with the time of death when we know it. Now, could I ask you to sit where you were last night when you came in to get Barnaby? Put the

64

professor's dog on your lap if she'll come.'

Barnaby comes readily enough. Wong slumps tiredly in the other armchair. He explains quietly that his men left everything exactly in place as they found it and asks me if anything looks different to the way it normally looked when the professor was alive.

We sit in eerie silence. Bernard's shoes are still at the back door. He always slipped them off when coming into the house and usually used the back door. His typewriter is at his desk, a blank sheet of paper inserted. The way he left it when going to bed – ready in case inspiration or insomnia drove him to the machine during the night. The chair is pushed back from the desk as if he has just risen from it.

'The fan,' I say and turn it on at the switch by the front door. 'Bernard always had it on lowest. He used to say that its slow creak matched the turn of his mind.' The super says nothing and we sit on. Barnaby cocks her head from side to side as if the familiar sound of the fan will bring Bernard out of the kitchen. I look along the old prints of the Straits Settlements on the wall and linger on a fading black and white photograph of Bernard in his mid-twenties and the anti-Japanese leader Chin Peng in their wartime jungle hideout. 'Apart from the fact that the shutters are closed in the daytime, I would say everything is as it usually was.'

'Take your time please, Doctor Haddock. We'll leave the shutters closed, the way they were last night. Something might come to you. In the meantime, perhaps you can tell me about Professor Fox; I knew him but not as you knew him.' The superintendent's manner is friendly, as if we are working together to solve the mystery of Bernard's death; clever, that.

'Where shall I start? There really was so much more to

Bernard than our shared years at SU. I got to know Bernard well during these last two years but I have only a faint idea of his early years.' Better, I think, to stick to the idea of Bernard as close friend of two years than go into our lifelong secret relationship.

The super speaks gently. 'Start anywhere. I don't take notes or use a recorder. A failing of mine. I often have to return and ask the same questions. It helps me build up an overall picture. Start anywhere you like. Did he, for example, as a pessimist about the human race, exhibit any prejudices himself?'

'Certainly, no racial prejudices. At worst, he might be accused of a dislike of the Japanese – but not all Japanese – and a paternalism towards Malayan aborigines. He spent three years with them during World War II and, until his health deteriorated, now and again went back into the Perak jungle to spend time with them.'

'How did he get to Singapore in the first place?'

'He came down from Oxford in 1940, age 21, and was declared unfit for the armed forces. Probably his eyes. He always wore thick glasses to read. There's a pair beside you on his desk. He usually left them there, next to his work. He passed his civil service exams, was given a Malay dictionary and packed off to colonial service in Malaya. He'd just about got settled in when the Japanese invaded and Bernard found his bit of the Empire had changed emperors.

'Bernard told me he passed the war in the jungle of Perak with Chin Peng, his anti-Japanese guerrillas and the local aborigines. He was surprised at the end of the war to be given three years' back pay and – like Chin Peng himself – receive an OBE for his time with the stay-behind forces. Bernard developed a great respect for Chin Peng. After the war, he stayed on throughout the Emergency, but asked to be placed in a position that would not require him either to support or betray Chin Peng, who by 1948 was leading the communist forces against the British; so he was offered a job in Singapore U at that time.'

'So that's how he got here,' the super punctuates my monologue. 'But do continue. Everything you can tell me about the professor might be relevant.'

'Bernard placed friendship above anything else, even above his country. Chin Peng and Bernard became close friends when the Raj left him to the mercy of the Japanese. And Bernard did not make friends flippantly; he spoke Malay fluently but could not befriend Ra'mad – I suppose because of their opposing sides in the war. Bernard knew my family – my father was in the colonial police.' I do not mention that Bernard was my mother's brother and my only uncle. We kept our relationship secret when alive and I can think of no good reason to announce it now he's dead. 'My parents spent the war in Ceylon but came back when Japan surrendered. I was born in Malacca but went to the UK for school in the 1950s, so I never really knew Bernard until I got the job here.'

The super is studying the picture of young Bernard with Chin Peng. 'I wonder what Acting Dean Chin's father made of Chin Peng.' Now, why, I think, bring my department head's dead father into an investigation of Bernard's death?

'Your guess, Superintendent, is as good as mine. I heard Chin's father died just after the Japanese surrender, so you can't ask him. There are rumours he prospered during the Japanese years through collaboration and other rumours he was really working against the Japanese, passing information and funds raised by the Chinese in Singapore to Chin Peng in the jungle. I don't suppose we will ever know the truth. Does it really matter? It was so long ago.'

'Do you think Harry Chin would know?' Clearly, Wong attaches some importance to knowing.

'Harry would have been a baby when his father died, he's not that much older than me. But if he knows, I doubt very much he will admit to either version of his father, collaborator or communist. Singapore is still a place where the sins of the father carry over to the son.'

'But wasn't Chin senior more a nationalist than a communist? He made substantial donations to the Chinese University here.'

'But some say the money he gave was only part of the money he took from Singaporeans during the war and that most never found its way either to the university or to Chin Peng.' Why are we talking about Chin's father?

'Who's *some*?'

'Well, *one* might be a better word. Li Fang.'

'Would Professor Fox have known the truth of the matter?'

'If you had asked that question to Bernard, he might have replied: "It all depends on what you mean by truth." Bernard accepted that a person could be more than one thing but I rather gathered he saw Chin senior as a collaborator and didn't look any further. Not that he ever discussed Chin or his father with me.'

'Yes. But ... the money? Would Bernard Fox have known if Harold Chin's father diverted funds meant for anti-Japanese forces to the Japanese?'

'I don't know,' I say, wondering how the super has hit the nail on the head so quickly. 'Do you think it important?'

'It might be. At this early point in enquiries, everything

about Bernard Fox and his past could be important. We might get around to approaching Chin Peng quietly but I don't see how he or Professor Fox could have known in the jungle what was happening here in Singapore.' If the super doesn't see, I'm not about to tell him.

We fall into silence. Next to the typewriter, a glass of water stands half full, half empty. I look around again, searching for any detail that might give the super something to work on. A mental picture of Bernard at his desk forms and dissolves in my mind, reforms and turns to look at me. Bernard's lips are moving. Is he telling me something? No, he's eating! That's it, Bernard's eating.

'Bernard ate late. Either Li Fang would bring him something over from Guild House or his housekeeper would make something and leave it in the fridge for him. He almost always ate at his desk. Any time between 7.00 and 10.00 in the evening. He was a nibbler and he wasn't too fussy about cleaning up. He would leave his plate on the desk for Norsiah – that's the house-keeper – to clean up in the morning. She's devoted to Bernard and would never have suggested he change his ways to save her the trouble of clearing away the ants. She also cleans for me; she didn't come yesterday or the day before, so she must be away.'

'Norsiah,' the super says to himself as if making a note in his mind. He looks tired. 'Please go on. Detail is what catches criminals.'

'Well, if Bernard died before 7.00, he would probably not have eaten first, but any time after that and he would have nibbled at something, but I see no plate.'

'In the sink perhaps? To save ant trouble with the house-keeper away?'

'I'm sure you know exactly what is in the sink, Superintendent.' Of course he knows.

'Perhaps the professor planned to go out to eat somewhere?'

'He hadn't been off campus for ages. He was fanatical in his working routine. He was coming to the end of what he said was the best thing he'd ever written and stayed close to his work. He was on the final lap of his marathon and almost finished.'

The superintendent interrupts. 'Perhaps, Doctor Haddock, there is no plate because the professor did not feel like eating. If you were plucking up courage to end your life, would you call Li Fang to bring an egg fu-yong?' I would probably call for a lot more than egg fu-yong if I get to the point of suicide, but I say nothing; the super has a point. 'The detail of Professor Fox's eating habits is noted in my mind,' the super says tiredly, leaving me to think my observation of the missing plate is not a likely case solver. 'Any other anomalies with the professor's normal routine?'

We are in the same room but in different worlds. For me, Bernard's sitting room is a place of sacred memory, a temple to things past, for Wong it is a source of pendent discovery, a treasure-trove of hidden clues. We sit again in silence. Eventually, the superintendent offers a prompt. 'Was the professor's chair normally there at the desk?'

'Yes. It's exactly as if he just stood up. As if he will be back any minute. When Bernard was not at his desk, he would sit in this armchair, at least he would when I was here. His working chair would remain just at that angle, just the way it is now. It's as if he had finished his work for the day and stood up to go to bed.'

'Or to welcome a friend?' The point is a little too sharp for comfort but the super does not pause for an answer before continuing. 'And no other chairs are normally in the room?'

'No. Only the two we are sitting in and his work chair.'

'Please think carefully. When you came in here last night to get the dog, did you move any piece of furniture?'

'No.'

'You're sure?' the super insists. 'Nothing? Not even a cardboard box or something?' I realise where the superintendent's mind is leading.

'It was dark. If anything got moved, I am unaware of it. Superintendent, there was nothing between Bernard's feet and the floor and nothing near his feet that would have held his weight.'

'I think you understand, Doctor Haddock. If Professor Fox hanged himself, he would have had to step off something.'

'So, suicide is ruled out?'

'No. Perhaps the cleaner's not away at all and she put the chair back and cleaned away the plate after he hanged himself – or for that matter after she hanged him. Or there might be an explanation so far not evident … Or you might be lying.'

'Do you suspect me, Superintendent?'

'You must be considered a suspect. You live next door, you have no alibi, you had the habit of dropping in and you could get past the dog.'

'Motive?'

'At the moment, Doctor Haddock, motive unknown. There is no indication of a struggle and however well a killer – or a housekeeper – tidies up, it is difficult to hang a man against his will and leave no trace. The fan might not have held his weight if the professor had been struggling.'

'From what you say, it sounds like you suspect suicide.'

'It's the most likely conclusion to an investigation like this. A man kills himself and that's an end to the matter. Had you told me you moved a chair from near the body, that could be the answer that would satisfy everybody.'

'I did not kill my best friend.' I get in an early plea of innocence.

'I said moved a chair, not pulled a chair. There is a compromise scenario between suicide and murder that at this early point in investigations appears to encompass the facts we know so far – assisted suicide. You knew the professor was sick, you knew of his problems with the university authorities and how much they depressed him. If the professor had asked you, would you have helped him rig the noose? Helped him onto the chair. Watched as he kicked away the chair? Perhaps held his hand as he allowed himself to be strangled with as little struggle as possible? And then you put the chair back in its place. Like a Samurai assisting his friend at the end.'

I have just met the superintendent yet he seems to know me and Bernard only too well. It's a bit spooky. As if he has been listening in on our private conversations. Is he just fishing or can he read me so easily? I don't know.

'And then turned on the fan, Superintendent?'

'A bit ghoulish. But, why not? Maybe you wanted to deflect a conclusion of suicide.'

'By leaving the front door open?'

'That,' says the super, 'is more likely to support the idea of suicide than conclude against it. No murderer would leave the very public front door open on his crime. A suicide, however, might be considerate of those who find the body. In the dark, the scene would not be visible from the road unless, as happened, a bright light is shone inside. In the morning light, on the other hand, a passer-by could see the body and call those more used to dealing with such things. You said the professor's housekeeper is away; perhaps he did not want her on return to be the one to find the body, so he left the front door open. By the way, do you know where she has gone and when she's coming back? We need to talk to her. You say she was your cleaner too, so do you have a telephone number or address for her?'

'Sorry. I didn't even know she was going. She has a servant's room just behind Bernard's back door; there might be an indication in there. Maybe she's gone back to her village in Perak for some family reason, but it's odd Bernard never told me. It's near where Bernard was during the big war and he occasionally went back there. It's mostly aboriginal and I doubt there's a telephone. I don't know the name of the village. I don't even know the housekeeper's full name. Admin will have it – she'd have an identity card to work and live on campus; she's been here for years. And as for Bernard's front door, last night it was closed at 10.00, if we can believe the German at my window; he said he knocked hard on Bernard's door and got no answer.'

Superintendent Wong has set out a reasonable hypothesis of assisted suicide. I am aware that once the super has read Bernard's *Social History of Suicide*, he will have a clear idea of the sympathy and at times admiration with which Bernard wrote about those who kill themselves and those who assist suicide.

*   *   *

Where is my work? It's Bernard, back in my mind and now talking loud and clear. *Am I supposed to have destroyed it and then killed myself or what?*

'There is indeed something different in the room now,' I say.

'I'm listening,' Wong says.

I walk to Bernard's desk and open the cupboard below it. It is empty. 'Where did you put his manuscript?'

The super's expression sparks as I continue. 'Bernard had been working on *The Social History of Singapore University* for over a year. He always worked at this desk and kept the manuscript pages in the desk cupboard. Just one copy, he never made carbons, too much trouble. He did not talk directly about his work in progress but I got the feeling that some people would be wounded by what he wrote. Bernard was a very moral man but he did not set himself up as judge; he said he could not self-censor but was more than a bit bothered about his work being used for purposes other than those for which he intended it.'

'Which were?'

'As an academic work of history it was his child, his way of extending his life after what he thought a cruelly brief span; he was after all only 62, but with his heart problem he didn't expect to enjoy old age. It would also, he hoped, serve as a memorial to what will be lost if there is no Bukit Timah Campus. Over the past year, his life was this book. He had finished it and was checking, changing and polishing. I have never seen him as happy as over the last couple of weeks. The university establishment was treating him like a leper for opposing the relocation but he was in no way driven to despair. His heart obliged him to rest in the afternoons but this was not a reason to end his life. He knew he had written a powerful book. He told me this book was what he wanted to be remembered by.' The super raises his eyebrows at my last ambiguous words, as if still waiting for a sound argument against the suicide hypothesis and not finding it.

Get to the point! Bernard hisses in my ear.

'The point is,' I continue hurriedly, as Barnaby follows the super towards the front door, 'Bernard would never have killed himself before seeing his work published. You asked me if I noticed anything different about the room. Yes, I do. Bernard's manuscript is gone.'

The super stands in the doorway and turns off the fan. 'How many people knew the professor was writing this book?'

'Everybody knew he was writing something. Probably a lot of people knew he was writing a history of the university.'

'A history of the university...' Wong muses, looking very tired again as he moves out into the sunlight. 'Those words don't sound too threatening. There is a history of the Raffles Hotel about to be published and there must be a hundred histories of Raffles and Singapore but not one of the writers was murdered – although it might be tempting to conclude justifiable homicide if one or two had been.' The superintendent's ability to joke dryly about the deadly serious is something Bernard would have appreciated. I am caught off guard as the super slams straight back into a logical line of enquiry. 'Tell me. Apart from you, who regularly visited the professor? Who might know the book was ... what shall we call it? Something of a rendering of accounts?'

'Kingsley Woolf, sometimes called "K" – that's what we call him – was just about the only lecturer apart from myself who didn't back down on the issue of campus relocation. And David Bent used to pop in. Bernard was interested in the open discussion of homosexuality – but don't get the idea he was homosexual, he told me he was attracted to the abstract idea of homosexuality as an antithesis to the norm of reproduction inherent in what we think of as instinct and society. Agnes, the wife of the acting dean, also used to drop in occasionally in the afternoons. I think she's a bit lonely – understandable if you are married to Chin. Bernard's housekeeper saw the manuscript every day but probably had no idea what it was about. Li Fang, the Guild House manager, saw Bernard every day but he's no reader. I doubt if anybody apart from me knew much about the explosive nature of some of its contents.'

'Those people are all, like you, neighbours or regular contacts of the professor. Most murders, *if* this is murder, are committed by people who know the victim well. Murderers rarely just drop in, kill a stranger, and leave. That's why we focus on motive.'

'You asked me, Superintendent, who *regularly* visited Bernard. But you showed no surprise just now when I told you about the German. I never saw him before last night. He came to my house around 10.00 and said he had *tried* to visit Bernard. Perhaps *he* succeeded and was the last person to see Bernard alive.'

'That,' replies the super, 'was the distinguished criminologist Professor Von Führer Düsseldorf. You haven't seen him before because he only came back to Singapore last week. I met him earlier yesterday evening – so his alibi is gold standard. The Vice-Chancellor held a small reception for him. Professor Fox and Doctor Chin were invited but both declined; seems Düsseldorf's an old friend of Chin's father. We'd talked at the reception about long-term institutional memories in Singapore and I mentioned Professor Fox as one of the most important. I told him Professor Fox lives right next to Chin; he said he knew the house as Chin had mentioned it. He was familiar with some of the professor's writing and openly praised his work on suicide. You'll be meeting Düsseldorf professionally before long.'

The superintendent's car has been brought to Guild House for him. He reaches a tired hand to open the back door. 'Thanks for providing a motive for murder: theft or destruction of the professor's manuscript. By one of life's endearing little ironies, that motive also makes you prime suspect and your friend Woolf number two – supposing only the two of you had much of an idea about the contents.' He calls across the road into Guild House that the professor's house should now be relocked. 'You'll excuse me Doctor Haddock, I'd rather crash on my bed than in the car. We'll be talking again once I have seen the coroner's report – and once I have read *A Social History of Suicide*. Let me know if your cleaner turns up and so as not to disappoint your expectations,' he gives a wry smile, '... please don't leave Singapore without my okay.'

I walk towards home feeling the excitement of novelty rather than the disquiet of sadness; murder is anything but boring. Real grief seems as elusive as ever. Bernard's death has added spice to my life at a time when I am still young enough to enjoy an increase in adrenaline. Barns hugs my side as I walk. 'Well, Barns, I'm *prime* suspect and K is only number two – he'll be furious.' Christ, I am not only hearing voices from the other side, I'm also sharing confidences with a dog.

I know Venus is waiting for me in the flat, something of a role reversal, but I can see K's car still there and I don't feel like any company more demanding than Barnaby. It's time for a mad dog and a sort-of-Englishman to take a walk in the midday sun and have a little man-to-dog heart-to-heart.

7

Ice Cream and Orchids

I WALK ALONG the shaded open-air corridor between the two quads at the heart of what Bernard refers to affectionately in his manuscript as the 'imitation intimations of immortality associated with the great universities of the world'; I'm not quite sure what he meant by that, having gone to a very mortal place full of red bricks, sounds impressive though. Whatever Bernard meant, the imitation succeeded so unpretentiously in his view, he approved it. Certainly, nothing is overdone. There are no fearsome gargoyles on high or highly-placed people from centuries past lowly placed under flagstones in chapels for feet to walk over, but there is a harmony of structure and mood that any visitor from anywhere in the world would associate with a university of standing. The magic of the place is, to use Bernard's words: 'strong enough to take students out of the everyday without stranding them in never-never land.'

Bernard saw the university as a vital bridge between the abstract concept of learning and the concrete but pragmatically-changeable realities of Singapore. To him, the university's standing and mystique captured and held those privileged to be part of an institution older by far than any of them and much older than the Republic of Singapore, which at this time of Bernard's death is in its spotty teenage years.

The university is, Bernard had argued in a passionate address made when discussion on relocation had yet to become taboo, an institution that has much contributed to the formation of the city state, an institution that contains the wisdom of generations – a wisdom greater than any single person can hope to possess or fully comprehend. Bernard cautioned that because Singapore University is much older than Singapore, the nation should respect the university as a son should respect his father and keep it close to its heart. Although his arguments were conservative and cautious and fully in keeping with Asian values, Bernard must have known that Singaporeans do not like to be warned publicly they are making a mistake – and warned by an *ang mo* at that.

'Is this the way Bernard really saw the place, Barns? As substantively different from the modern structures that will be the new campus on the southern coast?'

Barnaby pauses as if considering her reply, steps off the path onto the harsh blades of tropical grass, stretches out her hind quarters and has a pee.

'Yes, Barns. I get your point. We must respect the path that brought us to this point in history and at the same time we should be free to step aside and have a pee when we want it. I wonder if Bernard went into that in his manuscript. I expect he did, his book isn't just a bunch of photographs and a list of great names – we know that much.'

'Sure thing,' says Barns. 'Master used to read out loud what he had written. I can only suppose he was speaking to me as I was the only one there. He went into everything, including my close encounter with a full-grown cobra. I sure respected that snake – just rose up in front of me on the cricket pitch of all places. A thousand people cross that grass on a normal day. And there in front of my eyes was a dancing cobra to remind me that any of us is here only because that snake and his friends allow us to be here. No reason we can't co-exist – given a little tolerance all round. People should learn tolerance at university. That's my special role, Professor Emeritus of Tolerance.'

'Yes, Professor Barnaby. I do understand. Is that why you walked along the lines of freshers when the Vice-Chancellor was welcoming them onto the campus and stuck your nose up all the skirts?'

'Don't forget, us professors have our little eccentricities. That's what gives a university character. The up-skirt welcome was a first lesson in tolerance. And one has to learn tolerance *before* discipline. It can't be learnt *after*. Once kids are pro-grammed to jump up and obey, it's too late to add on a vague slogan reminding them to be tolerant while they're at it.'

'How right you are, Barns. Tolerance is an understudied area in the social sciences. And the limits of tolerance. And of course, there's *cats*.'

'Cats! Intolerant and arrogant monsters. Must be kept in their place, lah. Singapore cats are okay, lah, you know, the ones without tails, they do their job and keep the rats down. But those long-tailed retrograde cats of Chin! They just cause trouble, lah. Worthless and spoilt, lah. No sense of values.'

'I suppose you're right Barns.' I wonder how often she and Bernard shared a good talk. I suspect quite often. 'And since I've got you in a talkative mood and since you are the only known witness to the death of your master, how about telling me just what happened last night?'

Barns looks at me as if considering my request, then folds

her legs and toboggans her rotund tummy down the steep grassy bank to the cricket pitch and rolls on her back.

★   ★   ★

I am loitering in the limited shade of the admin block, wondering if I should slide down the slope and join Barns in her rolling, when Chin's wife, Agnes, turns the corner and walks straight into me. I almost jump out of my skin. And Agnes almost jumps out of her shorts and singlet.

That first impact is memorable. I am day-dreaming about lots of things and my mind is far from prepared for the impression of Agnes's outstanding breasts as they bump into my tummy. The bit of a strange thing is – although I don't get bumped in the tummy by a pair of remarkable breasts every day so perhaps it's not so strange at all – Agnes gives just a little gasp of surprise and jumps, if jumps is the word, no further than a simple rebound from a well-cushioned impact. The tips of her breasts don't hang around in contact but they leave a lingering impression. Agnes then stands closer than necessary for polite conversation and much closer than Asian norms require for sexual opposites meeting in public. I can smell her moist sweat and feel sparkles of electricity playing on it and reaching across to me.

Agnes is no Venus. Of course not. But the firmly pronounced bosom and nice legs compensate for the fairly standard, if unusually fair, Chinese moon face. This face is set off under a broad-brimmed hat which, by accident or design, allows stray strands of hair to hang provocatively down her bare and attractive neck. She is shorter than Venus and looks up to me with the curiosity of a precocious child. Neither of us excuse ourselves. Agnes speaks first.

'Doctor Haddock. A pleasant surprise. I was beginning to feel like the last person on earth. Where are you going?'

'Just walking. Trying to put things into perspective. You know: the university moving and everything.'

'Me too. Just walking. I'm going over to the Botanic Gardens. There's a small café there. I sit among the orchids and eat ice cream. Would you like to join me?'

'Why not?' I answer with a smile, for some reason trying for a casual and sophisticated allure that's not really me – hell, not me at all. I don't ask Agnes why, if going to the Gardens, she is walking in the opposite direction. She turns and walks beside me. To escape the sun, we hug the shaded perimeters of the building and in order to maintain conversation, almost hug each other. Barnaby charges up excitedly, sniffing and sneezing at Agnes's bare legs and tightly-outlined crotch. I try to call her off.

'That's all right,' says Agnes. 'Barnaby always does that. It's the smell of Harry's cats.' She reaches down and ruffles Barns' neck folds with affection. More surprises; the two are clearly on crotch-sniffing and neck-fold ruffling terms. Barns licks the sweat on Agnes's inner thighs and Agnes giggles like a schoolgirl. 'I'm not usually ticklish but Barnaby's tongue sets me off every time.'

So, frequent wet contacts between the thighs of my head of department's wife and the tongue of my dead uncle's dog. And 'Harry's cats', I had presumed the beasts to be joint possessions, divisible on divorce. What further revelations await?

We have our ice cream among the orchids, with double helpings of chocolate for Barns. Agnes insists on paying, taking damp folded notes from a pocket inside her shorts and waving away the change. The only customers, we linger, sip iced tea and talk. I stick to the neutral 'you' rather than 'Agnes', and we talk about everything except her husband's rise in status and Bernard. But Bernard is there all right, coming between us or bringing us together, I'm not sure which.

I've never spoken to Agnes one-to-one before and, until we literally bumped into each other, had stereotyped the 5.30 evening jogger as a colourful appendage of a colourless man. I tend to do that: profile people. I know it's wrong but still I do it – it gives me some nice surprises when what emerges from the profile is so much more than the stereotype, and that's the case with Agnes. She demonstrates an independent intelligence that – as much as her lightly-clad boobs, or almost as much – make her attractive company. I learn about her family in Ipoh, how difficult it is to persuade Harry to drive her there and how when he finally does, he always insists the cats go along. I learn she went to Oxford University and studied English on a Malaysian scholarship that would normally have tied her into the army as an officer for seven years. I learn that she wanted to make a career in the military, a bit of a surprise, and had completed basic training when she accepted Chin's proposal of marriage and he bought her out by paying back the scholarship – even more of a surprise. I'm also surprised she's tall enough for the military, but I say nothing. Agnes is so open and full of surprises that in half an hour I learn far more about her than I know about Venus after two months. I say little about me in return.

'You must be looking forward to moving to a modern campus,' I say, conscious of inserting an element of controversy under the guise of small talk. 'Fully air-conditioned, sea breezes and all that.'

'I shall hate it,' she replies. 'I love this old place. Singapore is so lucky to have a real university. It's ridiculous to give up this heritage for a place with no history.' Agnes pauses. The word 'history' seems to trouble her.

'And are you happy here after Oxford?' I ask, playing the controversy.

'Happier than I might be elsewhere. I enjoy the self-contained aspect of campus life. I can walk every day in beautiful green surroundings, go for a run in the evening, pop into the library and read the foreign papers. And we do have a nicer house than we might get in Oxford.'

'Biggest on campus, isn't it?'

'I think it is. There's even a guest apartment attached with its own entrance. But that's a double-edged sword.'

'How so?'

'Guests!' says Agnes in explanation.

'You don't like guests?'

'Normally, I welcome them.'

'Normally?' I'm now intruding, but it's as though Agnes wants me to intrude.

'Our current guest sits in the living room with Harry speaking Mandarin with him for hours on end.'

'Is that a problem? You speak Mandarin with Harry, don't you?'

'Yes. Wouldn't get far if I didn't. But the Baron never stops talking. The man knew Harry's father and keeps saying what a great man he was and what a shame for Singapore he was murdered. Of course, Harry loves to hear that. But I don't. I wasn't born then, in Singapore in World War II, but I know it was horrible. The Baron was here throughout the Japanese Occupation and seems to think it was the greatest of times.'

'The Baron?'

'Baron Von Führer Düsseldorf. You haven't met him?'

'No. Doesn't sound very Chinese.'

'German. Speaks fluent Mandarin but says nothing of interest in it and takes forever to say it. He came by a week ago and Harry seemed to think his saviour had come to the door; invited him to stay with us and he shows no signs of leaving.' The image of the German who didn't say *thank you* comes into my mind; if he is staying at Chin's, why did he not use their phone to call Bernard? And he went off in the opposite direction to Chin's house.

'I think he came to my window last night at 10 o'clock. Said he was trying to visit Professor Fox but Bernard didn't answer the door. He was in a beautiful old Citroën. I had no idea he was staying with you. He drove off Tanglin way.'

'He likes the Tanglin Club; loves anything top drawer. Last night he'd been to a reception with the VC and other VIPs like the Superintendent of Police you've just been with – I noticed you with him as I left the house just now. Harry was invited to the reception but didn't go; it would have been a speak-English do; Harry hates them. Bernard was invited too, but didn't go – I suppose he didn't feel like it if he was contemplating suicide. The Baron had been trying to button-hole Bernard for days, even asked me to arrange a get-together with Bernard for him, but Bernard wasn't interested and took to locking his back door and placing his phone on answer-machine mode. Don't blame him at all. Whenever I visited Bernard, I had to knock; Bernard would come to the back door and I would have to say it's me before he opened it.'

Bernard? First name terms? Well, it sounds like Chin has a

guest who's overstayed his welcome, at least with Agnes. Now I know why Bernard's back door has been locked lately. I don't pursue the subject. Must be the criminologist the superintendent says I'll meet soon; he sounds deadly boring.

Agnes drops the Baron from our conversation in favour of giving me an enlightened account of the different life styles of the orchids around us, a subject I find more interesting than the plants themselves. One of them looks particularly small, weedy, colourless and insignificant: a bit like her husband Chin – there I go stereotyping again, surely Chin must have something interesting about him if Agnes gave up her own ambitions to join him in his. Not that Chin strikes me as ambitious; I don't share K's views there – I can't really imagine Chin deliberately wheedling himself into Bernard's chair; he might be happy to have it but I don't believe he'd kill to get it. Agnes tells me it, the weedy orchid that is, is now found only in Perak State, where it grows near the tops of the tallest trees in the primary forest, far from the eyes of Man. 'Isn't that sad? Something so fragile and beautiful and people never know it's there.' Agnes speaks with the wistful implication that both of us should identify with the plant's romantic isolation. I hold my tongue. All I can see is an unappealing straggler in a fast-moving world. Rare, wild orchid it might be, but it seems an act of mercy for the pathetic rootless wonder to be forever exiled from the human eye. Of course, I just nod my head and let her continue. 'Bernard brought me a couple back from the jungle. One died, the other I treasure.'

Bernard, she says again. And Bernard, who cared not at all for the jumble of weeds in his own garden, bothered to bring wild orchids from the Perak forest to give to the wife of Chin, his worst enemy. Curiouser and curiouser. Should I dig further

into the relationship between my uncle and the girl next door?
She who knocks and says 'it's me' and Bernard opens. But I
don't – with Bernard's name spoken as if he is still alive, I find
that catch in my throat again.

'Anything wrong?' asks Agnes.

'No, nothing wrong. It's just hearing Bernard's name spoken
as if he might suddenly appear when we both know he won't.'

'You two were very close, weren't you? I can understand. I
couldn't sleep at all last night, kept crying. I, too, felt close to
Bernard. I'll miss Bernard terribly.'

There's a moment's silence. The ice cream and ice tea are
finished so we have nothing to do with our hands on the table
other than look at them. Agnes says she is going to walk around
in the only patch of mosquito-infested virgin forest left in Singapore, at the heart of the Botanic Gardens, and would I like
to come. I remember Venus at the flat, feel a bit guilty – not
sure why – and say *love to but I must get back*. She reaches for
my hand to say goodbye and holds it a lot longer than social eti-
quette requires. She holds it, I suspect, until she detects a spark
of interest in my eyes – probably several sparks – and then she
lets it go with a finger-tip-palm-slide, a smile on her lips, and
next time then.

I watch her disappear into the trees – Agnes can, like her
tree-top orchid, be sure of being alone in there – and turn my
attention back to Barns. 'I'll have to think of finding you a home,
old girl. Your friendship with Agnes surprises me, but it might
take more than that to keep you on campus. You were tolerated because Bernard protected you but you're not the dean's
dog anymore: you're the enemy of the acting dean's cats. Maybe
Venus will take you? I'll ask her. Would you like that, Barns?'

Barns looks at me as if I have taken leave of my senses. 'Take me away from the university?!' she snorts. 'Isn't it empty enough already? Take me away and there will be nothing left.' With that, Barnaby runs off after Agnes into the darkness of the forest. There is such a lot I don't know about such a lot of things.

I walk back quickly. It's a long way in the heat of the day and I skip from shade-patch to shade-patch. My mind is full of Bernard, but it's also now full of Agnes. She wasn't in the crowd outside Bernard's last night. Neither was Harry Chin. Neither was the Baron. Bernard's death was announced only this morning by the VC. She must have heard about it from somewhere last night; if not, how come she couldn't sleep all night because of it?

*   *   *

On arriving home alone, I am relieved to see K's Mustang gone from outside my door and equally glad to see Venus waiting for me. 'Where's Barns?' Venus asks. 'Wong kept you for ages. Was it a real grilling?' She is wearing the older of my two sarongs, tucked in *selapas mandi* style above her small firm breasts and flowing down to her beautiful knees. The old and flimsy cloth is almost transparent in the strong sunlight and clings to damp parts of her body. She is comb-surfing the gentle waves of her *Peranakan* hair. Everything about Venus, the dark flashing eyes, the honey skin, the round buttocks, everything, it all radiates natural sexual attraction – maybe I've said that before, maybe I'll say it again, maybe I'm infatuated. And if I had felt arousal during an innocent ice cream with Agnes, I am now feeling hopelessly sinful in the close proximity of Venus.

'Crazy dog. Gone digging for treasure in the jungle.' Did I

say that? I must have. 'Yes, Wong had a lot to say but asked me not to repeat any of it, so I'd better not. Was the breaking news shown live last night on TV?'

'You don't know much about television, Tom. The Singapore Broadcasting Corporation packs in at 11.00. Siggy would need to take the film back and it would be processed and edited if a technician could be found in the early hours. It just about made the 7 o'clock news. It could have been on radio a bit earlier, but it wasn't. Still, it beat the papers by a day.'

So, I'm thinking, Agnes didn't see it on TV. Her night of crying must have another explanation – maybe the Baron knocked on her door when back from the Tanglin Club and said *by the way, there's been a hanging next door.* Although, if he did, how did *he* know about it? 'Need a pee,' I say.

'And a shower!' she adds.

*   *   *

The bathroom is sultry with the lingering presence of Venus. I look in the steamy mirror, extract a couple of Agnes hairs that have somehow attached themselves to me and dispose of them through the grill covering the ever-open window and stand naked under the cold water to wash away the aroma of Agnes lingering guiltily in my nostrils.

My bathroom is empire scale. I could give a lecture in there – with the size of my Economic Anthropology class there would be room to spare. Size, it seems, does matter, or it did to the Empire. And so does age. Age spots pock-mark the wall of weathered Javanese marble surrounding a brown-stained enamel cold-water bath. It's a room of multi-barrelled adjectives. A room that has seen smarter days but retains the dimensions and mood of faded imperial dignity. My Singapore bathroom alone is larger than the entire bedsit (shared toilet downstairs along the corridor) in which I survived as a student-in-exile in London. In London, my one sun-deprived pot-plant hung its leaves in constant depression – in the City State, a husked coconut in one corner of the bathroom survives on humid air alone and shoots its own tree up towards the sunlight of great, open windows; in sultry Singapore, it grows like the living goddess of Kathmandu, without once touching the ground.

I look out at lush, green Singapore. Surrounded by nature, I soap up and think I am a pretty lucky guy what with Venus just outside the door and all. An apparition of Venus forms spontaneously in the veins of marble that surround my nakedness. I often see images in the marble; like an Englishman in England sees them in the flames of a fire. This particular image of Venus is eating ice cream, has strands of hair falling from under a wide-brimmed hat and is surrounded by lonely orchids.

The reality of Venus is in the kitchen, from where she calls out and asks if I know K has taken David and Toshi across to Johor Bahru for the day since the university is closed anyway? No, I do not. But how like the man! To ignore the VC's request to stay available to help the police. Still, none of my business.

*   *   *

Venus has been in my flat since breakfast. Her first breakfast at my place and she brought it with her. I feel a twinge of guilt at having left her alone and the Agnes interlude. Although it was an accidental collision of breasts against my tummy, the memory of it is no accident, nor the ice cream that followed. And, a bit of a surprise, and not by accident, I now know more about the relatives and husband of Agnes after a casual ice tea than I know about the relatives and husband of Venus after two months, particularly that husband, enigmatic Richard, more inaccessible than the remotest orchid.

Venus has showered before me and wears my old sarong as if by right. No woman ever wore it before and, given its threadbare state, it's a sure bet no woman will ever wear it again. Only Venus can make that old rag look the height of fashion. Her skirt, her blouse and her underwear are draped neatly and provocatively around the many bathroom hooks and rails. No way I can ignore them. I lift the knickers to my lips and rub my nose in them – men are like that when nobody's looking.

Bathroom appearances suggest we are in the familiarity phase of cohabitation – but appearances are deceptive when it comes to Venus. I do not want to blow everything by pushing too hard or for that matter pushing at all. I am waiting for Venus. Chase her and I feel she might run away.

I can't be certain my encounter with Agnes doesn't have as much to do with it as the soft feel of Venus's knickers, but for whatever reason, I am aroused. Am I, I ask myself, man enough to walk out, *Homo erectus*, and carry Venus off to my bed? K would no doubt advise such direct action; I can imagine his words: 'Any wench who leaves her knickers in a chap's bathroom and floats around naked under his flimsy sarong is obviously gagging for it.' I make a token dab with the towel, have a quick mouthwash, and fresh and wet step into the bright new Javanese sarong that Venus had not selected for herself. I walk out cleansed, suggest a siesta under the fan would be nice, take the slim hand of Venus and gently lead her to my bed. She comes like a lamb.

'You don't mind my closing the shutters, do you Venus?' I ask as casually as my enthusiasm allows. She minds. Why did I ask? Because I really am not all that good at leading lambs to slaughter. Venus says to let the air in, outside is so green and fresh, it's a pity to cut ourselves off from such a pleasant world. How to argue with that? So, the shutters stay open and she tells me to lie down and rest – after that long questioning by the police – and she will watch over me like a guardian angel.

I lay on my back, sarong loose around my waist, something rising under the cloth like a snake from an Indian's basket. The guardian angel notices; it would be hard to miss. She sits on the bed, legs tucked up under her and tries to talk it down. 'I'm sorry, Tom darling. It's just, you know, I can't – well – betray – you know. *Betray*'s not the right word. Oh Tom, what do I really mean?'

What Venus really means is *take me, I'm yours*. But I don't tell her. I know the kind of response she is expecting and give it to her – to score points. 'Maybe what you mean, Venus, is that you feel you would be betraying yourself, maybe betraying your dreams and hopes from the past, your love for a man who would probably still love you if only he could.'

'Thank you, Tom. For being so understanding. You put it beautifully.' She laughingly makes as if to pat my spontaneous levitation but pats only the air above it and says, 'Oh, sorry again. I shouldn't do things like that. Not fair to you, is it? Not fair to either of us.'

As if to control her hands, she lies down on them. Front down, inches from me but not touching, her eyes looking straight into mine. I am torn between the beauty of Venus's eyes and the curves of her backside. I am not the only thing tearing apart. I can see a hole in the old sarong slowly expanding, silently pulling itself open until it forms a perfect frame for Venus's right buttock. I turn on my side towards her. It's time. I sniff her cheek in an Asian kiss and feeling no resistance, work my lips towards her mouth and there we are, like two fighting fish, mouths locked together, a sucking, hungry vacuum between us. No more words. No more talk of betraying Richard. I run my hands softly over her body, loosen the tuck of the sarong and feel her lips press harder. And then, *and then*, as far as it is possible to do so a few metres above sea level on the equator, I freeze.

'Ah. Doc-tor Had-dok. Li Fang come.'

We do not move. Maybe if we play dead, Li Fang will go away.

'Doc-tor Had-dok. Madhu he phone say I come you.'

Is Li Fang in secret league with Richard? Can't the man see I am within a pubic hair of bedding the most desirable woman in Singapore? Does the man have no sense of decency?

'Madhu phone.'

Venus recoils. I turn towards the familiar backlit shadow, swing my legs off the bed, tighten the sarong around my waist, hold my temper firmly in and cross the room. 'Yes, Li Fang, what is it?'

'Madhu come see you 5 o'clock.'

'He wants to see me here at 5 o'clock?'

'Uh.'

'Thank you, Li Fang.'

I squeeze Li Fang away from the window. He begins talking excitedly in Hokkien and is still rattling on when I finally get the shutters closed and locked. I look back at the bed. Venus is still there but sitting, sarong realigned, the apologetic look back on her face.

'I'm sorry, Tom. You know how it is.'

Richard wins again. Like Harry Chin, I think unkindly, poor Richard can win without lifting a finger. In fact, Richard wins because he *cannot* lift a finger.

'Hell, Venus. I *don't* know how it is. I just don't understand. I mean, do you want me or not?'

'Please, Tom, it's not as simple as that. Please don't be angry. It's not what I *want*. There's something holding me back.'

I dress grumpily. Maybe I should take another walk to the Botanic Gardens and accidentally bump into Agnes in the virgin forest. I'm sure she won't have too much holding her back. Barnaby, back from her walk in the woods, pads into the bedroom, lays her head on Venus's lap and looks at her in sympathy, one woman who knows what another is going through.

'Barns is hungry, let's go have lunch,' says Venus. Barns and Venus share a love of eating. I wonder vaguely whether Barns ever had a beautiful figure and whether one day Venus will be all roly-poly. Maybe they should shack up together. Barns sitting beside Venus on prime-time news – something to stir the interests of the nation's apartment-bound dogs – and then they can both go for a late supper at Newton Circus. 'Give me a few minutes.' She disappears into the bathroom to redecorate and make herself less attractive.

I go into the kitchen; might as well have an early beer. And there on the worktop I find a bulging carrier bag. Venus said she found the dog collar there last night but didn't mention any carrier bag. I call through from the kitchen, 'Venus, did you see this bag here last night?'

'What bag, where?'

'Here on the worktop thing, counter, whatever you call it.'

'Yes. Saw it. Next to the collar. Why?'

'Nothing.'

I look inside. Crumpled old Malay school exercise books, lots of them, giving off the pong of old paper badly ventilated. What are they doing here? Each is numbered on its front cover: 1 to 27. Number 1's on top. I flick through it. Bernard's handwriting. It seems to be some sort of log. Now, I tell myself, here's a mystery. I start to read.

*   *   *

'Intriguing, Li Fang's message,' Venus calls from the bathroom.

'About as intriguing as any note inside any Chinese cracker,' I reply cynically, already lost in Bernard's world of 1942.

'Well, Li Fang intrigued me if not you.' Venus speaks with just a tinge of annoyance.

'Venus,' I say, feeling, and probably sounding, testy. 'I don't know what you are talking about.' My eyes are still fixed on the open exercise book. I'm hearing Venus but reading Bernard.

'Well! What Li Fang said, of course.'

Like many Singaporeans – Harry Chin a notable exception – Venus is so perfectly at ease in several languages she sometimes doesn't notice what language is being used.

'Okay,' I call out. 'What great revelations in Hokkien did I close the shutters on?'

'Only that Professor Fox wasn't really hanged at all.'

8

On the Wireless

TODAY WE ARRIVED at Chin Peng's jungle camp. It looks more like a refugee camp than a military base. I've yet to meet the famous Chin Peng. About the only attractive thing here are the young aboriginal ladies; maybe in time I'll get used to being surrounded by naked breasts, but I hope not. One gave me this school exercise book and a pencil.

Since I have absolutely nothing to do other than stay alive, I intend to write a sort of diary of my time here, hoping it will be very short. At the moment, boredom seems a greater enemy than the Japanese. I should begin my story last week on the first day of 1942, since that is when I encountered the remarkable Li Fang.

It was not a happy new year for me. I was sitting in Tanjung Malim waiting for the Japanese to be defeated or take me prisoner or worse, and fiddling with the knobs on my huge wireless set, trying to get a human voice within the static. Kuala Lumpur's just forty miles away, but it takes forever to get somebody on the wireless there.

There's a knock on the open door. I look up and see a young Chinese at the door. 'What do you want?' I say in English, following up automatically, since I don't speak Chinese, with 'Apa yang awak mahu?' in Malay.

'You,' says the Chinese in English. 'You go now. Me go also.'

'What do you mean?'

'You go now. Me go also.'

I spent two years learning Malay yet I'm constantly reduced to guess-work conversations in ten-word English. 'I'm not going anywhere. I just arrived here last week. And the wireless doesn't work so I can't go anywhere. If you don't want anything, please don't want it somewhere else.' I know the kid at the door doesn't understand but say it anyway because there's nobody to speak to but myself.

'Me go also.'

I lift myself tiredly from my chair and move to close the door. In Tapah, as Batang Padang District Officer, there'd been somebody to protect me from such time-wasters. I put a hand on the boy's arm and gently ease him out of the doorway as I close the door.

'No,' says the boy. 'You go now.'

'Go – there,' I say, pointing to the closed door of the person who's supposed to be my assistant. 'He speaks Chinese.' The boy doesn't move, confusion on his face. Well, too bad; I have my own problems. 'Please leave my office.'

The confused look on the young face before me slowly dissolves into a smile. 'Got you! I think I'd best introduce myself … if that's all right with you.'

I sheepishly open the door. 'You'd better come in.'

★   ★   ★

'I'm Li Fang. I've just graduated from the special school in Singapore. I was told to come to see you. Took the bus up to Kuala Lumpur yesterday and came on this morning. You must have been told I was coming? Wireless message, no?'

97

'I'm afraid you've got the better of me. Why the games? Your English is perfect, but I'm not expecting you or anybody else. The wireless doesn't work, so I haven't got any message.'

'They would have sent you a signed coded fax as backup.'

'They might have. There's a fax message waiting for me to decode. Haven't got round to it yet.'

'Show me … if you don't mind.'

I'm caught between showing a stranger an official message and my curiosity about this young man who looks like he belongs in school but speaks like he graduated from Oxford. It's coded anyway, I tell myself, so no harm, the boy won't understand; I've got no idea myself what it says. I take the message from the fax machine and hand it across to the schoolboy in front of me.

Li Fang looks at what must be mumbo-jumbo to him for a full minute then speaks. 'District Officer Fox from Control. You will be visited today by an important member of the Malayan People's Anti-Japanese Army, Mr Li Fang. It has been decided that your current position is not secure. You have to move again. Where you go is up to you. You can return to KL and then to Singapore or you can go with Li Fang to the place he directs you and wait until the Japanese are defeated. You should let us know your decision today by wireless.'

I'm amazed; my face must show it. 'You decoded that by sight? I can't believe it.'

'I'm fresh off the course and we spent a lot of time on codes. Where we are going, I doubt we'll be using written messages like this – perhaps just as well. You can check it with the code book and use the wireless for confirmation. You have a telephone but I wouldn't trust that too much.'

'I don't trust it. But as I said, the wireless doesn't work.'

'I'll look at it while you decode the message. We also spent quite a bit of time on wireless transmission, although where we're going there's no electricity, so there'll be no wireless.'

I'm not technically minded, the wireless set is a mystery to me; no harm in allowing this clever young man to try and do something with it. Then I sit at my desk, take the code book from a drawer and start with pencil and paper.

*   *   *

It takes 10 minutes. Li Fang goes out, comes back and sits quietly waiting.

There must have been wonder on my face as I look up at him. 'It's exactly as you said! I can't believe you sight-read a coded message. Is that what's taught at that special school?'

'The course was only three weeks. Should have been six months but the Japanese wouldn't wait.'

'You learnt in three weeks to decode a message on sight? Then the code must be worthless.'

'I can't say I learnt a lot in three weeks. What's written there, what you just showed me, it's all gibberish to me.'

'But you decoded it!'

'Because I *en*-coded it myself, last night in KL at Control. Didn't I tell you?'

'No, you didn't.'

Li Fang smiles. 'The wireless should be okay now. It was the antennae. Wind had blown it down.'

Why didn't I think of that? I turn the set back on, wait for it to warm up and twiddle knobs. 'Fox to Haddock, come in.'

The wireless speaks. 'Haddock here. How are you, Bernard? I was trying to get you last night but no luck.'

'The antennae was down. The chap you sent just fixed it. You did send him, didn't you? And the fax. That must have been you.'

'It was. Li Fang's there already? Our best student. Learns very quickly. Almost as if he knew everything already. Beautiful English. He should be entering university in Singapore right now but won't, of course, not until we've sent the Japs packing.'

'Beautiful English, yes. But when he came to the door just now he spoke like a coolie in the market place.'

'We told him to talk to any stranger like that if he's approached in English. If he's picked up by the Japs it won't look good if he's educated with fluent English. He can play the fool very well. Don't be fooled, he's no fool.'

'Well, his act worked on me. I almost sent him packing.'

'Lucky you didn't. Now, what have you decided? You going to stay behind or retreating? Your sister will be happy if you come here, but it's up to you – has to be.'

'I haven't decided yet. Big decision to make. I presume Li Fang is in one of the stay-behind groups, right?'

'That's right. He's from Ulu Slim. Seems he knows the area inside out. Fluent in Malay and Semai. That's really why we hooked him. Don't be fooled by his babyface. He's only seventeen but wise beyond his years and eager to kick out the invaders. He's already something in the communist party; quite important, apparently. Don't be put off by the word communist. It's the communists who might save Malaya.'

'I'm not put off by the word, George. I wouldn't have survived Oxford if I were.'

'Yes, I seem to remember we worried about you for a while; your sister still does.'

'Tell your wife not to worry. As for going anywhere, I'm not at all sure what's on offer. You know I've only been here a week. I was expecting to return to Tapah. Quite miss the place.'

'I'm sure. But return might take a while. The point is, Bernard, you know that neck of the woods and the people there, you speak Malay damn good and you're somebody we can trust. Won't ask you to go into the woods behind enemy lines, but that's what it might come to. Right now, the Japs are massing to take Trolak and Slim River. They've even got tanks. Won't do them much good in the jungle but Trolak is not prepared for tanks. We're trying to get some air cover but things are stretched. Don't know if you've heard but there's a huge battle in Kuantan and most planes left flying are over that way. If Kuantan falls, they'll be coming at you from the east as well as the north. You might be cut off. That's why it's time you left. It's all happened so fast.'

'You can say that again. But shouldn't be too long now before the Americans are with us in real terms. That should change things.'

'We can hope so. Truth is, Bernard, everybody's far more interested in what's happening on England's doorstep. Nobody thought Japan would really be able to attack Malaya. Seems Thailand let them do it from there. Now we're desperately snatching at whatever we can get to delay them.'

'Like me and this young man here! Must be desperate indeed.'

'Right, better get off the air now. Lots to do. Call me back when you've made up your mind.'

'It would help me if you could tell me where I'm supposed to go and what's waiting for me if and when I get there.'

'Can't do that, would spoil the fun. Your visitor can put you in the picture. Bye for now. Over and out.'

'I'll call later and let you know, wireless or phone. Look after big sister. Out.'

I turn to Li Fang, waiting patiently. 'Thanks for the wireless repairs. Thing's never worked as well as today. Now, maybe you'd better tell me a bit about this stay-behind option. Got to say it sounds more like left-behind than stay-behind.'

'For me,' says Li Fang, 'It's more like going home. I was born in Slim – actually Ulu Slim, then school in Ipoh. I went to Singapore expecting to enter university next term. That won't be possible if the Japanese win, so I'm fighting the Japanese.'

I hold out my hand. Li Fang takes it.

⋆　　⋆　　⋆

'Madhu's here already.' Venus is calling from the sofa.

I close the exercise book on Bernard reluctantly and put it back, almost reverently, on top of the crumpled pile of books in the carrier bag. I've had a glimpse of Uncle Bernard a few years before I was born, when he would have been the age I am now. It's strangely familiar but it's a world that existed before I existed. Must be Uncle Bernard's writing style; I can hear every word as if he spoke it, as if he's inside me reading it to me with his Oxford vowels.

9

How Barnaby Got Her Name

I LEAVE BERNARD inside his exercise books in the kitchen and go through. Madhu's at the door. Barns grumbles a bit but stays on her armchair. Venus stands up, ever the polite hostess, and tells Madhu not to bother taking off his shoes. Her control of household norms is, I think, a mite premature given the progression of our romance, and Venus has contradicted one of my mildly-held principles: shoes off at the door. It's not as if I have so many principles I can just toss one away.

Madhu has the sense to slip off his shoes before padding in. In the East, where shoes come off at the door, I wonder if toeprints are ever taken along with fingerprints. For all I know, there might be a whole forensic department devoted to criminals' feet. The fact that I can't remember a single movie detective asking, 'Can you describe the man's feet, Sir?' means little. Cinema screens preach that feet, in or out of the home, belong in shoes; footloose cultural bias.

My ruminations are by no means irrelevant, I tell myself. If Bernard's killer entered Bernard's house at Bernard's invitation as the super suggested, he would have done so in a cultural context and since Bernard had no greater love for shoes in the home than I, the killer might well have left behind footprints.

'Something on your mind?' Venus asks me sweetly.

'Feet,' I reply.

'Funny place for them. And whose feet are on your mind? Mine?'

'Right!' I answer with enthusiasm as Madhu looks as if maybe he has come to the wrong party. 'It could have been a woman!'

'Are you sure you're all right?'

'Fine, Venus. The killer. He could have been a woman. I mean *she* could have been a woman. You see what I mean?'

'Ye-es,' says Venus, meaning no.

'A question of feet. Women have feet.'

'My dear Tom, with such observations, I think you had better leave investigations to Madhu and Wong.'

'I think I should tell you that I'm here officially, on duty,' Madhu says. 'I'd better make that clear.' Sounds like feet are off the menu. 'The super knows we are friends and that I'm quite involved with several people significant to the case and he thinks that can be both useful, since I have the lay of the land, and problematic, since I need to stay objective. He thinks on balance being conversant with the place and people in it over-rides the objectivity thing. The super himself is also familiar with the university – he did History here twenty years ago under Professor Fox and has stayed in touch with him ever since. Between you and me, Tom, that might be why he's personally in charge of the case instead of Inspector Ong, my direct boss; the super admired Bernard. I'll be running the investigation team from Guild House because the super asked *me* to do it.'

'And your boss, Inspector Ong, is he also involved?'

'No. The campus falls within Ong's territory but Wong's in charge of this one; I'll report only to him. I don't mind telling you, I'm quite happy with the secondment – Wong's more fun than Ong and murder trumps a blitz on dirty car number plates any day – if it is murder, of course. But my feelings are irrelevant; I want it to be quite clear, Tom, I'm now a cop before a friend.'

'Got it. But you'll have a beer while we talk, Madhu?'

'Just one glass then, can't see that would hurt.' Madhu will drink the beer of the prime suspect but remain a copper. Good cop, Madhu. Good beer, Tiger.

'I'll get us some refreshments,' says Venus and heads off to the fridge. Madhu takes out his pen and pad.

*   *   *

'The super told me to inform you of the coroner's report and the blood test on Barnaby – and *note your reactions*.'

Drops of condensation fall from the cold beer glass onto Madhu's notebook, blurring my reactions before they are noted. He reads from his notes in a serious stutter-free voice. 'Death occurred between nine and ten, of heart failure.' Madhu looks up at my face for some reaction to record. Perhaps he's expecting a Victorian wringing of hands and a knitting of the brow. I'd oblige but I've never quite learnt how to do either. 'Not hanging?' I say.

'Not as a cause of death, no. He was dead when hanged.'

'Why hang a dead man?' I ask. I don't expect an answer and I don't get one. To help Madhu out, I suggest he tell the super I'd already heard gossip that Bernard died before being strung up on the fan and therefore took the news calmly. Madhu flicks his head happily in sub-continental agreement and pours a second glass of beer. I sense he is about to tell us something we don't know. Something perhaps not even Li Fang knows.

'Stretching of the neck and marks left by the rope on the skin suggest no struggle at all, not even the involuntary movements of a suicide. They also indicate the body was hung up on the fan sometime between nine and ten-thirty p.m. – soon after death occurred.' Madhu pauses to allow this revelation to sink in. 'Contents of the digestive tract suggest the ingredients of a steak and kidney pie and a quantity of sedative that would knock out a man of the professor's size but not normally kill him. However, the heart problem was possibly aggravated by the drug and death probably occurred while the professor was unconscious and before the hanging.'

'It's a relief to know Bernard did not suffer greatly,' I say. Madhu writes *glad to hear it*. 'That's quite a surprise about the steak and kidney pie. As far as I know, Li Fang has no idea what a steak and kidney pie is. It's certainly not on the Guild House menu and I rather doubt Bernard's housekeeper could knock one up or that Bernard would ask her to do so.'

'I don't know anything about that,' Madhu says apologetically, failing to write these wonderful clues in his notebook. 'Maybe he had an old pie in the fridge and just snacked on it.'

'Maybe an old poisoned pie?' I suggest.

'That we don't know, lah. Maybe he took the drug independently of eating the pie – it's a strong sedative, maybe he took it to get to sleep. We didn't find any of it in his house but we are checking all recorded prescriptions now. It doesn't look like a suicide attempt – that's what the super said – because not enough of the drug was taken to kill a normal person. Anyway, the super says a man intent on killing himself by drugs does not sedate his dog and hang himself in a noose just to make sure, especially if he is already dead.'

106

'Astute chap, your super. But what makes him think Barns was sedated?'

'The super said something about all sorts of things happening to the professor but the dog did not bark. When I asked him what he meant, he said as a detective I should read Sherlock Holmes. Does that make any sense to you, Tom?'

'Absolutely. *Silver Blaze*.'

'Err?'

'That's the title of the Sherlock Holmes story. I've got it somewhere; I'll dig it out for you. Barnaby would never have sat by and let anybody string Bernard up. Not without a hell of a fight. She only started howling towards midnight; maybe she woke up and found Bernard circling.'

'Well, from the blood test results, the dog's a real junky – the injected tranquilliser you gave her last night, masses of Valium and the same drug found inside the professor. If it were human, that dog would be in for obligatory detox.'

My eyes are distracted towards the window for a moment as Agnes jogs by. I look at the clock. Exactly 5.30. I could set the time by Agnes's breasts bouncing by – not that I look out for them, but they are difficult to ignore. Madhu finishes his beer and Venus opens a second large bottle. 'Anything else of an *official* nature, Madhu?' I ask.

'Well, the super said to find out what I can about the dog. Maybe you can help me there?'

'Not much, Madhu. Age unknown. Neutered bitch. Fat. Singapore breed – you know: part Chinese, part Malay, a touch of Tamil and a sprinkling of others. Short brown hairs that fall out in bed, curled-up tail, genitalia on public view. Whimpers when dreaming. Adopted by Bernard about three years ago, before

107

I entered the scene. Known on campus as Professor Barnaby, well-liked by students and tolerated by the authorities. Faithful. Name of Barnaby given by Bernard.'

Madhu scratches down what he can of this. 'What was the last thing?'

'Name Barnaby given by Bernard.'

'Yah, that's it, lah. The super wants to know why a bitch is called Barnaby. Was she named after someone?'

Venus stops practising provocative curling and sits up in her armchair. 'The story of how Barnaby got her name. Last night you promised to tell me, Tom. Now you have to – police orders, isn't that so, Madhu? It will make a nice human-interest piece – "The Professor's Dog". I'll get Siggy to take some footage of Barns. She's really quite photogenic – maybe a red filter to put some gloss on the coat and a little moisturiser on her nose. Please do tell us, Tom.'

I can't refuse Barns her fifteen minutes of fame – a dog robbed of her master's protection might benefit from public exposure. Perhaps offers of a rich and comfortable home will pour in. Maybe a billionaire Irish Wolfhound will propose marriage. Anyway, no harm in the story, although any relevance to finding Bernard's killer eludes me.

Barns moves her head quizzically from side to side as her name is bandied about. She gives a long yawn as if to say, 'I suppose nobody's going to ask what I think?' No, Barns, nobody will ask you. You just trust us to do what's in your best interest. That's what being a dog's all about.

'Okay. Fill your glasses and sit comfortably. *How Barnaby got her name*. As narrated by Professor Bernard Fox and stored in my memory.' I sit back and let Bernard do the talking.

★   ★   ★

'Barnaby – at that time a dog with no name – appeared on campus a few weeks before taking up residence with me. I used to throw her lunch-time scraps from my table in Guild House and she caught them. She hung around Guild House and the student canteens. I noted from the first moment that she delighted in chasing those fancy cats of Chin. I think she saw something oddly demonic in cats with tails, as if only dogs should have them. Maybe she drew parallels with the image of a betailed devil. Barnaby's aversion to cats with tails suggests she had never been out of Singapore in her life. Few Singaporean cats have real tails so perhaps Barns had never seen a cat with a tail until she set eyes on Chin's imports.

'I met Barnaby before the doctors warned me to cut out drinking before it cut me out. At that time, I was far along the alcoholic trail, collapsing into sleep each night and getting up late in the mornings. It was during one of those morning slumbers that I was awakened by a kiss. Several very wet kisses. I opened my eyelids to see two big brown eyes and a nose as long as Granny's in Little Red Riding Hood. Behind the big brown eyes were two men in uniform. The men were blurred – my early morning world was a blurred place. From the uniforms, I supposed the men were police. It turned out they were dog-catchers called by Chin to rid the campus of a stray and dangerous animal – not me but the dog.

'I heard mumbled apologies and excuses for entering my house and bedroom without permission "in hot pursuit of the outlaw dog". I reached for my eyeglasses and saw one of the men was armed with a long stick with a noose at the end and the other with a rifle. They explained the rifle only held stun darts. "We don't kill them, lah. Just take them back, lah. Nobody claim, gas, lah."

'I saw the big brown eyes appealing to me and heard a voice – I sometimes heard voices when the alcohol level dropped. "They will drag me away and gas me." There was, I thought, already too much dragging away and gassing in twentieth century human history without extending it to the canine world. I ordered the men out of the house. They said they would go as soon as they had secured the dog, explaining they entered the house because all doors were open, which was how the dog got in, and that they were there to protect me, not harm me.

'"It's my dog," I told them, lying in defence of decency. The men were checked. They couldn't noose a professor's dog in his own bedroom, at least not when the professor was lying in his bed. On the other hand, they didn't really believe it was my dog. One asked to see the rabies vaccination certificate and reminded me that *every* dog in Singapore should wear a collar at all times. "*What! Even in bed?!*" I flung at them, knowing sarcasm rarely works in Singapore.

'My defence clearly annoyed the dog-catchers. They listed the complaints against the dog made over several weeks, all by Chin, and described how they had tried several times to catch the dog without success. At no point during those weeks, they said, had I claimed ownership of the dog. The dog snuggled closer and appealed to my sense of justice and my dislike of Chin. I again ordered the men out of the house. They reluctantly turned to go but one of them dared to tell me that as there was a complaint against my dog, they had to file a police report and therefore needed the name of the dog. That's not quite the way they put it. I remember something more like, "What dog name, huh?"

'I was not used to thinking until after a few cups of morning tea and was getting annoyed at having dog-catchers in my bedroom. I muttered "barbarians", referring to the men, not the dog. One of the catchers said, *Barbara*? I could have left it at that but I found Barbara a stupid name for a dog, so I corrected it to *Barnaby*. The other catcher pointed out that the dog was a bitch. I looked underneath and found that Barnaby was indeed a bitch. I decided I had been more than tolerant of an invasion of my bedroom and responded: "And what bloody business of yours is the sex of my dog?"

'Thus, Barnaby found a name and I found myself a dog.'

*   *   *

Venus is oozing. 'I love it. And the way you told it, I wasn't sure if it was you or Professor Fox speaking.' I, too, am not quite sure who was speaking. 'So, Professor Fox and Barnaby were united against Chin from their first moments together. It's almost as if Chin and those foreign long-tailed devil cats drove Barnaby into the professor's arms. We might be able to play the long-tailed foreign devil bit on the box – subtly, of course. It's something Singaporeans can respond to without feeling racist.'

My own long-nosed foreign devil response does not leave my lips. It is stilled by a loud human scream coming from the back of the house.

10

Rats and Maids

MADHU COCKS HIS head on its axis in his gesture of enquiry. Barnaby responds in exactly the same way.

The scream screams again.

'It's all right,' I say. 'Just the cleaner finding another rat in a cupboard – happens all the time.'

Venus gives me a long sideways look. She is not yet mistress of my life, but she knows Norsiah discreetly cleans up my mess in the mornings not the evenings, and even in my flat cleaning is no cause for screaming. She also knows there is nobody in the kitchen since she just brought in two bottles of beer from the fridge.

Luckily, at that moment Madhu remembers something he forgot to tell me and diverts his own attention. 'Tambiah will be reading Professor Fox's Will tomorrow at 10.45am and your presence is requested at his chambers on Shenton Way – know where that is?'

'I do,' says Venus.

'Tambiah also requests the presence of Barnaby.'

'Reading of the Will so soon after death?' I am surprised. 'I thought such things took ages.'

'It can be done any time,' says Madhu. 'After death, that is. It doesn't *need* to be done at all, but you know Tambiah, can't

112

resist a touch of Victorian drama. Superintendent Wong will be there to see who gets what; it might indicate a motive.'

'I'll be there with Barnaby.' I say.

'Then I must go too,' Venus chirps. 'You can't expect Barnaby to ride on the crossbar of Tom's old bike. And Tom would never find the place.'

Venus knows me – Shenton Way's skyscrapers, even in 1980, are a different world and one I don't much care for. But how does she know about the bike? I haven't taken it out of the store room for months. I know next to nothing about her and she knows about my invisible old bike.

A series of moans of increasing intensity come to us from the back of the house, capped by another scream, followed by silence.

'More beer, Madhu?' I ask quietly.

'What was that noise?' Madhu questions, in a tone expecting a reply.

'Probably just the TV.'

'You don't have a TV.' Madhu demonstrates his powers of observation.

'Oh. You mean that yelling out back?' I play for time.

'M-m-moaning and s-screaming more l-like it. I-I-I'd better take a look.'

'Better not, Madhu. You'll only frighten the maid. She doesn't even realise she moans and if you walk in on her, she'll really scream the house down. It's all Ra'mad's fault. He's experimenting with different types of rat poison. Since his kitchen is directly above mine, my kitchen gets to be the final resting place of tortured rats. Whenever the maid opens a cupboard, a half-dead rat falls out. Can't blame her for the occasional shriek.'

'S-s-something m-must be d-d-done about it,' Madhu suggests slowly but firmly.

'Well, I can't gag her, you know.'

'I m-m-m-mean about R-r-ra'mad's ex-x-p-periments.'

'We could call the loony bin and have him put away.'

'I-I-I…' Madhu swallows. The stutter-gauge is flicking dangerously high. There is the silence of a stalled aircraft and then the sudden rush down an imaginary slope in the sky as the words fall over themselves. '… I should look in the kitchen.'

Madhu stands up but before he takes two steps towards the kitchen, K walks in from the back of the flat. Venus rises to greet him. A mistake for any woman, doubly so for one as lovely as Venus. K kisses her on the lips as if they are old lovers. He tosses Madhu a *hiya* and pats Barns on the backside.

'What about rats in the kitchen?' Madhu asks K, with no trace of stammer.

'Er … I'm not too fond of rats anywhere.'

'How's the maid?' Madhu says, leaving K staring.

'*My* maid, Madhu?' K asks in confusion. 'She's well as far as I know.'

'*Tom's* maid. You came in through the back door and through the kitchen. Is she all right now? Rather disturbing this business. I shall have a word with Ra'mad.'

K recovers his composure and tries a shot in the dark that is way off target but better than Madhu searching the kitchen for rats and maids. 'You should have more than a word with him. Lecherous old git. We don't like to complain about a colleague, but the girl could get seriously hurt. May already be psychologically damaged.'

'Exactly,' agrees Madhu. 'Rats are no laughing matter.'

'Rats?' says K. 'Aren't we talking about maids?'

Venus has the sense to interrupt and although I know she is curious about the screams from the back of the house, she says she must be going. 'Not because you are here, Dr Woolf, but because I have to work tonight. If I don't go to work, there will be no news. I'm sure Madhu won't mind me mentioning the coroner's report and the new facts surrounding the death of Professor Fox. Perhaps I'll pop in a mention of the plague of rats scaring the life out of campus maids.' K rises as if to embrace Venus again but I beat him to it. 'See you for supper?' she says to me, knowing there is no need for a reply. I'll be waiting. 'And you, Doctor Woolf, could I drop in on you very early tomorrow morning with the cameraman and get your eulogy to Professor Fox? The expected theme is the great historian. No more than five minutes, 8 o'clock okay?'

'My dear, nothing would give me greater pleasure,' says K. 'But the Ghurkhas are chopping the head off a bull at dawn. They do it every year ... not the same bull, of course. Then the superintendent is coming by to see me at 8.30. So sorry, it seems I'm just too popular early in the morning. Later on, perhaps.'

Venus leaves, Madhu says he must get back to the Guild and K and I are alone.

*   *   *

'K, if you must roger your students in my place when the police are here, you might try to keep the volume down.'

'Students? That would be taking advantage of my professional position and the fact that some of these little cuties would do absolutely anything other than study to get passing grades.'

'Well, if not a screaming student, who was in the back room with you?'

'I'd rather not say, Haddock. Chivalry, you know. Start disclosing confidences and before you know it, there are no confidences to disclose.'

Agnes is into her return run, jogging around the corner from the back of the flats and along the road in front of my window. Bouncy and sweaty, she never breaks the stride that will take her back to the anaemic world of Harold Chin and his demon-tailed cats.

'Is whoever it is still there in my back room?'

K looks past me to the retreating image of Agnes' bouncing backside. 'Obviously not,' he says.

No, it can't be. Not the sweet little wife of K's worst enemy. 'Not...'

'Why not?'

'But I had ice cream with her earlier.'

'You bounder!'

'She's nice. Not at all like Chin. Don't tell me Agnes was screaming in my back room.'

'All right, I won't tell you.'

I feel sort of deceived. Not by K, he beds anything that comes his way, but by Agnes. I had her pegged as somebody worthwhile. Or maybe I just fancy her.

An awkward silence.

'Oh, come on, Haddock. There's enough of Agnes to go around. To each his own. I've never shared an ice cream with her. And my little affair might bear some useful fruit, apart from the obvious, ha ha. You'd be surprised what a woman lets slip just before she hits the heights. Depends on the wench – and the man of course, ha ha – but I would say there are twenty seconds preceding climax when a wench doesn't know what she is saying and truth will out.'

'So, I suppose we advise the super that anthropological research recommends interrogating wenches in the twenty seconds before orgasm?' I am being sarcastic.

'I'd need more empirical data before going that far. After all, some wenches fake orgasm all their lives just to please some fish of a husband or to get it over with. But not the screamers – and Agnes is a screamer.'

'Yes, I noticed. Double orgasm, wasn't it? About a minute between them and the second much deeper than the first?'

'My God! You weren't watching, were you? Have you made spy holes in the bedroom wall?'

'No need, old fruit. We could hear every moan from these armchairs.'

'You could have warned me Madhu was here,' K says lamely.

'I thought *you* were in Johor Bahru.'

'Only for lunch by the sea. I didn't want to stay for the night-life with a couple of faggots – nice guys that they be. Making hay with delectable Venus, are you? Now, there's a wench I could eat alive, if you don't mind me saying so. Not that I would of course, at least not until you've chewed your fill.'

'Well, I haven't chewed my fill,' I say curtly.

K tries a conciliatory tone that only works on those who don't know him. 'Not bitchy about my brotherly embrace of your beloved, are you? She didn't respond you know … not much anyway, ha ha ha. You know I *never* roger the wenches of friends. Enemies don't count.'

K never leaves room for compromise. People love him or hate

117

him. Only I do both. Sometimes I find his incredibly light view of life attractive. At other times I find him unlovable. This is one of the other times, and I'm not sure if my feelings are spawned by Venus or Agnes or both of them. 'It's all some great game to you, K, isn't it? Bernard's dead, the police are investigating and all you can do is take a couple of homosexuals off to lunch by the sea and roger Chin's wife.'

'Well, that's not bad is it? I mean, be reasonable. It would be difficult to fit a lot more into one day, ha ha ha.' K isn't at all put out by my tone. But then he is hardly ever put out. He disappears into the kitchen and comes back with a bottle of beer and two glasses.

'Haddock old chap, of course it's all a game. We are anthropologists, after all, so we should know. We know all anybody does is play roles. Might as well enjoy the theatre. You – unless things have taken a sudden turn for the better recently – act the part of unrequited lover forever waiting for Venus. Tell me, is there a touch of masochism there? Do you enjoy the role? Is anticipation of the honey more satisfying than the taste of honey? Is deferred gratification the real aphrodisiac we all seek?'

'None of your damn business.'

'Struck a nerve, did I? Just advice from an older brother. Venus is a beauty. Best thing you've laid hands on, or should I say not laid hands on? It does seem a bit weird though, your spending time with the most desirable woman in Singapore and not bedding her. You'll agree that needs explanation.'

'The explanation is simple enough. Her husband Richard is in a coma in the special annex of Holland Village Nursing Home. He'll never come out of it but she is not ready to cuckold him.'

'Holland Village Home you say? Bit of a coincidence there. Old Ra'mad's wife's been there for two years. He goes there every Sunday morning with a bunch of flowers.'

'I didn't know that.' I now know where Venus meets the mad chemist on Sundays. 'That's kind of noble of the old bugger, isn't it?'

'Yes, of course it is. Every Sunday morning for one hour old Rat-Mad plays the noble role. A lot harder for your young Venus. But sounds like she's playing a role too – the faithful wife who won't betray her husband – though if comatose, no way he'd ever know she did and must be beyond caring. Society applauds her for keeping values most of its members happily break in private. And you, Haddock me lad, expect her to behave in the way you've weirdly got used to. Having a comatose husband is bad enough, no need to compound the dear lady's problems with a comatose boyfriend. Anyway, what's the story behind this husband? How'd he get into a coma?'

'I don't know.'

'And you're not curious?'

'Of course. But all I know is what Venus has told me. His name is Richard, but I know nothing about him. Only that he became comatose two years ago and is not expected to come out of it.'

'And what do you know about Venus? She is, after all, one of the best-known faces in Singapore.'

'Almost nothing. She's several generations a *Peranakan* but apart from that I've no idea about her family or history. She has a house but I've no idea where it is and I've not met any of her relatives.'

'Any children?'

'She hasn't mentioned any so I presume none.'

'Haddock, you amaze me. You are besotted by a married woman you are not bedding and you know next to nothing about her. What on earth do you two do together?'

'Eat. We went to the zoo once – had breakfast with the orang utan and Venus interviewed her. I swear it's true: she asked Ah Meng, that's the orang utan, questions and Ah Meng answered, with Venus translating for the camera. She likes animals. Seems to love Barnaby.'

'Well, that explains why she's with you. But have you never asked her about herself – school, family, home, you know?'

'I've tried but never got much. She studied here – left the year before you came, fortunately. She studied alongside her cameraman, Siggy, who seems to be her best friend but nothing more – he's gay. She did some of Bernard's courses. That's about it. I don't want to appear pushy. I suppose when she's ready, she'll tell me.'

'Venus is a very sexy woman. From what you say, she's been without it for two years. Believe me, neither of you can wait for ever. If a wench is with you all the time, she wants it. The longer you wait for her, the less chance you'll get what you're waiting for.'

The world according to Woolf is a simple one. We all act all the time. The roles all involve getting it or not getting it. I want to scream there is more than that to life, but I don't. He might be right.

11

The Reading

THE MORNING after the screams of the evening before I am sharing a large pot of the best Javanese coffee in my kitchen with David, who never needs an excuse to drop in. I took to Javanese coffee after I read Tom Stamford Raffles planted it when he was Lieutenant-Governor of Java. My drinking Javanese coffee would please my father – Dad called me *Tom* after his hero; pity he didn't call me *Sir Stamford*. Anyway, it's good coffee.

I'm telling David about the rats story I invented to explain the screams from my back room when – coincidences do happen – Ra'mad pokes his moustache around the back door. 'Good morning, David, Doctor Haddock. You haven't seen my rat by any chance? It's past time for his antidote you see and I can't find the little fellow anywhere.'

Ra'mad was at Aberystwyth University during WWII, which explains his accent and choice of words. His regional English is perfect to the point of punctuations like 'you see', upon which Ra'mad hangs a lilt from the dales. I half expect him to throw in a *boyo* or two but he never does. It's almost as if he has barely spoken since leaving Wales – at least not to humans, rats are another matter.

'Lost a rat, have you? Would that be Socrates, Sophocles or CP Snow?' My sarcasm makes David snigger and I immediately regret my words. Nobody with a bitch named Barnaby and coming from a long line of Haddocks should make fun of the way a man names his rats.

'Snow, the white one. He's the only one I let out regularly. He never leaves the flat.' Ra'mad sounds concerned. 'He's well past time for his antidote.'

'What happens if he doesn't get it?'

'I'm not 100% sure you see, not with Snow. He's a strong one. An ordinary rat would die, you see. And I would not want Snow to suffer. He's been with me now for two years.' So have I, I think.

I suggest we look through all the cupboards, of which there are an imperial number. It is David who finds Snow, curled up with his nose under his tail, like Barnaby asleep. He must have come down the waste pipe and is in the cupboard under the sink.

Ra'mad picks Snow up by the tail. It hangs limply. 'It's dead,' he says, sadly stating the obvious. I can't quite manage regrets and condolences, although the little body does look more like a child's beloved pet than a mad scientist's experimental rodent. 'I killed it,' Ra'mad continues. 'Do you think it suffered?'

'How would we know?' David retorts unkindly. 'I suppose if you poison a rat or poison a person, there will be suffering involved.'

'Not necessarily, you see,' Ra'mad replies. 'If a rat suffers, it *always* cries. Not like humans. Did you hear any squealing or sobbing coming from the cupboard?'

'No,' I say in a comforting voice. 'We've been in here half an hour and heard nothing. Barnaby would certainly have reacted if a rat had started to squeak.'

'That's very good. Very good news indeed.' I swear Ra'mad's

eyes glint. 'No pain you see.' He holds the rat up to the window, inspecting its face in the light. 'Yes. I'm sure there was no pain. You just went to sleep and didn't wake up. That was the way of it, wasn't it, Snow?' Ra'mad the scientist thanks me quickly and leaves with his rat. Barnaby follows him to the threshold and stands guard there.

'I suppose he's going to cut it up and do an autopsy,' David remarks. 'What a way to get your jollies.'

Tooting aborts our dissection of Ra'mad's motives for killing his favourite rat. Venus is here. 'Come on, Barns,' I say. 'We're off to the reading of Bernard's Will.'

★   ★   ★

Venus finds a place to park far from where we want to be and we walk, Barnaby heavy in my arms because I have yet to buy her a leash and can't have her running into the traffic or befouling the pavement. Venus eventually says, 'Here we are,' at a building I swear was not there the week before. We duck out of the street and under the down-blast of one of those cold curtains that restyles your hairdo and reduces your body heat by 50% in one second.

Mirrored walls and ceiling and non-slip high gloss plastic flooring reflect each other into infinity. Helpful signs in four languages direct our behaviour: no smoking, no spitting, no loitering, no littering and, of course, no chewing gum or peeing in lifts; but nothing about dogs.

Little cameras on glassy walls track our progress – I wonder if the new high-tech university will be like this. The names of a hundred agencies, organisations and companies are listed alphabetically on one wall, each with its floor and access lift represented by a white number and a letter of the alphabet in a little black box that looks like it will flip over to display a time of arrival or departure. Venus, surprisingly at home in this alien landscape, explains to me, the wild colonial boy, that we have only to match the letter for Tambiah's office, an F, against the ranks of high-speed lifts and get out when we get to the floor number. Simple.

Barnaby is huddled in my arms, shivering with cold. We are looking for lift F when a whistle sounds and I know it sounds for me.

'No dogs.' It's a female guard with 'SECURITY' stretched around her chest.

'Dogs?' I echo, looking down at the brown eyes and curly tail of my somewhat overfed baby.

'That!' Security clarifies, jabbing her chin towards Barns. 'Outside.' And then, perhaps catching sight of the banner proclamation 'Courtesy is Our Way of Life', snaps with courtesy: 'Dog in street, lah.' Such discrimination directed against a dog who doesn't smoke, spit, litter, chew gum or, as far as I know, pee in lifts.

Venus explains in firm, clear Singaporean that we have been told to bring the dog to a reading of a Will and gives Tambiah's name and phone number. Security says, 'Wait'. I bet she knows I'm good at waiting. She unhooks a phone from a wall, taps in numbers, whispers, listens and says, 'Okay, lah. Lift F. Keep dog off floor. Get out twenty-six.'

Lift F is long hair carpeted, the colour of an Afghan Hound. The presence of a Malay lift pilot stops me peeing and ensures Barnaby doesn't leave my aching arms to make love to the carpet. Shedding hair freely in the air around us and looking with confusion at the infinitely mirrored images of herself, me, Venus and the lift boy, Barns sneezes into the stream of Arctic air blowing down on our heads from the glass ceiling. The pilot swings his control lever around one hundred and eighty degrees for maximum G-force and we take off with a resounding ping that sends numbers rolling in the digital display above the lift door. We arrive before our stomachs.

I had been expecting Tambiah to hang out in a couple of character rooms off Serangoon Road, somewhere between Komala Vilas – all the vegetarian food you can eat from a banana leaf for a Sing dollar – and the twin Sodoms of Bugis Street and Johor Road. But somewhere inside this anonymous structure sits a jolly Tamil with enough of Bernard's confidence to be entrusted with his Will.

On leaving the long hair carpeted lift, we tread onto good old Singaporean-pragmatic hemp carpet, made to last and you can smoke its sister. The long corridor has the clean and functional aspect of Mount Elizabeth Hospital. Prints of sailing boats on Lake Geneva are screwed tightly to the walls at precise intervals; why, I don't know. When we finally come to a glass-panelled door labelled 'Tambiah', I feel I should be carrying a get well soon card instead of a large shivering dog.

Venus opens the door and we walk into anti-climax. The extent of Tambiah Chambers runs to one room the size of my main bathroom and less genial; no toilet or bath. Tambiah is back to the wall behind a desk. Piles of books and bundles of papers tied with string fill available space. I feel like Alice stepping into a filing cabinet.

Li Fang and I exchange looks of surprise at seeing each other. The super, wearing casuals, sits next to Li Fang. Both look frozen. Tambiah rises and crosses his chambers in two strides. He closes the door behind us and says I can put Barnaby down if I like. I do like – my arms feel like lead. Barns immediately starts to dig through the matting. I rebuke her. She shakes a flurry of fine hairs and sneezes, spreads herself out as flat as she can and pushes herself along the matting. Tambiah bears it stoically. Perhaps his clients normally begin procedures with a roll on his rough-textured carpet and a sneezing fit; maybe a dog sliding across the floor is the ceremonial prelude to any reading of a Will. I rather doubt it but it's the first time I attend such a rite. Indeed, my first time in any chambers. Tambiah's squat little one-room office high in a techno tower does not meet my expectations. To me, *chambers* implies a plurality of rooms and, by the semantic implication of pots to pee in, a toilet – of which I feel a need coming on. All the cold air has got to my sacred parts – or maybe it was the temptation to pee in the lift.

I ask Tambiah to turn down the air-con or open the window; Barnaby's aroma goes best with open windows. Tambiah, snug in his wool suit, regrets there is nothing he can do, the air-con is centrally controlled and the window is sealed. I'm getting a taste of the future.

Tambiah tells us we are there for the reading of the Will of Bernard Fox and that Superintendent Wong is present as an observer. He notes Venus is not mentioned in the Will and is not a witness to it. He asks if anybody objects to her presence and pauses. The super seems to be searching for courteous words to do just that.

During the pause I wonder why Venus *is* there. If she wants to know who got what, she could ask me afterwards. I also wonder, a bit morbidly, what she stands to get when Richard finally croaks. Perhaps the house she lives in now? Perhaps a fortune in investments? I know so little about her and nothing about Richard, I can't begin to speculate. Yet here she is, about to find out what Uncle Bernard left me.

Pause done, Tambiah says, 'Well, then, all right,' and Venus is in by default. Fitted tightly into his reinforced Windsor chair, Tambiah puts on a serious face and opens a file. The reading begins.

The Will, Bernard's first and last, is dated just three days before his death. Bit of a surprise, that. We are then guided through the sound mind bit, which has more the stamp of Tambiah than of Bernard, then it's into cash flows. Li Fang comes first. Bernard refers to him as his trusted friend of many years, not as the cook across the road; I remember their first meeting as Bernard described it in the exercise book. He gets one hundred thousand Singapore dollars. Nobody seems more surprised than Li Fang.

Next comes Norsiah, just Norsiah, no surname. Norsiah missing-whereabouts-unknown; she gets the same as Li Fang. Thanks to Bernard's generosity, Norsiah the cleaner need never wash my knickers again. She must be in her mid-thirties. With her new-found wealth, she still has time to make a good marriage if that's what she wants. I never looked at her much. She comes when I'm out, she cleans, she takes away my dirty clothes and by magic they reappear clean and ironed in my wardrobe. Never have we had anything approaching a chit-chat. She's fairer of skin than most Malays and might, I suppose, be considered attractive. A little devil in my head wonders if there had perhaps been somebody other than Barnaby to share Bernard's life.

127

'You don't know the half of it,' says Bernard in my mind. 'Not yet you don't.'

Then it's my go. Bernard refers to me in terms that close my throat. 'My very close comrade who has helped me do what I needed to do, to think, to have ideas and to stay alive until the end.' He leaves me his entire Central Providence Fund Retirement Benefit, which Tambiah states he has valued at about one hundred thousand Singapore dollars, placing me on par with Li Fang and Norsiah. In Singapore 1980, to a young lecturer, it is an enormous amount of money. Two conditions are placed on the bequest.

Firstly, that I care for Barnaby and give her a home. Tambiah adds in his own parentheses that what happens to Barnaby is between me and my conscience since 'care' and 'home' are loose concepts open to interpretation that nobody is likely to contest. Nobody except Barnaby, I think. I am sure Barns has very clear ideas on what care and home mean. 'And so do I,' says Bernard in my head.

The second condition, Tambiah states, he had advised Bernard against, but Bernard had insisted on it. 'You must ensure publication of *The Social History of Singapore University* as I wrote it.'

Tambiah explains. 'I understood from Professor Fox he had completed a manuscript on this subject and he had discussed some of the contents with you. Unfortunately, the professor declined to leave a copy of his manuscript with me and Superintendent Wong informs me the original manuscript has disappeared and cannot therefore be published. This opens the possibility the Will be contested, if anyone were to interpret the conditions on your bequest in terms of payment for services.'

Tambiah looks rather embarrassed at his failure to tie Bernard down to legally binding specifics. 'This possibility seems remote and would involve a legal tussle. There is, for example, no way to know if any publication on this subject is, in the professor's words, "as I wrote it". The only basis I see for a significant legal problem arising is if the original manuscript turns up. Suppose, for example, Professor Fox gave it to a third party for safe keeping and that party publishes it without your involvement. However unlikely this sounds, I suggest you avoid possible legal problems by allowing me to place the total of the bequest made to you in an interest-bearing trust to be redeemed on publication of the professor's work if it comes to light, or after one year, which will provide time for any objections to be raised. I will advertise for the professor's manuscript with a reasonable reward and that way, nobody can later accuse you of not trying to comply with the terms of the Will.'

Tambiah then produces three sealed envelopes, gives one to Li Fang, one to me and states that the third will be held by him for Norsiah. With as much an air of mystery as he can muster, he explains that the envelopes contain no money or valuables, only letters to each person. Superintendent Wong immediately requests us to read the letters in private before leaving the premises and then to allow him to read them, since anything and everything might have a bearing on the case. Neither of us refuse.

Reading the letters in private poses a problem given the confines of Tambiah Chambers. The super suggests he and I go outside into the corridor, where thankfully we find a toilet free of Arctic air. I break the magic beam at the urinal and water flushes to present me with a nice clean bowl to pee into. A further automatic flushing follows my withdrawal from the stall. After the

129

symbolic washing of hands that men do in public toilets when others are watching and after a liberal dose of the hot air dryer, I open the envelope. The letter is to reveal how little I know my best friend and only uncle.

12

Dead Man Writing

MY DEAR TOM,

You should know that Norsiah is my daughter. Bet that surprised you! She was born end-1942 in the Perak jungle. Norsiah's mother, Syep, was a Semai aboriginal Malay. Her mother and I were together during those happy years in hiding from the Japanese. We had a Semai wedding, nothing on paper so no evidence of paternity. When our daughter was born, I was there and helped her out. There was a dog licking her as I tried to clean her up, so I named my daughter *Syou*, which means *dog* in Semai. I thought at the time that if she ever found herself in England, she could simply be Sue.

Syep was caught by the Japanese shortly before they surrendered in 1945. She used to carry Chin Peng's messages to a small town on the edge of the jungle, where Li Fang would collect them on full moon days. The messages were all verbal. Li Fang would remember them, return to Singapore, encode them and send on by radio to British forces in Sri Lanka. Messages would come back to us the same route in reverse.

With Chin Peng in the jungle it was all pages from a boy's own comic – tommy guns and blowpipes and the occasional sabotage attack on Japanese positions – tremendous fun. Until Li Fang's resistance cell in Singapore was caught and tortured by the Kempeitai; the information they gave was enough for Japanese soldiers to pick her up as soon as she appeared in the contact village. Li Fang witnessed her arrest and ran back to warn us. She couldn't tell the Japanese anything other than the report she carried in her head but she could lead the enemy to us, which is why we moved camp. Later, other Semai told me she was raped, tortured and murdered. It is something I have lived with all this time.

My wife was just one aborigine among many passing through a tiny Malay town. The Kempeitai must have been tipped off. At first, I suspected Li Fang. He could have fed us and the British forces misinformation that would sabotage the whole resistance; since messages were verbal, he could easily have changed them. But, Chin Peng argued, the Japanese would not have cut short a valuable and unwitting source of disinformation and Li Fang at any time could have led the Japanese straight to us had he wished – so I knew it wasn't him. Plus, Li Fang loved Syep as much as I did. He could not return to Singapore after his cover was blown, so Li Fang stayed with us and fought bravely until Japan surrendered.

After the war, it seemed kinder to leave my daughter with the Semai than bring her to an uncertain civilisation. Following Japan's surrender, I was stationed in Singapore. It was a lawless time. Greater-Malaya nationalists found themselves uneasily allied with the mostly-Chinese communists who had fought against the Japanese. I maintained my friendship with Chin Peng but there was no place for me in the politics of the time. I never found the Japanese who tortured and killed Syep; but I did find out who betrayed Li Fang's resistance group in Singapore and I took my revenge.

After Japan surrendered, many scores were settled. Collaborators were knifed in the street or hanged outside their houses. Singapore then, for a few lawless months, was a totally different place to the safe haven you know now. Another war followed, this time British and Federation soldiers against Chin Peng. It was not dignified as 'war', it was 'Emergency'. It was 1960 before the Emergency was declared over and I could revisit forest villages in Perak State. Only then did I find my daughter.

When I found Syou, she was already widowed. She had married at puberty and given birth to one child. Her village continued to assist Chin Peng's guerrillas and many people, including her husband and child, were killed in a reprisal attack by British soldiers. It is impossible to describe the shame and guilt I felt on hearing that. I tried to make things right by supporting Syou, but it ended with her supporting me. Her mother killed by Japanese because she carried messages *for* the British, her husband and only child killed *by* the British. None of it made sense. Even now as I write, history seems a compound of mistakes.

When Syou came to live with me in Singapore, it was as my Malay servant not as my Semai daughter. I didn't want her involved in any second-generation reprisals. Syou changed her name to Norsiah for obvious reasons – Malays don't name their children *dog*. We have now got used to the name Norsiah and please use it, not Syou, when talking to or about her. People think of her as Malay and she is – aboriginal Malay. In addition to the money I have left my daughter, I have given her a letter certifying that I am her father – it might be useful to her residence in Singapore, since I am now a citizen, although there is no documentary evidence of paternity. But unless she decides otherwise, our relationship should remain secret. There are still men who would take revenge on my remaining family if it's too late to get me.

Li Fang never talks publicly of his anti-Japanese role. As Chin Peng's key liaison person, he risked his life every day. I got an OBE and three years' back pay after the war. Even Chin Peng got an OBE – before he was cast as a communist villain. Li Fang got nothing. He has always been a trusted friend to me and to Norsiah. He is the real Singaporean hero – unrecognised.

I have not included in my Will things of a sentimental nature. Please offer the early pictures of me to Norsiah. Behind the picture of me with Chin Peng, you will find pictures of Norsiah's mother as a young girl in our jungle home. They too should go to Norsiah. In the same place are pictures of Li Fang in the jungle with Chin Peng. Even now, I am not sure how safe it is for a Singaporean to admit to close association with the rebel leader. Give them to Li Fang quietly.

For my funeral, Tambiah will handle it. No religious ceremony. I would prefer not to have any funeral but simply live in the minds of those of you I love and think of as family. What I would much prefer would be not to die and while I have a kind of premonition of death, I hope I'm wrong. If I am right, please ensure my book, and through it the university, lives on without me.

I think you and Barnaby and Norsiah are the three who will most miss my presence. Were it possible to do so, I would miss you too.

As ever (well, not quite),
Bernard

*   *   *

I turn to a separate last page to read a simple PS that surprises me; it contradicts what I saw the afternoon of Bernard's death. An automatic flush of water tells me the super is at the urinal. I glance quickly in his direction and wait for him to shake his peg, an action that requires men to turn down the eyes. As the super jiggles, I hastily fold the single page PS and slip it into my shirt pocket. If he sees it, it will complicate things.

My cleaner is Bernard's daughter; that makes her my cousin, so I'm not completely alone in the world. Why had Bernard not told me when alive? Why tell me now he's dead? Does she know we are related? Where is she now? And I'd better destroy that postscript – it suggests Bernard had prepared himself for leaving the world. A great pity, I think, that his preparations didn't include copying the manuscript to which he attached such importance.

Super Wong has been patient. I pass him the letter and wander out of the toilet and along the corridor. Having read the letter, Wong finds me and gives me a sympathetic look along with the letter. 'What's in there better remain confidential. It's an interesting last letter. Informative, realistic and human. The way I remember the professor.'

'You remember him?'

'Professor Fox taught me history twenty years ago and we stayed in contact.'

'Does the letter have any bearing on the case, do you think?'

'I'm not sure. If he was planning suicide, perhaps he sent Norsiah away – the Will being made just three days before he died supports that – although that letter doesn't read like a suicide note, and there's still no explanation for the fan turning. Maybe we would have more of an idea if we could read his lost manuscript. The confidence he places in you to see the work published would seem to counter any suggestion you stole it.'

'I'm not prime suspect anymore?'

Super Wong gives another of his wry smiles. 'Well, you, Li Fang and Norsiah are equal beneficiaries in the Will, so you all remain suspects. You saw the professor on the evening of the day he signed the Will. Did he mention anything to suggest he had just made it and how he might divide his estate?'

'Not a word. Bernard said nothing about a Will and being left this money is a great surprise to me.'

'What I find strange is the Prof's silence about his daughter all this time and telling you only now. And as far as I know, only you; *why you*? Norsiah is certainly a case of Asian genes taking precedence; it takes a good look to see she had a white father.'

'So, you have seen her?'

'I mean her campus ID photograph. Why do you think he kept the relationship secret?'

'Maybe, as he says in the letter, Bernard felt there remained some danger through association with Chin Peng in the past.'

'Right,' says the super thoughtfully. 'Same no doubt for Li Fang. If Li Fang could deceive the Japanese, what's to say he is not even now passing messages to the remnants of the Communist Party of Malaya still in the jungle? And somebody might question Norsiah's years in the jungle with the communists. Indoctrinated as a young girl, married to someone killed by British anti-communist forces who also killed her only child, she takes on a Malay-Muslim name and comes to Singapore pretending to be Professor Fox's servant not his daughter. With the professor, Li Fang and Norsiah living in each other's pockets, it would take a lot less for some people to cry *communist cell*.

This letter of yours could raise difficult questions.'

'Are you going to raise such questions, Superintendent?'

'No. I don't want a witch-hunt on campus. Please keep the contents of your letter to yourself. I will advise Li Fang and Norsiah, when she gets back, to do the same with their letters. You really have no idea where she might be?'

'Sorry, no. If anybody knows, it's Li Fang. He and Norsiah were very close … *are* very close I mean.'

Since the super seems about as friendly as a policeman investigating you for murder can be, I venture an enquiry. 'Would it be out of line to ask if you are close to catching Bernard's killer?'

'Not to ask. But it would be out of line for me to answer. Right now, we are concentrating on campus links – Professor Fox had few recent contacts outside of university life. In this regard, I would like to ask you about Dr Woolf.'

'I believe you interviewed K early this morning.'

'How do you know that?'

'K told me yesterday you were seeing him at 8.30.'

'I did and I'm concerned about Dr Woolf's alibi. He originally said he was at home watching a video with his wife the evening of the professor's death and they went to sleep around 11 o'clock. Things seemed to check out at first. He left a Drama Society meeting before 8.30 and his wife said he arrived home at 9.00 and they watched a video before going to sleep. But the video she described was entirely different to that described by Dr Woolf this morning. Their maid said that Woolf arrived home late. When I tackled Woolf about this, he admitted he had not arrived home before 11.00. His new account of the evening is one that can only be confirmed by you. He says he just floated around Singapore in his car, parked near the Padang and walked down by the river. He picked up a transvestite by the bridge, name unknown, twenties or thirties, Chinese, took her to your place, parked his car round back out of sight, entered through the kitchen and left after ten, dropping the transvestite on Tanglin Road before going home. Can you verify that?'

I frown.

13

Beyond Surprise

'SORRY, SUPERINTENDENT,' I reply. 'I can only confirm K's story is perfectly in character. He has a key and uses my flat whenever he wishes. He does cruise around in his car. What he calls "going wenching." When he has a wench, he doesn't ask if I mind him using my back bedroom – that would be vulgar. Sometimes he comes through for a drink after, with or without his companion, but if he has picked up someone he'd rather not show off – which happens often enough with K – he simply leaves as quietly as he came without disturbing me.'

'Then you don't know if Woolf was in your place and he doesn't know if you were there?'

'That's it, Superintendent. Sounds a bit weak doesn't it?'

'To say the least. Dr Woolf tried to point out that this was the strength of both of your alibis: had you invented an alibi, you could both have done a lot better. Not a great line of defence, particularly following his lie about being at home with his wife.'

'That's K, Superintendent. Knows he can always count on his wife to support him. It's hard to imagine a wife more tolerant. She's expecting a baby and doesn't go out much, whereas K can't bear to be locked up at home. I'm surprised their marriage works but it seems to.'

'Woolf's marriage is not my concern. I'm only trying to establish if he was in your flat that night. Nobody saw his car or him. I suppose that's a precaution he might take to cover his adventures. Woolf says he heard music coming from inside your flat. Can you name any of the music you played that night?'

'I played Pink Floyd most of the evening. *Wish You Were Here* and *The Wall*. I turned the music off at 10.00 so as not to annoy Ra'mad upstairs, but before then K might have heard music. Whether he was paying attention to what was playing, I doubt.'

'On the contrary, that is exactly what he says he heard.'

'Does it clear him?'

'It helps. It helps Dr Woolf and it helps you. Had you answered differently, Dr Woolf would be helping us with our enquiries before the day's out.'

I feel sorry for Wong. He's a decent bloke, this is perhaps the most publicised murder he's ever had, and he sounds literally clueless. I'm sorry I had to lie to him. I've played nothing but the same two pieces of Pink Floyd for weeks now – and K knows it. But on the night of Bernard's death, I had not touched the old record player that K gave me along with those same two Pink Floyd long-play records – the *only* music I have. There had been no music as I waited for Venus. K lied.

What really worries me is that around 9 o'clock I had gone into the kitchen for a refill of ice and seen the door of the back bedroom wide open. There had been nobody inside. Of course, K might have mixed up his timing – and there was that mysterious hour between ice at 9.00 and Von Whatsit at 10.00, when even I have no idea where I was.

*　　*　　*

Barnaby launches herself at me with the canine equivalent of hugs and kisses as I re-enter the chambers. She is my dog now and we stand to share a lot of money together. Venus does a bright round of goodbyes and accompanies me out, dog in arms, waiting until halfway down the corridor before she speaks.

'This is fantastic. Li Fang's an unsung hero in the fight against Japan. And you, Tom darling, what did you do to deserve so much money?'

'I suppose you've been reading Li Fang's *private* letter. I can't show you mine as the super's kept it. It doesn't say anything you don't know. Talks about his time in the jungle with Li Fang.' I don't tell Venus that Bernard's maid is his daughter, not yet. And I have the letter in my pocket – my first lie to the woman I want to trust.

We step out of lift F as the super leaves the neighbouring lift. How that is possible I have no idea. Barnaby squirms in my arms, anxious to be out of the cold. 'Miss Goh ... Mrs Goh,' the superintendent calls. 'Please remember everything about today's proceedings is private. That means *not* for public consumption unless you get my okay.'

'Of course, Inspector,' Venus coos. 'Not to worry. Although it would be nice to have something *tangible* to report on the investigations.'

'I promise that when there is something, you will be the first informed.'

'And, while waiting, there isn't some little scrap, perhaps something not 100% *tangible*, something that I could report without quoting source?' Venus will hold off on her scoop, if the contents of a Will are a scoop, but she wants more in return than a promise to be first with the news when nobody will be interested.

'What you can safely say, Mrs Goh, is that the police have made significant progress in analysing the drugs found in Professor Fox and the professor's dog. That can be on record.'

'And off record?'

'You are, I believe, interviewing people who knew the professor. I suppose you have already talked to Doctor Ra'mad?'

'No, I haven't. Should I?'

'I have to go now. Your audience might be more interested in drugs than in dry legal proceedings, don't you think?'

'Definitely,' Venus chirrups.

While Venus is bargaining with the super, I notice a familiar wide-brimmed white hat at the entrance. Wisps of hair flutter in the cold-air curtain's breeze, lick at the exposed neck and flick onto a simple white dress. I feel a guilty interest as she recognises me and comes towards me all smiles.

'Why, Doctor Haddock, what a nice surprise. Bumping into you here was the last thing I expected.' Agnes ignores Venus. 'And carrying poor Barnaby in your arms. Where have you been?' She strokes poor Barnaby's head. Barns turns her right ear to be scratched, a sure sign of familiarity.

'Just looking up an old friend,' I reply. 'Have you met Venus?'

'No,' Agnes says simply, turning to look briefly at my love in waiting. 'Hello. Sorry, got to dash. I have a meeting with my solicitor. You know him, Tambiah of Guild House fame.' Agnes flashes me a conspiratorial smile and moves directly to lift F.

'And who was that?' asks Venus, with the stress on *that*.

'Oh, that? Harry Chin's wife.'

'The little partner of your satanic enemy? Bit friendly, aren't you? I mean, all things considered.'

'Chin and I are not enemies. Being friends with K doesn't

142

make me enemies with my head of department. Anyway, I wouldn't heap a husband's sins on his wife. Neither would Bernard. He and Agnes were quite friendly in a neighbourly way.'

'And you, Tom?'

'What?'

'Friendly in a neighbourly way?'

'Not really. Only know her to say hello. Like you and Ra'mad, I suppose.' I can see Venus thinking. Must be thinking about Agnes. But no. Venus is thinking about Ra'mad. She surprises me by turning to Miss Security and asking in the politest Mandarin if she can use the house phone to make an urgent call. The guard surprises me even more by lifting the phone and handing it to Venus in an almost reverential manner that Singaporeans can affect if they really, really want to. She must, I think, have recognised the star of TV news.

'Ra'mad's phone number, Tom. Do you have it? Oh, you wouldn't, would you. I've got to get to Ra'mad before he's tried, convicted and hanged.'

'Venus. Calm down. Li Fang is still upstairs but call the Guild if it's so important. Somebody there will carry a message to Ra'mad and ask him not to get hanged until you've interviewed him.' In Li Fang's absence, anybody sitting around in the Guild answers the public phone. This time, the anybody is K.

'Doctor Woolf, what a lovely coincidence. Could you do me a great favour and pass a message to Dr Ra'mad?'

'Of course, my dear. I'm anyway about to drop in on Haddock.'

'Please tell him I'll be along as soon as I can get there, within the hour, and I'm then going to the Home to see Richard. I'd like to give Dr Ra'mad a lift to see his wife. It's not Sunday but a break in routine surprise-visit might jog the responses.'

'I'll tell him that if you like, but I rather think Ra'mad's wife is beyond jogging,' K answers dryly. 'Ra'mad has, by coincidence, already done what you have just suggested. He paid his wife a surprise visit yesterday evening. She died during the night.'

14

Roasted Ra'mad

AS VENUS PULLS UP, we see Ra'mad through my window, sitting in my best armchair. Venus runs to him, ignoring K and David. I have no idea what everybody is doing in my flat; seems it's now a community centre.

'I'm *so* sorry, Doctor Ra'mad. So *very* sorry.' Venus apologises as if it's her fault that Ra'mad's wife has finally *left the world*, as Malays do instead of dying. Venus really looks sorry: the beautiful mouth and eyelids turn down and her voice descends with them. Her consolation of Ra'mad is distraught enough to invoke reciprocal consolation from the bereaved.

'There, there, dear lady. Please don't upset yourself, now.'

'You poor, poor man, Doctor Ra'mad. Everybody knows how devoted you were, how you stood by your wife until the very end.'

Ra'mad is beaming under his sorrow. Consolation clearly sits well with him, particularly from the full lips of Venus. His Welsh-ness becomes so prominent that I have to remind myself he will be following Muslim custom and dropping his missus in the grave he will already have ordered, not placing her rouged-up cheeks on show for a viewing after chapel.

'Thank you, my dear. But it is God's will, you see. There was nothing any of us could do. It's a blessed release really. She'd been in pain, you see. A lot of pain. With no chance of getting better. She's at peace now.' Ra'mad puts as much emotion in his voice as if his wife is late getting back from the fish and chip shop. But he didn't even burst into tears this morning when his favourite rat was found curled up for the sleep of its life.

As a scientist, Ra'mad naturally wants his devotions quantified. 'I never missed a week. During two years, I never missed a week.' Never missing a week is a pretty good empirical record, I give Ra'mad that. Quantitatively, Ra'mad is beyond reproach, although he does rub things in a bit on the qualitative side. 'I saw her suffer you see. Week after week, watched her terrible suffering. God had mercy on her and lifted her up to Him.'

'When's the funeral?' Venus asks with sympathetic softness. She's really tops at sympathy. She even extends the sentiment to those around her. 'Of course, you can count on our help.' The sister of mercy speaks for us all.

'That's Ra'mad's problem.' K the anthropologist speaking. 'Muslim custom says the body should be in the ground before the next sunset, but the police won't release it. Ra'mad's upset that Wong has ordered an autopsy.'

'My wife died in the night you see,' Ra'mad complains, 'but the hospital only thought to tell me twelve hours after she died. They came out with some nonsense about not being able to get in touch with me. But they managed to get in touch with the superintendent quickly enough. And he just orders an autopsy without a by-your-leave. Can you imagine?'

Venus looks unsure if she is to imagine or not to imagine and settles for a little tut to indicate general disapproval. I can't manage even a tut. A husband who passes his time poisoning his best friends, all of them rats, steps out of the Sunday morning routine and visits his wife on a weekday evening a few hours before she dies and nasty Wong orders an autopsy; appalling. The image of Ra'mad holding the dead Snow comes into my mind and stays there; funny Ra'mad never mentioned his wife's departure this morning.

Ra'mad hesitates. He wants to complain but not complain too much, an understandable position in 1980 Singapore. 'What gets me, you see, is the attitude of that superintendent. I've been home all morning. He didn't even bother to give me a call. I had no idea my dear wife had gone.' So, if he can be believed, Ra'mad didn't know his wife was dead when he sent Snow to join her.

'But the autopsy?' Venus coaxes. 'Do you know the findings?'

'That's the ridiculous thing. The initial autopsy showed traces of all the drugs that the home was treating her with. Well it would, wouldn't it? It seems one of the drugs found in my wife was the same as the drug that killed Professor Fox, or knocked him out or whatever. Since the Home was prescribing the drug, you would think the police would question the doctor. But that superintendent, without a by-your-leave orders a full autopsy and sends Madhu to grill me.'

Toshi appears from the kitchen and stands in the doorway. The avid learner of English is trying to follow the conversation. He frowns. I know today David-san is teaching him the special language of the fucking kitchen. If he understands correctly, Toshi's face tells me, the police in this country have grilled the good doctor. No doubt Toshi finds this form of interrogation very passé. The image forms in my mind of Ra'mad spread-eagled over charcoal brassieres as Madhu fires questions in Ra'mad's ear and fans the coals.

147

'According to Madhu, the sedative found in Professor Fox and in my wife was the same as one I use in my experiments. That's hardly reason for police to enter my flat and seize my drugs. I am a certified *research* chemist. My work depends on drug availability.'

'You keep a supply of the drug?' Venus keeps the incredulity low in her tone. She is the only one prepared to humour Ra'mad further. The rest of us have already found him guilty: the wife-killer chemist.

'Quite legally, yes. Every gram under lock and key with its use accounted for in my logbook. As I pointed out to Wong yesterday, the only quantity that went out of my flat was that given to the Chins. If the police want to float accusations of murder, they could begin with Chin, not me.'

Venus, perplexed or playing at being perplexed: 'But, Doctor Ra'mad, why would Doctor Chin kill your wife?'

Ra'mad looks at Venus as if he cannot blame her for being stupid, she is a woman after all. 'Oh. Not my wife. My wife died of natural causes. I'm talking about the death of Professor Fox.'

'Ah, you think Doctor Chin might have had something to do with the professor's death?' Venus plays the dumb woman so well I'm not sure she's playing.

'Of course, he does, Venus dear,' K butts in. 'It doesn't take a genius to connect Chin to Bernard's murder but Superintendent Wong is more interested in what music young Haddock played on the night of the murder. Went on and on about it this morning. Practically accused *me* of killing Bernard because I wasn't sure I could remember all of Haddock's weird taste in music. Gave me a real grilling.'

Toshi frowns again. These Singapore policemen seem to be

grilling all round. He looks from Ra'mad to K, perhaps searching for visible scars.

Venus opens her mouth to speak, but K has the bit between his teeth and is galloping into the jungle. 'The police have been grilling practically everybody.' Toshi looks positively alarmed. K continues in his thespian tone of self-indignation. 'Wong more or less called me a liar to my face.'

'More, or less?' I ask sarcastically. 'Did he really call you a liar?'

'Not in so many words.'

'Pity.'

'I appreciate your sense of humour, Haddock,' K says in a tone implying the opposite. 'But it looks like everybody except Chin is getting the treatment. David has been told to be at home for interview tonight. I'm sure he'll be grilled in the same way. The police will probably even roast Toshi if they find him in the Mess.'

'Roast Toshi and grilled David, quite a menu.' I can't resist. 'I suppose Haddock will be battered and fried in oil.' Toshi's face is white. I turn to Ra'mad. 'So, you think Chin's Bernard's killer?' I bowl the question towards Ra'mad. It is caught midfield by K.

'Yep. I'll lay it on Chin. Chin wanted to be dean and supports the campus move to that wasteland.' At K's words, Ra'mad winces. Few have been more vocal than Ra'mad in supporting the new National University location. Ra'mad's views on relocation are identical to those of Chin, although their motives for supporting the move are not. Chin supports it because he's for all officially-sanctioned plans. Should the plan change, Chin's views change to fit. Ra'mad, on the other hand, believes the move signals an upgrade. Chin acts like most academics in following the winds of change. If wanting to be dean and supporting relocation indicates Bernard's killer, then nine out of ten of Singapore's academics are suspects.

K then clutches at the weakest straw. 'And there's Barnaby,' he says. Barns raises her head at the sound of her name. 'Bernard's dog is always chasing Chin's fancy cats.'

'So, Chin killed Bernard to protect his cats against Barnaby?' I speak as flippantly as K's line of prosecution merits. Barnaby, at repeated mention of her name and the total abandonment of discursive logic, withdraws with a shake of the head into the kitchen.

'Whose side you on then, matey?' David fires at me. 'Chin had the opportunity. Chin lives right next door. Chin could have known Bernard's housekeeper was away and he would not be disturbed in his dastardly deeds.'

'The super made precisely the same points about me,' I throw in. 'And most of them, plus some, could be made against any of us here.'

'Yep, maybe,' says K, 'but the important thing is: *we* didn't do it. So, Chin must have done it.'

'There's more,' says Ra'mad loudly and pauses to signal a big revelation coming. Surprisingly, Ra'mad introduces a note of sanity into the Kangaroo Court. 'Chin had access to the sedative that knocked out Bernard Fox and his dog because I gave it to his wife and noted down in my log exactly how much I gave. Some four weeks ago it was. Agnes came to me and asked for something to keep the cats quiet on the twelve-hour drive to Ipoh. Twenty-four hours that drive is, there and back. A quantity to put those cats out of action for twenty-four hours would be more than enough to knock out a man and his dog, if you see what I mean?'

'I do,' I say. 'But can you imagine Chin being physically and mentally up to murder?' I pose the question and it draws a vacuum of silence quickly filled by K.

'You have a point there. Loathsome fellow that he be, it's hard to imagine Chin having the nerve for premeditated murder … on his own. Perhaps he had help.'

'Such as?' Venus chips in.

'Agnes,' K chips back. 'She's a strong wench; perhaps she's the driving force behind Chin's ambitions. A real Lady Macbeth that one.'

'Come on, K, you can't be serious.' The image of my lady of lonely orchids is in my mind. 'Agnes might be a Madame Bovary but she's no Lady Macbeth.'

'As you will, Haddock. But both women drove their husbands to desperation. Yes, perhaps you're right, ha ha ha. Doctor Bovary maimed by incompetence. I can see the incompetent Chin doing by accident what he wouldn't dare do by design.'

Venus, having never read Madame Bovary, looks unpleased with my defence of Agnes, bestows a smile on K and purses her lips; three actions in such rapid succession she must have practised in a mirror. 'Aren't we forgetting the important thing?' She speaks quietly and calmly. Another one of those pauses. We all wait to hear what the important thing is – just about everything unimportant has been thrown into the witches' pot, a spicing of something important can do no harm. 'If it were Chin, how would he get the professor and Barnaby to swallow the knock-out drug? It's not as if the two of them were neighbours who dropped in on each other for tea.'

This has everybody stumped except Ra'mad, the expert on poisons. 'Perhaps Fox's housekeeper is involved. She could easily have put it in his dinner and in the dog's food. Who knows what went on in that house? An attractive Malay girl and an old Englishman; perhaps she couldn't take his abuse anymore, so killed him and fled the country.'

'Don't forget, Doctor Ra'mad,' says Venus. 'Professor Fox was Singaporean, not English. And the housekeeper disappeared *before* his death.'

Ra'mad then lapses into the academic's disease of defending his thesis past reasonable refutation. 'How do we know when she went away? Even if she is away, she might have left something behind for Fox to eat, in the fridge like. I heard Fox died after eating a steak and kidney pie. She knew she would be far away when he ate it, the perfect alibi.' K and David nod like donkeys.

'Cunning,' I speak acidly – the rat-poisoner is accusing my cousin of killing her father. 'The housekeeper sedates Bernard long range with a steak and kidney pie and Chin keeps popping his head around Bernard's door to see if he is ready for the noose.'

Toshi enters, cutting short a dialogue that has outlived itself. Barnaby frisks around his legs in delight as he places a large steaming tray in the middle of the table. We stare at it.

'Runch,' says Toshi.

Venus looks dubious. Before her is not the fine Japanese cuisine she loves. 'What is it?' she asks, trying to sound polite.

Toshi swells with pride and declares: 'Steak and kidney pie.'

*   *   *

The superintendent's car pulls up outside my windows but he hasn't come for lunch. We sit in silence, expecting him to appear through the open front door; he doesn't. We hear his shoes click up the tiled stairs of the hollow stairwell and the bell sound on Ra'mad's door overhead. 'Maybe there's news about your wife, Doctor Ra'mad,' Venus suggests as Ra'mad's face registers suppressed alarm.

'Or maybe it's time for another grilling,' K adds unhelpfully.

Ra'mad is still. But evading the long arm of the law is not so easy. The bell upstairs stops ringing. The click of shoes marks the super's descent and in he walks. 'Ah there you are, Doctor Ra'mad. I wonder if I might have a word. In your flat.'

Ra'mad rises sheepishly, a bit like Barnaby when she has done something naughty. 'We'll keep you some pie,' K calls after him.

David nods me toward the kitchen. 'Look matey, chances are Ra'mad's kitchen door's open. If we go up the back stairs, we'll hear every word.'

'Despicable, David. Fiendishly cunning. Well done, indeed.' Barns looks torn between joining us and staying where the food is; no contest. David and I climb the stairs dog-less.

*   *   *

Ra'mad's kitchen door is wide open. We creep in like a couple of ninjas. The flat is the precise image of mine, except his kitchen is dominated by a huge padlocked fridge with 'poison' written on the door. Rats in cages sniff at intruders.

'It must be about the death of my poor wife,' I hear Ra'mad say sadly.

'No,' replies the super, sounding for the first time like a tough cop. 'It's about the death of Bernard Fox and Harry Chin's father.'

'Harry Chin's father? That's going back a bit, isn't it? Would you like an orange juice? There's some fresh in the fridge.'

'No. The death – murder – of Chin's father takes us back to the end of World War II, but the case has never been closed. Chin Senior was hanged after being tortured and forced to swallow a massive dose of opium that might have killed him before his head entered the noose. The similarity with the death of Bernard Fox is obvious.'

'Maybe so. But that was surely before your time on the force?'

'Before I joined the police, yes. But there are a lot of confidential files dating from that period that remain active, including one on you, Doctor Ra'mad.'

David grips my arm. I'd love to see Ra'mad's face but don't dare poke my head around the kitchen door. I imagine chocolate draining white. Ra'mad's voice sinks so low I strain to hear his answer. 'I wouldn't know about that. I suppose the police have their job to do. I wouldn't know about your files.'

'But I do, Doctor Ra'mad. Or should I call you Ali Ridzuan?'

'Lots of us took aliases during the war, Superintendent. I did so in the hope the Japanese would not connect me with Ra'mad who had studied in England and returned in 1944, landed secretly in Johor and crossed into Singapore with the idea of grouping Malays for an uprising to coincide with an allied attack.'

'Others don't give you such a noble role,' the super says sharply.

'I'm not sure I care for your tone,' says Ra'mad, sounding politely indignant. 'And that has nothing to do with the death of my poor wife. I'm going into the kitchen to get a drink.'

'You sit down!' The super almost shouts and I imagine Ra'mad sits down pretty smartly. 'And since there is nobody to hear us and this is off record, I can tell you I don't give a damn if you care for my tone. Either we have our talk here or at Police Headquarters. It's all the same to me.'

'There's no need to get confrontational, is there now? I'm always willing to help the police.'

'Like you did in Wales?'

'You've lost me, Superintendent.'

'Janet Jones. Suffocated in her sleep after taking a sleeping draft. You were living with her. Slipped out of the country damn fast, lah. Paid your passage on a cargo ship to Ceylon, connected with the *anti*-British forces there, slipped into India and made your way to Burma, from where you took a boat to Singapore with the blessing of the Japanese. Don't give me crap about working with the British forces. We know you were wanted by the British police.'

'I never killed Janet. It was her husband. He came back in the middle of the night. She'd told me he was already dead, killed at Dunkirk. I ran out of the house leaving him inside. Anyway, that's all long ago.'

'Yes, Ali. Long ago. Not much chance of British justice catching up with you now, is there, Ali?'

'Why do you keep calling me Ali? I've told you that was a pseudonym adopted during the war.'

'Adopted when? Precisely when? Before you left the UK? When the ship docked in Ceylon? In Burma?'

'All right. I changed my name to Ali before getting on the ship to Ceylon and used Ali in Malaya.'

'Not in Wales?'

'I took the ship from Southampton in England.'

'You enrolled in Aberystwyth University as Ali. Your first degree is in the name Ali. Stop playing games with me or I'll arrest you for your wife's death. Even if that one was a mercy killing, the result will be the same. In Singapore, killers hang. Tell me the truth!'

'All right, Superintendent,' says Ra'mad, a resigned whine in his voice. 'You are right, I was born Ali Ridzuan and went to the UK under that name. That doesn't change the facts of my life in Wales. It's as I told you, I swear it. I changed my name to Ra'mad to avoid that raging husband. I left as soon as he turned up. There was no reason to stay, I'd got my degree. I didn't even know Janet was dead until the war was over. I took a cargo ship to Ceylon using the name Ra'mad. It was my grandfather's name. My father was Ridzuan Ra'mad. I kept the name Ra'mad bin Ra'mad after the Japanese left Singapore because I had signed on for a doctorate in that name with Hull University. They had a special programme and grants for ex-servicemen after the war.'

'Ex-serviceman? You?'

'Well, not in the sense of regular army. But I was able to give the British forces useful information on the Japanese in 1945 and they showed appreciation with a grant.'

'And you showed your appreciation by conspiring to sabotage the Malayan Federation before it got started.'

'I opposed the idea of a Federation at the time. But not once it became reality. I have never been disloyal. I just wanted a greater Malaya. One that included all the British, Dutch and

Portuguese colonies. At the time the colonists were coming back and I thought we should unite with our Indonesian brothers against imperialism.'

'From a fishing town in Yorkshire!'

'Times were complicated, Superintendent. And I needed to further my education to serve my country after its birth pangs.'

'You spent three years back in the UK and returned to Singapore only after Chin Peng had taken to the jungle to oppose the Malayan Federation. With Chin Peng out of the way and the worst of the revenge killings over, you felt safer returning to Singapore than remaining in a country where you were wanted by the police who might at any time connect Ali and Ra'mad.'

'I just don't get you, I'm afraid. One minute you are accusing me of conspiring to sabotage the Federation and the next you are implying that I fled Malaya to avoid revenge by those trying to sabotage the Federation.'

'I would call that covering your bets. You worked with the Japanese and against them by helping Chin Jin-Hui – Harry Chin's father – to pass information to Chin Peng in the Malayan jungle. And along with the information went funds to support Chin Peng's operations – although you never passed over very much of what you collected, did you?'

'That was a lie put about by Chin Jin-Hui in 1945. He blamed me for stealing Chin Peng's funds to cover the fact that he stole it. Chin Peng chose to believe his clan relative against a Malay. Jin-Hui managed to save his neck, but only until the Japanese surrendered. During those lawless days between the Japanese surrender and the return of British forces, Chin Peng worked out that Jin-Hui had been betraying him for years and justice was done.'

'But there is nothing to suggest Chin Peng was behind that revenge killing; I suppose we could ask him yet again and mention your name or names. But he's living in Beijing now and while Beijing and Singapore are friendly, we have yet to become the best of friends. And you might brush up on your history. Chin Peng was born Ong Boon Hua – like you, he adopted an alias. He did not take the word of a clansman against that of a Malay, since Chin Peng was never a *Chin*.

'The large sums salted away by Chin Jin-Hui – with or without your assistance – were never found. Millions of dollars' in gold and silver collected to help resistance against the Japanese remained with Chin Jin-Hui until his death and then mysteriously disappeared. Since you were working with Jin-Hui during the last year of the war, perhaps *you* got your hands on it.'

'If I had the money, I would have spent it by now. You see how I live. Half my salary went into keeping my wife alive. I don't even have a car. Anyway, if Chin Peng had been suspicious of me, I would not have lived longer than Harry Chin's father.'

Silence. Point to Ra'mad.

'Who killed Harry Chin's father?' the super demands bluntly.

'How would I know,' Ra'mad whines.

'Because you worked with the Japanese on their death list; people to be eliminated as enemies of Japan.'

'I had to do that. They'd have killed me if I didn't. I only gave them names of people safely in the jungle with Chin Peng.'

'One of whom was Bernard Fox. And another who had never been in the jungle in his life. You worked with him in Singapore. Harry Chin's father, Jin-Hui.'

'Yes. But Chin's father was playing a double-game and the Japanese knew it towards the end, so I told them what they

158

already knew. They let him live because he was important in business circles. They used him to give orders to Chinese commerce and to pass false information to the British in Ceylon. But I warned Ceylon. None of the false information he passed to the British was acted on, but the Japanese did not know that and Jin-Hui escaped with his life until after the Japanese defeat.'

'When somebody came for him, tortured him and strung the body up outside his own house for everyone to see the traitor. Who did it?'

'I don't know who did it but I can guess who ordered it done.'

'Go on.'

'Bernard Fox. With the blessing of Chin Peng. Rumour had it the two of them were hand in glove, even at the height of the Emergency.'

'How would you know?'

'I said rumour. Word was that Li Fang, that idiot at Guild House, continued to act as messenger for Chin Peng throughout the Emergency. I would guess Fox took advantage of the lawless period between Japanese and British rule and had Chin Jin-Hui killed – and Li Fang led the execution party.'

'You're saying Fox, a colonial civil servant awarded an OBE for his anti-Japanese role and one of the first Singapore nationals after Independence, was working against the British and against the Federation?'

'Chin Peng got an OBE at the same time as Fox. A lot of men played double games.'

'That's true! But if Bernard Fox and Li Fang killed Chin Jin-Hui, what happened to the war loot after Jin-Hui died?'

'If you are asking for my opinion, Superintendent, just for my opinion mind, I would say either the hiding place died with

Jin-Hui or someone took the stuff. Perhaps there wasn't all that much and Jin-Hui gave it away. He did leave large amounts to the Chinese University and to his son, Harry Chin. On the other hand, maybe Jin-Hui talked before he died and the treasure passed into the hands of Li Fang or Bernard Fox.'

'Professor Fox left no great treasures in his Will. As for Li Fang, he doesn't act like a man with a fortune tucked away.'

'Who would? There are still people around who would settle old scores.'

'Perhaps you are one of them, Ali. Was it to repay an old score that you killed Professor Fox? Or was it in the hope of getting your hands on the loot you thought he might have?'

'I did not kill him, Superintendent.'

'You have no alibi, had the opportunity and had what nobody else has – a motive. Perhaps two motives. The lure of gold and to ensure Bernard Fox remained silent about your past. Perhaps three motives: you were next in line to become dean.'

'You might say the same for Harry Chin. Now, with or without your permission, I am going to get a cold drink from the refrigerator. If you want one, the offer is still there.'

Barnaby picks just that moment to charge into Ra'mad's kitchen and cannonballs into the back of my legs, blocking my retreat for two vital seconds. David's hyperactive reflexes have already taken him out onto the staircase. Ra'mad walks straight into my face.

'What the ...? How long have you been here?'

Before I can think of a reason for my presence, Ra'mad calls out to the superintendent. 'Doctor Haddock has just come up to say it's already very late and they are waiting for me to join them at lunch. Any objections, Superintendent?'

The super is with us instantly. I must look guilty as hell. 'The invitation extends to you, Superintendent. There is plenty for everybody.'

'Thank you, Doctor Haddock, but I must decline. As for you, Doctor ... er ... Ra'mad, I will speak to you again very soon.'

*   *   *

Ours is not the jolliest of lunches. Ra'mad, David and I are mute. Ra'mad picks at his pie until he sees the super drive off, then pleads that he has much to do if he is ever to get his wife into the ground and scurries off back to his rats. K and Venus immediately ask what I overheard in Ra'mad's flat. My suspicions raised by K's false alibi rise to the surface of my mind, advising caution.

'Do you mind if I don't tell you just yet?' I say lamely.

'Of course we mind!' Venus retorts.

'Come on, David,' K coaxes. 'If Haddock has gone weird, you tell us.'

I shoot David a look of ferocity. It's Bernard's look rather than mine.

'I'd rather not say,' David answers. 'Sorry.'

I know David's resistance will last no longer than the steak and kidney pie. I am not sure why I do not want to share the news. But I don't. 'Lovely pie, Toshi,' Venus says pleasantly within the tension. 'Pity I've got to be off to work. Anybody like a lift into town? David? Toshi?' They both almost rush out with Venus, who is sure to winkle everything out of David before they clear the campus.

I grab K before he too can leave; I feel more than a bit annoyed with him. 'Look, K, it wasn't clever of you to invent such a pathetic alibi, particularly after your first one failed. Saying you were here when Bernard died was stupid. What if I had told the super the back bedroom was empty that night?'

'Now, now, Haddock, don't be rhetorical and hypothetical, especially at the same time. I *was* here. You simply did not see me here.'

'I did *not* see you. I also did *not* play *any* music that evening.'

'Is my word not good enough for you?'

'Have you told the superintendent who was in the back room with you?'

'No.'

'Why not, for heaven's sake?'

'Maybe I didn't feel like it, Haddock. Now, stop asking questions and tell me what you heard upstairs.'

'Maybe I don't feel like it.'

'Please yourself.' With that, K walks proudly out to his car, drives off and disappears.

15

Bernard's War

ALONE. K HAS GONE and I'm glad; sometimes he's just too ... too ... K. Venus is at work, making news. David and Toshi are playing away. Agnes jogs back home. The sun sets. The cicadas start screaming. I retreat to the kitchen. Bernard calls me from his carrier bag. I pick him up and carry him through to my bedroom. I switch on my reading light and stack the notebooks beside me on the bed in the order Bernard wrote them. Time to find out what he was like at my age, so very long ago.

A world war is raging but Bernard gets only snippets of news in his jungle seclusion; snippets brought back by his wife after meetings with Li Fang. His initial boredom is replaced by Syep; the girl who gave him the first notebook and keeps him supplied with fresh ones and pencils. By book twenty-seven, into Bernard's third year in the jungle, they are a couple and have a two-year-old daughter, the one Bernard mentioned in his post-mortem letter: Syou – also known as Norsiah, the cleaner. Far from the rest of the world, Bernard keeps track of the calendar as days move into months and years. He's no Robinson Crusoe. He has plenty of company; he calls it splendid company in splendid isolation.

It's all there: *sumpatan* blowpipes, poison-tipped darts, quiet kills in the forest, clear mountain streams, comradeship around an evening fire, split-bamboo beds, shaman's magic, nose flutes at sunset, stories told as mothers suckle their young. Beautiful people ... naked breasts. As I read on, I feel I am there with him.

Some things he finds unlovable, like hunting monkeys and grilling them over a fire; Bernard says they look like children and refuses the meat. His wife loves it; the two do not agree on everything. One book is full of Semai words, a sort of dictionary, with the English and Malay equivalents and notes on syntax. He learns Syep's language and uses it.

Back propped against pillows, I'm happily in another world. Looking at my clock, it's after 10.00. Will Venus call by after work? Maybe she'll send a message through Li Fang. I'm learning such a lot about him from Bernard's journal. He wasn't with Bernard most of the time, not until towards the end, when he daren't return to Singapore. Bernard writes about him as a welcome visitor and as Syep's childhood friend. Seems Syep and Li Fang had a history, although Syep never went to school and Li Fang got the best education available. Bernard wonders if there was anything more to their relationship, but doesn't seem worried if there was.

Bernard saw more of Chin Peng than of Li Fang. He calls him Boon in the texts – a reference to Chin Peng's birth name, Ong Boon Hua, but I only know this because Wong mentioned it when questioning Ra'mad upstairs.

Bernard and Chin Peng seem to spend more time playing chess together than planning sabotage. Unlike Li Fang, Chin Peng had gone mostly to Chinese-language schools before the war; he is keen to improve his English and does so with Bernard. The two discuss widely – politics, history and philosophy – and Bernard is impressed. The undisputed leader of the stay-behind forces teaches Bernard to use a tommy gun but won't allow him to practice with scarce ammunition; he insists the training is only for Bernard's self-protection in case the camp is attacked and he refuses Bernard's pleas to accompany sabotage missions with the words, 'You're just the wrong colour'.

Bernard worries whenever Syep is away from the camp. She is the contact person who meets Li Fang in a small town three hours' jungle walk away. Li Fang carries news about the larger war from Singapore, obtained over covert wireless sets tuned into allied forces in Ceylon; he also relays operational messages like supply airdrops verbally through Syep. In return, she gives Li Fang news of sabotage activities and Japanese troop movements. All goes well until one day Syep fails to return by sundown.

★　　★　　★

'Syep's late back today.' I say to Boon, seeking reassurance as I move my queen.

'You're not concentrating,' Boon pins my queen to her king with his protected rook. 'Don't worry, Syep is safe with Li Fang. She'll bring us good news, I'm sure. Maybe the British counter-attack has begun.' He pours another splash of *arak* into my enamel cup and tops up with water. 'Cheers.'

It's at times like these that I feel myself less the white man's burden as the burden of being a white man. I can't go looking for my wife because of the way I look. A white man in the jungle is just too noticeable, too tempting to report to the Japanese for a reward; if seen, I would risk the entire camp by being white.

'Be nice if that counter-attack does materialise,' I say. 'But I've been sitting here for three years waiting for such news, so I'm not holding my breath.' I lift Syou into the air and swing her from side to side; she loves that. I should be fighting Japanese, not drinking *arak*, playing chess and babysitting. 'Can't you let me go with you on your next sabotage do? You taught me how to use a tommy gun but won't let me fire it.'

'Once the Japs are on the run, I promise you can come with us and hurry them along. It can't be long now. With the Germans on the run, it might be just days before America opens an Asian offensive. Let's see what news Syep brings back.'

'I'm worried. She's never been this late before.'

Boon suddenly jumps up and runs to the edge of our clearing. I look up. Li Fang comes out of the trees. He shouldn't be here. That's not in the plan. He looks exhausted. The two of them yammer urgently. Boon goes to the alarm rod and bangs it frantically, yelling in Hokkien, 'Alarm. Emergency. Move camp. This is not a drill.'

Li Fang approaches me, 'Tom, I'm sorry...'

* * *

Empty pages follow. I am left wanting to know what happened. I skim through the other 26 books in case I somehow missed book 28. I haven't. I must imagine the rest of Bernard's war. I hear a familiar car outside my shutters. Venus. Time for a Tiger.

16

Enter the Baron

WHEN THE TAMIL GIRL who makes tea comes into my office and says, 'Doctor Chin wants to see you,' I'm surprised. It's rare for Chin to call for one of his staff. 'He just wants you, now, in his office, without Barnaby.' She offers to Barnaby-sit. Thus, dog-free, I approach the chamber of Chin and knock at the door.

Chin sings out a merry '*jin lai*'. Why's he speaking Chinese to the backside of his door? Even Chin can manage 'come in', he knows I'm not Chinese. I press down on the handle slowly. '*Jin lai ba*,' Chin calls again. Hesitantly, I open the door.

Four people sit talking in Mandarin. Chin, Super Wong, Li Fang and the ageing bronze god with the finest of patinas who wanted to use the phone I don't have, the one with the VW problem. The Adonis sports an immaculately tailored short-sleeve shirt and a pastel flowered tie of matching silk; both look as casually expensive as his golden skin. It's the first necktie I've seen on open-neck campus in two years. His close-cropped hair denies rather than defies age. An Aryan nose – of course. A firm jaw clean-shaven. A square head, clean-angled. Muscles well-toned. I put him around Bernard's age but much better preserved. He's the kind of physical jerk who plays tennis every evening, swims ten lengths before his morning muesli, goes sailing at weekends, skis down Mont Blanc in avalanche season, punches sharks on the nose, never wears a condom and takes daily water-soluble Vit C. I dislike him instantly.

'Doctor Haddock,' Chin says, as if explaining a regrettable smell.

The stranger stands, stretches out a golden hand and I have to surrender my palm to its firm and solid grip as his eyes – ice blue, wouldn't you know – fix on mine and his thin lips part just wide enough to show a gleaming set of real teeth. His head inclines briefly forward and I half expect him to click his heals. He is horribly assured and upper crust. The cruel thought crosses my mind that this is the genuine Übermensch version of the man K pretends to be. I am chilled. Chin's air-con is too cold.

'Von Führer Düsseldorf,' he says.

'What?' I ask, wondering for a moment in what language Zarathustra spake.

'*Baron* Fon Fu Rer Du Se Dof,' Chin repeats the introduction and then corrects himself, '*Professor* Baron Fon Fu Rer Du Se Dof.'

'*Herr* Professor Baron Fon Fu Rer Du Se Dof,' Bernard says in my mind. From the tone, it sounds like Bernard likes him less than I do.

'Call me Adolf,' says the Baron.

Chin rattles a rattan chair; I sit on it.

'Adolf will teach anthropology,' Chin says in English.

'Where?' I ask, aiming my question between Chin and the Baron. Only K and I teach anthropology in Singapore. Maybe, I think, he's just passing through on his way back to Düsseldorf after swimming the Pacific. Wishful thinking.

'I vill lecture here. Doctor Voolf's courses. Ve vill be vorking together, you and I. Harry has invited me to be Visiting Professor. I understand you vill give me the run down on the anthropology here, yes? I look forward to our social intercourse.'

'Coffee?' asks Chin, reaching for the pot.

'Tea,' I say, just to be awkward.

'We must call the girl,' Chin says in Mandarin – I can just about understand that much.

'Never mind,' I say magnanimously. 'Coffee is fine.'

'I have known Adolf a long time,' Chin says. 'And father.'

Since Chin never knew his father, I gather he means his father knew VD; must have been a WWII connection. 'You'll be working with Doctor Woolf and me?'

'No, Doctor Haddock. I'll be vorking only vith you.'

'What about K ... Doctor Woolf?'

My question is answered by the super.

'You don't know Doctor Woolf disappeared four days ago?'

'Disappeared? He didn't say anything to me.'

'That's what I wanted to know,' says the super seriously. 'Was there no indication he might suddenly disappear? You see more of Woolf than anybody.'

'None at all. I can stand in for his lectures; I have before.'

'Not necessary now Adolf is with us,' Chin informs me, delight in his voice.

'When was the last time you saw him?' the super asks.

'When we had lunch with Ra'mad, four days ago.'

'Not since? I thought Woolf was in and out of your flat all the time?'

'We are usually in regular contact.'

'He'd have told you if he planned to go away? Asked you to take over his teaching duties and so on?'

'Normally, Superintendent. But maybe he drove off for a short trip and his car broke down.'

'He would have telephoned,' says the super logically. 'And he did *not* take his car. That's still at the Mandarin Hotel where he left it after dining with Professor Düsseldorf. There's also no indication that he passed through immigration on the causeway or at the airport.'

For K to go off by himself and leave behind his pregnant wife is one thing but to leave his beloved Mustang in a hotel car park sets wrinkles on my brow.

'I can see you are concerned,' the super notes. 'That's why I am here and that's why Doctor Chin asked you to join us. That and to meet Professor Düsseldorf. Nobody has seen Woolf for four days. He just disappeared.'

'What is Li Fang doing here?' Bernard speaks in my head and out my mouth.

'I asked him to come,' says the super. 'Li Fang saw Woolf and a woman dragging Professor Fox into the back of his house around 9.30 on the night of his death. They were on the back path from the flats where you and Doctor Ra'mad live. Li Fang told me what he had seen only after the reading of the Will; his civic duty overcame his reluctance to get involved. I swore Li Fang to secrecy and had Woolf followed, hoping he would lead us to the woman. But he must have realised we were onto him and disappeared. I wonder, Doctor Haddock, if you have any idea who this woman could be?'

I am speechless. I have no idea who the woman could be. The only possibility that enters my mind is Agnes. But to mention it in front of Chin is out of the question. 'No,' I say, 'I have absolutely no idea. What did she look like, Li Fang?'

'I don' know,' says Li Fang, back in his I-know-nothing alter ego. 'I see Doc-tor Woof. See OK. He big man. Don' know woman. Dark.'

'Li Fang couldn't see the woman's face. Too dark,' the super repeats. 'Tall with long hair, that's as far as he can go.'

Slowly, I realise the implications. K and an unknown woman have been seen by a reliable witness dragging Bernard from my flat or Ra'mad's flat along the back path to his house within the time bracket the coroner set for Bernard's death and when I was sitting alone in a dreamlike state waiting for Venus.

'Sorry, Superintendent,' I apologise. 'I don't know any tall, long-haired women who might have been with K. I was sitting at the front of my flat and I saw nobody the whole evening other than Professor Düsseldorf, who came just after 10 o'clock.'

'But your back door was open? And anybody could have come and gone and you might not have noticed?'

'Yes, Superintendent.'

'That's all for now, Doctor Haddock,' Super Wong says. 'But should Woolf contact you, get in touch with me immediately. Meanwhile, I wish you a useful partnership with a criminologist. I understand the sociology of crime is a developing subject.'

'Sociology of Crime,' the Führer says. I don't know if he's echoing the super or naming the title of a classic work on a subject about which I know bugger all. 'Ve vill see each other, yes? There is much to talk about.'

As the super rises to go, I excuse myself and accompany him to his car. 'This is all very confusing, Superintendent. Might I ask why you chose to drop the bomb in the presence of a stranger, not to mention Chin? Won't word now go all over the place that K is missing and implicated in the death of Bernard?'

'Yes. Perhaps that is necessary. After all, nothing was moving in this case until Li Fang's revelation. And Woolf *is* very much implicated.'

'It's all a mystery to me, Superintendent. I've no idea what's going on.'

'Well, it looks like only Woolf or his unknown companion will be able to put us in the picture. Unless our new criminologist has any bright ideas.'

'What's he doing here, Superintendent? That Von Führer whatsit.'

'Chin told me he's an old friend of his family. Speaks excellent Mandarin. Japanese too, it seems. He knew Chin's father in the war. He was stationed here as German liaison officer. Young at the time of course, like Professor Fox. But opposite poles politically – Professor Fox was anti-Fascist, anti-Japanese and to the left. Our file suggests Professor Von Führer Düsseldorf is anti-communist and was a firm supporter of the Third Reich. I can't imagine he'd have had much time for Chin Peng or for Bernard Fox, if, of course, he'd met either during the war, which seems most unlikely.

'We now have two missing people: Woolf and the professor's daughter. We knew already Norsiah had not left Singapore through any formal channels. The Malaysian police traced the aboriginal villages near where Fox spent much of the war years. They tell us she has not been seen there. So, we don't know where she is. We've put out an appeal for anybody who sees her to contact us, but nothing so far.'

'That's very worrying,' is all I can find to say. It is; disappearances are multiplying and I don't believe in coincidence.

And then another coincidence I don't believe in: Agnes walks around the corner.

'I think your husband is engaged,' the superintendent says, trying to be helpful.

'Thank you, Superintendent. But I never disturb Harry at work. I'm just off for a stroll in the Botanic Gardens. Good afternoon to you. And to you, Doctor Haddock.'

Anybody going for a stroll between the Chin household and the Botanic Gardens need *not* pass the department building. I go back inside long enough to release Barnaby and slip out the back way to cut off Agnes.

17

Androgynously Inclined

BARNS GREETS AGNES with the dance of joy. When I catch up, the two are muzzling each other. 'I'm glad you could come,' Agnes says. And in my naivety, I thought I was catching up with her. Truly, a man chases a woman until she catches him.

It is only when we have taken seats at what's becoming *our* table among the orchids that it all flows out. 'What happened to K?' she asks, concern dripping from each word.

'I was going to ask you the same question.' Agnes had come to the department in the hope of finding K. I see no point in keeping what I know from her, particularly since Super Wong announced his suspicions about K in front of her husband. 'Things don't look too good for K,' I start. 'I think your husband is trying to get rid of him. That's the interpretation I put on Herr Professor Baron Von Führer Düsseldorf taking over K's lectures – and I doubt Harry intends the arrangement to be temporary.'

Agnes takes off her hat; there is no need for it in the well-shaded garden. Her hair falls down and she tosses her head provocatively to send it into order. There among the lonely orchids, tears welling, she looks very vulnerable. She also looks especially attractive. 'My husband has long wanted to get rid of K. Now he's acting dean and K seems to have broken university rules – just popping off without a word – Harry thinks the chance is here.'

'I don't know. K has only been gone four days. There could be a simple explanation. K has a contract and when he returns he can take up his teaching duties again – unless your husband can find a serious breach of discipline.' I stop myself from adding *like rogering the wife of the acting dean* and look at Agnes. Her concern is real. 'You have no idea where K might be?'

'No. I only wish I did. To think that of all people to replace K, Harry has to pick that repulsive German.' Agnes's vehemence surprises me.

'Well, I agree old Von Führer Düstbrush is a bit full of umlauts but I'm surprised you call him repulsive. I don't care for him myself but I would have thought him good-looking to women.'

'You mean a good stand-in for K?'

I blush; I had been thinking precisely that. If Chin suspects his cuckolding by K, replacing K with the archetype superman seems a pretty dumb idea – even if the Hun speaks Han.

'You don't know the German.' Agnes adds to the mystery, leading me to assume that she does know him. 'He's staying with us. And that creates problems.'

'Does he try it on with you?'

'Of course not.' Agnes looks at me as if I'm stupid. 'I can't wait for him to go. Now he is temporarily on the staff he's moving into Wolverton Mess, next to your friend David Bent.'

'Next to David. My God! David will be on his knees slobbering as soon as he sees the Teutonic hulk. He'll be in agony; I can't imagine him getting a snifter except in his imagination.'

'Don't be too sure,' Agnes wrinkles her nose and goes on to

pronounce what sounds like a Schoolboys Own spy contact-pass-word. *'The German is androgynously inclined.'*

Agnes studied English at university. Thus, she has the better of me when it comes to words dressed in Greek lingua-drag. 'Do you mean he's queer?' I ask. Best to be clear about these things, especially where Greek words are concerned.

'It depends on what you mean by queer,' Agnes uses words that could come straight from Bernard. 'Adolf likes hermaphrodites. Not straight men. Men yes, but those who exhibit a feminine side. He's a bit of a bully.'

'Wow, David really will be in his element. He doesn't like straight women at all, this German?'

'I'm quite sure he doesn't.'

'And straight men are safe?'

'I wouldn't bet on it,' Agnes says impishly, breaking the gravitas. 'How's your feminine side?'

'Still in hiding,' I reply. 'And does hubby Harry know about these proclivities of his father's friend?'

'He most certainly does.'

'But how can you be sure?' Too blunt. It sounds like I'm questioning Agnes's morality rather than that of the German. And Agnes's morality, being known, is not in question.

'Curiosity got Man into the mess he's in,' comes the reply. *No need to remind me, Bernard.* I know then that Bernard is speaking – or to put it less mystically, his thoughts are speaking – through the mouth of little Agnes. They must have discussed more than orchids on her afternoon visits.

'Are you going to satisfy me?' I ask her.

Agnes looks at me super-coquettishly, as if considering my request. 'Maybe. But not just yet,' she answers. 'Right now,

we have to consider K and how to help him. If he's still alive.'
Agnes's face clouds once more and her sadness returns. Barnaby places her head sympathetically in the fold of Agnes's lap. K
dead? I suppose a lot of people don't like him and some might
wish him dead. But would anybody kill K? 'I don't think it's a
coincidence that K disappeared just after meeting Adolf. There's
a lot you don't know.'

There sure is; how did Agnes know K had met Adolf? Agnes
takes a small stick from the tiny purse she carries and rolls mosquito repellent onto her legs. Funny how a man can see a woman
jog by in shorts almost every day and hardly stir, yet the sight of
the same woman lifting her skirt and a glimpse of inner thigh
holds the power to turn him on. Talk about distraction; what was
I thinking about?

'You don't know it, but Düsseldorf tried to visit Bernard
on the night he died. He says he couldn't get in. Oh, he's ali-
bied right up to his crew cut – you couldn't set up a better alibi
however hard you tried – reception with the Vice-Chancellor
and Superintendent Wong. He even stopped at your window
to prove he had nothing to hide.' I do know it but don't know
Agnes knows it.

'Düsseldorf's visited us a couple of times in the past and
always called on Bernard. Always about the same thing as you
know, offering to arrange transfer of the war loot out of the country in exchange for a half share.'

Whoa! One minute we are talking about a ginger German
and an absent K, the next it's treasure-trove time. The conjunction is missing. Agnes is telling me what she thinks I don't know
when she suddenly moves into territory about which I haven't a
clue but which she seems to assume I do. A warning bell tinkles

in my head, Bernard's PS to his letter glows neon in my mind and I keep quiet in the hope she will tell more. She does. 'Now that Bernard is dead, Adolf will be onto you with the same offers and threats.'

I nod knowingly and say simply, 'Do you think so?'

'It makes sense, doesn't it? You're the only one who knows where the loot is.'

'But how do *you* know that *I* know?' I sound confusing, even to myself, but hope Agnes makes sense of it.

'News travels fast. Bernard's sealed letter to you. It must have disclosed the location of the war loot – Tambiah is an open book. I was expecting Bernard to pass on the secret to Li Fang. But I suppose that was too obvious. He would avoid the obvious. Li Fang has been his keeper all these years, making sure Bernard did not run off with the stuff himself. I suppose Li Fang is now performing the same function watching over you.'

Agnes's words seem to connect with the PS of Bernard's letter to me, but catching their meaning is like putting together the pieces of a jigsaw puzzle with no idea what the picture is supposed to be or if all the pieces are there. Agnes casts me as a leading actor in some drama and I don't even know the plot. Bernard's PS must be a central piece in the puzzle, as might be what I witnessed the afternoon of Bernard's death, but I can't think where either fits in with the German. So – when ignorant, bluff. 'Whatever Bernard said or wrote to me was private and I can't disclose it.'

'I'm not asking you to disclose it. Certainly not to me. I don't want them getting at me. I couldn't care less about this stupid war loot. I just want to warn you to be careful about the German and his boyfriend – and my husband.'

'And Li Fang?'

'Bernard trusted Li Fang. You would only need to worry about him if you intend to make off with the loot.'

Time to find out what we are talking about. I chance a serious take-it-or-leave-it ultimatum. 'Agnes,' I say, ignoring my resolve to avoid first-name familiarity, 'unless you tell me everything you know about this affair, I think it might be better we stop talking about it and get back to seeing if there is anything we can do to help K – presuming he is not dead already.'

'But how can we talk of one thing without the other? You know the German was good friends with Harry's father during the war. You know the role played by Bernard and Li Fang in the war and you know the suspicion that one or both of them murdered Harry's father.'

Wow! Bernard, are you listening? The plot has thickened so much I could stand WWII upright in it.

'I did not ask you what *I* know. I must know all that *you* know.'

'Yes. I'm sorry. I thought you knew already how far Bernard had let me in on things, since the two of you were so close.'

I'm the only one in the dark and Agnes thinks I'm the only one fully enlightened. 'Bernard told me everything,' I lie. 'But he never told me he had taken you into his confidence.'

'And you want to be sure of me? Yes, I understand that. Very sensible. After all, who can you trust? It makes sense to be cautious. Bernard told me that Chin Jin-Hui, Harry's father, had betrayed Chin Peng. Jin-Hui had collected from the Chinese in Singapore gold and silver and anything valuable that would aid the anti-Japanese struggle. Some of the more portable bounty was sent with Li Fang to Chin Peng in the jungle. Some

179

of it was handed over to the Japanese. Neither the Japanese nor Chin Peng suspected they got only part of the total collected. Chin Jin-Hui gave the Japanese the names of anybody who refused to contribute, presenting them as anti-Japanese. It was a protection racket: the big contributors were guaranteed safety. The Japanese were happy with Chin Jin-Hui, in spite of the small amounts he handed in, because they had a regular supply of Chinese to hang. Chin Peng was acquiescent because those Chinese who opposed him were being dealt with by the Japanese. Only Li Fang suspected Chin Jin-Hui and he kept his suspicions to himself until he told Bernard. But you know all this.'

'Yes, I do,' I lie confidently. Somewhere in my mind, a connection is forming between what I overheard in Ra'mad's kitchen and the revelations of Agnes. 'But I'm surprised *you* know it.'

'Bernard told me the full story after I told him of Harry's suspicion, based on what Düsseldorf told him, that Bernard had killed his father and stolen what Harry sees as part of his family's wealth. It was Harry who first encouraged me to visit Bernard socially – he would not have been welcome himself – and nose around for any clues as to where the treasure might be. Harry actually thought Bernard would be stupid enough to hide it under the mattress. The Chinese used to do just that with their wealth, bury it in their house and live on top of it; Bernard was not Chinese but he could hardly deposit trunks full of gold, silver and jewels in a bank deposit without attracting suspicion. There must have been quite a volume, since all types of payment were acceptable to Chin Jin-Hui: gold necklaces, art works, silver tea pots, even porcelain. I imagine Bernard could have opened an antique shop if Li Fang had let him.'

'Did you ask Bernard why he kept the spoils rather than simply tell Chin Peng to take it all away?' I risk this question, as Agnes seems to have all the answers.

'No, but I can guess there are two possibilities. Firstly, that Bernard was himself a bit like Chin Jin-Hui and Ra'mad during the Emergency; he was not sure where his loyalties lay. He didn't want to make a present of the loot to Chin Peng. On the other hand, he was not going to betray Chin Peng. He could not give everything to the British and couldn't bring himself to finance anti-British revolutionaries. Secondly, perhaps Bernard received orders from Chin Peng to hang onto the loot rather than risk its loss through movement – there was never a time that Chin Peng looked like winning his war and he kept moving around. And Bernard knew Chin Peng had set Li Fang to watch over him. Bernard could not make a move without Li Fang knowing. Li Fang didn't know the location and was therefore tied to Bernard. The two were synergetic. That's why they lived right opposite each other.'

Agnes is full of Greek words but things are becoming clearer to me and raising new questions. 'Did Bernard tell you what he intended to do with the stuff eventually, if he had lived? After all, Chin Peng is in Beijing and the Emergency is long over.'

'From what he told me, Bernard waited years for Chin Peng to achieve respectability and enter the democratic political arena; then I suppose he would have needed all the funds he could get. But the Malaysian authorities would not hear of allowing him back into the country, even if he surrendered. They had beaten him and were happy to let him live out his life in Beijing or Bangkok or anywhere outside Malaysia. So, the treasure stayed with Bernard and was never claimed.'

'Right,' I say, feeling a confirmation to be appropriate. 'But where does the German come in?'

'Adolf must have known of Chin Jin-Hui's profitable double-game during the war. From what Harry says, seems Jin-Hui wanted to be friends with both the Germans and the Japanese; he thought they would take over in Singapore in place of the British and install a Mandarin-speaking government throughout the region. Bernard told me he knew about Adolf from Li Fang, but only as a minor player, more of a diplomat really, concerned with Germany's conquest of the world more than helping the Japanese chase Chin Peng's tiny group through the jungle. Adolf was on Chin Peng's blacklist – death list – but according to Bernard, such lists were almost routine at the time and Adolf was not involved in the diversion of resistance funds. If he had been, leaving the country would not have protected him from sharing the fate of Chin Jin-Hui. After the war, Adolf perhaps wanted to forget about his wartime role. He became a professor; but during the Emergency he returned to Malaya and Singapore to advise the British forces on the suppression of Chin Peng and the Malayan Communist Party. His earlier visits to Bernard after the war were all made to get information on Chin Peng. I doubt if Bernard let much slip. After the Emergency was officially over, Adolf's visits had a very different motive. He tried to tempt Bernard to make a run with the treasure, offering to fix Li Fang and at the same time fake Bernard's death and take him out of the country in a chartered plane to Indonesia – at that time in confrontation with the Federation and safe for criminals from Malaya. When bribes failed, he threatened to expose Bernard as keeper of the war loot. But both he and Bernard knew that such exposure could have led to the permanent loss of the treasure and the threats were empty.'

'And do *you* think Bernard had something to do with the death of your husband's father, Jin-Hui?' I know I'm pushing things, but Agnes is in a talkative mood.

'That's the logical link with the treasure. Chin Jin-Hui had the stuff, he was murdered and Bernard had it afterwards. Li Fang might have been involved. I can't imagine Bernard personally torturing Jin-Hui to get the treasure and then hanging him outside his family home. On the other hand, much as I like Li Fang, I *can* imagine him doing it. Bernard would never tell me. You must know.'

'I'm as much in the dark as you as to who killed Chin Jin-Hui,' I say. 'But if Bernard risked everything to kill him and get the loot for himself, it's strange he didn't make off with it. If he couldn't do so at the time because of Li Fang, it would not have been difficult during the years since. Bernard has many times been off by himself into the Perak jungle. For all we know, he moved the treasure bit by bit out of Singapore. He had strong links with the aborigines. Perhaps he gave it all to them to make up for what they suffered from both the Japanese and the British.'

Agnes looks quizzical. 'Are you saying you *don't* know the location of the treasure?'

'Right you are, Agnes. I don't know.' I felt quite pleased with my newfound ability to lie convincingly.

'Are you telling me the truth?'

'Ah, it all depends on what you mean by truth.'

'I hope for your sake that you do know where it is. Something tells me the German will waste no time in visiting you and he'll get very nasty if you don't tell him.'

'Would you advise me to tell him, Agnes?'

'I suppose I should advise you to tell all you know to Super-intendent Wong. But an enormous treasure is very tempting, particularly if nobody is going to notice you take off with it – as long as you give Li Fang and Adolf the slip. On the other hand, it might be safer to settle for half of it and have the German take care of Li Fang and other problems.'

'From hearing you, my impression of Von Führer Düsseldorf gets nastier by the minute. Is it possible that he had anything to do with the murder of Bernard?'

Agnes does not pause in her reply. 'Very possible. Although the version the police have worked out is wrong. I heard Wong throwing out the idea to Harry yesterday that the German put K up to drugging Bernard and searching his house for the treasure, and that Bernard accidentally died and was hanged to make it look like suicide. Adolf's dinner invitation four days ago was to warn K he had been seen dragging Bernard's body from your flat and to get out of town.'

'Do you think K beyond a little drugging and searching if a lot of money is to be had?'

'K didn't drug Bernard. He phoned me from the Mandarin. He said the German had tried to get him to persuade *you* to reveal the location of the treasure and I was to warn you.'

'And you took four days to give me the warning?'

18

Take a Letter, Adolf

AFTER SEEING Agnes off into the Botanic Garden's postage-stamp jungle for her quality time alone, I walk home across the cricket field through a light rain, trying to make sense of Agnes's avalanche of revelations.

Driving smoothly around the edge of the field is the old Citroën, wings waxed and gleaming, chevrons shining, gorgeous and menacing. Its roll through decades of history halts where I always cross Evans road before reaching the flat. A back door opens. Barns presses against my legs, growls rising. I wait for an SS officer with skull on hat to step out in full-length leather coat, take off his gloves and slap them on one palm. It doesn't happen, but a familiar blond head pokes out into the misty drizzle. 'Doctor Haddock. How are you?' Von Führer Düsseldorf sings out in Wagnerian tones of comradeship and victory.

'Well, all right. Nothing much has happened in the two hours since we met.' I put a hand on Barns to calm her.

'Good. So good. Do you like the car?'

'Lovely. Was it left over from the war?' I think I'm joking.

'Yes. How clever of you to guess. Harry Chin managed to pull the strings for me and get it out of the auto museum and back on the road. The very same car I had here until 1945.

"Traction Avant"; best thing the French ever made. Hop in. Ve vill take a spin.' Quiet as a ghost, the Citroën creeps forward and the Führer beckons me into his time-machine. 'I'd like to talk to you, Doctor Haddock – Tom. Perhaps we could eat together? I invite you to the Mandarin. Please to come in.'

'Sorry, Adolf. I'm busy. Another time, okay?'

Adolf looks like another time is not okay. He remains polite as he waves an envelope. 'I have something here of interest. I vish to discuss matters of mutual benefit.'

I see Ra'mad watching from his balcony, binoculars dangling from his neck. Poor old bugger, I think, the threat of a downpour will make the girls think twice before setting out on their run tonight. 'I can't make it tonight. Maybe some other time,' I intend to reply, something reasonable like that. But Bernard – doing the behind-the-scenes thinking for me – comes through loud and clear with what is really in my mind. 'No way. Eating with you makes people disappear.' Hey, Bernard, take it easy. That might be construed as provocative.

The square head flushes under its tan. Thin lips purse. Cold-blue eyes narrow as Adolf does a fair impression of a cobra preparing to strike. 'Reinkommen!' He hisses in my direction. 'Im Auto!'

The front door of the car smashes open against my thigh and I fall back into the puddle I'd just jumped over and Barnaby just skipped though. I look up into the hard eyes of the Japanese driver, who is out of the car and talking in perfect English. 'Please get in the car. It would be a pity to have unpleasantness … An unfortunate fall. I do apologise for opening the door carelessly. Here, let me help you up.'

An arm reaches toward me and Barnaby sinks her teeth into

it. I struggle to my feet as the driver retreats into the museum piece and re-appears at the open window holding a pistol. I can't believe it. Only the police and very desperate criminals carry guns in Singapore. And this gun is waving in my direction. It fires. Barns yelps and falls into the puddle. The puddle turns blood red.

I grab at the car's door handle. It's locked. 'The next bullet vill be for you. Learn manners. Pig.' The Führer spits out the window at me as the Citroën drives off.

Barns is struggling; the water, alarmingly red. The heavens pick that moment to open. I cradle Barns' head and kneel there in the rain, feeling a strange mix of anger, love and helplessness.

'Why, Bernard, why? Why did you have to provoke them?'

Two figures close in on me.

'I had to show you. Now you know their true colours.' I am asking myself questions and answering them.

Two people are bending over me.

*   *   *

'Christ, mate. What's happened?' It's David.

'I saw it all.' It's Ra'mad aka Ali. 'That disgusting German!'

I stagger through the rain, Barns in my arms, David and Ra'mad fussing around me. 'I'll kill them, Barns. I'll kill them both.' I speak with no prompt from Bernard.

Into the flat, I place Barns on my bed. Blood and mud on clean sheets Venus changed yesterday. My dog is dying and has to be saved. Ra'mad disappears upstairs to get the tools of a trade he's not licensed to practice.

'Shouldn't we get a real vet?' David asks. 'Ra'mad's Muslim. Can we trust him to treat a dog?'

'I don't know,' I reply. 'But Ra'mad only poisons people doesn't he, not dogs?'

'Don't forget his best friend, Snow the rat,' David reminds me. 'What if he decides to go for something of intermediate size?'

Barnaby is snapping at her wound.

'David, you're not inspiring confidence in the patient. We have no car and God knows how long it would take to get to a real vet. And Barnaby has a bullet inside her. We don't have a choice. It's obvious Ra'mad hates the German. Let him patch her up and then we'll get her to a real vet.'

Ra'mad comes back with one of those black grips that all doctors carry in the Westerns. He examines the patient carefully. 'Lucky she's a bitch,' he says. 'Otherwise it would be much more serious.'

'Why?' David asks.

'She'd have lost her dick, man.' We laugh. Barns looks a little offended. 'We need to calm her down. I'll have to dig around a bit to get the bullet out then clean the wound. I'll put a dressing on it and she mustn't go ripping it off and licking the antiseptics before they have time to do their job. They do, you know. However much you tell them. Animals and children. Just can't stop playing with their wounds.'

Ra'mad seems to know what he's doing with the swabs and bottles. I hold Barn's head and David holds her hind legs. 'Can't see the bullet. Must have gone straight through the fat and out the other side hitting nothing vital on the way, so a clean and a rest should work wonders. I'll give her a mild sedative. She'll feel much better afterwards.' Ra'mad reaches for a hypodermic. David and I exchange glances. I consult my inner voice but Bernard is having a celestial nap. 'By the way, when I was upstairs, I took the chance to telephone a real vet. He'll be along but not for an hour. I also called your friend Madhu to report the shooting. He's on his way.' Ra'mad shows a public spirit that surprises me. Barns slips into unconsciousness. 'Not much more I can do. She should sleep until the vet gets here. Just call me if you need me.'

I thank Ra'mad, vowing a total rethink of his profile if Barnaby recovers and his painful death if she doesn't. David says he could murder a beer and I go into the kitchen to get him one. The fridge door is open just a crack; closing it properly requires lifting the door on the hinges – second nature to anybody who has dealt with it a few times. Nothing is missing inside. The hall is the real giveaway. A trail of wet footprints leads from the perpetually damp floor of the bathroom. The outline of a man's shoes. In spite of the urgency of the situation, David, Ra'mad and I had automatically kicked off our shoes at the door. Somebody has been inside my home; somebody in shoes!

★   ★   ★

David follows me as I pull from the massive blackwood sideboard the single great drawer where for two years I have thrown any document that didn't go into the rubbish. The only order is most recent on top. On the top had been Bernard's letter; I'd put it there. It is missing. I quietly congratulate myself. 'David, did you notice anyone in the flat before I arrived?'

'That German. He was on his way out. Said he would go to meet you and drove off in that Citroën. Seemed like the nice, polite sort at the time. Never thought he was a dog killer. Quite fancied him, actually.'

'He's your new neighbour, David.'

'I know. He told me. Invited me to drop in for a drink tonight. Of course, I said I would.'

'According to Agnes, the man's androgynously inclined.'

'Not German?'

'Come on, David. You're the fucking English teacher. The bloke goes for the sexually ambiguous.'

'Do you mind if we have a chat before Madhu gets here?' David suddenly changes the subject away from the thing I think would most interest him. 'The super hauled me over the coals this morning. I'm sure he thinks I killed Bernard. You know I would never have hurt Bernard, don't you Tom?'

'Of course you wouldn't. This isn't one of your fantasies, is it David? Just because K's disappeared following a fingering from Li Fang, there's no reason for you to imagine yourself in a similar predicament. I'm not in the mood for fantasies.'

'I don't know what you're talking about. Has K disappeared?'

'Yes, but get on with what you want to tell me, David, before the flat fills up with police and vets.'

David looks serious. 'I was there, at Bernard's, on the day he died. Li Fang saw me going in. I had no reason to hide.'

'No reason at all,' I interrupt with impatience, leading the way back to Barnaby's bedside.

'The super wanted to know what Bernard and I talked about and I told him.'

'So?'

'We talked about you, squire. Bernard was more than academically interested in homosexuality. He loved you.'

David pauses. Barnaby is breathing calmly, I'm not.

'We also talked about Bernard's old days. Not that old but

before you came on the scene and before Bernard's heart problem. He used to get drunk. When he did, he was a different person. Aren't we all? Bernard always had to get drunk before taking any of us girls on. But since he was drunk every night that didn't limit him much. When he cut out the booze, he found the yearning still there but couldn't do anything.'

'Short version, David.'

'He was ashamed. Not for what he'd done. But because he couldn't do it anymore, I mean because he needed alcohol to free his mind. He was also deeply sad because he couldn't declare his love for you.'

'You told the super all this?'

'Yes, matey. You know how persuasive that bloke is.'

'And you told him I'm not ginger?'

'Well, no, not exactly. I mean, you can never really tell for sure, can you?'

'So, Bernard was a suppressed homosexual. If true, David, it's yawningly interesting, but it doesn't nail you for murder.'

'Not in itself. But I felt sorry for the old sod, so I went back to see Bernard in the evening. As I told the super, I'm not sure of the time. It must have been around 9.30. Bernard's back door was wide open. I went in. I thought he was asleep. He was in his armchair. I didn't want to disturb him, so I crept out. Li Fang must have seen me.'

'David, think carefully. Did you see anything on Bernard's desk?'

'I don't have to think. The super asked me the same question. Bernard's manuscript was there and a plate.'

'So, the manuscript was still there when you left. And what about Barnaby?'

'She looked as if she'd had a hard day. She was lying at Bernard's feet. Lifted her head, saw me and closed her eyes.'

'Look, David,' I say in a calming tone. 'It was stupid not giving Wong this information earlier. We now know Bernard's manuscript was taken after you left. I can understand the super being annoyed. But don't worry. You're not the last person to see Bernard alive. K was seen dragging Bernard into his house nearer ten. A woman was helping him.'

'Who says so?'

'Who do you think? The same person who saw you. Li Fang.'

'The same person,' David speaks as if struck by lightning, 'who raised the alarm! Christ, matey, Li Fang must have done it. I saw Bernard asleep in his armchair before 9.30, he would have had to get up and gone out if K really was dragging him back in before 10.00. There's only Li Fang's word for that.'

There's no time to consider David's deductions before Madhu and the vet come in the front and Ra'mad bounces in from the back. The vet is a quiet and serious man. He places a thumb on each of Barnaby's eyebrows in turn, shines a torch into her eyes and goes *hmm*. He removes Ra'mad's dressing, touches gently around the wound and goes *hmm*. He listens to Barnaby's heart and goes *hmm*.

'There is nothing I can do,' the vet says.

I gulp. David gulps.

'Who put the dog to sleep?' the vet asks.

'Ra'mad!' David and I sing out accusingly.

'Doctor Ra'mad? The famous chemist?'

Ra'mad nods modestly to confirm his name and fame.

'Very pleased to meet you, Doctor Ra'mad. You will be aware that the drug will soon wear off. The dog is likely to worry the wound. I will leave a longer-acting sedative to keep her quiet. No need to give it for an hour yet. Perhaps, Doctor Ra'mad, you'd be so kind as to administer it. There is nothing I can do in addition to what you've done already. I expect the dog to be running around within twenty-four hours. But if there is anything, please call me, Doctor Ra'mad.'

I thank the vet heartily. He says all my thanks should be directed to Doctor Ra'mad and refuses any fee – Singaporeans do that sometimes.

Madhu quickly gets into the reason for his visit. 'A coincidence that Doctor Ra'mad called just when he did, since the super wants to see you, Tom. I'm to take you there. First though, tell me briefly what happened with Professor Düsseldorf.'

I tell Madhu more or less what happened, leaving out Bernard's interjections. Madhu draws from my account the salient points for the Prosecution. 'The driver opened the door, knocked you off balance, apologised and stretched out an arm to help you. Barnaby bit it and he shot Barnaby. A biting dog gets an automatic death sentence.'

'But the gun, Madhu? Isn't possession of firearms in itself a very serious offence?'

'It is. *If* possession is illegal. But maybe the driver has authorisation.'

'Why would he?' I ask, bewildered. 'He's obviously Japanese?'

'The f-fact that s-somebody originates from J-Japan – or Tamil Nadu or Ch-China or P-P-Putney for that matter – does n-n-not m-make them any less S-S-Singaporean.' Madhu speaks with stutter-inducing passion. Nothing unites Singaporeans as much as their differences.

'Very sorry, Madhu. I realise Singapore's greatness is thanks to its ethnic synergy. I was not to know the driver has authorisation to carry arms.'

'I said m-maybe he does. We'll check. If he is authorised and makes a complaint, your dog's in trouble. Now, it's well after dark and the super is waiting. Can we go?'

Barnaby is left in the loving care of David and Ra'mad and I leave, as they say, to help the police with their enquiries.

★   ★   ★

No flashing lights, no sirens, no handcuffs, no police markings on the car. We head towards Changi, a distant suburb known, in 1980, only for the sailing club, a middle-income dormitory estate and its prison. The road, at that time, is unlit and narrow. My stomach rumbles. Madhu says, 'Don't worry; you'll get fed where you're going.'

We pull up in front of an unassuming house on the anonymous housing estate. 'Does the super live here?' Madhu gives a laugh in reply and leads me through a small neat garden like the small neat gardens of the houses on either side. Inside is exactly what you would expect from the outside. A sitting room dominated by a television, a tank of tropical fish, a large print of horses pulling logs through the snow and various family souvenirs in a well-dusted showcase. If it's not for the tiled floor and the turn of a ceiling fan, I might be in suburban London.

'Come and sit down,' the super's voice rises from the back of an easy chair. I prop myself on the edge of a sofa facing him. 'Make yourself comfortable, we have plenty of time.' The super's at ease in T-shirt and shorts, his bare feet raised on a padded rattan stool, a frosty glass of beer on the arm of his chair. Looking equally at home next to him is K.

19

Helping with Enquiries

THEY ARE WATCHING a football match on TV. K grins broadly as if he has succeeded in playing one of his brilliant practical jokes on me. He wears a clean neckerchief, freshly ironed shirt and looks fully relaxed. 'Madhu,' the super says, 'would you mind getting a glass for our guest. And bring more bottles from the fridge, would you? Oh, and now Doctor Haddock is here, we can eat. Tell the girl to bring in dinner.' It sounds like grilled Haddock is off the menu.

The super is in no hurry to begin and for once K holds his tongue. The TV is clicked off as the many courses of a Chinese meal are clattered together, *nasi padang* style, on the coffee table. Madhu brings the beer and leaves without eating. 'I'll drive you back later,' says the super. 'You must be wondering what we are all doing here.'

'Yes,' I answer simply. At the super's wave of invitation, I pick up chopsticks and begin to eat.

'Do you have any idea why a superintendent is on this case?'

'No. I know in the movies it's usually an inspector who heads an investigation. Maybe things are different in Singapore.'

'Not so different,' the super replies. 'Murder is a status thing even in egalitarian Singapore. If a dozen building workers are axed by a labourer running *amok*, I would be kept informed.

When professors and vice-chancellors are involved – fortunately not often – or when there is a strong political element, I get dusted off for the spotlight. This case has it all. The confidential file on Bernard Fox alone was enough to raise the stakes.' The super pauses for effect.

K remains unusually quiet. Is he deferring to the super? I can't remember K ever deferring to anybody. I follow his lead and do not interrupt. I know the super will tell me all he wants me to know, no more, no less.

'You find yourself at present in what your movies might call a safe house. When we need to accommodate somebody in secret, we simply move them into a vacant house with a cook and a guard. This is such a house: it allows Doctor Woolf to disappear for a time while helping with enquiries. I should make clear that your friend is here voluntarily. I spoke to him before his dinner with Düsseldorf and took that opportunity to invite him to leave his car at the Mandarin and enter our care. The main reason for the pretence at his disappearance is to draw out Düsseldorf and Nagasaki.'

The super looks across to K, his cue to speak. 'The super means: leave the axis with nobody to attack but you, ha ha.'

'You have already had trouble with Düsseldorf. Madhu informed me immediately Ra'mad telephoned him. Düsseldorf's car was stopped soon after it left the university. He had in the car this gun and this letter; both were brought to me here. Do you recognise them?' The super opens a plastic bag lying among the beer bottles.

'That's the gun the driver used to shoot Barnaby and the letter is from Bernard to me, the one you read already.'

The super clicks the TV on again and turns up the volume.

The crowd roars and jeers, the umpire blows his whistle. Wong aims the gun at the umpire as he tries to separate two brawling players. He pulls the trigger. Bang. The brawl continues. The screen does not shatter.

'Imagine your statement in open court and the fun the Defence would have with it,' the super replies as he clicks off the set. 'The gun taken from the car only fires caps. It's a World War II Luger, but a replica, a toy if you like, it makes a decent bang but cannot fire a bullet. The driver used the gun to frighten your dog – he says he had been bitten when trying to help you up. My men have so far failed to discover any bullet near where the incident occurred, but they did find a scrap of wood with a rusty nail through it in the water where the dog fell. I explain this not to accuse you of lying but to demonstrate that Von Führer Düsseldorf is a very wily bird. His explanation for the letter is that you were holding it when you fell against the open door of the car and it dropped inside. When Düsseldorf tried to return it to you, you abused him and he drove off.'

'I can see how it would look in court,' I concede.

'Why did you not show me the PS along with the rest of the letter? And what does the PS mean? It must make sense to you. Let me refresh your memory.' The super reads slowly from the last page of Bernard's letter. 'PS. In the forest of virginity, you may dig out a greater treasure than hidden by any pirate. To find it, follow the way of a lonely orchid. Branch left, continue to the dog stone and uncover the ground.'

'It doesn't mean anything,' I say. 'I made it up and forged Bernard's handwriting. There was *no* PS on the letter. I added it only because I wanted something to show *if* they came looking for war loot. I would have shown them the letter and said I don't know where the treasure is – which is true. I didn't expect the letter to be stolen from my flat and I did not deceive you. I never showed you a PS because there wasn't one.'

'Okay, so *you* wrote this PS. We can check the handwriting. Whether or not you know where the so-called *war loot* is, that's one thing. But how do you know there is any such thing?'

I hesitate.

'The super's got you there, Haddock,' K intervenes. 'I certainly knew nothing about any treasure until Herr Umlaut tried to bribe me with a share of it in exchange for persuading *you* to reveal its location. The deal, he said was to be 50% for us, you and me that is, and 50% for him and his boyfriend. In exchange, he would deal with the problems involved in moving the whatever, converting it into US dollars and overcoming any problems with Li Fang, who was in some weird way the guardian of the loot and Bernard's keeper. I, of course, wanted nothing to do with the proposition. Although I might have done – if I had not already found the treasure!'

'*You* found the treasure?'

'I say, Haddock, don't gape like that; you'll trip over your bottom lip. Somebody had to find the stuff. Why not me? I, of course, handed it over to the police.'

'When my men picked you up with it!' The super added.

'I only carried it around for the sake of feeling extraordinarily rich for a time. I always intended to hand it in. After all, it wasn't mine. Although you have mentioned, Superintendent, that some of it might find its way back to me in terms of an official reward. I'll explain it all to you, Haddock. But first I believe you should answer Superintendent Wong's question. How come you know about the loot?'

'Agnes told me. She thought I already knew about it and where it is and warned me Von Düsseldorf might try to discover its whereabouts and will be angry if I deny knowledge of its existence. She said you had phoned her from the Mandarin and told her to warn me.'

'That was four day ago, Haddock.'

'Yes, she waited until today to tell me – seems she expected you to call again and whisk her off to paradise. I left Bernard's letter in my drawer so I'd have something to show Düsseldorf if he got violent. But Düsseldorf stole the letter rather than my giving it to him. That's perhaps why he seems not to have questioned whether or not it was written by Bernard.'

The super listens intensely. 'When did he steal the letter?'

'Today. David saw him leaving my flat.'

'When you were with Agnes? I presume she made the great revelation after we had met in Chin's office?'

'Yes.'

'So, the timeline is: Agnes reveals all, Barnaby gets shot, Madhu brings you here. Between which of those events did you manage to write a convincingly fake PS to Fox's letter to you?' The super punctures my timeline.

'Er, none of them. I wrote it before.'

'Before Agnes told you about the treasure and warned you about Von Düsseldorf?'

'Yes.' Wong and K both look at me, waiting. 'Alright, I mixed timing. She told me the day after K called her and told her to warn me – she phoned me in the department and told me to beware of Düsseldorf, because he thinks I've got a map to the treasure he wants. I thought it a silly invention of K's – one of his games – so I went along with it. Didn't draw a map – that really would have been a bit too schoolboy-ish – but made up a meaningless riddle. She gave me the full story only today.'

'So, you were half expecting to be called on by the Gestapo, but never thought to let me know or even to lock your door.'

'That's right, Superintendent. It was Agnes passing on a message from K – I thought he'd put her up to it – one of his elaborate practical jokes. When I faked the PS, I wasn't really expecting trouble from Von Düsseldorf, I thought I'd show the letter, with the PS to K and string him along in his joke.'

'The games children play!' The super sounds exasperated. 'The important thing now is that Düsseldorf thinks he has a real clue to the war loot's location. Tell me, when you wrote it, did the PS come to you out of thin air or were the clues intended to lead somewhere – even if only in your imagination? That might be important in getting our hands on Düsseldorf. At this time, we have a whopping great file on the man and can find nothing he has done against the law.'

'Then why are you so interested in him, Superintendent?' I ask.

'Because he's always around when something nasty happens: Chin Jin-Hui's wartime protection racket, Jin-Hui's death and the death of Bernard Fox are some of the things you know about. There are others you don't know about. In return for his help to the British after the Japanese surrender in Singapore, Düsseldorf saved one Japanese who would otherwise have found himself at the end of a rope. One you have already met. He was known then as Takemura, now Nagasaki. He was Kempeitai and worked with Jin-Hui during the war, torturing and hanging whoever Jin-Hui fingered as anti-Japanese. All of the files on Nagasaki held by the British were destroyed to please Von Düsseldorf, his boyfriend during the war. Nagasaki's the one who denies having shot your dog.'

'And you can't lay anything on them?' I ask bluntly.

'Officially, Von Führer Düsseldorf performed a diplomatic function during the war and later assisted Singapore and Malaysia to defeat communist insurgency during the Emergency. Had he not been German and ex-Nazi, he might have been decorated along with Bernard Fox, with an OBE. Nagasaki remained in Singapore after the war, helped the British and received a pardon from the colonial authorities. His continued residence qualified him for citizenship on Singapore's Independence – just like Professor Fox. He owns a security firm which protects the property of many well-off people in Singapore. They are both wealthy men. Nagasaki is *not* the German's chauffeur; he just drives the car. Neither of them needs work. They do so as a hobby. In the same way they search for the wartime loot. Both are squeaky clean.'

'Superintendent, I will of course do anything I can to help, although I can't think what.'

'From what the super tells me,' K interrupts, 'you can be a great help. You will be a decoy. Don't forget, they don't know I have already found the treasure – and don't tell them that, even if they twist your goolies.'

'But why *not* simply make public that the treasure has been recovered? Surely that would stop their chasing around looking for it.'

'You're right,' says the super. 'That's why we do *not* tell *anybody*. There is a more important issue than recovery of war loot: justice for those thousands of Singaporeans who were executed with the involvement of Nagasaki. The British pardoned him but such pardons are not binding on today's Singapore. We need to catch him actually doing something *now*, not thirty-five years ago. Once detained, we'll get the full story.'

I drink my beer. 'Before I agree to act as a decoy in whatever plan you have in mind, I want to know how you, K, just happened upon the loot and what you are doing in a suburban house watching telly.'

My big question remains unasked. How could K have handed in the treasure when only Li Fang and I know where it is?

20

They Stole the Guard Dog

'THEY CAME IN through the open front door when Barn-aby was still sedated on your bed under the watch of Ra'mad.' David's account, told to me later, of what is happening back at the flat as I drink beer in a distant Changi suburb. It is David's account, not mine – *David* speaking, *not* me. I believe half of it.

★   ★   ★

Old VD tells Ra'mad, 'Doctor Haddock has been detained at the police station, ve vish to assist him by bringing his dog to a spe-cialist for more expert examination. Ve know, Doctor Ra'mad, that in the past you have seen many unfortunate cases of people dying unnecessarily because correct care vas not available. I need only mention the case of Harry Chin's father, Jin-Hui, a good friend of mine. You are vell avare that Jin-Hui died unnec-essarily aren't you, Ra'mad?'

'Dogs are not the same as people,' Ra'mad says.

'I vould agree,' says the German. 'But some sentimental Englishmen value dogs above human life. This seems to be the case with our Doctor Haddock. Ve vould hate anything to happen to his precious Barnaby. The unfortunate accident ear-lier this evening led to Mr Nagasaki here being bitten and to Barnaby hurting herself when she fell. Mr Nagasaki is villing to

203

forego his right to have the animal gassed. Far from thoughts of revenge, Mr Nagasaki is here to help the dog's recovery. He does so in the spirit of kindness. The dog vill be better cared for at an animal clinic. Do you agree, Ra'mad?'

Ra'mad agrees too damn quick. He says he'll immediately go upstairs and telephone you at the police station so you know your dog's in good hands, then he scarpers. This left me alone with the buggers.

'I think,' I tell them, 'we should wait until Doctor Haddock answers. If he says take Barnaby, then fine.'

'Dat's vhat *you* think,' VD says. '*I* think differently. So does Mr Nagasaki and so does Doctor Ra'mad. That's three to one. Now please step aside Mr Bent, unless you vish to assist Mr Nagasaki in muzzling the dog and carrying it to the car.'

I react instinctively and cover Barnaby with my body. This noble act leaves my backside wriggling around in the air and, I suppose, tempting the androgynously inclined. Next thing I know, the Führer pulls me Bermudas down, digs his nails into my backside, lifts me bodily and dumps me face down on the bed beside Barns. Barnaby's awake enough to lick my face as I'm about to be buggered. Nagasaki fastens a muzzle over Barnaby's head and forces her to watch. The fiend.

Then, as they say, the world explodes. I've never been raped before, and gang-raped at that, still you hetero-types probably wouldn't be interested in the details, would you. Enough to say that between the German and the Jap there's really no contest, the Jap wins Hans-down. Von Scheisskopf's got the dimensions, but the Nip keeps it going. I really can't complain. It's the first time I've had a nip in the bud. Exhausting it was. I don't know how long I lay there or when they took off with Barns. I only come round when I hear Venus. She finds me with my Bermudas still down and sounds ever so concerned.

'David, what's happened?' Says your much-distressed lady.

'I was raped by the evil German Baron and his sadistic Samurai sidekick,' I reply. 'And Barnaby has been stolen.'

'That's terrible, we must call the police immediately,' says your Venus.

'Ah, but I have my reputation to think about,' I answer her. 'If the whole world knows I've been raped, nobody will marry me.'

I'm expecting some compassion. But you know what your lady Venus says? 'It all depends on what you mean by rape.'

Well, I'm not one to argue. Women think they have an exclusive on rape. I reply I'd as soon not report it to the police. Venus actually laughs. Yes, laughs. 'Don't be silly, David,' she says. 'I don't intend to report whatever *you* have been up to. I'm thinking about Barnaby. Why on earth would anybody want to steal Barnaby?'

21

To Catch a Butterfly

'WE SHOULD ALL do what we do best,' K begins his answer to my question as to what he's doing hidden away in Changi. 'For my part, I've spent the last few days going through just about every tart in Singapore.'

'Metaphorically speaking,' the super qualifies. 'I wouldn't want you to think CID is running a house of ill repute.'

'Heaven forbid!' K laughs. He pats a mound of files beside him. 'Know what's in this lot? Mug and body shots of every transvestite ever pulled in for questioning and many who have yet to have that pleasure.'

A sample file is flicked open. Pictures range from formal prison-type faces of the scrubbed and unhappy through the grossly over-painted to the beautifully glossy. Many were taken, K explains, in Bugis Street and Johor Road, some in the chic cafés on Orchard Road. Big breasts and tiny waists, a buttock or two and some interesting tattoos; transvestites fondling their occidental clients as they drink their Tigers. 'I haven't found any familiar faces – or body parts,' says K. 'But the whole world is here as supporting cast.'

K shows several pictures of Von Führer Düsseldorf with a group of white men of similar age. 'There's little scandal value in such pictures,' K says. 'At worst, they might embarrass a man if shown to his wife. They were snapped openly in the street. Tourist souvenirs. Just to place things in perspective, here's one of the two of us with some of them. Quite an innocent evening, wasn't it? I had to think hard to recall it. You had just arrived on campus two years ago. As I remember, we'd just been to your welcome dinner at Chin's and needed amusement. Snapping one second out of an evening can give the wrong idea, no?'

'Yes,' I reply. 'I suppose this explains why there are so many photographers around.'

'Right,' says the super. 'We buy up their unsold pictures and they cut their losses. We also have one or two men of our own taking pictures. We like to ensure as complete a coverage as possible. Surprising how many men take a ladyboy to a hotel and then complain they were robbed. If they can remember where they were picked up, there's a good chance we can provide a set of pictures for identification. These files are by location. Butterflies-of-the-night have their territory and generally stay in it. If we identify a picture, we usually get the thief. Not always, there are some who don't fit the pattern. They work alone or encroach on the territory of others until they get chased out. Some of them can only look the part in the shadows and some have criminal records and keep on the move. Doctor Woolf has been searching the files hoping to come across one in particular of these lone she-wolves.'

'But why?' I ask.

'Doctor Woolf can explain things in his own words.' The super picks up a chicken wing, dips it in black sauce and sits back in his armchair.

'I expect you remember, Haddock, the last meal we shared at your place. It ended with you getting into a huff and being unreasonable.' Typical K, rewriting history.

'I've never objected to your using my back room. If you used it the night Bernard died, it's odd that you didn't come through and say hello. I like to have a look at your crumpet.'

'That particular bit of crumpet was well beyond its use-by date. Not up to standard. I was pissed. I can never take that sort unless I'm in my cups and then I can't resist them. It's hard to find a real woman with such well-polished breasts and such total vulgarity.'

'So why didn't you come through and show me those well-polished knockers?'

'Because, Haddock, after the quenching of the fire, that particular source of lust disgusted me and I wanted rid of it as soon as I could. That's often the case. I don't want them rubbing my balls and covering me in cheap lipstick and smelly perfume; their clip-on wigs, their pong, it all disgusts me. I just want shot of them, never to see them again.'

'Christ, K, you sound like Jack the Ripper. I hope you don't bump them off when disgusted by what you can't resist.'

K peers down his nose at me. 'Have you looked in the wardrobe in your back room lately? Full of discarded butterflies pinned to the wall.'

'All right K, you know I'm joking. If they turn you off that much after you've dipped into them, I'm glad you didn't bring a particularly bad one through.'

I don't want to destroy our joint alibi, but there remains a crucial hour that doesn't fall into place and I feel now is the time to shed light on it. 'I went into the kitchen for ice around 9 o'clock that night. I noticed the door to the back room open and looked inside – it was empty.'

'Oh, Haddock!' says K. 'Is that what's bothering you? Can't you put two and two together?'

'I can, and it's not making four. Why are you here searching for a transvestite you never want to see again? And why did you say you were with it at my place when you weren't – at least, you weren't at 9 o'clock.'

K sighs. 'Did you check your bathroom?'

'No.'

'There you are then. I needed to wash and took that one into the bathroom. Not for any thrills but to make sure she didn't pinch anything worth pinching – if you've bought anything worth pinching lately. Now: serious. The super has told you Li Fang reported seeing me and a tall, long-haired woman apparently dragging Bernard along the back path and into his house?'

'Yes.' I look at the super sitting quietly. 'He asked if I have any idea who the woman might be. I do not ... do you mean ...?'

'Right, Haddock. At long last. It was Madam Butterfly. Bernard stumbled into us in your kitchen just as I opened the back door to get her out. At the time I thought he was drunk. He wasn't himself at all – kept muttering your name, Tom, not Haddock; had a carrier bag in one hand and was waving a dog collar around with the other. I supposed he was looking for his dog. His hands were full and he dropped a little pouch on the floor. I picked it up and put it in my pocket to keep it safe for him. He dropped the collar too; I picked it up and put it on your counter alongside the carrier bag of books. Before I knew what was happening, Bernard had his hand down the front of the transvestite's dress and was playing with the glossies. I thought he had simply gone back on the booze with a vengeance – he seemed happier than he had been for ages.'

'Why didn't you call me to help?'

'I don't think Bernard wanted your help. He forgot you as soon as he saw the tits. Since he seemed pretty keen on having my leftovers, I gave our companion an extra fifty dollars to service him. As we approached his house on the back path, Bernard lost his footing a few times and I again put that down to booze. In the end, we were practically carrying him – not dragging him, but I can see how Li Fang got that idea in the dark. When I left him inside his place on his bed, he smiled at me and I really thought the old chap would have a harmless good time. I waited outside his back door for twenty minutes for the butterfly to reappear. She said Bernard was asleep in his armchair wearing his sarong, so I took her back to my car and dropped her on Tanglin Road before going home with the windows wide open.'

'Could she have taken the manuscript from Bernard's?' I ask.

'The super's asked me that. I don't see how or why she could or would. I searched her handbag when she came out to make sure she hadn't lifted anything of Bernard's. Anyway, I can't imagine she laps up academic manuscripts.'

'But there's some reason for hunting this person now?'

The super comes in. 'My men picked up Doctor Woolf from the Mandarin car park and brought him in for questioning as soon as Li Fang informed us of what he had seen. Fortunately, Doctor Woolf was still carrying around the pouch of Bernard Fox. It was full of diamonds. Does that surprise you?'

The super looks at me. Trying to judge my reactions no doubt. I look surprised.

'At first, I was prepared to believe Doctor Woolf had killed the professor for the diamonds and strung him up to look like suicide. It was the only motive we had. But when faced with

Li Fang witnessing a woman accomplice, Doctor Woolf came clean with the story as you've just heard it, diamonds and all – although I'm not sure he'd have included the diamonds had we not found them in his pocket. Li Fang was able to identify both pouch and diamonds. It seems that a few years ago he changed the old war loot into far more portable diamonds and Bernard Fox kept them safe.'

'But,' I interrupt, 'I thought only Bernard knew the location of the treasure and he could not do anything with it as long as Li Fang was watching him.'

'Who told you that?'

'Chin's wife, Agnes,' I admit with a feeling of betrayal.

The super smiles. 'Let her and everybody else continue to think that. Certainly, Li Fang was some kind of watch dog over Bernard Fox and the war loot immediately after the death of Harry Chin's father in 1945. I suppose you know about Chin Jin-Hui's role in amassing the loot in World War II?' I nod. 'Agnes?' he asks. I nod again. He continues, 'Professor Fox and Li Fang had long since decided there was no point in keeping heaps of loot in several locations for a cause long lost. They made their own arrangements. The diamonds stayed with the professor, and he and Li Fang swore an oath that neither would touch them as long as Chin Peng was alive or until he sent word. They also swore secrecy for as long as both of them lived. As far as other parties are concerned – people like Düsseldorf and Agnes – there is *no* little pouch of top-quality diamonds. Düsseldorf, I am sure, is still looking for a pirate's chest under a spot marked X.'

I jump as the phone rings violently. The super laughs and lifts the receiver. His expression changes but he says little, signing off with worrying words, 'Get onto all the animal clinics. I

211

know it's late. Wake them up if you have to. Good work, Madhu.' He puts down the phone and continues as if he never lifted it. 'You now see, Doctor Haddock, why we took Doctor Woolf out of circulation and why we need your help.'

'Yes and no,' I say. 'I can see K behaved suspiciously but I don't really get what he's doing here, obviously not under arrest, and I've no idea what help I can give.'

'For Christ's sake, Haddock! I'd have thought you of all people would be more supportive. I've told you what I'm doing here. Looking through hundreds of photographs in the hope of finding that one trannie I picked up that night. Not an easy job. I picked it up along by the River. You know what kind you get down there. The no-home-territory sort. There's simply no file on the riverside. Too dark. No tourists hang around there. And I can't describe what she looked like. Everything about them is false. Wig, eyelashes, rouge, lipstick, moveable beauty spots, pop-in dimples. Change the pieces around and you have a different face; it's like playing potato-woman. I might recognise the bum, but to pick out a mug shot is proving impossible.'

'Seems so,' confirms the super. 'We've already brought in four of them for Doctor Woolf's closer inspection. One even had to undress! Unless we find the person, we might never know what happened during the last moments of the professor's life. It could be that *she* hanged the professor; so we must find her.'

'David will be very pleased to hear this story,' I say. 'He thinks he saw Bernard dead at home and is under suspicion because Li Fang saw him leave Bernard's house.'

'David Bent saw the professor drugged. Li Fang entered the house after Bent left, made some strong coffee and got the professor walking up and down a bit. He was dozy but otherwise okay when Li Fang left him. I suspect Professor Fox then went out his back door to your flat, carrying the pouch of diamonds. Perhaps, given Düsseldorf's recent return to Singapore, the professor wanted to hide them in your flat – perhaps also the reason he made his Will, just in case, three days before his death; anyway, it seems he was still affected by the drug and none too aware of what he was doing. Don't tell Mr Bent anything about tonight. I do not want him gossiping – that could drive the transvestite underground – if she's not there already.'

'So, this whole thing is to catch a butterfly. I still don't see where I come in.'

'You will be a decoy, Doctor Haddock. I would expect Düsseldorf or Nagasaki to be calling on you. After you got that post-mortem letter, they must think the secret lies only with you and you might turn in the loot or take it out of Singapore. They can't hang around.'

'How do they know about the letter?'

'Your friend Doctor Woolf told them.'

'What? Why? And how could he? I never told K I got a letter.'

'Because *I* told him and I told him to tell them,' says the super. 'I told Woolf you had received a letter but not what was in it. I told him when he informed me he was dining with Düsseldorf – which he did after the two of you had your little fight about you refusing to let him in on what you had overheard when snooping on me and Ra'mad. I told him that Düsseldorf *might* simply be inviting a fellow anthropologist to dinner and just talk about anthropology – in which case he should let me know – or there might be a more sinister meaning for the invitation. I told him the German might raise the subject of the treasure directly or ask about you, and that even if he doesn't raise things directly, Woolf should find a way to casually reveal you got a letter from Professor Fox and are keeping the contents of that letter to yourself.'

'So, you set me up, both of you!' I try to sound indignant.

'You could say that. I had to draw them out; after all this time being unable to pin anything on them. I did intend to warn you, but Düsseldorf acted quicker than I expected. Lock up your flat from now on, but allow Düsseldorf and Nagasaki in if they visit you. Microphones will be placed in your flat – with your permission – before breakfast tomorrow. We'll change the locks on your doors too, and don't give fresh keys to anybody. A policeman is stationed upstairs in Doctor Ra'mad's flat; he'll be able to hear every word. All you have to do is let your visitors talk. The officer will have a key to your back door in case he needs to intervene, so don't bolt it, just keep it locked with the key out.'

'He will hear *everything* that goes on in the flat?' I am thinking of Venus.

The super smiles. 'If you need privacy, just switch your kitchen light off. That will switch off the whole system. Our officer will understand when he cannot see the light from your kitchen. Just remember to turn it on afterwards and to leave it on day and night. By the way, what was in that carrier bag in the kitchen?'

'Just some books Bernard had borrowed.'

'And while you are sitting comfortably at home switching the kitchen light off and on,' K jumps in, 'yours truly will be prowling the streets looking for one butterfly in thousands.'

The telephone rings again. The super completes a conversation of grunts and turns to me. 'Your dog…' he begins.

22

The Dog Stone

'YOUR DOG. Vhat do you call it? Barnaby? If you vant it back, ve must be cooperative.'

I have just said goodbye to the super outside my flat. After locking and bolting my door on him as I'd promised I would, I walk straight into the ghosts of WWII.

So much for the great entrapment plan; the microphones will be installed 'before breakfast' and the only one entrapped is me. Nagasaki has in his hand, pointing at my head, the same gun I had seen a couple of hours before in Wong's hand. How is that possible? I don't know. It only fires caps I know, but a gun pointed at the head definitely has it over intellectual debate when it comes to deciding who fears and who sneers. And beside Nagasaki, posing with bronzed hands on hips, is Adolf Von Düsseldorf of the Thousand-year Reich.

'What do you want?' I ask stupidly. Well, *nice to see you, Adolf* seems out of place.

'Let us stop playing games,' the Führer declares. I didn't know I was playing games with a couple of androgynously inclined leftovers from the wrong side of WWII. 'You vill be a good boy and reveal me a riddle. You vill tell us vhere is the treasure. In return, you get back your filthy dog.'

'One filthy dog for a fortune in treasure,' I improvise. 'You keep the dog and I keep the treasure.' Sorry, Barnaby, basic bargaining strategy in play.

'You can add in Fox's daughter. Syou or Norsiah or whatever you call her.'

'She went away before the professor died.'

'Ve know. Ve can bring her back.'

'Well, my sheets do need washing but it's still not much of a deal. Tell you what: Norsiah, Barnaby *and* we go fifty-fifty.'

'Seventy-thirty.'

'Okay, Adolf, it's a deal. Girl and dog first.'

'Treasure first.'

The German takes a paper from his pocket and unfolds it. 'I copied it myself from the letter to you. The police have the original. Listen. *In the woods of virginity, you may dig out a greater treasure than hidden by any pirate. To find it, follow the way of a lonely orchid. Branch left, continue to the dog stone and uncover the ground.* You vill reveal the riddle.'

Now is the time for a drop-kick to the rising sun and a forearm smash to the iron jaw – or I could just reveal the riddle. 'It refers to the Botanic Gardens. There is a path in the virgin forest known for an orchid that only grows alone and far above the crowd. A bit like a wandering *samurai*. The path branches and on the left branch there is a stone that looks like a dog. That's where the treasure is buried. I have not looked myself; I'm being watched by that little creep Li Fang and the police.' Surely only Long John Silver could ever take this nonsense seriously. 'Fifty-fifty, Adolf. Okay?'

'I vill give you the one-turd share. That vill stop you going to zee police.'

'One turd?'

'Vun turd für you. Vun turd für me. Vun turd für Nagasaki-san.'

'Fair enough. Fair turds all round. I hope you find the treasure.'

'Ya, I hope so also. Ve vill go togezer.'

'Better I wait here. Li Fang's spying on me.' My mind is racing. What's the policeman in Ra'mad's flat doing? He couldn't have missed that car outside but no sign he's about to come in guns blazing. Must be waiting to catch them actually doing something against the law … like buggering me. I hope Ra'mad hasn't absent-mindedly slipped a sedative into his cocoa. 'Now tell me where are Norsiah and Barnaby.'

'I tell you later, after ve see the treasure.'

'What guarantee do I have that I will get a third share?'

'The vord of an officer of der Turd Reich. Enough für you, I think.'

'Quite, Adolf.' Who could ask for anything more?

I hope the policeman in Ra'mad's flat or Li Fang in the Guild is looking as I'm shown into the back seat. I could run for it now – but Norsiah and Barnaby might never come home; Von Düsseldorf would just deny everything. The gun is now in Düsseldorf's hand and he sits beside me as the Citroën moves silently off to the cuckoo's nest.

*   *   *

We leave the car and walk through bodies half-visible in cloud-masked moonlight. The Gardens provide a spooning ground to any couple whose passion merits a thousand mosquito bites. I could scream for help but if I do the only witnesses will vanish into the foliage.

At the collection of deserted concrete tables until now known only for ice cream, iced tea and glimpses of thigh, I point along Agnes's path into virgin forest. 'The way of lonely orchids,' I say. Nagasaki has brought a spade and torchlight from the car; I am the treasure map. He lights the path and the Führer prods me onto it. Should I make a run for it? Would they shoot me in front of lonely orchids? But that gun fires only caps, so what if they do? But more likely the Divine Wind will fly through the air and head butt my vital parts. At least I'm out of the flat. The darkness of the forest should offer an escape if needed. After all, I tell myself, I sort of know the paths and I presume they do not.

I fork left. The path skirts around a very tall and wide megalithic-like boulder that must be four metres high. It looks as good as any other big rock we are likely to come across.

'The dog stone,' I say.

'Ver is der dog?'

'Look, Adolf. There's its nose sticking out. And a curly tail at the bottom.'

'Not dog.'

'In the dark, maybe not. More dog in daylight.'

Nagasaki walks around the boulder to the other side. He's Japanese; he knows his rocks. 'Dog Stone,' he declares.

'Up to you, Adolf,' I say cheerily. I'd welcome any hint of discord within the odd couple. 'We keep walking or you try digging here.'

'*You* dig,' the Führer orders in a tone of *Arbeit macht frei*. Nagasaki-san passes the shovel.

'Where?' I ask, swinging the metal head absently. Nagasaki social distances himself.

'The ground,' says Adolf. 'Dig up zee whole fucking rock if necessary.'

The black, soft humus is almost like sand and within half an hour, there is something worthy of the name hole around one side of the rock. Once the surface soil has been removed, however, roots and stones stray in the path of the spade and the digging gets tough.

I slowly dig myself deeper. The boulder looms over me. The axis powers look down on me. This is their big moment. They will reverse the fortunes of a war in which they carelessly lost the world. I know they won't find it here. Pretty soon, I figure, my captors might sense it too.

Whenever the spade chinks against a stone, I get a few seconds' rest while the torchlight plays on imagined golden chalices. The digging is easiest near the boulder and I find myself tunneling under it.

'Goot. Treasure may be under rock. Continue.'

I continue. My hands are sore. I suggest this might be the wrong place or the wrong side of the rock and am told to dig deeper, wider and under the rock. Now and again, I glance up uneasily at the rock towering over me. The moon comes out behind it and it looks now less like a dog and more like the grim reaper stooping over to watch me at his feet, digging my own grave. The hole gets deeper; so do I.

I am in the hole up to my armpits when the spade vibrates against metal. The torchlight beam reveals a metal plate with Japanese writing. Animated discussion in Japanese. Nagasaki jumps down beside me and takes the spade, waving me out of the hole and handing the gun up to Von Düsseldorf.

Maybe I've struck treasure after all. Nagasaki caresses the

plate lovingly and gently, cleaning away the earth around it. A metal oil drum. Skull and crossbones. Must be treasure!

'What's the writing say?' I ask.

'Danger. Explosives. Smoking verboten.'

I lean my aching body against the dog stone and imagine it moves ever such a little bit. 'Explosives! Shouldn't we get out of here, Adolf?'

The Führer looks down his nose at me from the infinite superiority of a man who would destroy the world to prove he is the best thing in it. 'Don't be afraid, little Englander. Der pearl is in der ugly oyster.' I cower behind the boulder. The last of the master race laughs at me and laughs in the face of danger as he stands at the brink of the hole, straight, feet set apart, braced for a glorious posterity.

Nagasaki-san uses the spade's head to lever open the drum's top. The Führer levels his Luger at me. I quiver against the stone and it quivers back. I push against the rock and it trembles. A stream of Japanese invectives. I look round to see Nagasaki raise an ammunition shell above his head.

'Get in der hole!' Adolf yells at me, gun unwavering. His wartime treasure is unearthed but he is not jumping for joy. I flatten myself against the rock, trembling; the rock trembles back. An idea from a boys-own comic surfaces in my mind. As the moon scuds behind a cloud, I will slip around the rock out of view and run into the forest as the evil Nazi looses off round after round into the darkness. Then I remember the gun fires only caps. I prepare to run.

Powdered rock hits my eyes and I hear the Luger crack; those caps are damn realistic. Von Düsseldorf could have shot my balls off. His steely-blue eyes bear along the barrel of the gun and into my head. The moon obligingly scuds behind a cloud but I scud nowhere. Through the darkness, Nazi eyes shine fanatically. I look into the hole. It has final solution written all over it. Von Düsseldorf, the spoilsport, seems to be giving up on the treasure hunt. 'In der hole!' he spits, and his knees buckle, the gun flies out of his hand and he falls into the hole onto Nagasaki.

Li Fang's rugby tackle to the rescue, or rather, Li Fang's alter ego in black overalls complete with face mask, goggles and tropical diving gloves. He tells me later he was cleaning out the cesspit at night while the Guild was closed when he noticed the Citroën pulling away towards the Gardens, went to my flat, found the door open and ran here. I hear cries from the hole as Li Fang adds his weight to mine and the rock topples neatly down.

*   *   *

'You okay?' Li Fang asks, removing his mask and pointing the Luger at the fallen boulder to stop it getting up. I assure Li Fang that I am really, really, really glad to see him.

I hear the spade digging under the stone. The earth at the rim of the fallen rock crumbles and the head of Von Düsseldorf appears. Less arrogant now. 'Please to help us. My friend is trapped under der rock. His leg is perhaps broken. Der rock fell on us.'

'It didn't fall,' I say. 'It was pushed. And now Li Fang has *your* gun, full of *your* fingerprints, pointing at *your* head. He has only to pull the trigger, toss the gun into the hole and let Tokyo Rose explain to the police – if he should ever be found alive.'

'I vill make der deal,' the German speaks to Li Fang. 'Let us escape and I vill tell who killed Chin Jin-Hui and why.'

221

'Okay, deal,' Li Fang agrees. Personally, I could not care less who killed Chin's father.

'Out hole first.'

'Name first,' counters Li Fang. He aims the gun directly between the Führer's eyes. The Luger looks at home in his gloved hand. Both he and Düsseldorf seem to know it doesn't fire caps.

'Ya, okay. Jin-Hui vas killed by Bernard Fox. Jin-Hui gave names to der Kempeitai of those who refused to contribute to his resistance fund. Fox kill him good. Revenge. That's all. Quits. All over long ago. Fox got treasure; you can keep it.' Düsseldorf widens the hole enough to get both arms out and pulls himself up towards us.

'Who kill aborigine wife of Fox? Who torture girl?'

'Okay.' Düsseldorf pulls his shoulders clear of the hole and starts to climb out. 'It was Nagasaki.'

A violent roar from the depths of the earth and the German struggles. 'Help me,' he calls in English. 'Or you will never find the girl Norsiah.'

'I know where she is,' says Li Fang quietly.

Inch by inch, Nagasaki pulls Düsseldorf back under the stone and we do nothing to stop him. A gurgling scream suggests the Turd Reich is being strangled by its axis partner. And then the stone slips again.

Bernard is now fully avenged for the death of his wife if not himself; I hope now he can find peace and stop buzzing around in my mind. I listen carefully. I can make out a faint scraping under the stone.

The spadework becomes appropriately frantic for a man with a broken leg about to be entombed forever. The head of the spade appears briefly and Nagasaki's eyes flash in the moonlight. I watch fascinated as Nagasaki works to widen the hole. The edge of the hole crumbles again. The huge stone settles down, a dog making itself comfortable.

I walk around the stone. It fits perfectly into its hole. Horizontal, it looks like Barnaby in recline – the dog stone. Li Fang stands, Luger in hand, savouring revenge. 'Wait here, Li Fang, I'll go get the police – there's a policeman in Ra'mad's flat. They can get something to lift the rock and arrest them.'

'No. No police.' Li Fang squats by the stone, gun in hand.

'Give me the gun, Li Fang. I'll put it in their car and dump the car.'

Li Fang takes a rag from his pocket and wraps the gun in it. 'Don't touch it,' he says. 'This never happened.'

★   ★   ★

The Citroën is waiting. Much as I love pristine antiques, I am glad Düsseldorf replaced the vintage starting handle with a key switch electric start and gladder still he left the key in the ignition – too late now to search through his pockets. I put the wrapped gun beside me on the driver's seat. The campus roads are empty, the moon has gone to sleep, any leftover lovers are too occupied to notice a black car pass silently through a dark night. Holding the wheel in my handkerchief, I drive quietly through the sleeping campus. I stop the car outside Chin's front gate, turn off the ignition using the handkerchief and pop the keys into Chin's mail box. He'll think Düsseldorf parked it there and is asleep in the guest bedroom. I wonder how long it will be before Chin finds the keys and the gun, and realises his father's friend is never coming back. As I take the back way to my flat,

I hear an explosion from the Botanic Gardens – I hope Li Fang is okay.

★   ★   ★

Barnaby comes back next morning, personally returned by the superintendent of police. He comes with the technician to install the recording equipment and change the locks. 'Do you have any idea how many animal clinics there are in Singapore? Half of the Singapore Police Force has been looking for your dog overnight.' I thank him. That still leaves Norsiah unaccounted for. Does Li Fang really know where she is or is she waiting somewhere for the German to feed her? 'When the technician's quite done, you'll feel safer and we might get something to lay on the two of them.' Don't worry, Superintendent, I feel safer already and something's already laying on the two of them.

23

Barnaby's Babies

MURDERS ARE a fickle business. Within Singapore's bamboo ivory towers, the alarm bells sounded by the death of Professor Fox fall silent as staff realise his was a one-off and none of them is next in line for the fan-murderer's noose. Death loses its sting when police officers are to be seen every day in Guild House, sitting at desks and shovelling papers; reassuringly familiar activity. As long as murders can be reduced to the written word, quantified, classified and filed, the mystery of solving them takes on the dimensions of, say, a socio-demographic study of Toa Payoh housing estate. Bernard's killer has been absorbed within the academic environment, the perfect hiding place. He has become a hypothesis, his existence to be proven. Nobody bothers too much about an abstraction of the mind.

Off-campus curiosity about the death of Bernard has an equally brief life. The death is now popularly accepted as 'an obvious case of suicide dressed as murder' and never mind who dressed it up by turning on the fan. The news editor of the Singapore Broadcasting Corporation suggests Venus 'let up on eulogising a relic of colonialism'. At the request of Superintendent Wong, her last mention of the case on national TV is an appeal for anybody with information as to the whereabouts of Norsiah to contact the police. I see my cousin's picture on Guild

House television; it's from her work permit and must have been taken some years before – she looks quite attractive. I don't ask Li Fang where she is; he would never tell me, if he knows.

★   ★   ★

'I must, I must, I must increase my bust, my bust, my bust.' The morning chorus of what David calls the *Guild House Rozz-ers' Male Voice Choir* is heard for the last time by the dorm girls in their morning group exercise as they fling thin arms back and trim chests out. The investigation team boxes mounds of papers and, with visible reluctance, decamps for pastures less pleasant.

Li Fang says he misses the policemen: they were more fun than academics. He particularly misses their happy hour after they closed down their day's work, opened up their evening beers and eyed the procession of jogging shorts led by the strong thighs of Agnes. With the police retreat, only the sunset glint of binocular lenses from among the potted plants on Ra'mad's balcony suggests anyone is monitoring the rites of Bukit Timah's aspiring Amazons.

Students are more interested in making up lost time than mourning an ancient Briton. Ra'mad manages to get his wife buried and overcomes his remorse at losing his favourite rat. Venus presumably continues her Sunday morning devotionals at Richard's bedside, since she is never-on-Sunday and our rela-tionship remains forever amber. I respect her wish to remain true to the one man she can never have again. I love her the more for her fidelity to my only competitor. K continues his marathon review of Singapore's butterflies; neither he nor Wong seem to know the axis threat is buried forever.

I manage both my own and K's lectures and tutorials in the mornings; I like to get teaching out of the way by lunch, leaving my afternoons free. Venus begins her working day in the early afternoon, so we fall into a routine of late suppers after her 10 o'clock news slot. Agnes, on the other hand, has her afternoons free.

It is on one such cloudy afternoon that I sit at my open window marking essays and see her walking by in that signature hat. She smiles, I smile, she walks on, crossing the cricket pitch; crisp, white summer dress; short skirt, long legs. My eyes follow her figure; she knows it. She reaches the corner of Wolverton Mess and looks back. She waits a full minute then waves before disappearing. I leave my desk and with Barnaby at my side, take a walk to share ice cream among the orchids. And the next day and the next; repeat performances but never boring with Agnes. She tells me one day that a peculiar thing has happened, a very large rock inside the jungle walk has been turned from vertical to horizontal – 'Honestly, these gardeners must have nothing better to do.' We feel the physical and mental attraction pulling us together; but it doesn't progress beyond eye-games flirtation and friendship; we both seem to prefer it this way … at least for now. We talk a lot about Bernard, a little of K, nothing of Venus. I am happy to be Bernard's platonic replacement. Agnes never comes into my flat; I am not K and we both know that might ruin everything.

David continues to mourn K's absence; I can't tell him there is no cause for concern, some gossips just can't be trusted with the truth. K had called his wife on the first night of his absence and knows he can rely on her silence. Toshi continues to live with David but in the closet; he builds up a small private clientele of university people who appreciate Japanese massage without dirty things.

An open verdict is quietly declared on Bernard's death – suspicious but cause unknown – and Bernard is cremated after an unmoving ceremony sponsored by the University Staff Association. Attendance is dictated by professional obligation and even Chin and Ra'mad are present, in opposite corners. Barnaby is locked in my flat; I don't want her sobbing and howling through the funeral. As few words as can decently suffice are said by the VC about Bernard's contribution to scholarship in Singapore. The only wreath comes from Venus, who wears a contrasting white corsage pinned to the bodice of a stunning long black dress. Siggy stays away, aware the event has zero news value. Only Agnes, in mourning white, cries openly.

The staff troop out dry-eyed from the short goodbye: Professor Bernard Fox, historian, is history. K stands quietly at the back of the memorial hall, his reappearance almost unnoticed. Superintendent Wong has told him he can resume his teaching duties again as both Düsseldorf and the transvestite cannot be traced.

Apart from the absence of Norsiah and the police tapes sealing the doors of Bernard's house, so strong is the air of normality that the mystery of Bernard's death and the turning fan might have remained forever academic ... had Chin contained his ambitions. The memorial service might have been the final act in the psychodrama of Uncle Bernard's life and death ... if Chin had behaved himself. An 'acting dean' is supposed to sit quietly, be nice to everybody over tea and hope to be confirmed in place while denying any real wish for the office. But Chin can't mark time. No sooner has Bernard been given his final honours then Chin strikes.

The strike starts with a direct attack on the easiest target. David is told by the English Department Head he can resign and get one month's pay or face the consequences of official dismissal, crime to be announced. David takes the money and comes to us crying.

K drives off in a rage to the VC to demand the reason for the attack on defenseless David. He is back within the hour, possibly for the first time ever lost for words. He shows us a letter the VC had all ready and waiting for him. The letter informs K that his contract will not be renewed on expiry in one month's time. I am left unhassled. Nothing Chin does contravenes regulations and, while K would not go out quietly, I feel Chin might just get his way if he stops at this point. He does not.

The day after my two friends are hacked by Chin's invisible *parang*, I receive a pre-publication copy of a weighty volume, courtesy of the Singapore University Press, with an invitation to contribute comments which might be used in the book's launch the following week. A quick flick through the pages is enough. I snap shut *The History of Singapore University* by Harold Chin and call a war party.

Courtesy of Li Fang's telephone and guessing it is bugged, I contact Venus, K and David. Meet me immediately at the flat. Come now, Barnaby has just given birth to twins.

*   *   *

K's Mustang and Venus's Starlet pull up outside as David arrives on foot. I open my front door to allow entry and close it immediately, turning the key in the lock. In spite of the strange disappearance of Düsseldorf and Nagasaki, I am still bait for the axis powers until Superintendent Wong decides otherwise. K whispers a reminder for me to turn off the light in the kitchen.

Toshi is appended behind David and K as if I might not notice him. Venus asks me where the twins are and I explain they are imaginary puppies; she says she'd still like to see them. Toshi with a bow hands me a tray of Japanese sweets and says *congratulations*. This gives me a twinge of conscience but not a strong enough twinge to soften my resolve to exclude him from the conspiracy about to happen. Tosh gives Barns a cuddle and the tart, who hasn't even given birth to twins, rolls over for a post-natal nipple massage.

David stands rock still and confused. 'Is there something bleeding awful wrong?' he asks. Venus, K and Toshi cling to him in solidarity, all look at me as if I have cracked my eggshell.

'I have certain communions to make which had best be retained twixt four bonces rather than five. Our council of this hour and endeavours on the morrow will embroil a profundity of Anglo-Saxon and must preclude perchance miscomprehensions. Thus, it be optimum to eschew the element of the rising hot cross bun.'

'What on earth are you trying to say?' Venus asks.

'Yeh,' adds David. 'Why cancha talk proper?'

K is the only one to understand. 'I think Haddock is asking if Toshi would be so kind as to make us something to eat in the kitchen. Right?'

'Right,' I say. 'But there's very little in the fridge. Two doubtful eggs and half a stale chapati.'

'Never mind that, matey,' David rejoins. 'No need to go all Richard the Third on us. We don't usually come here expecting a banquet. As long as you've got the beer in, don't worry about the grub as long as Tosh is around. It just so happens our Tosh is now into the Japanese fast-food and steak and kidney pie delivery business. No-dirty-things-massage an optional extra. You now see in his hands a Yaohan bag full of goodies to celebrate Barnaby's motherhood – I presume it was a miraculous birth as she's neutered. Just let Tosh into the kitchen and see what comes out.'

'Okay,' I compromise. 'But the kitchen door and shutters stay closed and locked.' The last person I want poking his moustache around the door is Ra'mad; he will have seen my flat closed up, the familiar cars outside and the listening device switched off and his curiosity is surely aroused. 'And Toshi, on no account, absolutely no account, turn on the light.'

'Turn on the light?'

'Yes. No. Do *not* turn light on. Very important. Understand?'

'Tom Haddock,' Venus butts in. 'You have everything closed up and expect Toshi to cook in the dark? What on earth is wrong with you today?'

'All right Toshi, open one shutter, but no electric light and no door.'

'What?' says Toshi.

K leads Toshi by the hand to the kitchen, opens one shutter, takes the key from the lock of the back door and shakes his head and hand at the light switch. Toshi seems happy enough, but it's easy to tell the three musketeers see his exclusion as requiring an explanation. 'This doesn't sound much fun,' David complains. 'You banish Tosh to a darkened kitchen, yet you allow Barnaby to stay.'

'Barns can't talk,' I say.

231

'And where are her babies?' Venus lightens things up by play-ing the dumb beauty. At least, I think she's playing.

I have, somehow, to inject an air of the serious into a group bonded by frivolity. 'What I have to say must remain confiden-tial. Just the four of us. No news on TV, Venus. No blabbing to your boyfriends, David. No crossed lines on the 5.30 express, K.'

'Blimey,' David whines. ''Oo elected the Generalissimo? Sounds worse than the girl guides. In case you've forgotten, we are your *mates*, squire. If you can't trust us, who can you trust? Why not tell us what it's all about and we can decide whether to hear it or not. I don't like all this secrecy stuff. Gives me the creeps.'

K and Venus confirm their sentiments are with David. I'm getting a bit peeved at my allies. 'If I'm a generalissimo, I can only say few generals in Asia would be stupid enough to hatch a conspiracy with a Japanese masseur in the kitchen.'

'I think you might be wrong there,' K cuts in. 'I believe there is a fine tradition of Japanese masseurs present at plots going back before the Tokugawa Shogunate.'

'That's beside the point, K,' I respond lamely.

'Well, Haddock, how are we supposed to know what is on or beside the point if you don't tell us what the point is?'

'The point is ... *Chin*,' I say simply and loudly and find myself in silence. I raise the copy of the book and hold it before me like a tombstone. 'The reason for my atypical behaviour: *The History of Singapore University* by *Harold Chin*. Title sounds familiar, doesn't it? I have over the past two hours had a good look through this book. Much of the content bears the unmistak-able imprint of Bernard. Look at it yourselves. Apart from *Social*

232

knocked out of the title and some obvious editing, it's written in the painstaking English of Bernard Fox. No way Chin could have written this book.'

I put the book on the dining table. K imperiously clips on his pince-nez and leads three heads into it. I allow them a few minutes to skim the pages and see the same disbelief on their faces I had experienced earlier.

K raises his face. 'Continue,' he says in authorisation and command. I do.

'Bernard's manuscript disappeared when Bernard was hanged. It was the only thing to disappear. I know Bernard himself feared its revelations might be unacceptable to some. The police haven't found Bernard's manuscript.' Heads nod, eyes fixed in disbelief on Harry Chin's name in large letters across an aerial view of the campus on the cover of the book. There are no interruptions and I continue. 'I give you a hypothesis. Chin stole the manuscript and Bernard was killed in the process.'

'I told you. I told you it was Chin.'

'Yes, K, you did,' I agree. 'But you never said why.'

'All right,' says Venus. 'If your hypothesis is correct, why would Chin so desperately want his name on this book? Desperate enough to kill for it?'

'Why Chin would want his name on the book is clear enough,' I answer the first of her questions. 'It will make his reputation as an academic. Whether or not he would kill for it, I don't know. But Chin had the opportunity and knew the tempting prize was there. He knew Bernard never discussed his work much before he published and he possibly knew from Agnes there was only one copy and where Bernard kept it. But why *kill* Bernard? Why not just steal the manuscript? Bernard would have found it hard to argue that the book was his and not Chin's. Chin could have let it be known that he was working on a history and changed a lot more of the text and the style than he has. He could have waited until the move to the new campus before publication. But Bernard's death and Chin's rise to acting dean offered a chance he could not resist. By publication now, Chin will be acclaimed and his position as dean confirmed. But why *kill* Bernard? I don't know.'

'Okay on everything you say,' David comes in. 'But why not just inform Super Wong and let the police handle the whys and what-nots?

K gives a snort and answers David. 'Because, nincompoop, the original manuscript is missing. Chin would just deny any knowledge of any manuscript other than his own. Unless we find the original.'

'But isn't the original manuscript likely to have been destroyed already?' Venus strikes a blow for logic.

I falter. Only a fool would leave evidence lying around. And only another fool would look for it after the police failed to find it. But anyway, I make out a case for the continued existence of Bernard's original manuscript. 'You might be right. Chin is no fool and there's no reason to expect evidence to be handed to us on a plate. On the other hand, with Bernard dead there would be no rush to destroy the original, since Bernard wouldn't be complaining about its loss. Chin could not have destroyed it immediately – there would be no point in stealing it just to destroy it. He probably didn't dare even read it until the pressure let up. And when the heat was off enough to allow Chin to work at chopping out what he didn't like in the original and retyping, he perhaps felt no need to destroy the manuscript. There was perhaps no reason for Chin to be unduly concerned even were the original manuscript discovered. Bernard never wasted time typing his name on pages and never made a copy. If the police were now to find Bernard's manuscript, Chin could simply say it's *his* original draft which he has since revised.'

'So, what if *we* find the manuscript?' K asks. 'Wouldn't the same apply? I mean we would have to go to the police, wouldn't we?'

'I have a feeling that if we find the manuscript, we will have Chin. Perhaps something very simple. Matching up the manuscript with Bernard's typewriter for instance. Chin's typewriter is unlikely to have a broken 'm' and a high 's'. That's a job for the super. But I think it would be difficult, without a very good reason justifying a warrant, for the super to look for the manuscript in the place it's most likely to be.'

'Where's that?' Three speak as one.

'Think.' Time to prove what a clever dick I am. 'Chin has just bumped off Bernard and stolen his script. The distance from Chin's door to Bernard's is fifty metres at most. Chin's alibi says he was in bed with his wife. Where do you think he hid it?'

'In his bed?' David ventures.

'Chin was not seen out that night; he didn't take his car out. I think he hid it *somewhere* in his house.'

K looks at me over his pince-nez with begrudged recognition of my genius. 'Brilliant, my boy. Precisely the conclusion I came to weeks ago but nobody would listen. So, what do we do now?'

'We find it and we take it,' I answer energetically as Toshi comes in with a plate of sushi. 'We take it in the same manner Chin took it from Bernard.'

'You're not planning to string the geezer up, are you? I'm not quite into that.'

'No, David. We find the manuscript in Chin's house and we discredit Chin. Discredit Chin and we might all keep our jobs and get revenge for Bernard.'

'What is re-ven-gey, David-san?'

K chimes in before David can explain, 'Revenge is a dish best served cold.'

'Ah,' says Toshi, face alight with understanding, 'like sushi.'

24

Agnes Squeals

K TELLS ME Agnes called him to reactivate their 5.30 liaisons and that after so long without him, she'll be 'gagging for it'. He then revamps his weird pre-orgasm theory that a woman can't control what she is saying in the seconds before climax. He wants to install a tape recorder in the wardrobe of my back bedroom to register Agnes's unguarded moments.

'You sit in the wardrobe, Haddock, and try not to get too excited. You'll be witness that nothing is fabricated. Agnes will admit she and Chin killed Bernard. We use the tape to blackmail her to get Bernard's manuscript and there you are: the hard evidence we need.'

'No way. I'm not doing that to Agnes. I like her. We are friends. I don't believe she killed Bernard. If you imagine I'm going to sit in my own wardrobe watching you screw a confession out of Agnes, you don't know her and you don't know me.'

'No need to get on your moral high horse; I'm doing this for Bernard. It will be all the same whether you witness it or not. All I'm doing is what we've been doing for ages, plus using my Uher. Recording normality; us anthropologists do it all the time. All this work on *my* part is to get that manuscript *you* think Chin's hiding in his house. Better Agnes gets it for us than we smash our way through her house looking for it – which is *your* super plan.

You can at least be a bit useful and take Barnaby for a walk for half an hour; I don't want her scratching at the bedroom door throughout my farewell performance.' And that's what I do. I take Barnaby to sit on the Guild veranda.

At 5.30 precisely, the lithe legs of Agnes Chin resolutely jog past the veranda. Good firm strides that advance her directly into the center of a despicable plot about which I can pretend I have no part. I blame K for what happens.

*   *   *

Half an hour later, she jogs back, red and furious. She doesn't glance in my direction but turns straight into her garden. I wait another 10 minutes just in case K's plan has worked and she reappears carrying the manuscript, but she doesn't and I return to the flat; K has showered and is sitting drinking my beer on the back room bed. The wardrobe doors are open and the two large spools of the Uher beckon. 'Well…?' I ask.

'Well! I'm just about to listen to what we got. You're welcome to join me – unless it would offend your high moral principles, of course.'

'Okay, let's hear it,' I say. After all, the dastardly deed can't be undone and, let's face it, I am curious.

'Better get yourself a beer. I'm not stopping the machine and it's an all-action show.' I do and sit beside him on the bed. K pushes play.

I hear Agnes pant into the bedroom. Hot and sweaty, as K would say, 'gagging for it'. She turns the fan on full. I hear the wardrobe door flicker on its hinges and am glad I'm not inside witnessing Agnes strip to reveal the neat, firm and powerful body I so often imagine.

'I've missed you terribly,' Agnes moans.

'Ha ha ha, I bet you did.' K's laugh makes the needle on the Uher jump. 'Then it's a double package for you today. And as a treat, you can choose both of them.'

'Oh, Percy, you naughty boy. I'm going to punish you for going away and leaving me. Do it again and I'll bite you right off and gobble you up.' Percy? I might learn more about K from this recording than I will about the manuscript.

'Well, what's on today's menu?' K asks. Neither of them seems interested in old-fashioned foreplay. Theirs is scheduled adultery. Each has a spouse and dinner waiting at home.

'Sixty-niner and doggie.' Agnes orders rapidly, like a businesswoman who must have lunch but does not have time to consider the menu.

A long silence. So much for the chance of letting confidences slip; both mouths must be full. The needle on the recorder registers only the constant revolutions of the overhead fan. Five minutes in and I'm pouring myself another beer when Agnes must have let Percy slip. I hear her squealing, leading up to a piercing scream that sends the Uher needle flying to the top of its scale. Well, I think, thank god that's all over. Far from gushing confidences, Agnes spoke no words at all. 'Just wait a bit,' K reassures me.

I hear Agnes drink water like a horse filling up between gallops. She speaks as I have never heard her – the tone of a commanding foreman ordering a navvy to reposition the pile-driver. 'Now, stoke my fire. Quick. Woof, woof.' Woof, woof?

With her mouth free, Agnes is no more spontaneously informative than with it full. 'Don't stop,' seems to be the limit of her coital vocabulary. 'Faster.' I begin to think we might have got more out of her by kidnapping and ransoming her favourite orchid, the pathetic survivor that Bernard gave her. Why is Bernard suddenly in my mind? Did his afternoon rests include the occasional tryst with Agnes? No, he must be back because he's disturbed at what's happening.

'Agnes, what are you going to do when I'm gone? Be a bit frustrating, no?'

'Talk after,' gasps Agnes. 'Don't stop.'

'With me gone, your love life will be over. You know that, don't you? Is that why Harry's kicking me out?'

Groan. 'No.' Groan. 'He just hates you.' Groan. Well, Agnes tells the truth there. A long pause presumably filled with action I don't want to imagine.

'Now he's acting dean he thinks he's God. Can't we pull him down a bit?'

'Damn it. Keep moving.'

More pauses broken only by Agnes's cries of *faster*. 'Talk now, Agnes. How can we bring Chin down and keep me in a job?'

'You mean – gasp – groan – lose the dean position?'

'Would it kill Harry not to get it?'

Groan. 'Fuck him.' Gasp. 'It would bring *me* down ...' Groan. 'I'd be just another ... university wife.'

'Is that so bad?'

'Ask your wife!'

Reference to K's wife is the spur K needs. I can almost see his sneer. 'Better than a charge of murder, no?'

'Murder?' Agnes gasps the word.

'Wong's been confiding in Haddock. The two of them are great buddies. It seems you – you not Harry – asked Ra'mad for poison. The poison that killed Bernard.'

'Old news. Sedative for cats. That's all.'

'Chin says you never gave any to the cats.' Pause. 'Harry says *you* baked the pie and gave it to Bernard. Harry says *you* went out for half an hour before 10 o'clock.'

'Bollocks! Wong would never tell Tom.'

According to his theory, K has to break Agnes' power to lie rationally by banging her up as close as possible to the heights of climax without quite ringing the bell. His words become as hard as the treatment he's giving Agnes. 'You'd better believe it! Chin wants to get rid of both of us.'

'Harry won't damn himself. He knows … I won't sit quiet … if things come out.'

'If what comes out? That you and Chin *both* drugged Bernard and hanged him on the fan?'

'I did not hang him … I wanted to call an ambulance.'

It sounds like K is working hard. The momentum must have been broken and he has to get it back. In spite of the noisy fan on full over his head, I can hear him snort – I can picture the sweat running down his face. He must be giving the show of a lifetime. Sitting beside me he is clearly pleased with his own performance. But Agnes has admitted nothing other than wanting to call an ambulance – and I'm glad.

'Save yourself, Agnes. Scarper back to your folks in Ipoh.'

'There's no evidence.' Agnes hits the nail on the head.

'There *is* evidence,' K sounds brutal.

'Don't stop. Faster. Harder.'

K's words are laboured but clear. 'You bake pie. Put in drug. Give Bernard. You. True or no?'

'Yes! No. Yes.'

'True or no? You baked the pie. Chin stole the manuscript.'

241

'Yes! Yes!'

'Chin made you bake it?'

'Yes! Don't stop. Oh my god, yes!' A long scream drives the Uher needle beating against maximum. The groans subside, the Uher needle retreats.

K stands and takes a bow.

Another pause in which Agnes must be dressing. Then I hear the wardrobe door open and K speak. 'It's all there, all recorded. The confessions of an acting dean's wife. I can give the tape to the police or to your husband or maybe broadcast it though the Guild House speaker or I can give it to you. What would you prefer, Agnes dear?'

'Bastard,' yells Agnes. The sound of scuffling. Agnes grabbing for the tape spools. Sounds as if they are fighting.

Apology is clearly not in K's deck of cards. It sounds like he is restraining Agnes by force. 'Agnes, we do not *want* to use this tape *but we will if we have to.*' I wish he had not used *we*. 'There is no reason at all to think *you* killed Bernard. All you did was bake a pie. If Bernard died by pie, there is no reason you should hang for it or spend the rest of your life in Changi Prison. You get the tape and our lips are sealed. All you have to do is give me the manuscript that Harry stole from Bernard. Chin can be dean if that's what you want. He can even go ahead and publish his book. For you, nothing need change – not even our afternoon meetings. With the manuscript, I'll confront Chin and get my contract renewed. That's all that's important. I'm offering you a deal: the manuscript for our silence. Now, I'm going to let you go.' K remains calm. Agnes must be sitting quietly on the bed as K continues. 'As I was saying, Agnes, you give us the manuscript, we give you the tape. Simple as that.'

Agnes speaks with surprising composure. 'That tape would not be acceptable in court. But it would ruin my reputation. It would also ruin *your* reputation. What about your life and your wife?'

'My wife has no grand ambitions. She's happy as a *university wife* as you say. She will forgive a man's transgressions. More important for her is to have a home and for me to have a job; she's giving birth soon. I've been at Singapore University for six years: I should be getting tenure, for Christ's sake. Getting the sack instead will not help my reputation. Just jog off home, stuff the manuscript in your shorts and get it back here. Five minutes and it's all over.'

'I'd give you that damned manuscript. But I don't know where it is.'

'Look for it when Chin's out of the house.'

'Harry won't leave it lying around. Anyway, there are piles of papers in his study, I wouldn't know it if I saw it.'

'Can you let us into the house when Chin's away? Haddock would recognise the manuscript sure enough.'

'It would do no good. Harry would have hidden it well and his maid will be onto you in a shot. She never leaves the house. She's Harry's maid, nothing to do with me and she doesn't like me.'

'Okay, Agnes. We need a rethink on this one. I hope we don't have to ask Chin to make the exchange. I hope we can spare you that. But if the manuscript gets destroyed, you can be sure we will be inviting Superintendent Wong to listen to the tape. So, not a word to Chin and no tricks.'

K opens another beer as if we are celebrating. I don't see that anything has been achieved. And there will now be no more ice cream with Agnes.

'So, having failed to get the manuscript the easy way,' I say, 'we go ahead with plan B?'

'No choice, Haddock. But one change. Agnes is now warned and who knows what she'll do. It has to be tonight. Off you go to the Guild and phone Venus and David. The caper's on.'

25

Men in Stockings

DAVID IS INTO stockings but K prefers balaclava helmets. He insists balaclavas are more professional. Toshi asks what a balaclava is. 'Ninjas wear them,' David tells him. This exciting news inspires Tosh to venture a rare opinion and say David will look nicer in a stocking and K in a balaclava; very diplomatic.

'The question,' K states authoritatively as leader of *the caper*, on the basis we are in his house and in his junk room, 'is not how nice we look but how functional the alternatives are.'

'Well, if it's a question and not a royal decree,' says David, speaking confidently on the topic of men in stockings, 'stockings are better in the tropics than balaclavas. Bleeding obvious. You'd sweat to death in a wooly helmet. Really, K, when was the last time you saw anybody wearing a balaclava?'

'This morning – as it happens,' K sneers. 'A line of chaps swinging their arms around like windmill sails with sickles on the end of long sticks, cutting the university grass. Balaclavas keep out the sun and soak up the sweat. So, quite appropriate for the tropics – as it happens. When was the last time you saw a line of chaps in stockings?'

David responds by mimicking K's sneer. 'Early this morning – as it happens.'

'The difference, David, is the men I saw wore balaclavas on their *heads*.'

I intervene to get down to the crime at hand. 'I'm sure you each have experience of stockings in your own way and I doubt either of you has experience of balaclavas. I also doubt we have any balaclavas. If we don't, this discussion seems pitifully academic.'

K curls his lips. 'And what's wrong with academics having an academic discussion? Don't say you've joined the anti-academic academics?'

'Any moment now Venus will call us with the signal. Then we've got to move fast. So, do you or do you not have any bala-clavas?' K and David look at me as if I am constantly out to turn life into something less than a game.

'So, stocking-tops it is,' says David triumphant. 'If we have any, of course.'

And, of course, we don't. The closest K comes up with is his long-suffering wife's only pair of tights, worn once. He cuts off the feet with scissors. David and K get a foot each; the toes stick up like a cock's crest on the top of their heads. I get an open-ended thigh. Toshi gets nothing on the grounds he'll be outside keeping watch and should not look more suspicious than he normally does. He looks confused but does not seem too disappointed.

With stockings rolled down we look at each other. I complain about getting the thigh and K rebukes me. 'When a chap invites you to get inside his wife's thighs, it's not done to complain, old man. Anyway, thigh suits you. You look like a melon with a crêpe cushion cover in the supermarket.'

Looking in a mirror, I would not like to turn a dark corner

and bump into any of us. Even David looks like a stop-at-nothing thug. Barnaby growls. 'There you are,' K says, 'even Barnaby can't recognise us.'

'Gawd, even me Mum won't know me,' agrees David and no more is said about balaclava helmets like what ninjas wear. We roll the stockings up onto foreheads as crooks do in movies and Barns calms down.

K reveals his apprentice burglar's tool kit: a six-inch cold chisel, a sledge hammer, a torch with fading batteries and an old Swiss Army knife with compass. K's plan for getting in is brilliant in its simplicity. He will smash open the door.

'What about gloves?' David suggests. 'So's we don't leave fingerprints.'

'Good point,' K acknowledges and holds up a pair of wicket keeper's gloves with the flexibility of a Singapore judge pronouncing a death sentence. He looks at them respectfully but declares them out of play. An island on the equator is not the place to hoard gloves.

'What about condoms?' suggests David.

'David,' K says in avuncular tones. 'The problem reposes on the finger not the dong. Mankind, even yours truly, has yet to perfect the art of swinging sledge hammers using only the male member.'

'K, you don't need the sledge hammer,' jokes David.

'Well, it might have opened a few doors in its time but never by force.'

There being no time to dash off to Fitzpatrick's for latex gloves or finger-size condoms, we decide it is enough to go equipped with a K neckerchief to wipe anything that has to be touched and might retain a print. K disappears for a few minutes to select from his stock. These he ties onto our wrists. Toshi will not enter the scene of the crime and will not therefore be dabbing his prints about. He stands awkwardly kerchief-less, disappointment on his face. We are beginning to understand the sensitivities of David's Japanese appendage. Toshi doesn't mind about the stockings but feels left out over the kerchiefs. K generously ties a rather spiffy one onto Toshi's wrist and his face brightens.

The acceptance of K's prized bandanas, the anthropologists among us are well aware, marks acceptance of K's symbolic leadership of the tribe. However, when K suggests locking up Barns on the grounds she might make a noise if Chin's cats come into view, I concede the possibility but insist Barnaby be with us. If anybody can sniff out Bernard's manuscript, it's Barnaby.

K drops the tools in a black bag and we repair to the sitting room and its dress mirror, stockings on heads and kerchiefs on wrists. 'Oh me gawd,' David exclaims. 'The Neckerchief Gang. We look like blooming Morris dancers. Got any bells, K?'

K's wife, who melts away when visitors call, waddles in looking as if she is about to give birth but won't do so just yet as she doesn't want to be a nuisance. She doesn't blink at the stockings on our heads and the kerchiefs on our wrists. K's Drama Society exploits have granted her immunity. 'There's a lady on our telephone who won't give her name but wants to speak to you. Says it's urgent.' The resignation in her voice suggests this is not the first time she has carried similar messages to her wayward husband. We crowd the earpiece.

'The celebrity couple has arrived.' Venus speaks.

'Roger, over and out,' says K and hangs up.

And off we go to the scene of the crime-to-be.

26

The Caper

'A SINGLE BLOW, like a single gunshot, will be impossible for any listener to locate.' K informs us as we huddle in coven outside Chin's back door. Not that there are any listeners. It would take a lot more than a bang to disturb the chattering Tamils in the serious drinking room at Guild House. The quarters of Chin's maid are nicely distant from Chin's house and no light shines from her window. All is deadly quiet.

K raises his arms to strike at the lock and freezes, hammer high, like a proletarian statue on a Soviet traffic circle. Loud and clear, a wench wails the first lines of a Chinese song about unrequited love. Poor peasant girl deceived by glib talker. Can't be Agnes bemoaning K's treatment of her, Venus had insisted she accompany her husband to the recording studios of the Singapore Broadcasting Corporation, leaving the house empty and waiting for a cool, clean break and enter ... at least, that's the plan.

I tiptoe around the corner of the house towards the lamenting. A light in the bathroom. I look through window bars that protect Chin from people like us and see a young girl under the shower. Very svelte. K is quickly by my side and raises eyebrows in appreciation. The girl turns towards us, curls long hair up on top of her head, allowing water to splash onto her face and into her open mouth before dribbling down her neck to drip from tiny nipples. Chin's maid is taking advantage of her mistress's absence to soap and perfume herself like the lady of the house. We withdraw into the darkness.

'I see now where Chin gets his jollies,' K breathes into my ear. 'This means mission aborted. If we smash our way in, she'll scream the place down.' We return to the back door where David and Toshi and Barnaby are waiting. 'It's off,' K says simply, 'the maid's in the bathroom.'

Barnaby, one of the very few beings who could give K lessons in obstinacy, does not give up easily. She has her nose stuck into the cat-flap and is snorting the Chin air. 'Good try Barns, but I'm afraid what's big enough for your snout is too small for the rest of you, no matter how you try.' K's voice holds the bitter disappointment we all feel.

'What we need is a cat burglar.' David makes an attempt at humour in the face of adversity – what the British like to think of as their innate ability to rise above the dumps and the rest of the world considers evidence of genetic deficiency.

'We steal cat?' asks Toshi, logic straining at the leash.

K is as reluctant to leave as Barnaby. He shines the torch into the door lock then down at the cat flap. 'There's a key in the lock, all we've got to do is turn it from the inside. Who has a long enough, thin enough arm ...?'

We all look at David. The longest, thinnest arm in Singapore.

David gets down to cat-on-ground level and inserts his arm through the cat flap. Toshi is sent around to look at the girl and warn us if she starts to leave the bathroom. David's head is pressed against the door's foot. 'Another inch, that's all I need, just another inch and I'll be there.'

'That's what they all say, David. Not your fault. Stop straining, you'll not make it an inch longer by straining.'

David yelps and whips out his arm as if it has been scratched
by the devil, which in a manner of speaking it has. Chin's Sia-
mese tom flies out, setting the flap bouncing on its springs.
Barns pounces and sinks her teeth into that wretched foreign
tail. The cat screams, turns, spits, slashes at Barns' snout and
flies off into the darkness. Barns lets it go, chuckling to herself.
First blood to Chin's cat, second to our dog. The humans have
yet to score.

Four nasty trails of oozing red mark the place on David's
arm where a bicep might have been had the arm not been
David's. K shines the torch on the wound and makes a sucking
noise between his teeth. I think for a moment he is going to
kiss it better. Even in the dark, I can sense David's shame. He
let us down by not having an arm one inch longer. We all feel
annoyed. Not with David. Not with the maid. Just with our
rotten luck. The British spirit is foundering and Japanese inge-
nuity is busy looking at a little girl's tits and perhaps wondering
why they don't turn him on. In frustration, K rattles and curses
the handle. The door swings open.

'It was open all the time,' our leader states as if David
and I are cretins. Masks down we creep in. 'We go room by
room,' K instructs. 'Study first, then bedrooms, then living
room and kitchen. Stay together in one room. If the girl
comes out, she might leave by the back door without noticing us. She'll deadlock the door after her and we'll have to
smash our way out. That's why I brought the hammer.'
We roll the stockings, already uncomfortably hot and
sticky, up onto our foreheads. By torchlight I can see the

excitement in the eyes of my comrades. I feel it too. The caper is on.

While it spurs the adrenaline, fading torchlight is not the best way to search a littered study for a manuscript; it would take a week to go through the mounds of papers that lie in tied-up bundles around the room, reminding me of Tambiah's Chambers. The windows are shuttered; K turns on the light.

I can hear singing and running water from the bathroom; the girl seems set for a deep clean. If Toshi's not enjoying the view, at least it might help him out of the closet. Precisely how he is to warn us if the girl looks about to leave has been left to Japanese resource. We keep ears open for an unknown warning signal. K fiddles with his Swiss army knife in the locks of Chin's desk drawers. 'The bugger's locked every one of them,' he whispers. 'Must be more paranoid than I thought.' Light sledge-hammer taps on a cold chisel are enough to destroy the mahogany veneer forever and reveal the contents of each drawer to be nothing worth locking up. While K and David use a similar approach on the cupboards, I go quickly through the bundles of what turn out to be exam papers. It's the work of minutes to see Chin has not slipped Bernard's fat manuscript into the neatly-tied piles of thin scripts.

'Nothing here,' K decides. 'To the bedrooms.'

Barnaby is before us, her nose into a basket of dirty washing. 'Not much to interest you there, Barns. Unless you're a more perverted dog than I thought.' K lifts up a pair of knickers and curls his lips. 'I remember these. Yellow with little red hearts.' David tut-tuts that we are not here to sniff the underwear.

The bedrooms yield nothing. We leave behind a trail of broken locks on our way to the heart of the house, the most vulnerable point in the topography of larceny, a large living room with doors all round. If the girl leaves the bathroom, she cannot help but see us.

The living room cupboards are not locked. David looks behind a picture of the Great Wall of China and discovers a family of cockroaches. K scatters piles of magazines from the coffee table. I look under the Persian carpet and feel the lining of the curtains. Nothing. The telephone rings twice. The singing stops. The telephone stops. The singing starts again. The telephone rings again. The bathroom door opens.

K nips off the light. We all run into the kitchen, pull down our stockings and look out from the darkness. The girl trips over K's black-bag burglar's kit in her haste to pick up the phone. It's Venus: two rings, hang up, ring again; Chin has left the studios. Wrapped in a towel, the girl says 'Hello' into the receiver then drops it back in place. That she does not notice the vandalism is almost unbelievable. She steps over the black bag without giving it a glance and returns to the bathroom leaving the light on. I am holding the snout of quivering Barnaby. From a distant darkness we can hear a Japanese accent call, 'Rook out. Girl come. Rook out.'

K the gang leader looks resigned. 'We've found nothing and Chin's on the way. Time we're off.'

We retreat towards the back door. 'Come on Barns,' I sigh. Barnaby is whining beneath a table set against the wall and covered with a table cloth that reaches to the ground. I look underneath. 'Nothing here but the smell of cats. Come on, Barns.' I drag her out by the hind legs. She digs her claws into the wooden floor and leaves little tracks to mark her unwilling departure. 'Not now, Barns, for Christ's sake. For once be a good dog.'

Barnaby is not known to respond to entreaties to be a good dog. She breaks free and disappears completely under the table. 'Leave her,' says our leader.

'Fine. I might as well leave a calling card and a signed confession.' I pull the table away from the wall to get at Barns. At this stage, I am not beyond a little corporal punishment in the recipient's best interests; after all, this is Singapore.

K is opening the backdoor when I stop him. 'Look. K. David. Look.'

K gapes inside his stocking. Words elude this minor thespian of the Singapore stage. David stands in for him. 'A safe. Who would have thought of a safe?'

K lifts his stocking onto the forehead, a signal for us all to follow suit, and finds his voice. 'Obviously not you, Nincompoop. A nice discovery that does us no good at all since we left the gelignite behind.'

'What we need is a safe cracker,' David says.

'No doubt,' breaths K. 'I regret the subject was not covered at Oxford. Did either of you pick up the art at your red-brick universities?'

Ignoring K's pinprick sarcasm, David asks, 'How thick is the wall?'

'Not as thick as your head,' K rejoins.

'David's got a point,' I reason. 'Either the safe is a very thin one or it sticks out the other side.'

'I can't see what difference it makes, since we can't open it anyway,' K grumbles. 'But if it's going to make you happy, go back into Chin's study and look at the thing's backside. But hurry it.'

Barnaby hurries it. A leg-splaying run into the study, a

scamper through the exam papers and a skidding charge at a corner table. She sinks her teeth into a long cloth that covers a small table and snaps her head to one side. I catch a crystal vase of plastic flowers just before it hits the ground. A cat runs out. Barnaby ignores it. The corner table stands naked, and it's not a corner table anymore. It's the backside of the safe.

David runs his long, thin fingers along the welded edge of the safe and immediately wipes away his prints with K's kerchief. 'These seams aren't all that strong,' he states as if he knows what he's talking about. 'They are supposed to be encased in cement, not just sticking out naked from the wall and covered with a table cloth.'

'Now how, I wonder, did you come by that information?' K leers. 'Don't bother to answer unless you can open those flimsy seams with a Swiss army knife. Now let's get out of here while we still can.'

'I saw it in a James Bond movie. You cover the safe with a silk bedspread and chisel away at the seam.'

'A *silk* bedspread? Thai silk or Chinese? Any particular motif?' K's sarcasm is never subtle.

'There's a silk bedspread on Chin's bed,' I say. 'A nice heron motif for long life, luck and happy nesting.'

'Happy nesting, eh? Doesn't seem to have worked, ha ha.'

'Come on K,' David appeals. 'Why not give it a try?'

'I'd happily give anything a try. Well, almost anything. But we don't have time to lark around with silk bedspread magic tricks.'

'It won't take long,' David whines.

'How long?' asks K, resolve on the wane.

'Only two minutes.'

'Two minutes?' K repeats in disbelief.

'In the movie…' David explains.

I fetch the bedspread, fold the herons several times and lay the pretty padding on the safe's seam. In David's movie it no doubt deadened the noise of a safe being smashed open. K stands sledge in hands.

A car's headlights flash on the shutters. A car's engine approaches, slows and goes past. 'Okay, it's Venus in the Starlet.' I say. 'Chin can't be far behind, so let's get on with it.'

David has the six-inch chisel in place on the welded seam of the safe, his long fingers clutch the cold steel lovingly. 'Right,' he says, 'when I nod my head, you hit it.'

'A blow for Bernard's revenge,' K sings out dramatically and much too loudly as he swings the hammer to connect precisely with the head of the chisel. The chisel slices nicely through the layers of silk herons and bounces off the safe. David holds onto it bravely; I feel his fingers stinging. A resounding clang echoes through the house and the bathroom door opens.

'Is anybody there?' the maid calls out in Mandarin. I hold Barnaby's snout tightly closed to silence the reply I can feel swelling in her throat.

'Stockings down,' whispers K and we dutifully roll down our foot and thigh.

The girl continues to call out. I can't make out what she says. From outside comes a dolorous, 'Rook out'. The door opens and the girl comes two steps into the study.

The sight of three masked men and a dog take an eternity to register. The girl blinks. We all look at her as she looks at us: stupidly. In baggy Chinese pyjamas, her hair wet and long, she looks little more than a child. Barnaby, fortunately, has her wits about her and lunges. The girl screams and turns to run.

The full force of an overweight Barnaby bowls Chin's maid across the room. I wince as the girl's face strikes the door with her cute little snub nose, causing her only means of escape to slam shut. She turns her eyes from the barred fangs and presses herself against the door as flat as she can, which is very flat indeed.

David throws a string of deep-gutter Hokkien obscenities at the poor girl. I have no idea where he gets such words. I don't understand them and I doubt the girl does but the tone alone threatens a multitude of very nasty things if she doesn't shut her mouth and keep it shut.

'Was there a Chinese maid in your movie?' K asks David.

'No, just some massive Japanese butler with a killer bowler hat who smashes his way through the wall.'

'Can't quite see Tosh in that role,' quips K, preparing to strike his second blow for Bernard's revenge.

The need for stealth has gone. The silk bedspread is cast aside and K strikes with the full force of his considerable muscle. David winces but holds onto the chisel. The risk of an irreparably broken hand mixes with the smell of masculine sweat and the danger he shares with his hero. David is visibly more excited with every swing that K makes; I swear he's enjoying it.

'Let's hope there's something in this fucking thing,' K gasps between blows.

Worn over the face, nylon feet and thigh get indescribably sweaty in the tropics, unlike balaclava helmets. The sweat pools and dribbles where it can. My eyes are stinging. The chisel head and David's hand are a blur to me. By luck or judgment, K

257

distinguishes them and strikes with force, blow upon blow until a crack opens along the seam. And David the nincompoop drops the chisel into the crack and sucks his fingers.

'Jemmy! I need a jemmy,' K calls over his shoulder like a surgeon asking for a scalpel. He is now fanatically involved; the safe is a challenge to him and K would see us all in Changi Prison before he gives up.

'Jemmy?' I query, being unfamiliar with larcenist jargon. 'Can't you wait until we get home?'

'Jemmy! Not jimmy! I could have an effing jimmy right here and nobody would notice. I need a lever. A crowbar.' K is yelling. How am I supposed to know what a jemmy is? If he wants a crowbar, why not say so? Anyway, the chances of finding a crowbar in Chin's study are as likely as finding a good book.

'The golf clubs,' K cries in exasperation. 'In the corner, dumbo.'

A gleaming new set of golf clubs. Virgin heads sealed in moulded plastic, unkissed by any ball, untested on any green. They stand hugging each other like a group of pretty monarchists awaiting their turn at the guillotine, their heads poking proudly up from a tumbrel propped in the corner near the door beside the petrified maid. They are about to do a far, far better thing than they ever might have done in the hands of Harry Chin.

The girl shudders as I reach around her to select a putter. Battered to Death by a Golf Club – the headlines of fear in her young eyes. I'd feel sorry for her but don't have time.

K grabs the putter from my hand, inserts the head into the cracked seam and puts his weight on the handle. The head snaps off as easily as an Indian matchstick and clangs onto the chisel inside the safe. Another. It too is cleanly decapitated. Made in China. The third one puts up more resistance. Both K and David jump on it. The crack in the seam of the safe widens a bit before the shaft slowly bends. I am ready with the fourth. This one also bends, but in bending opens the gap wide enough for David to get his skinny arm into the back of the safe. The girl begins to sob uncontrollably. Barnaby stops growling and licks her hand. The girl shrieks.

'Keep the wench quiet,' K yells. 'Sing to her or something'.

'Sing?'

'Sing!' yells K.

David's lean hand pulls out a bundle of money. He tosses it to me and I hold it out to the girl, hoping the sight of loot will calm her down. She turns, looks up at my masked face and begins to beg for mercy, terror in her eyes. Silly kid. I am holding out to her more money than she might ever see in her life. Well, want it or not, she's going to get it. As her tears flow I reach for her pyjama top and drop the money into her slight cleavage. Her body is fear-rigid. I try to make a reassuring don't-worry-everything-will-be-all-right type smile, although it probably doesn't come through the stocking the way it leaves my lips. She shudders again. Lucky I didn't sing to her.

Barnaby bounds across the room as David's hand pulls out the manuscript. She looks about to eat it in her attempt to get to Bernard. 'This it?' K asks me. I nod. K throws the prize into the black bag along with the sledge hammer and orders an immediate retreat.

'Just a minute,' says David, pulling out a cloth-wrapped bundle; he drops it in the bag.

Three sweaty masked men and a hound coming towards her

to get at the door is the last straw for the girl. She screams hysterically; worse than Agnes. K brushes her from the door. He hands me the black bag and remains those vital seconds to take the key from inside the back door and lock it from the outside, delaying pursuit or entry and totally confusing detective Madhu as to how the villains entered and left with all windows shuttered and all doors dead-locked.

Repeated screams pierce the night. As I leave Chin's house and run along the dark back path, I see the Guild House lawyers spilling drunkenly onto the road to save a maiden in distress. Shadowy figures are pounding at Chin's front door and landing karate kicks at the louvred shutters. For the second time, Madhu will find himself first at the scene of the crime.

*   *   *

Venus is waiting in the flat as we troop silently in through the kitchen and turn off the kitchen light. 'Out of those clothes and under the shower,' she orders. I tuck the manuscript among some large-size volumes on my bookcase, where it looks happily at home. The girl's still screaming. If she was frightened by us, she'll be terrified when a dozen drunken Tamils led by Madhu smash into the house to rescue her.

K showers first while David looks on, ignoring K's advice to paint his scratches with iodine. Then I shower, while David looks on. Then David showers while K goes to select the least unacceptable items of my limited wardrobe and I go to rejoin Venus.

Only when we are all sitting around the whisky bottle and ice bucket and Venus has taken the black bag, sweaty clothes and nylon masks and dumped everything into a bath full of soapy water, does anybody think to ask what's become of Toshi. He never entered Chin's house and he must have had the sense to clear out at the sound of trouble. Should we include him in our alibi? We decide that unless he shows up, we haven't seen him.

Ra'mad pokes his head around the front door, which I have for the first time since the super's warning deliberately left open. 'There's an awful racket coming from Chin's place. Can't you hear the screaming?'

K replies cordially. 'Afraid we've been too engrossed in a discussion of Nietzsche. Now you mention it, yes, there does seem to be something going on down at the *acting dean*'s. What's Chin up to now? Torturing a student, I suppose. Anyway, none of our business, is it? Would you like to join us, Ra'mad? Orange juice, perhaps?'

'No, thank you all the same. I think I'll just pop along and see what it's all about. Never know like, I might be able to help. Sounds like somebody needs a sedative.'

When Ra'mad has gone to dispense sedatives, K raises his glass. 'Here's to the successful caper of the Neckerchief Gang and the release of the manuscript from false imprisonment.'

'Oh, blimey,' says David, glass frozen at his lips. 'I've just remembered. The chisel's still there in the bleedin' safe. It's covered in my prints.'

27

Three Men and a Dog

'MADHU. GREAT TO see you. Get in here and grab a glass.'
Madhu smiles like a little boy who finds himself wanted rather
than simply tolerated. K draws him into our circle.

Barnaby is pushed off her armchair and the cushion turned.
Madhu is centre stage. 'There's trouble at Chin's. The super said
to ask if you noticed anything out of the ordinary and …'

'Check our alibis?' K completes Madhu's sentence.

'… look around the flat to see if anything looks odd. But I
suppose there's no harm checking alibis while I'm here.'

'We've all been here together,' K begins. Madhu takes
out a notebook and pencil from his tote bag, leaving it open
and empty.

'Where's your gun, Madhu?' I ask.

'The super suggested I leave it at home when not on duty.'

'So, you're not on duty now?' K plops in.

'Well, yes and no. I am on duty *now* but I wasn't on duty
then.'

'When's *then*?' K's easy nothing-to-hide banter suggests a
confidence I do not share. Surely the maid recognised Barnaby
– who was not wearing a stocking – and there's that damning
chisel covered with fingerprints. Everybody on campus was fingerprinted after Bernard's death – how long will it take to link

262

the chisel to David?

'*Then* is when I left home and in the Guild House bar. I came on duty when a crime occurred.'

'An automatic cop. Turns on when crime occurs. I like it. Should save the taxpayer money.' K never takes his ex-student very seriously. 'What's the problem this time? Chin strung himself up from a chandelier in a look-alike suicide? Or something serious?'

Madhu's dusky face creases up. He's obviously had a few already and the large whisky K pours him should maintain his good humour. 'Nothing like that. There's a team at Chin's house now going through things but it seems clear enough it was a simple robbery. Three men got in and attacked the safe. They stole a lot of money. They also tried to rape the maid but her screaming alerted us at Guild House and we scared them off.'

'You saw them, then?' David enquires with an edge of nervousness to his voice.

'No, they went out the back way, the maid said. They must have passed your flat. Did you see anything?'

'What do they look like?' I questioned in reply.

'Three men and a dog. Hey, you're three men and a dog. Lucky you don't look anything like the girl's description. She says all three were massive great Sikhs who wore turbans and beards and spoke their strange language – she heard a couple of them say *Sing* – and the dog was a male bloodhound with a big red dick. That lets you out as suspects, but a trio of club-wielding Sikhs and a randy bloodhound should be recognisable. Can't imagine them getting far.'

David laughs. 'Sounds like a traveling circus…'

K interrupts David, 'It's pretty hard to mistake a Sikh. You

263

can rest assured we would have noticed three of them. And probably Barnaby would have lifted her head if a horny bloodhound passed within a hundred metres. She's neutered but has a good memory.'

'Right. And you've been here all evening? Nobody go out for a time?'

'Sitting right here, Madhu,' K continues. 'Discussing Nietzsche and whether Singapore might best be typified as one of Nietzsche's caves where the shadow of a dead God might still be seen or as the cradle of the new Ubermenschen.'

'How do you spell that?' asks Madhu, pencil at paper.

'U-b-e ...'

'No, the other thing.'

'Nietzsche?' K spells it and Madhu writes the strange name down.

'You noticed nothing odd. Sat here talking about ... God and Singapore. And nothing unusual in the flat?'

'You'd best look for yourself, Madhu,' I invite him. 'If there are three rampant Sikhs hiding under my bed with their bloodhound, I'd rather you find them than me.'

Madhu strolls into the kitchen as coolly as possible. I follow. 'If I were you, I'd lock that back door.' Madhu is not me, but I lock it and he seems pleased. We pass into the back bedroom which saw so much activity earlier and Madhu looks under the bed and into the wardrobe. 'Hello! A Uher. Haven't seen one of those for years.'

Madhu opens the bathroom door and pokes his head inside. Venus screams beautifully. 'It's all right,' I say reassuringly, 'just Madhu looking around. There's been a burglary at Chin's.'

'Please excuse me, Mrs Goh. I had no idea anybody was here.' Madhu averts his gaze but lets it linger on the mirror's reflected image of Venus up to her neck in suds.

'I'll get dressed and be right out,' Venus says pleasantly.

Madhu pronounces the house 'clean' – quite a stretch of imagination given my failure to replace Norsiah – and returns to his topped-up whisky.

Venus trips in wearing my best sarong tucked in above the left breast, Malay-style, her hair twisted up and held in place by a single chopstick. She sits with legs to one side, as cool, prim and proper as any married woman can be on emerging from her presumed lover's bath to face the police. She smiles so charmingly at Madhu he blushes. 'Been a break-in at Chin's,' he summarises.

'That explains the screams earlier,' Venus says as if that's okay then. 'But how terrible for them. I'd just been with them at the studio recording an interview. Doctor Chin's book about Singapore University will be officially launched this Saturday. We'll show the launch live along with a recorded interview with Chin and his wife Agnes. Anyway, notice was short and we could only fit in this evening. I don't see how the thieves could have known the Chins were away – unless their maid told them. I only called about 7.00 tonight and Chin came immediately. After the recording, I dropped by here.'

'And everybody was here, Mrs Goh?'

'Oh yes, even Barnaby. Just as they are now.'

Madhu thanks me for the whisky and returns to the scene of the crime. With Madhu gone, the flat secure and the kitchen light turned off, I bring out Bernard's manuscript and place it side by side with my advance copy of Chin's version on the dining table. 'Now let's see the difference between the master and the thief.'

Chin greatly assists our review. He'd left in place paper clips on those pages edited. We crowd over the manuscript as K turns the pages. It's like one of those games where you spot the differences between two pictures that on first glance look the same. The changes are easy to spot.

Bernard had gone into the Japanese occupation period in depth, naming all collaborators who had anything to do with the university. Some names are very familiar. Ra'mad is not given much space but is described as 'a brilliant young chemist who left a Welsh wife in the United Kingdom when he returned from exile to become a member of KRIS, a pro-Japanese anti-British movement that envisaged a Greater Malaya stretching from Thailand across Borneo and encompassing all the Indonesian and colonial islands as far south as Australia. Bernard's handwriting is clearly visible in the margin. He had noted, 'cut reference to Welsh wife, keep KRIS'.

'Why cut out the bit about a wife in Wales?' David asks.

'She was a wife but not Ra'mad's wife,' I explain. 'Bernard had not written to hurt unnecessarily; he intended to demonstrate the different types of nationalism that existed. Rather than write in the abstract, Bernard personified the political and racial currents. Chin's father is in the text as a supporter of Chinese nationalism.'

'You're explaining Bernard's self-editing,' K steps in. 'But how do you explain Chin's? Why would Chin have cut out anything about Ra'mad? Chin and Ra'mad are hardly mates. Past membership of KRIS and dallies with somebody's Welsh wife won't send Ra'mad to the gallows but it could shadow the last years of his career – some say KRIS gave information to the Japanese that led to the deaths of many Chinese. Chin's version names no collaborators.'

'Perhaps Chin got things cleared through security. Security might avoid discussion of race. The debate on a quota of places for Malays at Singapore University takes up twenty pages in Bernard's manuscript and is reduced to a two-line statement in Chin's book. Perhaps Internal Security had a hand in editing. What's more, the editing's in good English, which suggests Chin didn't make all the changes.'

The university's past involvement in anti-communist research, detailed by Bernard, is sliced out of the Chin version, as is any opposition to moving the university away from town. Bernard had set out the arguments for movement as well as the reasons for remaining. The decision to move is presented in the Chin version as beyond controversy.

Hardly a hint of nostalgia is to be found in the Chin copy, from which K reads the conclusion out loud. 'One era is over, another is underway. Faculty members have unanimously welcomed the opportunity to move with the times to the new modern campus. The university, like the airport, could not remain stuck in its past. Already plans for both airport and university are receiving international acclaim for foresight. It is such forward-planning that marks the progress of the university and Singapore.'

'One thing's for sure,' David says, 'Chin didn't write that.'

At two in the morning, we call it a night. The penned-in notes are all in Bernard's hand. The typeface will assuredly match that on Bernard's typewriter. There is evidence in abundance that Chin stole Bernard's work.

'Well,' yawns David. 'What do we do with this? Hand it over to Super Wong?'

Venus has a serious note in her voice. 'I'm not sure you realise publication of parts of Bernard's original manuscript might be considered against national interests. In Singapore, we have long memories and like to bury past mistakes, not publicise them. Reasonable people like Superintendent Wong – and me – think dirty clothes should be washed but not in public. Don't expect Wong to act outside of Internal Security.'

I say that nobody wants to take on the state security apparatus, only to nab Chin for theft and possibly murder. 'I feel sure Wong places justice before problems raised by the content of Bernard's manuscript.'

'Don't be too sure,' adds Venus. 'You don't get to be superintendent, acting dean, or news anchor with SBC or even manager of Guild House unless you run with the pack, or *appear* to do so.'

K, as usual, settles things. 'I hear all you say, Venus love. What's important is to bring Chin to justice. If that's done publicly or privately, never mind. Who cares if the cat is black or white as long as it catches mice.'

'Chin's cats are grey,' says David, helpfully deflating the serious tone.

'In that case,' K concludes, 'I'm going home for some beauty sleep.'

'Don't forget your bag and stuff,' I say.

'Where did you hide it?'

'In the bath suds with Venus.'

K disappears into the bathroom and returns with the bag dripping wet. In his hand is the package David had lifted from

Chin's safe. He makes a show of opening the cloth wrapping. 'Well, well, what have we here?'

'It's a World War II Luger.' I say, *'Don't touch it.'*

28

Sinking a Launch

'WHAT PLEASURE it gives me to see us gathered together this evening to recognise the work of a colleague.' The Vice-Chancellor, standing in K's living room, conscious of the bright lights and camera, inflects his speech like a dearly beloved vicar addressing his flock at harvest festival, about to unveil the winner of the biggest pumpkin award. It's normal enough: a reception to launch Chin's book. Very abnormal is that it takes place at the home of his greatest enemy.

'Doctor Kingsley Woolf, who will soon be pursuing his career in other parts of the globe, has kindly provided his home and hospitality for this launch of Dr Chin's latest book, which tells the story of our university. Doctor Woolf has asked me to lead this congratulation and I thank him for it. Doctor Woolf's wife is currently in the maternity ward about to give birth and Doctor Woolf will be leaving us early to join his wife. Because nature waits for no man, woman or child, I will give the floor to Doctor Woolf to lead the toast to Doctor Chin.'

Siggy's bright lights turn to K, tanned and muscle-tuned after weeks sitting in a suburban safe-house garden and energetic ping pong competitions with his minders. K's smiling face under silver locks denies his hatred of Chin. He leaves the company of Super Wong and goes to the VC's side. A slight pattering of applause.

'Thank you, Vice-Chancellor. Nothing gives me greater pleasure than to raise a toast to the author of *The Social History of Singapore University.*' K raises his glass high towards heaven. Nobody seems to notice K slipped 'Social' into the book's title. The entire Faculty of Humanities is here. K, ever the thespian, swallows off his whisky and looks towards Chin, his smile unwavering. 'Doctor Chin's book will be on the shelves of every bookshop in Singapore tomorrow. A truly remarkable achievement. Those of you who know Harry will wonder, as do I, how he managed to produce a work of genius. There is not much chance of him telling us. Doctor Chin is far too modest for that. Indeed, so modest is he that only the VC himself could persuade him to allow this little reception in his honour. Because Doctor Chin avoids the spotlight, a little subterfuge was necessary to obtain the original manuscript of this great academic work. Harry would be the last to display his genius for all to see and I hope he will forgive my asking his charming wife, Agnes, to sneak the original manuscript to us without telling her dear husband. This manuscript has now been completely photographed and on the walls you will see blow-ups which show clearly the author's comments and changes in his own hand. There is no better evidence of how the mind of a master chronologist works. This mind has done so much to capture the spirit of our university. We have here tonight members of the press. I would invite the media to examine the examples of genius that we have placed around the walls. I wish Doctor Chin all he truly deserves.'

K starts to clap, the VC claps and soon the house is full of clapping. Chin's face remains enigmatic. David, from a far corner, gargles a soft 'Speech', and the word spreads like a virus. Agnes is whispering in Chin's ear. All eyes are now on him. Chin coughs. 'Doctor Woolf, you are too much kind. Too much. I will never forget...' Chin trails off. He has forgotten whatever he will never forget.

Chin is saved by K's wife and the VC. 'Doctor Woolf, I have just been told that your wife is in labour. Please excuse my interruption.'

K thanks the VC, bids everybody eat, drink and be merry, and squeals off in his Mustang. Chin's aborted speech is forgotten as faces turn to the food and drink – K is never mean with his hospitality.

As guests split into conversational twos and threes, the super guides me outside the anonymous drone of intermingling conversations. He is in civilian clothes, personally invited by K and appropriately pleasant. He holds a drink and for all anybody knows, we are talking about the two subjects that pervade conversation in Singapore at this time: how to stop births at two or less and how to be courteous – there being no causal link between the two campaigns.

The super jumps straight in. 'Thanks for sending me an advance copy of Chin's book with pages marked for my attention. I read the book. Must say I thought it good. Quite a surprise though, it coming so soon after our failure to locate Bernard Fox's manuscript on precisely the same subject and just after the break-in at Chin's by three men and a dog.'

'I think, Superintendent, we were all surprised.'

'You'll be relieved to hear we won't be charging anybody with the robbery at Chin's. We found the money in the maid's room. She claimed the thieves had given it to her but could not explain why she hid it under her mattress. Chin accepts his maid's story that she can't remember. A girl who can't remember probably can't tell three Sikhs and a bloodhound from, say, three Englishmen and a street dog. Chin insists she not be charged and he keeps her on in her job. If the police are not to charge somebody caught red-handed with the loot, it's difficult to charge anybody else – but not impossible if we set our minds to it.'

'Mystifying,' I keep my reply as short as possible.

Wong continues. 'Yes. But not quite as mystifying as this party and this book's publication. I've talked with Chin many times since Fox's death and at no time did he mention he was researching exactly the same history as Fox and also writing a book. And why Chin's wife should give K the original manuscript of Chin's book is way beyond me. I know and everybody knows Chin and Woolf are enemies. Why this charade tonight?'

'Perhaps K is belatedly trying to woo Chin.' I say. 'You know his contract is not being renewed, don't you? Perhaps he thinks that if he makes peace with Chin, the decision might be reversed.'

'It would never work and Woolf knows it,' the super replies with a note of don't-play-with-me in his voice. 'I suspect this reception tonight is less a peace offering than the opening shot in some kind of academic war Woolf is waging. I won't question Woolf again until after the baby is born, but I would not want him – or any of you – overstepping the mark … again.'

'I'm not sure I follow you, Superintendent.'

'Then perhaps I should be as clear as Woolf's fingerprints on golf clubs, David Bent's fingerprints on a chisel and your dog's hairs all over a house she's never been in. Perhaps I should be as clear as ten to fifteen years in prison. Now, tell me why Chin's wife gave Woolf the manuscript.' When he wants to, the super can be pretty damn clear.

'Would you believe me if I say I don't know?'

'No,' the super answers. 'Although I *would* believe you if you tell me the four of you – Woolf, David, Venus and you – held a council of war at which you all decided Chin's book plagiarises Bernard Fox's manuscript. I would also believe you if you told me Woolf played a particularly nasty trick on Chin's wife, involving a Uher tape recorder in your wardrobe with your knowledge. I could also believe that you entered Chin's house while Chin and his wife were conveniently absent in SBC studios and stole the manuscript. I would also have no trouble in believing you hid the manuscript in your flat, had a bath and lied to Madhu.'

I gape. 'How...'

'How do I know? Don't forget your flat is wired. With your consent and for your protection.'

'But I turned off the kitchen light...' I stop.

'When engaged in conspiracy? Yes, I am aware that you've been turning on and off the kitchen light. Strange habit but not against the law.'

'Turning off the light deactivates the microphones.'

'Oh dear, you are mixed up. Our mikes are voice-activated. Turning off the kitchen light won't switch them off. Has somebody been giving you false information?

I look the super in the eyes. 'You did.'

'Did I now. I don't seem to remember.'

'So, you have weeks of my life on tape somewhere?'

'Yes. But nice and safe. I'm the only one who has access.'

'What about the policeman upstairs?'

'We moved him out as soon as we realised using you as a

decoy was not going to lead us to the war loot.'

'But you have it already. K gave it to you. I thought I was a decoy to catch Düsseldorf and Nagasaki.'

'That too. But, as you know, that particular threat was removed even before the listening device was installed.'

'Sorry, come again?' I am getting worried.

'You didn't know? Seems your persecutors fell under a large rock and then blew themselves up. Scared the shit out of the courting couples who reported it. Never made the news. One scoop your Venus missed.'

'If you moved out the policeman, who has been listening in on my private life? Not Ra'mad?'

'No, not Ra'mad. Everything said in your flat is relayed directly to a sealed recorder in my office. Only I have access.'

The super leaves no room for manoeuvre. He can clearly pull us all in if he wishes. Perhaps he is happy with the way things turned out; perhaps he is giving us enough rope to hang ourselves.

'Might I suggest, Superintendent, you keep the original manuscript and compare the typeface with that of the typewriter on Bernard Fox's desk. You might also compare the margin notes with Bernard's handwriting, which is quite different to that of Chin.'

The super's tone is friendly when he warns. 'Please leave things to the police from now on, all right?'

Before I can agree, Siggy moves in with his camera and Wong moves away. 'Doctor Haddock. Lovely to see you again. I've been trying to corner you. Venus can't come. She said you'd understand. She also said to tell you the Richard thing is over.'

'You mean Richard is dead?'

'Well, in a manner of speaking, yes. Good thing, too.'

'Good for me if not for him. I just hope Venus feels okay. Maybe she'll miss those Sunday sessions at the Nursing Home, but in the long run she'll be free of her past. I suppose now she'll have all the funeral stuff to get through.'

'Can't see her going that far. After all, it wasn't as if he really existed other than in her mind. I think the Sunday sessions will continue for a while, and maybe she'll need a bit more time before she jumps into bed. But you've waited this long, a bit longer might be on the cards, depends how she feels.'

'Why would the Sunday sessions continue? Or is Richard's body still there? They kept Ra'mad's wife weeks before it was released.'

'Eh? I'm not quite following you, Dr Haddock.'

'The body. Surely no need for an autopsy.'

'Body?'

'Richard. I can't see the need for an autopsy, not after two years in a coma nobody expected him to come out of.'

Siggy gives me a long look. 'You know all that stuff was just in her mind, don't you?'

'Sorry, Siggy, now I'm the one not following. We all know Richard was in Holland Park Nursing Home and he'd been in a coma for two years. I have no idea how he got into a coma, but I understand why she felt she had to visit every Sunday.'

Siggy is now looking at me strangely. 'Wait a minute,' he says and pauses, although not for a minute. 'You don't really think there ever was a Richard, do you?'

'Of course. Venus visited him every Sunday. Ra'mad used to see her there.'

'She visits the Home, yes.'

'Siggy. Could you backtrack and explain what you meant by "the Richard thing is over"?'

'What has Venus told you so far?'

'That her husband Richard is in a coma at the Nursing Home and not expected to come out of it. I know she visits him every Sunday but that's all I know. Whenever I try to get Venus to talk about her past, or even her present outside of the studio and you, she changes the subject.'

'I bet she does. Don't tell me you believed all that stuff.'

'Nobody would make up a comatose husband.'

'I think, if you don't mind, Doctor Haddock, I'd rather Venus explain it to you.'

'But is he dead or isn't he?'

'Since he never existed, he can't be dead.'

'Then who does Venus visit every Sunday? Is there another man I don't know about? Is he called Richard?'

'She visits her psychologist. Dr Lim, not Dr Richard – female. She never told you? You couldn't read between the lines?'

'I'm not great at reading between lines. You mean to say there never was a Richard? That Venus has no husband, comatose or not?'

'I know Venus tells everybody she's married and even wears a ring, but there is no husband and the ring is her mother's. Her father and mother have been dead two years now. Venus has trouble accepting their death. That's why she visits the psychologist every Sunday. You really had no idea?'

'No. I thought it odd that Venus never talked about her parents or anything about her family.'

'Venus never explained all those family pictures in her home?'

'I've never been to her home. No idea where it is. What

happened to her parents?'

'Died two years back. Car crash. Venus was in the car at the time.'

'Was Venus hurt?'

'Physically, not at all. She walked away. Psychologically, though, she was a wreck.'

'So, the sessions with the psychologist relate to survivor's syndrome?'

'Plus. Venus not only felt guilt at surviving, she felt guilty of killing her parents. You see, she was driving. Her father was in the passenger seat and her mother behind him. Her father was teaching her to drive. That's why they were over there in Johor – it's much easier to go for a spin without a proper licence in Malaysia. Had the accident happened here, there might have been more of an investigation. But everybody was busy getting the bodies back to Singapore, not in allocating blame. Not that anybody was to blame. Venus swerved to avoid somebody who'd stepped into the road but swerved the wrong way and into a lamppost. That lamppost took out both parents but left the driver's side of the car untouched. Not Venus's fault, but not anybody else's fault; that's been the problem. She never drove again until quite recently, when she got the evening newscaster slot and the Corporation gave her a loan to buy the Starlet, on condition she pass her test. She passed it just before you met her. Even now she's a bit nervous about pedestrians on the road.'

'Yes,' I say. 'I've noticed. It must be horrible for Venus, blaming herself for two years. Thanks for telling me, Siggy. It really helps. But what I don't get is why she invented a husband.'

'You'd probably need to ask the psychologist. Not that she'd tell you; patient confidentiality. I've known Venus since we were kids. We entered university at the same time and joined SBC the same day. If I were straight, no doubt we'd be married by now. I think I know Venus better than anybody. I've seen her use the Richard excuse with lots of guys before you. I think it just became a simple excuse that nobody argued with. She was very close to her parents and hasn't been able to talk about them with anybody, not even me really.'

'Does she talk much about me?'

Siggy laughs. 'Too much. Practically every day. I think once she'd started to use the Richard excuse with you, she couldn't easily get out of it. Nobody would want to talk about that tragic accident – or talk about why they're seeing a psychologist. Richard-the-comatose was an excuse nobody questioned. Fortunately, Venus has grown out of it, I'm sure seeing you has helped. My guess is she's ready for a relationship. But what do I know? I just record stuff on film, I don't see into minds.'

'Thanks, Siggy. I really mean that. I'll wait for Venus to tell me.'

'Yes, you must be good at waiting for Venus. Let her tell it her way, when she gets around to it. And don't mention I've already told you anything more than what she said to tell you: she can't come tonight and the Richard thing is over.'

I put my hand on Siggy's shoulder as a sign of my thanks. He sees David and turns to him. I'm feeling much happier about so much; I must have a stupid smile on my face. It is chopped off by Agnes, her angry eyes burning into me from across the room.

As Agnes moves towards me with daggers in her eyes, I duck through the French windows into K's garden. By doing so, I succeed only in removing both of us from the moderation of a crowded room.

29

Garden Talk

'WHAT THE HELL does your bastard friend want before he leaves me alone? After that horrible business with the tape recorder, now this nonsense about me giving him a manuscript. I suppose if I deny it, K has everything set up to broadcast the tape right now.'

This is my chance to say *I don't know what you mean* and hope to regain Agnes's friendship. But I don't think that fast. 'It seems like a reasonable precaution,' I answer.

Agnes's clenched fist begins its swing towards my teeth but stops mid-air. The dull light from the house catches her pale face and white dress. She looks like a marble discus thrower frozen in mid-swing. The effort to control her temper brings tears to her eyes. I take her fist and lead her away from the windows, into the shadows of the trees. I'm about to deny any part in the recording incident when Agnes suddenly morphs from K's tigress into my sweet lady of the orchids. She cries freely and stands with arms limp at her sides. I feel like saying *there, there* and other profound words of comfort. I place a hand on her shoulder. Agnes presses against me, sobbing. Each great sob throbs her breasts into my tummy. This is not at all in any plan.

'You don't really think *I* killed Bernard, do you Tom? Why would I? I loved the man.' Agnes pauses, but not long enough for me to answer her questions or to consider what she means by *loved*. She continues in a little-girl hurt tone that I, a naïve beggar when it comes to what women are capable of, think sincere. 'I know Harry and Bernard didn't get along. But Bernard wouldn't reject a wife because he doesn't like her husband. I often took Bernard cakes and things and we often saw each other in his home. On the day he died, I had taken him a pie and we spent an hour chatting. Bernard was a tender man who understood me. I cried bitterly when I realised he was dead.'

'Yes, I know,' I say, finding nothing better to say. Venus is occupied with a freshly-dead imaginary husband, K is busy birthing a baby and here I am with Agnes in my arms. My hand slips from Agnes's shoulder onto Agnes's firm buttocks and I leave it there, palm down, for want of somewhere to put it or reason to move it from where it seems welcome. Agnes's hair nestles under my chin just like Venus's does, and like Venus she smells nice … and sexy.

'You *know*?' She asks.

'I mean I know Bernard ate a pie before he died. The remains were found in his tummy. The only unknown is, if the sedative was in the pie, who put it there?'

Agnes stiffens a little only to relax and press deeper into me. 'Tom, you know it wasn't me, don't you?' I am only half listening. The other half is responding to the body pressed against me.

'Yes,' I find myself saying; I don't want it to be Agnes. 'It wasn't you. But the drug was there. You told the police of course? About the pie, I mean.'

'How could I, Tom? They might suspect me.'

'It wasn't you,' I say again, finding myself adding 'Agnes' and feeling her body-press reward. 'And since it wasn't you, Agnes, it must have been Chin.'

'Yes, Tom, it was. I was not to know. I told Harry I was making a pie for Bernard. He put the drug inside without my knowledge. It was a sedative that I'd got from Ra'mad to use on the cats during a journey. The cats had slept like babies without it and I had no idea Harry had kept it. Harry told me later he only intended to send Bernard to sleep for a while so he could steal the manuscript – the one you stole back. He wanted that manuscript so badly. I still don't know why.'

Agnes takes over the dialogue and leaves me only to agree. And every agreement ties us closer together. 'Harry has been a fool,' Agnes understates. 'He tried to get me involved. He knew I visited Bernard – his maid told him. He asked me to take the manuscript from Bernard's desk during one of my visits. When Bernard popped into the loo or dozed off in his armchair, I was supposed to grab the manuscript and run for home. I wish I had; Bernard might still be alive. But I refused and told Harry that if he wanted the thing so badly, he would have to steal it himself. And he did. He went to Bernard's house – he took my key without my knowing – found the manuscript on the desk and took it. He was back in a couple of minutes and if he had just acted normally, I'd have suspected nothing.'

'But he was not normal … Agnes?'

'Far from it. He came back with that precious manuscript all right but in such a state of panic I had to calm him down with a tranquilliser. Only then could I get any sense out of him. He said Bernard was slumped in his armchair and he thought he was dead. I told him he was talking nonsense. I needed to convince myself Bernard was all right. That's why I went back with Harry to Bernard's house. It must have been after 10 o'clock as I'd just been watching the news on TV. Bernard was slumped in his armchair just as Harry said. At first I thought he was asleep. I felt for his pulse but there was no sign of life. I wanted to call an ambulance from Bernard's phone but Harry said it would do no good now and would just cause problems for us, since we'd have to explain what we were doing there. It was then he told me about putting the sedative in the pie. The remains of the pie were there on the floor by the desk. And Barnaby was knocked out at Bernard's feet; I suppose she shared the meal with Bernard.'

'But why didn't you call the ambulance?'

'I should have. But Harry was in such a state because he thought he had put too much sedative in the pie or that Ra'mad had given me poison by mistake. Neither of us was thinking straight. And Harry got me frightened. He said that anybody could have seen me going to Bernard's house that afternoon carrying the pie. Our maid, who adores Harry but hates me, saw me go and Li Fang is always looking out from Guild House. The way Harry put it, it sounded certain the finger of suspicion would point at me not him, since I was the one who got the drug from Ra'mad. He said the best thing to do was to divert attention from the pie by taking away the remains and the plate and making Bernard's death look like suicide. He got the tow rope from our car – which was stupid as it would tie the hanging to us, but at the time we weren't thinking – and strung up a noose from the fan, then hoisted Bernard up into the noose. It looked so horrible. I was stunned. I couldn't move, couldn't do anything to stop it. Oh, it was horrible, Tom, horrible.'

'Then Harry turned on the fan,' I say, seeking a full explanation.

'No, of course not,' Agnes says. 'Harry wanted to make it

look like suicide. People don't hang themselves then turn on the fan.'

So, I'm thinking: if Chin didn't turn on the fan, if Agnes didn't do it, and Bernard certainly didn't do it, who turned it on and why?

'Did you and Harry leave Bernard's at the same time?'

'I ran out first, it was so horrible. I was crying.'

'Then Chin might have turned on the fan after you left?'

'He was just behind me. He was very upset, too. But why would he do that?'

Agnes is troubled at the memory and I find myself looking down into wet eyes turned up to me with the appealing look Barnaby uses when she wants something, wet eyes that beg for help.

'It was a terrible accident, that's all. I believe you, of course I do, but the police might think differently. Perhaps it would help if you go away for a time. Why not visit your family in Ipoh? With Bernard's manuscript now available, it's not going to take the police long to see the author was Bernard, not Harry. Then they will have a motive. It could be hard for you to argue you were not an accomplice, before or after the fact. Just for keeping quiet, you might spend your life in prison.'

'Oh, Tom, what should I do?' She sounds like a little girl who has just dribbled chocolate ice cream down her dress and is afraid mummy will find out.

'Distance yourself from Chin. Get out of Singapore and deny anything Chin says. And don't worry about me giving you away.'

'You wouldn't Tom, would you? I know you wouldn't. You know I couldn't hurt anybody, don't you?' Agnes has moved me deeper into K's garden and is just about as deep as she can be into me. She stretches up to kiss me. As I feel her lips touch mine, I freeze. Chin and Wong are walking towards us.

They stop just metres away, standing in the half-light, oblivious to what is happening in the shadows. Agnes and I stand embraced in silence like lovers turned to stone in Pompeii.

Wong and Chin speak in Mandarin and I can understand practically nothing at the time. Their entire conversation is retold to me in English by Agnes later that night. Then, she goes into such detail, she almost condemns herself.

*   *   *

'So, I hope you see now,' Chin says to Wong. 'That manuscript in there is evidence of nothing. It contains some things which Internal Security decided should not be made public – so I cut them out. It's an old draft I passed to Bernard Fox for his review – he is a historian after all – and he was kind enough to return it to me with his comments on it. All the notes you see there are his comments, in his handwriting. I had no idea my wife gave my original manuscript to Woolf. She knows my handwriting and knows the comments are not mine. It's as if she wants to raise suspicion against me.'

'And the typeface, Doctor Chin. Why did you use Fox's typewriter instead of the one in your study?'

'I did use my electric typewriter for later drafts. But I have only recently obtained it and I used my old manual for the first draft. I gave that old typewriter to Bernard Fox at the time he gave me back my manuscript. A sort of payment if you like. Bernard needed a better typewriter than the old portable he had.'

'Very generous of you, Doctor Chin. That explains a lot. As for the manuscript itself, I shall hold onto it for the time being. I

285

have no idea why your wife gave it to Woolf and I shall ask them both. It might be a genuine mistake – perhaps your wife was just trying to be helpful – but it might be something more serious. There have been attempts to link the manuscript and the death of Professor Fox. To put things bluntly, it has been suggested you put sedative in a pie, gave it to Bernard Fox to eat and when he was asleep, stole the manuscript and hanged him from the fan. Somebody did it. Who?'

'I have asked myself the same question many times, Superintendent. I should have talked to you before about this, but I kept telling myself it could not be true. The point is my wife has been behaving strangely for some time. Often disappears for hours on end, telling me she is going to visit someone or go shopping or something. Then I find out she has not been where she swears she was. I have suggested she see a doctor, maybe get some counseling or even psychiatric advice, but she doesn't listen. She resented all the time I spent on this book. I used to write at night, so perhaps I have been guilty of neglect.'

At this point, Agnes gags and I put my hand over her mouth.

'That's none of my business, Doctor Chin,' the superintendent responds. 'I suppose many marriages go through troubled patches.'

'That's what I've been telling myself. But Agnes does some strange things. On the day of Fox's death, for example, I found her baking something. It's unusual for her even to enter the kitchen. I asked if she was becoming interested in cooking and she practically forced me out the door. The maid does most of our cooking; she told me later that Agnes had baked a pie for Bernard Fox. Agnes used to drop in on Bernard from time to time. Quite often, actually. I don't think there was anything between them: Bernard was old enough to be her father. But if there was, perhaps their relationship might suggest a motive? Anyway, that afternoon she spent an hour with Bernard, according to my maid. She went out again that evening. I remember it was just after the 10 o'clock news. She told me she needed a walk and to be alone. She wasn't gone long, maybe twenty minutes. She came back with the pie dish.'

'Why didn't you tell me all this earlier?'

'I suppose I wanted to protect her. When you discovered sedative traces inside the body, I remembered that Agnes had got sedatives from Ra'mad some time ago. It was supposed to be harmless, just something to sedate our cats during a trip to Ipoh. We never used it on the trip and on return I put it away on top of a cupboard in the kitchen and thought no more about it until you mentioned the stuff. Then I checked and found it gone. Agnes must have put it in the pie she gave to Bernard.'

'Sedating Professor Fox is one thing, lifting an unconscious man is another. How could a woman lift a man up and hang him from the fan?'

'My wife, Superintendent, is a very strong woman. Jogs every evening. Press ups each morning. She completed military training and intended to make a career in the army until we got married. Physically, she is stronger than me. Mentally, I think she has problems. At times Agnes is like two different people with two different minds. Surely no *normal* person would drug a man, make a noose from her husband's tow rope, hang the man from the fan, then *turn on the fan*?'

At this point they turn back to the house.

⋆   ⋆   ⋆

287

'I'm taking you home,' Agnes orders. 'Your home.' She is again the resolute, strong Agnes. She leads me through K's garden gate to Chin's car in the drive.

'What about your husband? How will he get home?'

'Who cares?' says Agnes. Well, I for one do not.

30

Agnes Reveals All

BARNABY, LOCKED IN the flat, judging from the wood shavings on the floor, has been scratching all evening to get through the door. She gets her wish and rushes out as Agnes is shown in. The door closes and locks on her, and she immediately begins scratching to get back in. Dogs! I ignore her.

Agnes leads me by the hand straight to the bedroom, my one at the front, not the notorious back room. And there, sitting on the bed, she tells me exactly what was said in K's garden between Super Wong and Chin. There are lots of tears from her, lots of comforting from me and lots of agreement that she married a complete louse.

Agnes perhaps isn't the most objective interpreter in the world, but I believe her. If she's making it up, I tell myself, she would not make such a strong case against herself, reporting Chin's words about an unsound mind turning on the fan once Bernard's hanging from it. I know Superintendent Wong will, sometime, review this voice-activated recording and can compare it with what he heard in K's garden. Knowing the super will hear what is being said, I prompt Agnes to retell her version of events – the version in which Harry Chin does it. Only an hour has passed since she last told it but she doesn't seem to notice her two accounts are completely different.

⋆   ⋆   ⋆

'I innocently gave that pie to Bernard in the afternoon without knowing Harry had laced it with sedative. I knew Bernard's housekeeper was away and I thought he'd enjoy snacking on it. I didn't stay long, I needed to get back and change for my evening run. Much later, as I was watching News at Ten on TV, Harry came in carrying what turned out to be Bernard's manuscript. He was so nervous he couldn't speak and was sweating. I sat him down and he drank a litre of water before he could tell me what he'd done. He said he'd taken my key, gone to Bernard's, found him slumped in his arm chair and thought he was dead. I told him I was sure Bernard was just asleep. But I was worried enough to go back with him. We opened Bernard's back door quietly and went inside into the dark. The shutters were all closed and I couldn't see anything at first. Then the front door opened and I saw Li Fang.'

'Li Fang?' I ask with surprise.

'Yes. He was opening the front door from the inside. He went out and left it open. What I saw next almost made me faint. Bernard was not slumped in his armchair at all, he was hanging from the fan and the fan was turning. Harry looked like he was about to die. I recovered enough to turn off the fan and check that Bernard was really dead. There was no pulse. Harry refused to call an ambulance, saying it would just incriminate us rather than Li Fang and he turned the fan back on saying, "That's the way Li Fang left it." Then he said we should get out of there before somebody came in the open front door. We did, taking the pie dish with us and locking the back door after us. I had no idea what had happened or if Li

Fang had killed Bernard or come in as we had done and found Bernard hanging and gone out to call an ambulance from his phone.'

My ceiling fan is on fast but after that story I am sweating. We are both sitting fully dressed on my bed. I ask Agnes if she minds me removing my shirt. She doesn't mind at all; in fact, she helps me out of it. Then, clearly thinking ahead of me, she opens the buttons on her one-piece dress ... all of them.

'Tom, it's hot in here. Did you never think to get an air-con?'

'I never felt the need.'

'But everybody has an air-con these days.' The dress opens and slips from her shoulders. I notice Agnes wears no bra. I also notice her breasts are very firm ... nicely firm.

'Bernard never had air-con.'

'He did in the bedroom,' Agnes is purring her words. I've never seen those breasts before and they are every bit as my mind had pictured them.

'I never went into Bernard's bedroom.'

'No, I suppose you had no reason to.'

But you did? I think but do not say. In fact, I don't say anything.

'You should take these off as well. They look awfully tight.' They are indeed very tight. Agnes opens my belt and zip and rolls down my trousers. 'Now isn't that better?' Yes, it is.

Where were we? The story of her and Chin finding Bernard dead. Agnes has completely changed her story within the hour. She also seems to have forgotten completely what we were talking about. I suddenly remember Wong will be hearing all this and that in the new version Li Fang, not Chin, is the principal suspect. Some clarity is needed before I get up and turn off the kitchen light; then I remember there's no point in turning off that light.

'If you saw Li Fang leaving, why didn't you tell the police? You just went home and went to bed?'

'Harry said we should not get involved,' Agnes purrs slowly and reflexively, twisting fingers around my member in rhythm with her words. 'That Li Fang must have hanged Bernard during the time between Harry's first visit to get the manuscript, when Bernard was in his armchair and this visit, when Bernard was hanging on the fan. He said Li Fang was sure to deny having been there at all. So, I went along with Harry's idea that we say we were both together at home in bed; that was our alibi. When we got home, the maid was asleep in her room – we have so many rooms we let her have one; she doesn't sleep in the servant's quarters outside. We changed into pyjamas, then Harry woke her up and said it's almost 10 o'clock – although it was really 11.00 – and he feels like some corn flakes but can't find the packet. The maid found it, put some in a bowl, added milk and sugar the way Harry likes it and gave it to him. I was watching from the bedroom door and saw our alibi give Harry a sideways smile and look that she never gives me – the little bitch.'

'And the maid supported your alibi?'

'Yes, which means I still can't get rid of her. And after making a big thing about being home together, I couldn't change my story for that lovely superintendent.'

I think of the super smiling at those words. He'll be interviewing Agnes and Chin more vigorously after this. Agnes removes a familiar pair of yellow panties covered in red lovehearts and hangs them on my erection. I have a brief moment of conscience – Agnes is vulnerable and I've extracted a sort-of confession in a manner uncomfortably similar to K's escapade. But what worries me more is that Agnes had seen Li Fang leaving through Bernard's front door after 10 o'clock and he had not raised the alarm until over an hour later.

★   ★   ★

My head is bursting with competing images of Bernard swinging from the fan as Li Fang sneaks out the door and those very present breasts of Agnes and her hands which are expertly everywhere. I half-heartedly suggest she better make for home before Chin gets back, notices his BMW outside my flat and comes banging on my shutters. Agnes says, 'Don't worry, Tom, I'll never return to that fiend.' Actually, I don't want her to go just then.

We never get down to considering where Agnes might go if she is not to return to that fiend. Comforting and cuddling are not the same thing but come pretty close in practice, particularly after a few drinks and a touching of bare flesh. But as cuddling merges with fondling and one thing leads to another … a sharp *rat-a-tat-tat* hits the shutters.

I reach a hand to cover Agnes's mouth.

More heavy rapping from outside as Agnes shudders and almost bites my hand off.

31

Through the Window

'I'VE ALWAYS LOVED HER. Ever since she was born that day in the jungle. When Bernard helped her out into a very uncertain world and a dog licked her. I loved her as much as Bernard loved her, as if she were my child. I loved her mother too, in one way before Bernard came into our lives and in another when she gave herself to him. I loved them both: Syep – Bernard's wife and Syou – Norsiah I should say – Bernard's child. I'd cried along with Bernard when Syep was killed and I vowed along with Bernard to find her killer and kill him. When Bernard left the jungle after the war, I was a father to Syou. Bernard approved and I loved Syou as a father. And when she married and had a child, I loved that child as my own grand-child. And when that child was killed with its father, leaving Syou a widow, then I looked after her, cared for her, and began to love her, quietly, another way.'

⋆   ⋆   ⋆

Li Fang's telling me some of the bits I don't know. After he steps in for Uncle Bernard in my life, he's filling in the gaps.

⋆   ⋆   ⋆

'There's an uncertain tap on the glass, a pause, more timid taps, more hesitant pauses, then a decisive *rat-a-tat-tat*. Someone is at my bedroom window.

'I installed the glass window instead of the wooden shutters because I like to see outside at all times. Even lying in bed in the dark I can see Bernard's house opposite and the back path to it; I can also see up the road to the flats where you and Ra'mad are now the only occupants. If I approach the glass and look past Bernard's house down Evans Road, I have a full view of Chin's house, its front gate, its side parking space and its back path. Not that I spend my life at the window. When not in the bedroom or at the morning market, I'm always somewhere in Guild House with its wrap-around veranda, getting a clear view of anyone approaching or leaving.

'It's Norsiah at my window. I'm not surprised and indicate she should go to the veranda. It's 1 o'clock in the morning. I note Chin's car outside your flat and wonder what it's doing there. I'm relieved to see Norsiah; she would have walked on foot out from her village to the nearest road, taken local buses to KL and Johor Bahru, taken a motorcycle taxi through the rubber plantation to the Orang Laut aboriginal settlement on the "almost island", got an aborigine to boat her across the Strait to northwestern Singapore, then found a taxi into campus; exactly the no-passport route I used to take throughout the war – no taxis then, of course – and the route Bernard insisted she take in reverse when leaving Singapore; a route that leaves no paper trail. The Malaysian police had been searching for her in Perak aboriginal villages, but they had been looking for Norsiah, not Syou. She must be very tired. She must also be confused and worried at the police tapes sealing the doors of her father's house.

'I see her on the open, dark veranda before she sees me, the concern in her tired face too evident. I take from the fridge a pitcher of cold water and two glasses: this is not going to be easy.

'"Excuse me…" Norsiah begins. "I walked out many times to a telephone and tried to call Father but he never answered. I was so worried, finally I came back."

'Why didn't you call me? I'm always here.'

'"I know. It's stupid – I've never had reason to call you, so I don't know your number. I see police warning signs on Father's doors so I dare not enter…" words clog her throat.

'I'm very sorry…'

'"I can guess," she spares me. "Dead, right? His heart?"

'Yes, his heart. And other things.'

'"Please tell me. Tell me everything now. I won't be able to sleep anyway. I did not understand why Father insisted I leave here and return to the village. He had warned me to be careful, but not why."

'Your father sent you away the day before he died, but not because of Chin. A German who was here during the Japanese War had just returned to Singapore and teamed up with his old Japanese partner. They wanted something your father and I would not give them. Bernard was afraid they would use you to make him cooperate, so he sent you away to safety. It was the Japanese who killed your mother. Both the German and the Japanese worked with the collaborator Chin Jin-Hui – that's the father of the man you know as Harry Chin. Chin Jin-Hui paid for his crimes back in 1945. Harry Chin has been silent all these years but the German was staying at Chin's house, so the chances are he told everything to Chin. Your father wanted you out of harm's way until we neutralised all three. But they got him first. You can take some comfort in knowing that revenge has now been taken against both the Japanese who killed your mother and his German accomplice. You are safe here now. Your father died before they were removed, so he could not tell you to return and I could not get a message to you.'

'"Thank you," that's all she said. I swore her to secrecy, saying her cousin Tom was involved in the revenge and that you now know you are cousins. I told her she could talk to you freely when she felt up to it – but not in public.

'She wanted to sleep and I accompanied her to the maid's quarters behind Bernard's house. I checked out her room and told her to lock the door after me.

'Returning to my room, I saw Chin's car leave the flats and travel the short distance to park beside Chin's house. Agnes was at the wheel.

'Norsiah told me the next morning she was awakened by the noise of her father's back door opening, looked out her window and saw Chin going into Bernard's house.'

32

Panties on My Pillow

'COME ON TOM, open up. It's me, Venus, out here with Barnaby.'

O Lord, you write a nasty plot. The long-awaited love of my life, freshly widowed from her imagination, raps at my shutters just when the lady of the orchids is blossoming in my bed.

I push Agnes away and hold a finger to my lips. The smell of her must be drifting through the louvres to crinkle the lovely nose of Venus. I have never put on trousers so quickly. I speak through the shutters with a tired voice. 'Venus? Sorry darling, I was fast asleep.' I look back at Agnes. If she wants revenge for what K did to her, one word will be enough. She is sitting looking lonely, tears on pale cheeks. 'I'll open the door, Venus. Just a minute.'

'Make it the kitchen door. I don't want the whole world to know I'm here.'

I take Agnes by the hand and beg her to get dressed, go out the front door, get in her car and go home before I open the back door for Venus. She pulls her hand away and lies back down on my bed, naked. 'Tell *her* to go home,' she says. '...Tom.'

★   ★   ★

I open the back door, rubbing my eyes. Venus looks at me. 'Well, now what's going on?' I feel horribly sure she knows what's going on. 'Going to bed with your trousers on? And whatever's had you tossing and turning? Your hair's all scrambled.' Barnaby sniffs my crotch, sneezes, looks at me in reproach and follows her nose through to my bedroom in search of neck-fold ruffles.

'I didn't hear your car,' I say lamely. 'I had a lot to drink at K's. I just collapsed on my bed.'

'Don't I get a kiss?'

'I haven't cleaned my teeth.'

'Oh, Tom. You are hopeless. Now give me a hug and a kiss.'

With the smell of Agnes in my nose I peck at Venus.

'Not like that. Like this.' Venus reaches both hands to my neck and pulls me down to a sucking embrace. Her hair flows into the whiteness of a long dress I hadn't seen before – white dresses all round tonight, but this one doesn't open down the front. One leg lifts up at the knee. Why does she do that? I never do. Surrogate erection? I like it. It speaks of surrender and help-lessness. I doubt Agnes lifts a leg.

Venus finally releases me, takes a breath and says, 'I parked at the back.'

'Huh?'

'I parked the Starlet at the back. That's why you didn't hear me pull up. I didn't want Ra'mad monitoring my arrival, not tonight.' It's not Ra'mad you need worry about, I think, it's voice-activated Superintendent Wong.

It's early hours and Venus has come to me, free at last of the fantasy that kept her from me. My heart should be singing. It is pounding. This is the moment for the big love scene she's been putting off ever since we met. The moment when the earth will move, *tra-la-la*; it doesn't seem right to suggest another time might be more convenient.

299

With the cars of Agnes at the front and Venus at the back – I feel well and truly snared in my own deception.

Oh, what tangled webs we weave, when once we practice to deceive.

In Singapore, it never rains but it pours.

'I came to let you know Richard is dead.'

'I know. Siggy told me.'

'It means I won't be seeing you for a while.'

'What?' I say, confused. The phantom Richard is no more and she won't be seeing me for a while – did I miss something?

'The funeral,' Venus says. 'You know the way it is.'

I don't know the way it is but I agree I do. It looks for a moment as if I might get away scot-free. Venus has delivered her message; it's not very precise as far as details go but sounds like Richard the Pretender gets a pretend funeral. Maybe Venus needs a breather before she explains it all; maybe, having delivered the message, she's off to sit by an imaginary great Chinese coffin until the time comes to throw imaginary half-dead chickens around. I edge towards the back door and say I understand and I will and can wait and so on until she is quite ready. After all, Venus, we've waited this long, our love will endure. I take her by the hand and swing open the back door.

But the widow in white shows no more signs of departure than does Agnes in my bedroom. Quite the opposite. Venus looks at me as though I have just made a breathtaking declaration of devotion. She begins twirling the hairs on my chest around her fingers, back in character again, twirling between no and yes. But now the reason for no is dead and I can't take yes for an answer without spiriting Agnes out of my bed.

Come on brain, find something to say, to suggest the timing

is not quite perfect. *Hold it Venus, your old man is barely cold and you've got the hots, how about a few days of grieving?* Something like that but gentler. Something unselfish and caring: *I'm just thinking of your emotional state and how you might feel afterwards.* Something that will get her out the door but not forever out of my life.

'Are you going to keep me in the kitchen all night?'

I have no idea what I am going to do with her all night; the next few minutes are what concern me. So, I blabber. 'Actually, the kitchen is the heart of the home. The connection between cooking and sex is well documented you know, in anthropology that is, raw and cooked. Many languages use the same word for family and kitchen. It's almost impossible for an anthropologist to make love without thinking of the kitchen.'

'Well, you can think of your kitchen while we are lying on your bed! You can have me over the kitchen sink when the sink's not full of dirty dishes. Now come along ... Tom.' Venus leads me by the hand from the kitchen through the passage that runs past the bathroom to the bedroom ... and Agnes.

'How about a drink first? A beer to set you up. It'd give me time to clean my teeth and, er, straighten up a bit.'

'Bed full of girly magazines, is it? Never mind, lah. You know us Singapore girls. Tolerance itself.' I have a horrible feeling I'm about to discover the limit of my favourite Singapore girl's tolerance.

The toilet flushes.

'The toilet flushed,' says Venus.

'The toilet flushed?' I try to sound casual about the thunderous cascade echoing round the vast sound-box of my bathroom in the dead of night.

301

'It did. And it didn't flush itself, Tom, did it?'

'Er, well, it might have. You know what toilets are like. I think the ballcock gets stuck ... you know.' I sound pathetic. I hug her because I can't think of anything else to do or say. She's stiff but softens as the sound of the flush fades.

And Agnes chooses that moment to flit past. She passes within inches, silently, without a look, and disappears into the back bedroom like a ghost.

'Do you have somebody here?' Venus asks, meaning *You have someone here*!

'You mean ... her?'

'Yes, Tom ... *her*!' A sterner note in her voice as she breaks away from me. 'That woman!'

'Oh ... her! You don't think, do you Venus, that *I* and *her*? How could you, Venus?' I try my best to sound offended. A pathetic best it is.

'She's in your flat at one in the morning and wearing your shirt.'

Circumstantial evidence. There has to be a logical explanation – anything other than the truth. Barnaby joins us. I reach down and give her a playing-for-time pat. She looks at me suspiciously. Come on, brain, think. That's what you're for.

'My shirt? Are you sure?'

'Of course, your shirt. I gave it to you and that *person* is wearing it.'

'Oh, *that* shirt. I left it in the bathroom. I suppose she just put it on ... after flushing the toilet.'

'Tom Haddock! *Who* is that person?' A good direct question. Only one answer is possible and I give it.

'I don't know.'

'You don't know?' Venus looks as if she will die or kill. I don't fancy either. I think of making a run for it before Venus and Agnes reach an amicable settlement and cut me in two.

Bernard comes posthumously to my rescue, sending ideas into my mind from his unacclaimed monograph, 'The Big Lie'. You can fool all the people all the time if you tell big enough lies. Don't fart around with small lies. Small lies provoke big doubts. Big lies are certainties that people will defend to the death. According to Bernard, history is a compound of the biggest lies of all. Lies have to be big, brazen, uncomplicated and, most of all, what people want to believe. They are infinitely more powerful than truth.

'Yes, I don't know.' I sound quite convincing ... to myself. 'Be reasonable, Venus, you can't expect me to keep track of everybody who comes and goes around here. You know I never lock up.' There, the big lie is thrown out and Venus is checked. She won't call me a liar, will she?

'You've been locking up all the time since Wong told you to. You damn well locked up tonight. With that woman inside the house.'

Maybe Venus is not going to swallow The Big Lie after all. She is, after all, with the Singapore Broadcasting Corporation and perhaps knows more about such things than Bernard and I put together. Richard the Pretender wasn't exactly Big Truth – but not the time to mention Richard. I look to Barns. She stretches her head down onto front paws, sticks her bum in the air and tells me I can jolly well get myself out of this one.

'Barnaby...' I begin my explanation. Barns raises her eyes with a look of scorn. Well, there is nobody else to blame Agnes on; if it's not me, it has to be Barnaby. '... I had to get up and

303

open the back door to let Barns out for a pee. I must have left it open. I suppose that, er, woman came in through the back.'

Agnes is hearing every word. I wonder if she's laughing or crying or simply biding her time before appearing naked in front of Venus to claim me for evermore.

'So that woman came in the back, locked the door after her, flushed the toilet and put on your shirt. And you don't know who it is?'

'No. No idea.'

Barnaby looks at me pitifully and walks through the kitchen and out the back door. Want a simple life? Be a dog.

'Tom Haddock, I'm counting to three. It you don't tell me who that woman is and what she is doing here, I walk out the door forever.'

'Come on, Venus love. You wouldn't do that, would you?'

'One ...'

It's all K's fault, I think, as usual. Why does he have to have a baby tonight?

'Two ...'

'K ...' I say.

'Kay? Her name is Kay?'

'No. I was just thinking of K. You know, K, Kingsley Woolf.'

'K is here?'

'What do *you* think, Venus?'

'I think K's in the back bedroom with that woman.' Well done, Venus. Well done, Bernard. Well done, K. Well done, Barnaby. Don't, for Christ's sake, pop out now Agnes, please.

'Venus, you know K. He'll never change. He regards that back room as his own and he has a key to the back door.'

Venus looks relieved. Half as relieved as I feel. I take her hand to lead her through into my bedroom. Venus hangs back. 'Strange I didn't see K's car at the back.'

'Maybe he parked at the front tonight. Did you look at the front?'

'No,' Venus says. 'I suppose there's no reason he shouldn't park at the front. It's funny, that woman in the back room looks like Chin's wife.'

I swallow. Sometimes all people need to believe a Big Lie is a tiny truth. 'It might be,' I say. 'K sees her a lot.'

'And with his wife giving birth! That friend of yours takes the biscuit, doesn't he?'

'Yes, Venus, he certainly takes that all right.'

It looks as if the revolving door farce is over. I'll go into my bedroom with Venus and everything will be all right. Agnes will quietly exit the back bedroom and leave through the back door. That's how it might have been. Instead, Venus opens my bedroom door and freezes. On my pillow is a pair of little-red-heart panties.

I have zero seconds left to live.

'I can explain...' I say the immortal line as Venus rushes past me and out the back door. I stand at that door, no point in chasing her. As I hear her car drive off – it sounds angry – I turn back into the flat. I notice the door of the back room ajar. I look inside. The wardrobe is open and the tape spools from the Uher have gone. I hear Agnes driving away and return to the little-red-heart panties on my pillow, alone.

★ ★ ★

I can't sleep; who could? Rather than dwell on paradise lost, I write out the versions of events around Bernard's death as told

305

to me by Agnes and as told to Wong by Chin as interpreted by Agnes. The accounts agree on circumstantial facts; facts I already know. They differ on the most vital points: who put the sedative in the pie, who hanged Bernard on the fan, who turned on the fan. Chin blames Agnes, Agnes blames Chin in the garden version but blames Li Fang in the bedroom version. One must be lying, although Agnes could be both lying and telling the truth. Towards dawn, I fall asleep with the question in my mind: who turned on Bernard's fan? Only Chin's account answers that question, but I don't want to believe it.

33

The Fan Turns Again

I AM NOT EXPECTING to hear the voice of Agnes again so soon but there it is, echoing within the back stairwell. I'm in the kitchen with Barns making my morning tea and toast, and warming her pig's liver. The back door is open. Agnes is talking on the stairs to Ra'mad.

'Four cats,' says Ra'mad. 'Like last time. There's plenty of powder here. Going to Ipoh again?'

'Yes, that's right. I'd appreciate it if you don't mention this to Harry. You see, I'm going alone – with the cats that is – not with him.'

'I quite understand, my dear. You can depend on old Ra'mad. Be careful with the powder, mind. Remember: half that amount would send a man to sleep and the full amount if taken at one go, would knock him out in no time.'

'Thank you Ra'mad. I'm ever so grateful. Really, I am.'

I hear Agnes coming down the stairs and fear she might pop in. After last night, I don't fancy Agnes for breakfast. I risk poking my head out the door and catch sight of the lady in white disappearing along the back path. The kettle boils and the toast pops, and that's about the extent of sexual metaphor my mind can handle at this time of the day. I am a bit English that way and sex can't really compete with a nice cup of tea.

I turn back to breakfast. If homes can miss people, my filthy flat must be longing for Norsiah. I've always thought of her as the woman who puts the mop around, now I wonder if I'll ever see her again and if Bernard told her we are cousins. I had thought his insistence on secrecy was only to prevent accusations of nepotism on my appointment to university staff; maybe that was part of it, but now I know he feared for my safety and hers. Thanks, Bernard – that problem is buried now.

I pick up my shirt from the back bedroom and sniff it for the lusty aroma of Agnes but it just smells like any sweaty shirt; I throw it in the bathroom next to the germinating coconut. Perhaps, I reflect, I should have invited Agnes in for breakfast. But if Agnes has taken my advice and is going to Ipoh, that's the best thing for her, I wouldn't delay that. And Chin will be nicely furious when he finds she's taken his car and his cats.

I suddenly feel very much alone. I need to see somebody, anybody really. And there's that gun David took from Chin's safe. The gun I had taken from Li Fang at the rock and left in the Citroën for Chin to find. Now back in my hands, thanks to silly David and under my mattress because I didn't know what to do with it; I'd best get rid of it. But what to do with a WWII Luger? Can't just throw it in the rubbish bin, at least not in my own rubbish bin. I'll ask Li Fang; he'll know.

I wander down to Guild House. Li Fang is not there so I put the bagged gun down on a table and use his phone to dial Venus. An apology for last night is in order. Venus picks up and sounds like she hasn't slept. I say that hopelessly inadequate word: 'Sorry'.

'There is no need for pretence. I know you were just waiting for Richard to die and I'd appreciate your not coming to his funeral.' I wouldn't be doing that anyway, I think, since there won't be one, but I say nothing. 'I hope you'll be happy in your little-red-heart panties.' Then, 'click'. That click seemed to last a hundred years of solitude.

Venus is upset. Not about that phantom husband but about me and those panties. I need a plausible excuse for panties on my pillow.

I turn to Barns, my faithful comfort blanket. But she has crossed the road and is lying on the doorstep of her old master's house. The door remains sealed and still carries the police warning against entry. Barnaby is grieving again. I dial K's number. He'll have a solution to the panties problem.

'K. Did you get the boy you wanted?'

'It was a false alarm. By the time I got to the hospital last night, the contractions had stopped. I was hustled out so the missus could get some sleep. Now they say it could be any time in the next fifteen days. I went home, back to the party. Everybody was still there, except for you and Agnes. Chin was furious – Agnes had driven off in his BMW and he was the brunt of jokes. He called a taxi. The super took me aside and gave me a lecture. It seems he knows quite enough to send us away for a long time if he chooses. He doesn't seem keen to do so, though. He's taken the manuscript and you won't be allowed to publish; not yet anyway. On the positive side, the University Press is recalling all copies with Chin's name on them pending clarification of authorship.

'You still there, Haddock? Good. As far as the handwriting on the manuscript goes, Wong says Chin himself told him it's Bernard's. That throws our trump card out the window and brings us back to square one. As Chin now claims Bernard's typewriter is one he gave Bernard after typing the manuscript on it, there's still no evidence against Chin. There is, on the other hand, heaps of evidence against the Neckerchief Gang – if the super decides to use it.'

'Could we get together and talk about things, K? It's a bit difficult on the telephone. And I have a problem I need your advice on. It's a knickers problem.'

'Perhaps you should stop wearing them, old son, ha ha. I can't help you there. I'm a married man and about to become a father. I'm busy waiting for baby. When the boy's born though, we'll wet its bum in style.'

'We couldn't fit in a chat this afternoon? After your 5.30?'

'The 5.30 express has run out of steam, dear boy. Truth be told, it rumbled on beyond its best-by date. Anyway, the VC's asked me to drop by his place at five, baby permitting. No idea what for. He sounded friendly, though.'

'But K, I *need* to see you. I need to speak to you about Agnes.'

'That wench? What about her? Didn't bed her last night, did you?'

'As a matter of fact, K, I almost did. I feel lousy about it. It wasn't as if I set out to do it. I was kind of taken by circumstances.'

'That's what they all say, Haddock. Pathetic. At least act like a man. You wanted her and you took her. Wasn't that the way of it?'

'Not exactly. But Venus must think it was. She found little-red-heart knickers on my pillow; you know the ones. Agnes left them there. Venus went off furious without giving me a chance to explain.'

'A pair of knickers on your pillow doesn't mean the wearer of them was in your bed. So, whatever you do, *don't* apologise – just deny. Venus will never know unless you tell her. And believe me, wenches don't want you telling them that sort of thing, and apologising for it just makes it worse since they then have to forgive you. Tell Venus you'd bought those knickers for *her* and put them on the pillow for her to find.'

'I wouldn't have bought her second-hand knickers. These have clearly been worn very recently – there were even pubic hairs in them.'

'You had a good look then! But did Venus?'

'No, she just saw them and ran out. She'd seen Agnes coming out of the bathroom. I'd explained that away by saying she was in the back room with you. Then Venus opened my bedroom door and there were the knickers.'

'Did Venus believe I was there with Agnes? After all, my wife was, I thought, about to give birth; I was at the hospital.'

'Yes, she had no trouble believing it at all, in fact, she came out with the idea.'

'Well, don't worry. I'll back up your story. And while forever waiting for Venus, you can practice your performance with Agnes. You can keep my 5.30 appointments. Don't suppose Agnes will notice the difference an inch or two makes, ha ha.'

'No, thanks. Anyway, she's running away from Chin. I heard her talking to Ra'mad on the back stairs. She got more of that sedative stuff from Ra'mad today.'

'Maybe before she goes she's going to sedate Chin and hang him from the fan, ha ha.'

'She said she's going back to Ipoh and taking the cats with her. I advised her last night to get away for a bit; going home will be good for her. What I don't understand is, why's she taking the cats? They're Chin's cats. Agnes much prefers Barnaby.'

311

'Simple. She intends to poison Chin's cats and drive off leaving the bugger with only the maid for company. Women like to leave a consolation prize when they go. But whatever she does and whatever Chin does, there'll be no more visitations by rampaging Sikhs. The super made it clear enough – the vigilante trail ends and we leave things to the police. Hands off everything and especially *hands off Chin.*'

I wish K the best of luck in playing father-to-be and ring off. Having exposed Chin as thief and plagiarist, we are to act as if nothing happened. That doesn't sound like K. This baby thing has gone to his head. At least Chin's *History of Singapore University* won't be in bookshops today. That means the pre-recorded TV book launch will be on indefinite hold and middle-class Singaporeans will have to wait to have the book lying on their coffee tables – hopefully with Bernard's name on the cover when it gets there.

★   ★   ★

Li Fang pulls up on his motorbike, carrying bags of fresh food from the market. I tell him I used the phone and offer to pay for the calls. He says never mind and that it's bugged by the police so be careful what you say on it.

'Is there anything you don't know?' I ask him.

'Not much,' he says.

'Then you'll know what to do with this bag; it has a gun in it. The gun I took from you in the Gardens and left in Düsseldorf's car outside Chin's. Seems like Chin kept it and David, the idiot, took it from Chin's safe.' I hand him the plastic bag.

'I'll take care of it,' says Li Fang.

We stop talking as Norsiah steps out of the shadows and

helps Li Fang with his bags. My cousin is back. I should hug her or something. But she looks so serious I don't talk to her. I guess Li Fang has told her about her father; she must be devastated.

★   ★   ★

I cross the road to Barnaby. She is sniffing and sobbing, her nose pushed against the crack at the bottom of Bernard's sealed front door. If dogs could cry, tears would be rolling down her cheeks.

'Come on Barns, old girl. You can't spend your whole life grieving.' I hug her, I promise never to lock her in or out again. She will not leave the doorstep. I sit beside her in silence.

Bit by bit, I become aware of a familiar sound coming from inside Bernard's house. The slow click-click turning of the fan. A memory-flash of Bernard rotating in slow circles. I peer through cracks in the door and shutters but can see nothing in the shuttered gloom. I pause long enough to assure myself my imagination is not playing tricks, then run back across the road to Li Fang.

★   ★   ★

The police arrive in 10 minutes. It had taken only the sound of a fan turning inside the locked house to bring the super himself. An ambulance arrives as a constable opens the front door.

Daylight floods in. I notice first the lady's shoes, politely placed just inside the front door. The super turns off the fan. The rope slows its lazy circles. Long black hair flicks around a ghostly whiteness. As the constables slacken the noose and lift the body down, I see her face. The mouth is open; her eyes stare at me through heavy lids that wait to close forever.

313

*　　*　　*

The ambulance men pronounce her dead and close her eyes and mouth. Rearranged, Agnes looks quite peaceful.

Immediately under the fan, Bernard's desk chair stands erect. I know suicides kick away the chair – and Agnes knew it too, she had read all of Bernard's work. At any point in her death struggles, Agnes could have put her feet down on the chair and regained her life. If she had been conscious enough to do so.

I read the questions in the super's face. Who switched on the fan? Why carry shoes through the house and leave them at a sealed front door?

Chin arrives as Agnes is lifted onto a stretcher. His face as white as his wife's death dress.

'She's dead,' the super tells him.

Chin stares at the blue, nylon rope. 'Did she …?'

'We'll know the cause of death later. The medical cause, that is. The back door's unlocked. Did your wife have a key, Doctor Chin?'

Chin seems not to hear. He follows Agnes out to the ambulance mumbling that he told her not to wear that white dress. Ra'mad has heard the ambulance siren and comes to stand beside Li Fang and say, 'What's up now then?' Quite cheery, until he sees what's up and then he looks like he might die himself.

'Doctor Chin. Did your wife have a key to Professor Fox's house?'

'I don't know. It's possible. Anything is possible, isn't it?'

'Yes, Doctor Chin. Anything is possible.'

*　　*　　*

K never does things by half and the life-long male chauvinist takes to the role of father-to-be with the zealotry of a convert. I visit him in hospital where I find him holding his wife's hand and biding his son's arrival. It frightens me.

Venus now has an imaginary dead husband in place of an imaginary comatose one and, judging by remote extra-sensory perception, is ready to throw herself on an imaginary funeral pyre. I never see her, not even on TV, where her news slot is taken by a Sikh whose waxy turban and waxier moustache seduce no eyes to rise from the beer froth to the Guild House screen. I miss her.

Toshi disappeared the night he played Peeping Tom and David misses him; he blames himself for dragging a Japanese into an English-schoolboy game. Rightly so.

My mind is plagued by replays of the dirty tape-recording trick K played on Agnes. The face of Agnes keeps appearing in my mind, pitiful and pleading, the face of an innocent child. Gone.

⋆   ⋆   ⋆

The rumour spreads that Internal Security is holding Bernard's manuscript, which Chin had claimed as his own, and might be charging Chin with knowledge of things he shouldn't know. Such rumour would lead to booming book sales had the book-shops any books to sell. Perhaps it also leads the VC, ever a cautious man, to name the head of the English Department as the new dean.

Li Fang tells me Agnes's family comes from Ipoh, collects her things from Chin's house and takes her body from the morgue. Chin does not go with them for the funeral.

Norsiah returns to the routine of cleaning my flat in the mornings when I'm out; I leave it to her to mention our relationship and she doesn't, so I don't. I presume she's staying in Bernard's servant's quarters; I often see her on Guild House veranda, sitting with Li Fang.

Barnaby spends her life at the sealed front door of Bernard's locked house. In mourning for her old master or for Agnes or both. At night, I take her food and find it untouched the next day. I sit with her in the moonlight. Barnaby's head lays propped on the cement step like an opium smoker on a ceramic pillow, eyes set in the direction of Chin's house.

Chin's maid leaves one morning; I see a taxi take her away with a suitcase. Chin is now alone; his last source of comfort gone. He stoically continues his lectures, reading them out in English from notes corrected in advance by Agnes. He calls no staff meetings and spends no time in the department. Barnaby literally dogs his footsteps. Students tell me Barnaby attends all of Chin's few lectures and stares at Chin throughout. When Chin eats lunch – alone – in Staff House, Barnaby waits in his sight. When Chin goes to the library, Barnaby waits until he comes out. Wherever Chin goes on campus, Barnaby is there. Increasingly, Chin stays home as if under house arrest.

One evening, I see him walking to and fro in front of his gate, the little patch of mourning cloth pinned to a sleeve, a cat in his arms, alone and friendless. He must be suffering; he must be depressed. I find it increasingly difficult to focus loathing on the man. I am beginning to soften but Barnaby keeps her hate alive. She directs deep growls at Chin but she does not attack. She has a plan, of that I'm sure.

34

Suicide Dressed as Murder

BARNABY'S PREY IS isolated and vulnerable. She forays into Chin's garden; she circles Chin's house to scratch at the doors at night. Finally, she camps out on Chin's front doorstep. I do nothing to discourage her. With Barnaby, no point.

Li Fang tells me Chin tries to brain Barnaby with a golf club whenever he can. Barnaby always retreats, tail between legs, offering no fight. Li Fang explains that Barnaby acts out the thoughts of Chairman Mao, wearing down her enemy before the kill. It seems to me that Barnaby enjoys the blessing of Li Fang in her protracted war.

A golf-club length from Chin, Barnaby is always there, an unwanted appendage stuck like glue. A few times she misjudges, or as Li Fang and Chairman Mao would have it, *tests the enemy*. Even when clipped by a club or shoe, Barnaby does not retaliate. Li Fang explains: *to be attacked by the enemy is a good thing*. Barnaby is noting Chin's weaknesses while avoiding engagement. When she runs away whimpering, it's only to fool the enemy. Each time the dog-catchers come, Barnaby retreats to my flat or Li Fang's bedroom; eventually, I guess, the dog-catchers stop answering Chin's calls.

Meanwhile, life goes on. Li Fang quietly courts Norsiah. K receives an assurance from the VC that his contract will be extended after all. David and Venus, for different reasons, do not set foot on campus.

Chin's only 'crime' is being the son of Bernard's wartime enemy, and Bernard himself, it seems, removed Chin's father before I was born; of course, Chin stole Bernard's book, but you don't execute a man for stealing a book. With the suicide of Agnes – perhaps as much my and K's fault as Chin's – I lose any thirst for revenge. After all, I tell myself, Bernard's book will eventually be published with his name on it and if it's not exactly as he wrote it, can I really blame Chin for the changes? And Bernard's death, as explained by Agnes, was most likely accidental; sure, an accident that took Bernard's life but being disgraced as a plagiarist and losing a wife is surely punishment enough for unintended manslaughter? I, a man called 'hero' by the most beautiful woman in the world, should somewhere find the power of forgiveness. Explaining all this to Barnaby is beyond me. It should be possible with Li Fang, but I'm not sure it would change his point of view; although I'm not sure what his point of view is, and I don't try to find out. I do nothing … as usual.

Pleading grief at his wife's suicide, Chin reports in sick. He is given special leave and his duties are reallocated within the department. I see the food delivery van regularly outside Chin's. He never leaves home. His BMW sits in the drive; he goes nowhere in it. Nobody calls on him except Barnaby.

*   *   *

Four weeks after the death of Agnes, Superintendent Wong pays me a morning visit. He brings with him a technician to take away the snooping system. He tells me he listened to the recording of

Agnes's last night and asks me point blank if I think she, Chin or both of them were responsible for the death of Bernard; he doesn't mention Li Fang.

'If anybody, it must have been Chin,' I answer. 'He lied about the typewriter. Chin never gave Bernard the typewriter. I know because I gave it to him myself over a year ago. It never left Bernard's house; Norsiah can vouch for that. Chin drugged Bernard and stole the manuscript – just like Agnes said.'

'You think Chin killed the professor?'

'No, not killed. But maybe he *hanged* him. Bernard was already dead.'

'Why hang a dead man?'

'Agnes thinks … thought … it was to lay the blame on her. Chin suggested to you in Bernard's garden that Agnes was behaving strangely, perhaps insanely.'

'Agnes hanged herself and her suicide supports Chin's view of her mental state.'

'Maybe, but I believe Agnes – the first version as told to me in K's garden. Chin's not guilty of premeditated murder, but he is guilty of hanging Bernard's body in a noose.'

'Then you might need to hope he meets justice through karmic intervention. To put it bluntly, there's no evidence to persuade the Prosecutor that a charge of involuntary manslaughter would stick – I've tried. The case remains open but now that Agnes is gone and her testimony with her, it would be your word against Chin's regarding who gave the typewriter – and that's important to finding a motive; if Chin wrote the book, as he says, he had no motive to steal it and thereby no motive for murder or manslaughter. Even if Norsiah testifies you gave it to Fox, it's not enough for a murder trial.' Maybe so, but I doubt Barnaby will give up her fight as long as Chin is just down the road.

'I want you to know that after I leave here, I'll be turning both investigations, that of Professor Fox and that of Agnes, over to Inspector Ong; the campus area is within his jurisdiction. He might want to talk to you – knowing him, he will – although we have statements from you already. I listened to what was said in your bed and it's obvious you dislike Chin. I suggest you back-pedal on this dislike if questioned. Otherwise it might look like you have a vendetta against Chin'.

He asks me about Agnes's mood on the night before her death and I tell him she displayed mood swings between violence and childish tenderness. And that the account she gave in my bed is quite different from the account she gave an hour earlier in K's garden. 'I wasn't trying to bed Agnes to get at her husband. I was truly reluctant to sleep with her because of Venus and in the end I'm very glad I didn't, otherwise I would blame myself more than I do for her suicide.'

'In that regard, I would say Woolf, if anybody, carries some responsibility for her death. That stupid recording game and all those secret meetings in your back room.'

'K didn't kill Agnes but I feel that he contributed, as I must have done, to her death; perhaps, as they say, driving her to suicide.'

'I'm not a psychologist,' Wong replies in a measured neutral tone which sounds like every psychologist I've ever heard in academic seminars. 'I do, however, detect a marked air of communal guilt. Almost everybody I speak to seems to feel guilty about the death of Agnes. I doubt anybody was really fond of her, except perhaps Professor Fox … and maybe you in your own way. A few people state they thought her a whore. Perhaps that's why they feel guilty. And perhaps you are *all* guilty. But the police can't arrest the whole of society for the way it thinks.'

'You're sure it was suicide, Superintendent?'

'Can't be 100% sure of anything, but perhaps that's how Agnes wanted it – leaving behind the same mystery that surrounds the death of Bernard Fox. I spent a long time thinking about those shoes and why they were inside the sealed front door and not the back. If she was confused enough to give you two different versions of events in the professor's house and disturbed enough to kill herself, we should perhaps not expect shoes to be in their logical place. On the other hand, if someone had lifted her body to hang in a noose and the shoes fell off, that someone might have placed them by the front door – a mistake like the upright chair, perhaps a little too obvious to be a clue left by a murderer.'

'So, are you saying Agnes killed herself and left indications to suggest murder? If that's so, how did she manage to turn on the fan after hanging herself?'

'As I see the progression of events to support a conclusion of suicide: Agnes unlocked the professor's back door, then turned back towards her home and, presumably to implicate her husband, dropped the key on the path near Chin's house – my men found it there – before returning to Fox's. Inside, she mixed all the sedative given to her by Ra'mad in a glass of water and drank the lot, then washed out the glass. She used her husband's tow rope – not the one used to hang the professor as Chin had replaced his tow rope with a similar blue nylon one – to rig up a noose. It was amateurishly made – which suggests the second noose was made in a hurry. She tied the rope to the capstan, switched the fan on slow, climbed onto the professor's chair and placed the large noose over her head without pulling it tight. The noose swiveled around her neck. She stood there with the rope turning itself around her neck until the drug took affect and her legs buckled. The fan's movement carried her in an arc around the standing chair without knocking it over.'

'But what if Chin drugged his wife and strung her up, couldn't he also have left those clues?'

'He could,' says the super, 'had he not been with the vice-chancellor at the time pleading for his job.'

'And that thing about the noose swiveling around the neck until Agnes passed out, are you thinking that could also apply to the death of Bernard? Are we back with the possibility of suicide?'

'We are. The noose that held his body was much better made. It could easily have been made by the professor – I'm sure somewhere in the university library you'll find a description of a hangman's noose. The rope was taken from Chin's car in both cases, but Agnes as well as Chin had keys to that car. That it was Chin's rope suggests that Agnes got it for Fox and that Fox wanted to leave a big question mark over his departure, implicating Chin as killer. But in that case, because the better-made noose would not easily swivel around the neck – we tested it on Madhu – we can be fairly sure somebody other than Bernard Fox turned on the fan.'

'Same old question. Why would anybody turn on the fan?'

*　　*　　*

I am still sitting in my living room lost in a mind-replay of Bernard's death night, my waiting for Venus night, when, about an hour after the super has gone, another police car pulls up at my window and out step Madhu and two constables, all three in uniform. I go to meet them as they come in the front door looking very official. Madhu can't hide his embarrassment: he has been sent to pick me up.

Madhu leads me out and sits me in the back of the car. 'I'm sorry, Tom,' is all he says. There is 10 minutes of silence before the two constables join us. One is carrying in a clear plastic bag the little-red-heart knickers. Why had I kept them for four weeks? Just what sort of pervert am I?

35

Porridge

'IF PROFESSOR FOX killed himself, you told Madhu, he would have done things differently, with an overdose of sleeping pills *or something*.'

It's Inspector Ong firing statements at me. An acerbic edge to his voice so very different to the super's matey tone. We are facing each other across a table like chess opponents and I presume everything is being recorded. I'm here voluntarily they say, although I'd much rather not be here.

Ong is clearly annoyed at something – he's not trying to get my cooperation. He already has everything in a hundred files but seems ready to spend eternity going back over everything that led nowhere other than to the two of us sitting in a windowless room at Police Headquarters.

'I was simply making the point that Bernard hated violence and would not have hanged himself even if he had decided to end his life.'

'It's obvious he did *not* hang himself without your help. *You* helped him hang himself, using the noose he had made ready from Chin's tow rope. Fox wanted to die and at the same time wanted his death to serve a purpose – that purpose being to point a finger at his enemy, Chin. You did as Fox asked you. Whether or not you knew the purpose of the hanging is what will determine the judge's sentence. Come clean now and you get off with assisted suicide; deny everything and you'll face serious charges of manslaughter and defilement of a corpse.'

I realise why the super warned me to be careful. I'm not handcuffed. I can leave whenever I want, they tell me. But if I do, they also tell me, I *might* be detained. I guess they haven't decided what to charge me with yet. Successful suicide is not a crime in Singapore but Madhu told me abetting suicide can be punishable by up to ten years in prison; maybe that's what Ong is angling for. Or maybe he's going to charge me with turning on a fan. Ong, I feel, definitely wants to charge me with something; I'm not just here for a cup of tea.

'So, if I get things right,' I say, 'you are now working on a possibility that Bernard, for whatever reason, killed himself and deliberately left behind clues pointing to Chin as his murderer: *suicide dressed as murder*. Then Agnes kills herself in a copycat suicide and also leaves behind clues pointing to Chin, another suicide posing as murder. If you don't mind me saying so, Inspector, if the two deaths are so similar and *all clues point to Chin*, isn't the logical conclusion that Chin is the killer of both Bernard and Agnes? Rather than two suicides pretending to be murder, we have two murders dressed as suicides.'

'I *do* mind you saying so. Don't change the subject. You academics are good at that. Let me make it brutally clear to you. You mixed the drug into tea you made for Fox and he drank it while eating his steak and kidney pie in your company. You gave what was left over to the dog while you waited for Fox to fall asleep – all of this after or during having seen off the unknown transvestite, *if* there was one. Then you followed through and lifted Fox into the noose. Leave the suicide of Agnes out of

325

this. The only question is motive: did Fox ask you to help him kill himself or did you kill him to get the diamonds you knew he had.'

'Diamonds? I knew nothing of any diamonds until Woolf told me at the house in Changi.' I lie pretty well.

'The Chins were home all the time like they both said in signed statements supported by their maid and had no idea what was going on. Each was each other's alibi; you have none.'

'But Agnes admitted they were *both* there. She said nobody *intended* to kill Bernard, just to send him to sleep for a bit in order for Chin to steal the manuscript, not diamonds.'

'Whatever she *admitted,* she did so only to *you*, in *your* bed, at *your* urging, to please *you*. *You* knew it was being recorded, she did not. She said nothing to the police although she was questioned many times. You told her what to say knowing we'd eventually hear it. I'm sure she wanted to please *you* – not her husband. And what she said to you was within a few hours of killing herself. Chin's wife talked to you, in secret and in your bed, but not to the police; Chin implicates her openly to the police, not to you – get the difference? We are here to examine *your* role in the death of Fox, not the account of Chin's wife as given to you. And as for that famous manuscript you academics pretend is a motive for Chin to kill Fox, who's to say *you* didn't simply take it after *you* had hanged Fox and *you* kept it hidden until an opportune moment to suggest Chin stole it – *if* Fox ever wrote it and didn't simply make some comments on a manuscript written, as Chin says, by Chin.' At that point Ong stands up sharply, looking like an exclamation mark that has made its point. He opens a drawer in the desk and holds up a pair of panties.

'These were on your pillow. They belonged to Agnes. They are situational evidence. She was panty-less when hanged. A police search found her knickers *on your pillow*.' I know they were not on my pillow, they were in my locked desk drawer, but I say nothing, Ong is trying to trap me.

'I'm now in charge of investigating the deaths of Fox and Agnes, so everything leading up to their deaths – including your part in Agnes's theatrical confession – is relevant to *my* investigation of *you*. Now I'm going outside for a time. I'll have some tea sent in for you. You'll need to make a written statement before leaving here. There's a pad and a blunt pencil beside you if it will help you work things out. When I come back, I want to hear a different story. Ring the bell if you need the toilet.'

Well. Ong didn't waste any time pulling me in. He must have sent Madhu to get me the minute Super Wong handed him the cases. Or maybe that's the way Wong and Ong arranged it between themselves; good cop, bad cop.

I sit alone in an unfriendly room. It's introspection time. How far was I involved in Bernard's death? I must admit to myself that Bernard's death didn't come as a complete surprise. I spent the whole evening with Bernard the day before he died. We talked about suicide. Bernard was not suicidal. But I'm not sure what suicidal looks like, although Bernard never had Agnes's mood swings. We talked a lot about friendship. I was a bit embarrassed when Bernard said he loved and trusted me. He asked me – I thought it one of those questions academics play with – if, should he ever decide to kill himself and request my assistance, would I give it, holding his hand as his lights went out. I said I would.

When I saw Bernard after lunch the next day, he was happy, not suicidal – although perhaps some suicides are happy, I've

no idea. Then the diamonds came out in front of Li Fang –
although I'm certainly not going into that with Ong.

Was I so blotto on the night Bernard died that I visited him
without being aware of it? I don't think so. But then I wasn't
aware either that he visited me, left a bag of notebooks and a
dog collar, dropped the diamonds and took off with the transvestite. So, my not being aware of something doesn't mean it
never happened.

If I did pop out to Bernard's, as I've done so many times in
the past that I could walk there blindfolded, I was back in my
chair by the window when Düsseldorf came by around 10.00
– although Düsseldorf's not much of an alibi now. And if I did
visit Bernard on auto-pilot in a sort of sleep walk, why would I
erase that visit from my memory? Was it because I had found
him hanging from his fan? And did I then turn on the fan? No.
I wouldn't do that to Bernard, not even if he hanged himself,
which I don't believe he did.

Ong's right about one thing: there is no evidence that it was
either Chin or Agnes other than the word of Chin and Agnes,
and since both claim the other did it, they cancel each other out.
What if neither of them did it? It would have to be Düsseldorf.
But why? He wanted Bernard alive to reveal the location of the
loot. If Düsseldorf did it, it would have been in that very short
window of time between the transvestite leaving and his calling
at my window in the most recognisable car in Singapore, in full
view of Guild House and Li Fang. And if you have just murdered somebody, do you call at the neighbour's and ask to use
the phone to contact him? Maybe you do, if establishing an alibi.

The only thing that makes sense to me is the second account
given by Agnes, which she now can't substantiate – if it wasn't

Chin, wasn't Agnes, wasn't Düsseldorf and wasn't me, it was Li Fang. This is what I tell the bearer of a pot of tea and a plate of biscuits – the familiar figure of Madhu.

'I see your point, Tom. But if it wasn't anybody, it must have been suicide. I know Inspector Ong has already said this to you. The feeling here is Agnes's story to you was just what you wanted to hear; after all, she was in your bed. She left a very evident calling card on her pillow – we know that because you said so on the bugged phone to K – and you *kept* those knickers. Maybe what Agnes said to you makes sense within the circumstantial evidence. But so does Chin's account, now typed out and signed by him with Inspector Ong as witness; and given the suicide of Agnes, Chin's account has more credibility.'

'But whatever account makes more sense, I can't see why *I'm* here. You know, don't you Madhu, that I couldn't ever hurt Bernard?'

'Yes, Tom, I know you didn't *hurt* Bernard. That's not in question. But if Bernard had asked you, as his closest friend, to help him commit suicide, would you have helped him?' Good grief, I think, was Bernard's home bugged too?

I realise then that Madhu is playing good cop. This is no doubt being recorded so I try to sound confident as I answer him. 'No, Madhu, I'd have tried to stop him and called for help – *if* he had asked me.'

'It's all very odd,' Madhu admits. 'If Bernard didn't hang himself, somebody hanged him and then turned on the fan. You didn't find Bernard hanging and turn it on, Tom? That won't be seen as a serious crime in itself. You might say you were so distraught you turned it on without thinking, apologise for the trouble caused and after a psychologist's evaluation get off with a

deferred sentence for defilement of a corpse and probation; keep
your nose clean during probation and all reference is stricken
from records. You'd keep your job.'

I try not to pause too long before answering. 'No, Madhu, I
did not turn on the fan and I don't know who did. I see no reason
for my being here and no evidence at all to suggest I played any
part in Bernard's death. If Inspector Ong has anything more
substantial than Agnes's knickers to hold me here, he should
come out with it.'

'Tom. Things are more serious than you think. You can
indeed be held here; there's stuff you don't yet know.'

'Then, Madhu, now's the time to tell me.'

'Inspector Ong will do that. If anything comes into your
mind, jot it down. I think the inspector's hoping you come up
with something and we can close the case of Bernard's death
rather than link it to other things.'

'Other things that I don't yet know about and you're not
about to tell me. I have nothing new to tell you on the subject of
Bernard's hanging. I'm a teacher, not a detective.'

'Right – and I'm the detective.' Madhu is nice enough to say
it with a smile, then leaves me to finish my cold tea.

There is no clock on the wall and I never wear a watch. I
stew for a bit; I suppose I'm being processed. Then Inspector
Ong comes back and asks if I have any new thoughts. I say I
haven't. He goes through everything yet again and I give the
same replies to the same questions. I begin to fidget. And I begin
to feel annoyed. No doubt Ong can recognise the signs – I want
out of the room. And no doubt when he thinks I am sufficiently
primed, he sends in the bolt from the blue.

'What about Li Fang and the gun?'

I am tired, fed up and annoyed but now I am simply lost for words. Ong opens a manila folder and takes out a picture. 'Li Fang's here right now. Picked him up the same time as you. We made a thorough search of his room at Guild House and found this gun nicely wrapped up in a locked drawer; Li Fang is the only one with a key to his room and that drawer. It's an unusual weapon, can't be many like it in Singapore: World War II German Luger handgun. Ever seen it before?'

Suddenly I am out of the investigation of Bernard's death into the stoning of Düsseldorf and Nagasaki. Clear as day, my mind comes up with an image of Li Fang sitting at the stone with a gun in his hand, this gun. 'I don't know much about guns. It looks like the gun a Japanese called Nagasaki used to shoot my dog. Superintendent Wong showed it to me. It only fires caps not bullets.'

'Whatever you saw was not this gun. This is no replica, it's a working 9 mm Luger with an eight-bullet magazine. It's illegal to have this in your home in Singapore.'

'I don't have any gun anywhere. I wouldn't know how to use one.'

'But you know how to drive a car?'

'What's that got to do with anything?'

'Doctor Chin happened to look out his window at night and saw you arrive at his gate in a vintage Citroën car. You got out, posted the keys in his box and walked away, leaving the car outside the gate. Why did you do that?'

He's bluffing. Had Chin reported seeing me at that time I'd have been pulled in then not now. He must be bluffing. But he's not bluffing about the gun...

'Well?'

'I didn't do anything. I've seen the car around. Impossible to miss. If Chin told you that, he's lying. Why didn't he report it back then, if he saw me?'

'Back *when*? I just said *at night*.' So he did! So he did! I'd better be more careful. I remember Li Fang's parting words on that night: *this never happened.*

'No idea back when since I wasn't there. Maybe back last night?'

'Back on the night Düsseldorf and Nagasaki disappeared. We found their bodies, of course. You thought they'd remain under that stone forever? Both were in bits from the explosion of World War II ammunition under the rock; explosions in a contained space are very messy. It's the explosion what gives us precise timing, several people heard it. It's the explosion that Chin says woke him up; you must have heard it yourself.'

I realise then he's bluffing. I had heard the explosion as I reached my back door, not when I was in the car. But I say nothing.

'Chin made the report about you and that car the very next day. It's on file. He made it to the team in Guild House when they interviewed him about the car. The car was not immediately linked to the disappearance of Von Düsseldorf – not until identification of his body, which took some time.'

'Then maybe, Inspector, if the German's car was parked outside Chin's house not my flat and he was staying with Chin, Chin killed Düsseldorf as well as his wife and the professor.'

'You are not cooperative. Your friend Li Fang is more intelligent. He says he took the gun from Düsseldorf and kept it hidden. He is ready to make a full confession that implicates you.'

'I want to use a toilet,' I say.

'There's one in the cell.' Ong replies and calls, 'Constable' – just like that, calls into the air and the door opens and a uniformed constable comes in and takes my arm. Ong follows me out. 'I'll speak to you again. Meanwhile, you might focus on the shovel found buried alongside Düsseldorf's body. And why it is covered with your fingerprints.'

*   *   *

I am led down two flights of stairs to what must be a basement and into a barred cell; the door locks behind me. 'Toilet in the corner,' the constable says, pointing to a hole in the floor. The cement floor is furnished with only a sleeping mat. This can't be happening. But it is.

I sit on the floor. It's either that or pace back and forth like Steve McQueen in *Papillon*. There's a light on outside the cell but no windows. The air is stale and hot. I have no idea when the door will open and I'll be taken to Ong again. I know there is such a thing as *habeas corpus* in Singapore, but I never armed myself with the details. The walls are grey, my mood is black. There is absolutely nothing to fasten my mind on. It is silent. No sign of life.

Since I'm sitting cross-legged anyway, I pass the time trying to get back into meditation. I used to enjoy it – for twenty minutes. I don't want to do it for twenty years. It's when I'm just getting off somewhere other than a concrete cell that a man in overalls arrives and pushes a bowl of rice porridge through a slot in the bars, hands me a beaker and says just one word, 'Water'.

I look inside the beaker, it's empty. 'It's empty,' I say.

333

'Tap,' says the man, pointing over at the corner toilet and the tap beside it.

I ask him the time. 'Six o'clock,' he says, adding, 'evening'. Then turns and goes.

I eat the worst rice porridge ever and sip tap water, I notice a small camera mounted on the ceiling outside the cell pointed at me. From its corner position it must see every inch of the cell, every inch of me. No way to get to it; ceiling's too high. Right now, I'd love to be standing in my bathroom, twice the size of this cell, cold water flowing over me. I'm sweaty. My shirt sticks to me. I take it off and put it the only place to put it, on the floor. A mosquito buzzes in my ear.

This, I suppose, is all to soften me up. Would I like thirty years like this for the murder of Düsseldorf or would I admit to turning on a fan and get probation for eighteen months? Li Fang must be here, too, somewhere. I don't believe he would ever tell what happened in the Botanic Gardens. It would take more than a few nights in a cell to break him. If Madhu mentions this to Tambiah, I'm sure my time here will be limited; but maybe Madhu thinks I'm still drinking tea upstairs.

What to do for the best? What would Li Fang advise? I bet he'd advise silence. Tell them nothing. It never happened. But would the advice of Li Fang be all that useful? He kept a loaded Luger in a locked drawer in his bedroom instead of ditching it; pretty damn stupid. If things don't look good for me, they look really grim for him. All they've got against me is a shovel in a grave with two dead men – a shovel with my fingerprints on it.

Let's think of something to take my mind off all this. Let's think of Venus. But all that comes to mind are her last angry words on the phone: 'I hope you'll be happy in your little-red-heart panties.' Then that definitive click.

Think of Barnaby. Chin might be braining her right now and I won't know until I find her body in the drainage ditch if I get out of here.

I lie down facing away from the light and camera. Close my eyes and will myself to sleep away this huge waste of time. God, this mat is as thin as paper. My hip hurts. Try the other side. That damn light. On my back. On my front. It's a long night. A very long night. I see Inspector Ong's face in the grey wall and hate it. I know I must retain control. I'll say nothing next time, whatever he says, however long I spend in here. Nothing.

And as I'm drifting, I hear a noise at the bars. 'Bowl!' It's the porridge man. I poke my bowl through the hole.

'What time is it?'

'Six ... morning.' And off he goes. Will I stay here until 'six ... evening'? Well, nothing I can do about it – and if I can't do nothing well, can I do anything well? Look on the bright side; this is my chance to practice doing nothing. They took my belt when I came in. So, I can't hang myself from the bars. They even took my shoes. I suppose I could hit my head against the wall until somebody comes. But Ong might enjoy watching.

Nothing and nothingness. I wonder if Richard felt like this trapped inside his body. But Richard, I remember, existed only in the mind of Venus. She made him. She never had a husband; she just has a psychologist. And I believed her, everything she said. It all seemed real to me at the time. I wonder how real it seemed to Venus? What future can we possibly have if I believe every untruth she says? But did Venus imagine Richard, or did I imagine that she imagined him? After all, she told me he's dead, not that he never existed. Can I believe what Siggy told me? Did he really tell me or did I imagine he told me? Questions inside questions inside questions. Am I imagining all of this?

And as I sit there on the concrete, eyes closed, a pair of little-red-heart knickers floating within my mind's blur, I hear a familiar voice.

36

The Project

'DOCTOR HADDOCK.'

Standing on the other side of the bars in civvies is Superintendent Wong. Come to gloat? I don't stand up. 'Open the door,' he orders. I see on his watch it's 2 o'clock – four hours more to porridge. 'I didn't know you were here,' he offers. In explanation or apology? Isn't he in charge of all this? Doesn't he know who's in his cells? 'I'll take you home,' he adds. I don't jump for joy or say thank you – in case we get to the street and Ong leaps out to say *ha ha, fooled you*.

My belt, shoes and handkerchief are returned. The super says nothing as we climb the stairs. Ong is nowhere in sight. Along the corridor to the foyer-entrance, people in uniform stand to one side as the superintendent passes. And out into the glorious full light of the sun and into the super's nicely air-conditioned police car. Just the two of us.

'Can I stand you a late lunch?'

I give Wong a what-is-this look and say, 'My priority is shower, then Guild House for a beer and to see Li Fang; and I'm worried about Barnaby.'

'You'll find the Guild locked up. Li Fang is still detained. He had a gun in his room. It's the same kind as Nagasaki used to frighten you, but this one has live ammunition inside. Li Fang

337

denies any knowledge of it. But as only Li Fang has keys to his room or the drawer in which the gun was found, his claim the gun must have been planted on him won't stand up.' A pause and the super changes subject. 'Actually, I wasn't thinking of a restaurant lunch, it's a bit late for that. How about I call and order some food delivered to your flat? That would give us time to talk – after your shower.'

'Any chance of a steak and kidney pie?' I say.

Wong picks up the car phone while driving and pushes numbers. He knows the number by heart, must be used to ordering deliveries.

'And see if they have any kind of liver – no spices, just liver,' I add, thinking of Barnaby, although maybe she's still on her protracted war fast.

The super orders both, lots more, and apple pie with ice cream and gives my address. 'Everything for three.' Three? 'Put it on my tab: Superintendent Wong. Oh, and deliver a crate of Tiger Beer at the same time – with a couple of bottles cold and a bag of ice.' He hangs up and turns to me. 'Will be at your door by the time we get there and you've had that shower.' Sounds like the super is doing his best to make up for my time in the cell; I wonder why? As we drive into the university grounds and past the closed Guild House, I realise how much I'd missed my home terrain – and I've only been gone one night.

⋆　　⋆　　⋆

My front door is open with, surprise, Norsiah standing guard. Speaking Malay, I introduce her to the super as my cleaner. 'We've met, Doctor Haddock.' Wong surprises me by speaking passable Malay. They seem to be on friendly terms, odd that. I leave them chatting and get into the bathroom and under the shower.

I come out feeling comfortable. The food has arrived and Norsiah sets it out on the huge dining table I never use. There is a bucket of ice cubes and open bottles of cold Tiger. Norsiah serves onto three plates and takes a seat at the table, surprise number three. She has been in to clean mornings when I'm teaching but never invited herself to lunch. I suppose I should say something cousinly but Wong's presence stops me.

Norsiah takes the initiative, passing me a frothy Tiger and raising her glass of water. 'Welcome back, Cousin,' she says in Malay. Surprise number four. Wong doesn't turn a hair.

'It's good to be back. Have you seen Barnaby?'

'In the kitchen eating liver. Keeping her strength up to fight the forces of darkness.'

'It's long overdue that we three sit down together,' interrupts Wong. 'I have a lot to say that might surprise you, Doctor Haddock. I hope neither of you mind if we continue in English – my Malay's not what it used to be.'

'Not at all, Superintendent,' Norsiah replies fluently in English. I am stunned. The lady who puts the mop around can speak English!

'You ... you speak English?' I eventually manage.

'Of course,' Norsiah replies in English. 'I never needed English to wash your shirts. By the way, I hope you notice how spotless the place is. I took advantage of your absence to do a deep-clean. Now, would you prefer I call you *Sepupu*, Tom, or stick to *Dok-tor Had-dock* in Li Fang-speak?'

'*Sepupu* would be nice,' I say, using the Malay for cousin. 'I've never been called that. Didn't even know I had a *sepupu* until Bernard told me in his letter you were his daughter. Let's continue to do what your father wanted for the moment and use it just between us and only when we are alone. Superintendent Wong excepted, of course.'

'And I,' the super adds, 'will continue to call you Doctor Haddock.'

'Good. I'll call you Superintendent.'

'Great. Nice to have that *sorted* as they say in England these days. Now, if you don't mind my talking while we eat, let me begin the revelations.'

'Please do.'

'To start, I'd best revise the contextual picture you have of me. I asked you once why you thought this case merits the attention of a superintendent.'

'I remember. Wasn't it status? Bernard being a university dean, the vice-chancellor, media?'

'That was my excuse. It's the reason I gave the Commissioner and the VC. But I *wanted* to be involved – and not just because I didn't want Ong messing things up.

'Li Fang did call the police – but he did not call the emergency number; he called my home and spoke directly to me. He told me he had found Professor Fox dead in his home in what looked like suicide.'

'But how did Li Fang get your home number? I doubt it's in the phone book.'

'It's not,' says Wong. 'I gave it to him. I'd better explain from the beginning. For quite some years now, I've been quietly working with Li Fang and historian Bernard Fox and others on some of the outstanding questions from World War II and the Emergency period. Many scores were settled after the Japanese surrender. Some were revenge for crimes committed during the Japanese years, justified perhaps. Other crimes remain to be punished.

'Our findings are strictly confidential. The reason for this project is to identify potential danger areas to individual survivors of more anarchic times, neutralise such dangers and bring to account crimes of the past that remain unresolved. One of the survivors was Bernard Fox, your uncle – don't worry, your family relationship with the professor remains confidential. Another survivor is Harry Chin, or Chin Yao-Zu to use his birth name; but Chin is *not* a confidant of the project. His wife Agnes, on the other hand, unwittingly provided information on her husband and her husband's contacts – people like Düsseldorf and Nagasaki. Her information came to us indirectly through your uncle – the professor was more successful than Woolf in extracting information from Agnes. Your uncle hoped to make her a confidant of the project – which by the way was why Woolf was out of circulation for so long looking for his transvestite, I couldn't have him screwing things up between Agnes and Chin; I didn't want her popping off to Ipoh indefinitely.'

With the superintendent's words, much falls into place. 'Is this why you have been personally overseeing the investigation of Bernard's death?' There's no point in asking how he knows Bernard was my uncle; by now I wouldn't be surprised if he knows the name of my childhood *amah* in Malacca. '*You* and Madhu, not Ong and Madhu.'

'Yes. Madhu is not on our confidential project and neither is Ong. But Madhu's a good policeman. You know I got him seconded onto the case? Madhu did a good, independent job – independent of Ong, that is. Madhu's okay – but don't go talking

341

to him about this little chat. This stays between the three of us – although no secrets from Li Fang when you see him, which I hope is not too long.'

'If you don't mind my asking, Superintendent, why are you telling me now about a confidential project my uncle never mentioned to me?'

'Because now your uncle is dead, you might help us with some earlier things in your life – your childhood in Malacca and your regular visits from England to your uncle in Malaysia and Singapore ... yes, we are aware of them. You'll notice I'm speaking openly with Norsiah present – she has given us invaluable information about the Emergency and the retaliatory attack by British soldiers on her village; you never know when such information might be useful to Singapore – or to the UK – and perhaps belatedly right some wrongs of the past.'

From what I'm hearing, I wish I'd had the chance to sit down with Wong over a beer long ago. But is this secret project going to help my current situation much when there are still people like Ong around and a spade with my prints on it? Time to find out. 'Of course I'll help. But Inspector Ong accused me of burying Düsseldorf and Nagasaki, dumping their Citroën outside Chin's door and being somehow involved with a gun found in Li Fang's bedroom. And there was something about a spade. I rather suspect I'd still be in that cell had you not released me.'

'Had I known you were there, I'd have sprung you earlier. Between the two of us – the three of us – there was no valid reason to detain you ... other than the spade. There was nothing in the car to suggest your involvement. Chin's wife is on record to have said Chin had taken sleeping pills and was fast asleep that night and there were no fingerprints on the car from you but plenty from Chin. And more importantly, if you remember, I had placed a police officer in Ra'mad's flat to watch over you in case Düsseldorf tried anything before we got the recording equipment in place. That officer reported in writing that you were home and stayed home when we sent you back from Changi the evening of the explosion. Which means you have the best alibi possible – the word of a regular police constable set to watch you.'

'Why didn't I think of that yesterday?' I reply. 'That might have saved me from a night in a cell. After all, there's nothing to connect *me* to what happened in the Botanic Gardens.'

'Well, there *are* your fingerprints all over the wooden handle of a spade found under a heavy rock. Quite amazing the spade survived the blast that made identification of the corpses so difficult.' The super pauses dramatically. 'Fortunately, Norsiah will sign a statement that explains the spade. It's *your* spade, you intended to plant some flowers outside your windows when you moved in two years back – so of course it has your prints on it. Surely you remember?'

'Er, two years ago … I must have forgotten.'

'Easy to do. When Düsseldorf took Barnaby – when you were with me by the way – they also stole your spade. David Bent will no doubt back that up.'

'Now I remember. My fingerprints on that spade and *no* fingerprints of mine on that mysterious gun.'

'Not yours, no. Not Li Fang's either, which is lucky for him. But the gun was found in Li Fang's room following suspicions raised by Chin. Li Fang didn't wipe it clean, so there are still prints from Düsseldorf and Nagasaki on it. It's smothered with fingerprints. So far, they've only been tested against Düsseldorf,

Nagasaki, you and Li Fang. We should know before long if there's a match with anybody else fingerprinted following the professor's death. By the way, that gun has an eight-bullet magazine and one of the bullets had been fired. That supports your story that Nagasaki shot Barnaby on the cricket pitch – the missing bullet must have passed through, as Ra'mad said.'

My mind is back at the rock. Düsseldorf fired a warning shot near me – just one – that bullet ricocheted off the rock and must be somewhere in the primary jungle … but the way evidence seems to be stacking up or made to stack up, I believe it could just as well be found on the cricket pitch … if need be.

'Then I'm in the clear, but what about Li Fang? How does he explain that gun in his locked drawer?'

'He can't, that's the problem. He says it must have been planted when he was not home; he simply leaves all his keys hanging on a nail by his door.'

Yes, I think there's a nail by his door but I've never seen any keys on it. But right now, I'd swear I have.

'Neither Düsseldorf nor Nagasaki could have planted it there – although their prints are on the gun and the bullets – since both were dead by then.'

'Perhaps they gave the gun to somebody,' I comment helpfully.

'That's possible,' supports Norsiah. 'I saw Chin going into Guild House when Li Fang was at the market. You were there making phone calls – maybe you saw Chin? Two witnesses are better than one – and I'm just a Malaysian guest-worker, not a university lecturer. You wouldn't have seen him go into Li Fang's room, you can't see the door from the telephone, but you might have noticed him go past you?'

'Now you mention it, I did.' Until then, I'd always thought of memory as forged by the past, now I see how it can simply be forged. 'Chin came in, which struck me as odd since he never enters Guild House. He was carrying a plastic bag in his hand. He left by the other side, the side that leads across campus to the VC's house. Then Li Fang came back from the market.'

'Yes, that's right,' says Sepupu Norsiah. 'He came back soon after *Chin killed his wife.*'

I choke on my beer.

37

The Dog Dun It

DAVID SAUNTERS through my door hand in hand with Toshi in a complete non-sequitur that leaves Norsiah's dramatic declaration dangling in the air. 'Bad pennies always turn up,' I say.

'Well, there's a lovely greeting. Here Tosh and I are really worried about you and rush over as soon as we hear you're in jug and find you drinking with Super-Fuzz.'

'First time I've been called that,' says the superintendent. 'You can tell me later what it means, David. Get yourselves a drink. I have to make a call on the car phone. Okay, Doctor Haddock, if I get Madhu over here? He's still in headquarters pushing forensics to come up with surprises from all those fingerprints. I'll only be a minute.'

'I'll walk out with you, Superintendent.'

★   ★   ★

The super punches numbers on the car phone.

'Madhu? Good. Anything new on the gun?'

I can hear Madhu answer. 'You won't believe it. Chin's prints are clear as day.'

'Marvellous. That lets Li Fang off the hook. Bring Li Fang over here right now – to Doctor Haddock's flat. Jump in a taxi, don't wait to requisition a vehicle. I'll drive you home later. No uniform if you want to do justice to a crate of beer. Tell Ong I've cleared Li Fang's release.'

'Yes, Sir. But Li Fang's in a cell under arrest and Ong wants to charge him.'

'I'll call Ong now. He'll have to send men here to arrest Chin.'

The super hangs up and calls on the car radio, not the phone. 'Ong. Wong here. Chin's prints are all over that gun and Li Fang's aren't. So, release Li Fang *now* and send two men to arrest Chin right away. No reason to hold Li Fang. Expect to charge Chin before the day's out … What with? Murder of his wife, that's what … there's a witness … Tell Madhu to take Li Fang back to Guild House … No, *don't* you come too. And, Ong, you'd better apologise to him – we don't want bad publicity for wrongful detention of two university staff. Do it *now* and you'll get points for arresting a suspected murderer – keep Li Fang any longer and Tambiah will be raising hell. You got that? Good.' Wong hangs up.

As we return to the beer, I'm awfully glad the super is on our side.

* * *

By the time Madhu arrives in a taxi with Li Fang, the sun is setting. The mood around the beer table is almost that of school-boys together – Wong included. Norsiah is not drinking but seems doubly happy to see Li Fang.

As if to celebrate Li Fang's release, claxon bursts hit us in waves as K's Mustang skids to a halt inches from the super's car; behind it a little red Starlet shyly pulls up.

We all rush out into a darkening evening. Venus is all warmth and smiles; I hope it means I'm forgiven for panties on my pillow and not that Richard has come to life. K gives me an embarrassing man hug.

'Now what?' comes from above our heads. Ra'mad is on his balcony.

K calls to him. 'I'm a father, Ra'mad, will you not celebrate with me?'

'Boy or girl?' Ra'mad asks.

'A beautiful girl.'

'In that case, I'm coming down. A daughter might teach you something.'

⋆   ⋆   ⋆

'And now,' says K, 'let's wet baby bottom, lah,'

'Where's the baby?' I ask.

'With its mother, of course.'

'But how can we wet the baby's bum if the baby's bum's not here?'

'Metaphorically,' K says. 'Where to for a champagne fun-evening? My shout.'

There is ready agreement that baby's metaphorical bum is best wet in Bugis Street. I jump in beside Venus. This is the first time we are together for ages. 'You can kiss me, Tom.' I do, long. Tooting and cheering from behind. 'But where's Barnaby?'

As we pull away, Venus turns on her headlights and they fall on the locked and sealed door of Uncle Bernard's home. Barnaby is not there. Three policemen are sitting in their car outside Chin's garden gate, watching a duel between an ex-acting dean armed with a sharpened golf club and a street dog named Barnaby armed with her teeth.

Chin stands outside his gate in a do-or-die pose, a golf club raised like a baseball bat waiting to connect with Barnaby's head. Our car's full beam dazzles him. Barnaby seizes the moment and draws blood from Chin's thigh. Chin jumps back. Barnaby dances like a butterfly and stings like a bee ... until she yelps – Chin has landed a hard blow. 'Venus, stop. That maniac could kill Barns. I've got to help her.'

'Tom, be careful. Chin's dangerous.'

'He's after the collar.'

I leap from the car but K's Mustang is racing towards me and I can't cross the road to Barnaby's aid. Two sets of headlights now cone the contest like WWII searchlights fixing on a clumsy bomber tormented by a sprightly Spitfire. Jumping Barnaby taunts Chin to strike; he strikes and misses, strikes and misses, and strikes and hits, then brings the head of the club down with all his force onto a bloodied Barnaby. I hear the crack from across the road. Stunned, she lies where she falls.

I see him raise the club again, murder in his eyes, Barnaby helpless on the ground. Chin reverses the club and drives the spear down towards Barnaby's heart. K speeds past. I run forward but jump back again immediately, Wong's car is coming on fast – very fast. I can't get across to help Barns. The spear plunges down.

Norsiah smashes into Chin's back. The spear point sparks the road's surface harmlessly. She hammers Chin with her fists. Barnaby is up – I wince as she sinks teeth into Chin's groin. After that, it's clear my help is not needed. Barnaby tortures Chin's flesh. Norsiah claws at Chin's eyes. Lost in a piranha whirlpool, Chin spins like a top onto the road, hopelessly jabbing the club around him.

A grey, long-tailed cat runs in front of Wong's car. I see Wong at the wheel. Swerve left, he'll hit us. He swerves right. His headlights flash across the fight. Wong brakes. Chin folds over the bonnet of the police car. I hear his face smack the glass and I hear a crack. Chin's neck or the windscreen or both, I don't know. Madhu is once again first on the scene, conveniently with Superintendent Wong at the wheel beside him.

★   ★   ★

A bloodied Barnaby trots like a victorious bull across the arena, jumps into our car and onto Venus's lap. I see Chin slide slowly down the police car's bonnet, I see three men in uniform jump from the other police car and I hear Wong yell 'Call an ambulance' as he crouches over Chin and puts his face close to Chin's mouth. I also see Li Fang sweep Norsiah off her feet in a totally uncharacteristic expression of joy, the same grin on his face I'd seen at the dog stone. Mission accomplished; he's got them all.

'Venus,' I say as she starts up. 'Let's get out of here.' And as we pull away from the scene, it seems as good a time as any to see where we stand. 'About those panties on my pillow...'

'K called me to explain. They belonged to Agnes and he put them there as a joke when you were asleep – before I hit the shutters and woke you up. I'm sorry I flew into a rage without letting you explain. It won't happen again ... not ever ... as long as the only panties on your pillow are mine. And, Tom, let's celebrate with K another time. I'm taking you both home. My home. We need to nurse Barnaby's wounds and ... I want the three of us to be together for ever and ever.'

Barnaby sneezes. I gulp. Venus speaks.

'What was that you said about Chin wanting Barnaby's collar?'

'Oh, I was thinking of something in the PS of Bernard's letter. Düsseldorf stole the letter and must have shown it to Chin. Although, now I can think straight, he didn't show the PS Bernard wrote.'

'Düsseldorf? PS? Two PSs? Not following you at all. The collar. Why would Chin want it?'

'I'll explain later. You're driving, Venus; it can keep.'

Venus pulls over at the Bukit Timah entrance as an ambulance rushes in, stops and fingers Barnaby's collar. 'There, Tom. Now I'm not driving. This collar … it's awfully big and lumpy. And this lock looks like it belongs on a chastity belt.'

'Yes, doesn't it, Venus. Bit odd wearing a chastity belt around the neck. That's Barnaby for you.'

Venus gives me one of those looks. 'You're going to tell me aren't you, Tom?'

'It's a bit of a story, Venus. I'm not sure where to begin.'

'Well, it's early, so start at the beginning and I'll try to stay awake until the end.'

'You remember Von Führer Düsseldorf and Nagasaki?'

'Nope, never heard of them.'

'Never mind them then, we'll just skip World War II and the Emergency.'

'Might be better.'

'Yes, probably. You see, Bernard left me a letter to read after his death.'

'I know. I was there.'

'Yes, you were, but you didn't read the letter or Bernard's PS.'

'Okay, you've got me. What did it say?'

'It said Bernard had a small fortune in diamonds. He had sewn them into a big tubular guard dog collar with a secure lock and put it on Barnaby. On the night he died, Bernard came to my place with the diamonds and the dog collar. He was awake but heavily sedated. I never saw him. He dropped the dog collar and K picked it up and put it on my kitchen counter top, then K helped him back to his house.'

'Why would Bernard have a fortune in diamonds?'

'Well, during World War II…'

'Let's keep World War II for later.'

'Well, Von Führer Düsseldorf…'

'Keep him for later, too. So, Bernard had a fortune in diamonds. Why bring them to you?'

'He was afraid of Von…'

'He's for breakfast. So, you find the collar and put it on Barnaby?'

'You found it, not me, and you said I should put it on Barnaby. You remember how difficult it was to fasten the collar? That collar is the one in the PS to Bernard's letter.'

'Which you didn't show to the superintendent?'

'Yes, I didn't. Instead, I forged a different PS knowing that Von Führer…'

'Breakfast…'

'Well, that's it, Venus, give or take World War II, the Emergency, a Nazi emissary and his Japanese torturer-executioner boyfriend. I've kept Barnaby's collar on Barnaby.'

'So, over breakfast you can tell me all about World War II, then we'll have a look inside this collar and maybe go for a chat with Super Wong…'

'A late breakfast, Venus?'

'Yes, I think a very late breakfast.' Venus starts the car again. 'Let's go home, Tom.'

And so we do.

⋆   ⋆   ⋆

And after dabbing Barnaby with iodine, and after my being suitably impressed with Venus's home and garden, and after my carefully examining the bank of family pictures in which Lee Kuan Yew is standing cheek to cheek with Venus's father in Cambridge, a bank in which there is *no* deposit by Richard, and after a night that is the polar opposite of my night before – and that's all I'll say about it – and during that very late breakfast, with Barnaby's collar Exhibit A on the table between marmalade and tea pot, just as we are entering WWII, the phone rings. 'Now you know why I never got a phone,' I say as Venus picks up the receiver, says *uh huh* and puts a hand over the mouthpiece. I'm sitting there, waiting for her to say *It's Richard*.

38

A Nice Cup of Tea

'IT'S SUPERINTENDENT Wong calling from outside on his car phone. Can he see you here and now?'

'Tell him I'll call him later,' I say.

Venus uncovers the mouthpiece. 'I'll open the door, Superintendent. Just a moment.' Well, it's her door. I don't relish the old being dragged into the new, but whatever it is will taste better over a cup of tea with Wong than cold porridge with Ong.

'Superintendent Wong! What a nice surprise.' Venus speaking, not me.

The super kicks off shoes at the door and takes a seat at the breakfast table. Casual dress. Barnaby's collar is in front of him. Venus takes an extra cup from the dresser and says *Darjeeling* as she pours. Looks like it's to be a Courtesy-is-our-Way-of-Life consultation, not a grilled-Haddock interrogation.

'Apologies for disturbing you at home – I'd like this to be as informal as possible.'

'Should I leave you two alone, Superintendent?' asks Venus diplomatically, clearly loath to do just that.

'I'd prefer you stay. I have a favour to ask of both of you and an invitation to extend. But I'm here informally and confidentially – nothing I say should be repeated in any form by either of you.'

'Okay, we promise.' Venus again speaks for us both. The irresistible scent of raw news no doubt tickling her feelers.

Wong sips his tea. 'Good tea,' he says. We wait. Another long sip. 'Very good tea.' You said that twice. You've got all of our attention.

The brief tea-sipping silence is broken with a casually dropped bomb. 'I thought you'd like to know Chin died in the ambulance on the way to hospital. He got very talkative lying in the road with a broken neck. I had to put my ear right next to his mouth to get what he was saying, so I'm sure only I heard. He seemed to think I was his god judging him; he voluntarily confessed to killing both Professor Fox and his wife, Agnes. He said he was proud of what he had done and regretted only not doing it earlier in life and asked to be rewarded for honourable action.' I am taken back to Norsiah's interrupted *Chin killed his wife* – if ever a statement begged instant elucidation, it's that one; but David and Toshi walked in just then, Chin's fingerprints were found on the gun, K turned up wanting a party and Chin's neck got broken. But elucidation of the killing of Agnes can wait a bit longer, Bernard's death came first and comes first in my order of priorities.

'When you say Chin killed Bernard, do you mean accidentally? That he put too much of the sedative into Bernard's last meal? I thought the coroner had decided the amount Bernard had taken wouldn't normally kill him, but did so because of his heart condition?'

'No. The death was no accident; the coroner's statement was amended when Bernard's doctor was brought in – quietly – he thought Bernard would have woken up eventually with little chance of heart failure, and the fuller autopsy confirmed that.

Chin knew what he was doing. When lying in the road, he said he had meant only to send Bernard to sleep in order to steal that manuscript. But when Agnes told him Fox was dead, he checked the body himself. He knew better than Agnes where to find a very faint pulse and found it at the professor's neck. Instead of calling an ambulance, he told Agnes that Bernard was indeed dead, and that they should make it look like suicide to avoid suspicion. He got the rope from his car as Agnes told you, made a noose, tied it to the fan, then, with the help of Agnes, lifted the victim up into the noose. Professor Fox died by hanging – the coroner corrected the initial finding but I didn't make the cause of death public; I didn't want to alert the killer.'

Venus is clearly bursting with questions. 'But, why would Chin want the professor dead? He'd got the manuscript.'

'A matter of honour. Chin thought he was avenging his father.'

'I'm lost,' says Venus.

'It's as I was trying to explain,' I come in. 'Their house guest, Von Düsseldorf, had told Chin that Bernard killed Chin's father by hanging back in 1945.'

'Sorry I interrupted,' says Venus. 'Please go on, Superintendent.'

'That's it, really,' Wong says calmly. 'Revenge is a strong motive. Chin knew his father had been hanged and suddenly had the chance to take revenge.'

'So,' I say, 'Chin deliberately murdered Bernard. That, I can believe. But why would he turn on the fan? That surely would give the game away? Suicides don't turn on the fan after they hang themselves.'

'He didn't turn it on.'

'Agnes did?'

'I think you know better than that, Doctor Haddock. It was Li Fang.'

'Indeed, I had guessed. If it wasn't Chin, Li Fang was the only one who had the opportunity. But why do it, why turn on the fan? He loved Bernard.'

'Precisely because he loved Bernard. I did, too. Bernard was my friend, as well as my best informant on things past. Neither of us believed Bernard would take his own life ... or at least we had difficulty believing it.'

'But, why turn on the fan?'

'Because I told him to do so. The unexplained turning of the fan ruled out an easy conclusion of suicide. And it helped me argue that the case merited the close attention of a super-intendent. I couldn't risk Ong handling the case. So, when Li Fang called me that night, I told him to turn on the fan before telling Madhu.'

Wong drains his tea; Venus refills his cup. 'And Agnes?' she asks.

'On the morning Agnes died, Norsiah was just back from Perak. She came back in the middle of the night. Li Fang told her about the professor's death and she was very upset. She slept in Bernard's servant's room and was awakened by a noise at the professor's back door. She looked out and saw Chin pull the police tapes off the back door, open it with a key and carry his unconscious wife across the threshold. He had a length of blue nylon rope sticking out his back pocket. Fifteen minutes later, she saw Chin leave alone.

'She immediately went to see Li Fang but he was away at the market. She waited, saw you, Doctor Haddock, come in, make

357

some calls and go and sit outside Fox's front door with Barnaby. Then you suddenly crossed the road with news that the professor's fan was turning; Li Fang called me but mentioned only the sound of the fan turning. Only when Li Fang was arrested did Norsiah come to see me.' So, I think, *there's* the awaited sequitur to *Chin killed his wife.*

'The last time we talked about Agnes, Superintendent, you set out very convincingly the reasons for considering her death suicide. You also said then that she deliberately left clues pointing to murder rather than copycat suicide: the shoes at the sealed front door, dropping the backdoor key between Bernard's and Chin's houses, the upright chair and turning on the fan. You made the point that the clues *too evidently* pointed to Chin as her murderer and you explained how she drank sedative, let the fan turn the noose around her neck until she passed out and fell off the chair. Now you seem to think Chin killed her – the only witness being Norsiah, very tired after a long trip back from Perak and disturbed after hearing of Bernard's death. And Norsiah saw Chin carry Agnes into Bernard's house, not the hanging. If Chin were still alive, he might question why Norsiah failed to report what she had seen much earlier and called you only after Li Fang was detained.' I think I've been rather clever, so I pour myself another cup of tea.

'He *might* but he didn't get the chance – and he *chose* to tell me he did it. Had Norsiah come forward earlier it would have been her word – an aboriginal Malaysian guest-worker cleaner – against the word of Chin, a wealthy Singaporean university somebody. Norsiah was indeed disturbed at the time she witnessed Chin enter Fox's house. This, and her fear of Chin, accounts fully, in my view, for her delay in coming forward with the information. My earlier acceptance of the suicide verdict was wrong. We all make mistakes.'

'That's magnanimous of you,' comes in Venus. 'But I can't see why I can't report all this. Chin's dead and it is a good story.'

'You can – once our explanation of the death of Chin is officially accepted.'

'Is there any question about how Chin died, Superintendent? We were all there and saw it.'

'Exactly. That's why I am here. The three police constables sent to arrest Chin were sitting in their car and also saw everything close up. They told Ong I was driving very fast and erratically as if drunk. The campus speed limit is fifteen kilometres.'

'Do limits apply to police vehicles?' I throw in.

'Not those on urgent official duty. Madhu and I were in plain clothes and were not on duty, so strictly speaking we were driving an official vehicle for personal reasons. The vehicle was therefore my responsibility.'

'Well,' says Venus, quickly grasping the situation. 'I was on that road and right opposite Chin's gate and I would say you were doing a maximum of fifteen. Isn't that so, Tom?'

'Absolutely. You were crawling along. It was K before you who was going like a rocket.'

'And you'd be prepared to sign an official statement that Chin's death was an *accident*?'

'The death of Chin was accidental,' I say without hesitation. 'He ran out into the road chasing one of his cats and ... *bang*.'

'That's about it, Doctor Haddock.'

Venus adds, 'And I'm sure Li Fang and Norsiah will make similar statements. We'll all say the same thing.'

'Thanks,' says Wong. 'You realise I can't investigate the death myself since I was driving. Please make statements along those lines to Inspector Ong at headquarters. Four independent statements should do it; four to three, if it comes to it. We rely on eyewitness reports to establish the truth in accidents.'

Bernard comes into my mind, smiling, and says *depends what you mean by truth*.

'We'll go along immediately. Can't have anybody suggesting extra-judicial killing by the police.' Venus makes her broadest smile. 'You know what TV journalists are like. It would be easy for one to pop in a question to the Commissioner as to why two policemen, one very senior, off duty, out of uniform and well over the alcohol limit had they been tested, were speeding along a quiet campus road after dark in an official police vehicle when a university head of department in front of his own house got killed.'

'Quite. Of course, no such questions will be, as you say, popped in.'

'Not unless somebody suggests a certain biting dog be put down as required by law.'

'Dog? I saw no dog,' Wong corrects with a straight face. 'That was a *cat* in the road. Presumably, Chin ran across the road to get it. And Chin would still be alive and well, if in a police cell facing a murder charge, if Ong had sent officers to arrest him earlier.'

'Chin ran straight out. No way you could have avoided him. That's presumably okay to report on the news tonight? After we make statements, of course.'

'Of course, Mrs Goh.'

'*Miss* Goh, Superintendent.'

Wong looks confused. Venus holds up her ring finger, no ring, and her right hand with her mother's wedding ring on it. 'Excuse me, *Miss* Goh. I'm one of those people who mix up left and right.'

'A lot of people do, Superintendent.'

'Good to have that sorted,' I say. 'We'll be happy to give Inspector Ong his statements. But since things seem to be wrapping up nicely, what I don't get is why Chin would kill his wife just then.'

'You mean motive? Three come readily to mind. Firstly, the affair between Agnes and Woolf – a crime of passion. Secondly, Chin had been publicly humiliated the evening before when Agnes drove off in his car leaving him stranded and the brunt of jokes. And thirdly, to remove the possibility of his wife attesting as to his role in the death of Professor Fox.'

'Adds up,' I agree. 'But why get all that sedative from Ra'mad if Agnes hadn't intended to kill herself?'

'She told Ra'mad she was going to Ipoh with Chin's cats. I thought at the time this was her excuse to get the drug but now it seems she intended just that. It looks like Chin surprised his wife preparing to leave.'

'But didn't Chin have the perfect alibi because he was with the VC?'

'He was. The VC saw Chin at 8.00, but Chin had not made an appointment and the VC was in another meeting so asked Chin to wait outside his office an hour. Chin went home and found Agnes preparing to leave in his car, did the deed, then returned to the VC's office, short-cutting through Guild House – presumably dropping off a gun into Li Fang's bedroom on the way.'

'But how, then, did Chin get Agnes to swallow the drug?'

'I spoke to Chin's maid on the telephone just now. She heard Chin at the car; he asked Agnes to come inside and talk things over before leaving. The maid made them a pot of tea. They sat in the kitchen, talking. Voices were raised; the maid stayed out of the way. Ra'mad tells me that sedative is quick acting and has no taste when dissolved in tea. Chin must have put all of it in Agnes's cup.' The super looks down pensively into his own teacup.

'Darjeeling,' says Venus. 'We're out of sedative.' She tops up the super's cup. There's certainly nothing like a nice cup of tea to sort things out.

Sensing an air of conclusion, I ask, 'And the invitation, Superintendent? When you came in you mentioned an invitation.'

'Li Fang and Norsiah are both at Guild House. They want to invite you both to a special lunch there – Barnaby, too. A celebratory lunch. They will announce their engagement. Norsiah, Bernard's daughter, wants you, her cousin, to be the first to bless their union.'

'*Her cousin?*' says Venus, almost choking on her tea.

'I'll explain later.'

'Care to explain now? The cleaner is Bernard's daughter and you are her cousin? Did I hear right?'

'I was getting to it when the super called. Bernard was my mother's brother. He spent World War II in the Perak jungle where he had a daughter, Norsiah, who later came to live with him as his servant. He thought Chin and Ra'mad would argue against my appointment to the university on his recommendation – nepotism, you know – so he kept our relationship quiet. Chin's now out of the picture and Ra'mad has other things to worry about – like handing out sedative for use by a murderer. Bernard was also worried that his enemies like Von Düsseldorf might use me or Norsiah as bargaining chips to get him to reveal the location of the war loot, that's to say, the diamonds.'

'The professor your uncle! And Norsiah your cousin! Anything more I should know, Tom? We're not related, are we?'

'Not yet,' I say, giving my best smile. 'I haven't proposed … yet.'

Venus is also smiling and the super is caught in the contagion. One Smile Makes Two and One and Two makes Three – I think I've discovered Singapore's next campaign slogan.

★   ★   ★

As we watch Wong drive away, Venus sums it all up. 'That's nice, Wong coming out here to invite us to lunch with Li Fang. Of course, Li Fang could have picked up his phone and saved Wong the trip.'

'Yes. Maybe he really came for your special Darjeeling.'

'And,' Venus says, 'to make sure we get him off the hook quickly with that nasty Inspector Ong by making statements denying reckless driving of a police vehicle and causing the death of a pedestrian.'

'If that officious Inspector Ong needs statements, he'll get them.'

'You don't like Ong, do you, Tom?'

'No. But probably less than Super Wong. From what Madhu tells me, Ong and Wong hate each other's guts. They are the same age, joined the force together and became inspectors at the same time. Then, when the superintendent position became vacant, both applied and the commissioner chose Wong. Wong refused to consider Ong as his deputy, which is still vacant. Simple as that.'

'And Madhu's directly under Ong but working with Wong?'

'Yes, but not for long. Wong is getting Madhu transferred to his charge – one of the assistant superintendents – might be a promotion in it.'

'Good for Madhu. They make a good team.' Venus picks up the dog collar and looks at it. 'And what shall we do with this, er, *war loot*, Tom darling?'

'Put it back on Barnaby?'

'Aren't you a tiny bit curious to see what's inside?'

'Bernard told me.'

'In the PS?'

'The day before he died'

'And what did he tell you?'

'He told me what's inside.'

'Tom Haddock!' Venus reaches for a fruit knife, waves it in pretend-warning in front of my eyes and unrolls the tubular collar flat on the table, inner stitches upwards. We look into each other's eyes. I place my hand over hers, over the knife.

'Whatever's in there, I want you to know, Venus, I love you.'

'And I, Tom, love you … whatever's in there.'

Venus cuts the stitches. All is revealed.

'Peanuts!' says Venus.

'What were you expecting? Diamonds?'

'To-o-om.' Venus says my name as if it's a mile long. 'Last night in the car you told me the collar is full of diamonds. You said the professor told you so in his PS.'

'He did, in the PS. Which he wrote three days before he died. Then, having written the letters, he changed his mind, took out the diamonds and sewed in peanuts. He did it the afternoon of the day he died; I was with him. He thought a huge, fancy dog collar on a street dog might provoke curiosity. He took them out in front of me – they looked *very nice*, Venus.'

Venus looks me in the eyes. I see her lips move. She's counting to ten.

'And then…' I say at nine, 'he and Li Fang put the diamonds in two pouches. One stayed with Bernard, the other passed to Li Fang. I was a witness sworn to secrecy; I promised never to reveal where the diamonds are.'

'And you've just broken your promise.'

'Yes. But I swear you to secrecy.'

'So, Bernard told you about everything before he died?'

'No. He didn't tell me everything. I think he and Li Fang just wanted a trustworthy witness to their sharing of the diamonds. I already knew much of the background to their roles in World War II and the Emergency, and they knew I knew. But Bernard's daughter and the tragedies in Malaya, when Bernard lost his wife and Norsiah lost her husband and child, were revealed only in his death letter. He also didn't tell me about Von Düsseldorf and Nagasaki; perhaps he thought too much knowledge a dangerous thing. I'm inclined to think that when he felt himself go woozy on the night he died, he brought me his share of the diamonds in a pouch, maybe he wanted to hide it in my flat before calling an ambulance. He dropped the pouch in my kitchen, K picked it up and it's now with the police; but why he had this dog collar full of peanuts in his hand remains a mystery – perhaps he meant to explain that the death letter PS was incorrect on that detail or perhaps he wasn't thinking straight. Even Norsiah wasn't told about the collar.'

'But does Norsiah know about the diamonds?'

'No. Both Bernard and Li Fang are very protective. Neither would place her in harm's way. She knows nothing of any diamonds.'

'Good. Then she's not marrying Li Fang for the money.'

'Whatever her reason, it's not for the diamonds. Li Fang told me what he intends to do with his half now that Chin Peng can't use it and Bernard's dead.'

'Come on, Tom. Tell me.'

'Promise? Not a word?'

'Promise.'

'He's going to sell them bit by bit and put all the cash into the Bernard Fox Memorial Social History Scholarship Fund. That's pretty noble of him, don't you think?'

'I do. Li Fang's a pretty nice guy. I suppose that's why Norsiah's marrying him. He's generous and he's protective. Women like to feel protected.'

The phone rings again.

'Oh, no,' I say.

'Hello, good morning,' says Venus, again placing a hand over the mouthpiece and looking up into my eyes.

'It's Richard,' she says seriously, pauses long enough for me to turn green, and bursts out laughing.

About the Author

ROBERT COOPER is a British subject who has lived overseas most of his life in Malaysia, Singapore, Thailand and Laos. He studied French literature at the Sorbonne in Paris before switching to anthropology in the UK. He received a PhD in Economic Anthropology after two years with Hmong villagers in Northern Thailand and Laos. Following publication of *Resource Scarcity and the Hmong Response* (Singapore University Press, 1984), he was elected Fellow of the Royal Anthropological Institute.

Robert left an academic career in anthropology that included lectureships at Singapore, Chulalongkorn and Chiang Mai universities to join the United Nations High Commissioner for Refugees. He served with the UN in Laos, Geneva, Malawi, the Philippines, Thailand, Nepal, Bangladesh and Indonesia. In 2000, he became Head of the British Trade Office to Laos. He spent a year in Vietnam advising the government on poverty reduction, before returning to live and write in Vientiane, where he owns the bookshop *Book-Café Vientiane* and works on increasing literacy among young Lao. In addition to English, he speaks French, Lao, Malay/Indonesian and Thai.

Robert is the author of *CultureShock! Thailand* and companion volumes *Thais Mean Business*, *Thailand Beyond the Fringe* and *CultureShock! Laos*. He has also written cultural guides to Bahrain, Bhutan, Croatia and Indonesia, and three novels set in Asia and the UK.